THE PAW PAW TREE

On the subject of Reincarnation

Susan Fairfoot

Published in 2011 by New Generation Publishing

Copyright © Susan Fairfoot 2011

First Edition

The author asserts the moral right under the Copyright, Designs and Patents Act 1988 to be identified as the author of this work.

All rights reserved. No part of this publication may be reproduced, stored in a retrieval system, or transmitted in any form or by any means, without the prior consent of the author, nor be otherwise circulated in any form of binding or cover other than that in which it is published and without a similar condition being imposed on the subsequent purchaser.

www.newgenerationpublishing.info

There is a certain magic in the heart of South Africa's Natal, where a thousand hills interrupt the horizon, shedding a purple haze upon the valleys below. It is a place where the waters of the Umgeni have met with the Msunduzi over an immeasurable period of time on their way to the Indian Ocean, weaving a Neolithic landscape into its pattern of undulating hills.

Here and there houses perching on plateaus look down onto a backdrop of immense beauty. It is the end of summer and the grasses have dried to touch paper, tinder-hungry brittleness. In every direction among protruding rock and cliff edge, a brilliant blaze of colour from some wild flower lends a dash of colour to faded green and emerging dust-coloured grass.

A boy stands looking out into an endless vastness, absorbing all those hidden images that cross and flight the vision. His large conspicuous eyes betray none of the thoughts in which he has lost himself as he watches, subdued and full of intensity. He is small for his age and bears those wizened features where youth has lost its date, and death has been cast in shadows about his face. His scrawny build and shrunken posture accentuates the absence of normal animation for his age. His movements are slow and deliberate and so quiet, like some omniscient Deity silently privy to limitless, extensive knowledge.

Unnoticed by anyone, the boy goes each day to the end of the garden to water the Paw Paw tree that has so mysteriously sprung to life in the giant pot that stands there. The tree's rapid growth has usurped all other vegetation in its path, and in what seemed no time at all had outgrown the confinement of the man-sized tub it had been nurtured in. No one sees the boy lovingly cradle and touch the sides of the huge pot, waiting for life to burst forth from it. He was, after all, a child that was seldom taken into account by anyone in his family.

Within the space of one summer, the rapidly growing tree had sent cracks through the pot's structure, so that by the end of the following winter the pot was in several pieces at the sides of the globule of earth that had once surrounded it. A network of pale roots could now be seen above ground, where they had tested the greatest vulnerability of the pot as they crept around it, expanding and moulding into the pot's contour. Throughout its brief growth years, the tree had blossomed and finally yielded pendulous orbs of bright green fruit. Those fruits, untouched by the monkeys or birds, turned a bright yellow from the sun and matured to a soft mellow readiness to eat. Ripening happens so rapidly with the Paw Paw that the fruit is often overlooked, until it becomes so laden with its bounty that it drops to the ground, spilling its black seeds into the earth to become new trees. What ever else had been intended for this pot has been overtaken by the superiority of the Paw Paw tree, which had been richly fed by an over-large quantity of soft lime thrown in to the bottom. When the entirety of the pot had succumbed to its fractured parts, the hardened soil above the crumbling lime became splintered and was ready to submit to gravity.

"Just look at this, David. These Paw Paw roots have just pushed their way right through this pot," the boy's grandfather says, as he stands watching him hosing away at the earth that had maintained the shape of its three-year-long moulding. "Someone's dumped far too much lime to the bottom of this pot," the old man says, as much to himself as the boy.

As the lime washes away from the pressure of the hose, a fusion of frail white human bones fossilized in a foetal posture, imprisoned between the tenaciously probing roots, becomes exposed to the air. Loosed from its rotted scalp, long strands of dirt encrusted silken blond hair drains into the surrounding earth, encouraged by the flow of water.

"Betty, come out here at once!" the old man calls urgently towards the house, hastily turning off the tap. "Betty!" he shouts more urgently, as he runs towards the house. The boy is watching silent, motionless and impassive.

"What is it?" enquires an irritated voice from the veranda.

"It's Suki. She has been here all along."

"What nonsense - how can she be? Where has she been hiding all this time? Not the servant's quarters like her delinquent child? Not possible!"

"Come and see for yourself. She is dead, Betty; I have just discovered her body. Well...what is left of her."

The woman is middle-aged. A tight, greying perm frames her stern and furrowed brow. Thick horn-rimmed spectacles do little to add charm to the wry expression she has worn for most of her life, lending her face the expression of a character whose life has seldom reached her expectations. Drying her hands on an old tea-towel, she moves, suspicious and hesitant, out to the end of the garden where the small boy is still standing, disconnected and detached in the empty space he is lost within.

"Oh no! No - it's not possible!" the woman calls out, in stunned disbelief at what she sees.

There is a frozen instant of overwhelming dread of how life could become - in so short a moment - dissolved and changed. They stare at the gory remnant exposed now to a shocking fact. What once was a beautiful and vibrant life lies in twisted mockery before them, imprisoned in a network of yellow roots.

"That's her gold bracelet, the one we gave her for her twenty-first. Those rags...her dress she was wearing when..."

"No, don't touch anything - we need the police to see it first. Most of her clothes have rotted away, but we need as much as we can to identify her."

"Oh my poor girl, my poor child - what happened to you - how did this happen?" The mother weeps, converted now from her negative testimony.

"Perhaps you can take the boy back inside with you," her husband suggests.

"What's the point? Nothing registers with him. He has no feelings; you can see that now, can't you? Just look at him! You can see he has no idea what that is, or any understanding that it is his mother lying there. His father was right about the autism."

"His father! My God! What do we know of his father? Something here is wrong, so very wrong. Didn't he tell us she had already left to go with him that day? Come boy, come with Oupa. Will you stay there crying, Betty, or will you come back inside?"

Shock and grief transfer into a superseding irritation. There is no mutual empathy between this couple; theirs is a marriage that has remained shackled only by propinquity and habit. Affection and mutual understanding have long since become diverted, and now, in this tragic moment, they are separated by their own individual concerns with grief.

David
Chapter One

They say I can't hear them. They say I can't concentrate. They say I don't understand anything, that I am this autistic thing. They say lots of things. It doesn't worry me. It's not what they say that worries me. It is other things that worry me, things that I have bad dreams about at night.

Mama says I was born in South Africa, but I don't remember. She says we used to live with her parents till Papa sent for us but I don't remember any of that because I was still a baby, and when you are a baby you sort of forget things. Mama says her parents have a small house and her Mama was always saying it was too small for all of us, and that we must go back to my Papa. Mama cried, but we went back. Oupa cried too. I remember that. I remember a lot of things but they come and go, and mostly I forget them. But as I get bigger, they come back to me all the time now. I remember most when I am away in the dark space in Papa's study.

Papa started locking me away when we came back to him when I was small. He locked me away when Mama went out. He said he could not bear the sight of me.

Papa said Mama must go to London once a week to learn to meditate. Her thoughts are undisciplined he said. Mama is afraid of him, and she mostly does what he tells her.

He keeps telling her that I was a mistake and she must take care of it. She does. She hides me away from him most of the time. I know she loves me very much. She keeps telling me.

There is nothing you can do when you are little when someone big makes you do things. Like Ouma saying we must come back here to Papa. Papa kept writing and writing, saying he wanted Mama back, then he wrote to Ouma and she agreed we must go. He did not want her when I was born, but after, he said in his letters he has been missing her. That is what Ouma said and she said that the Bible says we must forgive.

There is this thing inside my head that knows things but I can't stop them. Not at first. It took a long time to learn to stop things. When Mama first went to London to her meditation Papa heard me in the kitchen and he called me to his study. He did not speak to me; he just took my hair and pulled it, so I had to follow it. He threw me in this dark stone cupboard in his study and closed it up so I could not get out. It was dark in there and I screamed and screamed, but no-one heard my screaming. I was frightened and somehow I remembered being frightened from before, but I can't say before when.

I screamed often after that. I can't explain why; it just sort of came out of me. It was like wetting your bed. You can't stop it.

Every time Mama went out, Papa locked me away there. He liked to pinch my arms so that I could not move and then locked me there, in that sort of stone cupboard. He said he had quite enough caterwauling when Mama went out and it was to stop me screaming, but it made me worse, and the screams shouted back at me, hurting my ears. I think he knows it makes me worse. It is what Papas do. I know that. It has happened before. Mamas are quiet people who do what they are told by Papas and are kind when Papas are not there.

At first when I was locked up I would scream until my throat was sore, then I would fall asleep in the darkness till I could hear Mama coming back. She would call me and I called back, but she never heard me. Then I would wake up and be in my bed. Papa was always there first. He said that if I said a word to Mama I would go back in that dark place forever. I never did ever say a word again.

After a while, I learnt to be quiet and listen when I am locked away. I can hear whispering when I am quiet. The whispering might be coming from inside my head, or it might come from that space of dark.

These days, I learned silence. I learn not to look into people's eyes any more. Eyes have a way of betraying all there is about people. I learned that I must be pushed into that hole every time Mama goes out - just to remind me, Papa says, and I learned to obey when I can do nothing about it.

Now I am five, I am not afraid of being inside that dark space. Being frightened is something else. You don't need it. It has a place that has a beginning and no end, like the darkness.

There are so many things inside my head that I know but I can't put words to. Millions and millions of thoughts come into my head, like I am a giant of thinking. I always feel strange and different from Papa and Lydia and Jake. They have their own special colours around them. Every person has their own different colour. That's what makes them all not the same. When I am with people I stare at those colours, and not at their faces. The colours make you know.

Papa always tells Mama that I am dull-witted, but Mama says I am as bright as a button and Papa has got it all wrong. Papa says that I will never be able to go to school when I am big because I have this autistic thing.

I like it most when Papa is away in London working. When Papa is in London, I can wander around the house all by myself. Papa's house has hundreds of rooms. I can only go inside a few, because most of them have handles that are too high for me to reach. Lydia lives away, in one part of the house I have never been to. I expect there are places as wide and big as foreign countries in this house, it is so big. I know I am not allowed in these places, but I know them already. I was in them before.

Mama says the house is old. I used to ask how old when I used to speak, and she said older than any of us. I think the house is even older than Lydia and she is a great deal older than Papa and Papa is already old, much, much older than Mama.

I like the library most. Mama finds books in there to read to me. My favourite book is the one about the animals that live by a riverside and they talk to one another. Mr. Toad is my favourite animal, because he is brave and does things that no one else can do.

These days, when I am locked away in that dark place and my thoughts begin to cram into my mind and the whispering goes on and on, I start to think of Toad and Ratty and Mole, and I know every piece of their story in my mind.

At night, sometimes I think of being locked up in that dark place and I am never found and I never come out and I die there, and then I wet my bed from the thinking of it.

Chapter Two

Things changed when I turned six. My thinking is better worked out, and I have begun to know how grown-ups want things to go their way. I can see all that when I look at their colours. I can see that Papa wants people to think I am this autistic thing, and by punishing me enough I will stay like that. Papa knows things about the mind, Mama says. That is his job. She says it's called psychiatrist. He says she must continue with her meditation class in London if she is to learn to control her mind, but Mama says he is just controlling it for her. They fight a lot and sometimes she takes me away to London to stay somewhere, but he always brings her back.

I hate it when she is gone all day to her meditation lessons. I must sit it that dark hole for all the time she is away. It is like a black cave. I just sit there and I bring my story to life. When I was a baby that dark felt like endless space, that went on and on forever, but now that I am grown up to six I can feel the sides, and I can almost reach up to the top of it if I stand on my toes.

There is nothing I can do about it. When Mama goes out, I have to go there. I can't hide. He finds me or gets Lydia to find me. Lydia cooks for us. She is mostly in the kitchen when she is not cleaning the house. She is mostly nice, but she has to do what Papa tells her or she will have to go. That's what she tells me, after.

These days, I never speak at all. Even if I try, there is something that blocks my voice inside, so I scream instead. Screaming just happens like a sneeze, you sort of can't help it, and it makes Papa mad. He can smack and smack and smack but the screaming won't stop. Lydia never comes to help me. She just makes a sort of clucking noise like a chicken, and goes away. When Mama is not here, no one will help. Jake is Papa's gardener and he hardly ever comes into the house, except the kitchen sometimes to talk with Lydia. I don't expect Jake would help either.

Mama still does not know what is happening to me when she is away; but Lydia does, and she says nothing to Mama. I expect Papa has told her also about me staying there forever if she does say. Most of the time Lydia is kind to me. She makes nice things for me to eat as if to make up for the bad time when I am locked away. I don't understand why she won't come to help me. I know she thinks about it because I can hear what people are thinking these days.

When Papa is away, we go out into the garden a lot, and visit the ducks and the geese in the wide pond. Jake likes to come and talk with us and tell us about the weather and about the plants he is growing. He talks most to Mama. He thinks I can't understand.

I have started to listen to the whispering. It comes from somewhere in the darkness. If I don't move too much I can feel air coming up from a small crack in the floor part. I try not to think about it. I sit quiet now and think of the book, and I say the words of the book in my head - The Wind in the Willows - and then I start from the beginning and say each word of the book to myself. I say it with my mouth but with no sound, and I don't think of the darkness or being frightened.

Today Mama left for London early, and Papa has come for me. I go with him because it is best to do so. I listen to Mama's car going down the drive and I feel heavy inside, like I always do when she goes. I think to myself, I don't see why I must go now when I don't scream any more - but Papa has things on his mind about me going there. He thinks it will make me the autistic thing.

I go. No fuss. Nothing. He still pulls my hair and I feel the scream wanting to start, but I will not allow it. No. I am learning. I am sitting on the hard bare space just arranging myself ready to go through the story of Toad and his friends. It's very cold and the stone underneath me feels cold and wet.

I hear the whispering. It has started almost at once today and I listen. I am not afraid of the voices; they speak another language, and I am beginning to understand it. They are louder today than I have heard them before. The sounds come echoing through my head like a tune that does not change. They are saying something I do not understand. It sounds like Ex tena-briss lix, no, lux...something like that. I seem to know the voice. It is from a long, long time ago, before I lived in these shadows. I stop the conversation in my head between Mole and Rat, and listen.

The sound is coming from the crack near the floor where that funny smelling air creeps into the hole. I put my fingers down and feel the crack in the floor. It's wider at one side. My hand goes in easily if I push it so...I can feel a funny kind of handle just underneath the crack, and it turns when I twist it. It is opening, slowly. It is getting wider, and I can see a bit of light down there with some steps made of stone. Some are going up, and some go down. They are very steep and not very wide, but it's okay for my size. Easy!

I am through. If I stretch my legs like this I can reach down to the next step. Now I am sliding slowly so I won't fall as I go down. The light is coming from high up, and it makes shapes on the walls way over there. I can see how big the space is now. Bigger than Papa's house, I think, down here. I wonder if I have come to Mole's underground house. I think I have been here before, because I am not frightened. I put out my arms to feel the way and I am creeping deeper and deeper into this new world, which is becoming lighter as I come to the end of the steps. A long thin light shines down like a torch through the dark. It's like a chimney of dark. I can see a sort of tunnel over there in front but it looks so black I don't think I want to go there. I am frightened. I am really frightened. What if I get stuck here forever and ever till I die? I mustn't be afraid, I am just going to walk and not be afraid.

It's very, very dark. Even the smallest light shows things in the shadows. I can see more tunnels like corridors and spaces like dark rooms that come off from the main corridor. It smells here, something like the old washing rags left in the larder - no – ugh, worse. I look inside some of the dark rooms but they are all empty, and so black inside you can't see anything anyway except where the light is. There is something over there - the light is just a little on it. It is something on the ground. It looks like someone sleeping there. I think it is a child. It looks small. I think he is my size.

Ugh - it's a boy's skeleton! I have seen them in Papa's medical books in his study. Oh, all his clothes have shrunken in. He looks so sad. He must have gotten lost down here and just sort of died. Oh, look, he has a toy engine in his stick fingers. I think it's my engine. I can remember it - yes it used to be my favourite toy once. But I forgot it all. I need to get it back but these stick fingers are holding it very fast. I am frightened. I think I am also going to get stuck here like the boy and no one will come for me even after I am very hungry and thirsty. Mama won't hear me scream and Papa will make me stay here forever. It's what Papas do. Mole, Toad...I need to start right from the beginning:

The Mole had been working very hard all the morning, spring-cleaning his little home…

Something is happening. It's so light, - so light I can't see. The light has filled all the dark spaces but I can't even look 'cos my eyes hurt so, and my knees are melted like butter on hot toast. I am falling. Oh, my eyes! There is a tall glowing sort-of-person standing in the light over me, and he is whispering. I don't scream. The sounds are getting louder and louder. If they don't stop, my head is going to burst from it. I must say my story in my head…

Why, certainly! said the good-natured Rat, jumping to his feet and dismissing poetry from his mind for the day. Get the boat out, and we'll paddle up there at once...

It's not working. It always works, but it's not working now - I can't concentrate. I think I am dying...

It's so cold. I'm freezing. It's dark again. I must have been dreaming about that light. It is still so quiet again, and so dark. I am not frightened any more. No, not one bit frightened. I know how to get back now. I know things. I am big in my mind now. Here are those jolly old steps.

I can feel things moving about in the shadows, but they don't frighten me any more. They are those hidden things that move about in the house. I feel them often. You sort of see them from the side of your eyes and when you look they are not really there, but I know that they are. Lydia said they are called Ghosts.

This is the place where I crawled out from the stone cupboard, but the opening has closed up by itself. I need to go up higher and higher past it. I'm not going back to that dark place again anyway. I have decided.

Now the stone steps have come to an end, and instead is a steep ladder of iron ring steps. Some of them are all rusted up and they crumble away in my hands when I grab them. Now I can see a light coming from a crack in the wall, just two more steps up.

I know there is a handle in the wall. I remember it. You pull it like this. It makes that old grindy noise that it made before, like cart wheels on a track, and the wall is moving like it used to and the light comes through from behind it.

I am in the library just from behind the back of a heavy book case. I am pushing it closed just in case Papa finds out I have discovered a way out. I can hear Mama's voice in the kitchen. She is talking to Lydia and Papa is there, but he won't lock me away or hit me when Mama is there.

Papa's face is angry. Mama has been crying. His colours are dancing about his head like fire and Lydia is just standing. Lydia is always just standing. I am not frightened and I don't feel a scream coming on.

First thing, Papa looks up, and like the only thing he notices is my toy engine. I see a thousand thoughts flashing across his face which makes his colours look like sparks from the fires that Jake makes in the garden. He snatches my toy from my hands and hits and hits and hits me without stopping, so I can't take a breath. Evil child, thief of graves, see what you are, what you have become...

Stop, stop at once Stephan, what are you going on about - thief of what grave? For God's sake, stop it! Mama is shouting and pulling at me. Then, as fast as his temper has begun, he stops. He turns around and goes out of the room.

My God, what is wrong with the man, Lydia?

Lydia just stands and does nothing and says nothing, like she always does when Papa goes mad like this.

Mama is sleeping with me in my bed tonight. I feel so nice and warm and safe with her warm body beside me, and she tells me that we are going away to Africa to my grandparents, but I feel I know this already. I lie still as still and cold and stiff from the pain all over me. Only when Mama's chest goes to a slow soft movement of sleeping do I close my own eyes.

When Papa next goes to work away in London, Mama and me will take an aeroplane to Africa, only we don't tell anyone.

Chapter Three

Mama's parents' house is completely different from Papa's house. It is small, very small, and I soon know every single room. I like it here and I like the rooms. They are warmer and nicer and the sun shines through all day long into window panes, and they fill each space with light. Outside, I hear chickens making noises and dogs barking. Dogs come to me, ready to play. Dogs speak without words. They give out so much love that humans can't. On the walls are strange photos of old people who have already died. They stare at me from the walls as if they will be here forever - just like that - staring out.

Grandfather says he is Oupa. Come into the garden with Oupa, he says to me every morning, and I go - not because I am afraid, but because I really like to be with him. He talks most of the time explaining things to me though he thinks I don't hear or understand but he likes to talk anyway. No one else listens to him otherwise. Ouma is grandmother. I know without explaining, because it's Ouma this and Ouma that, so that is how she is known. It's their language thing. Oupa's family came from somewhere called Holland, Mama says, and now he is Afrikaans. Ouma came from England somewhere when she was a little girl, Mama says, but she likes to think she is also Afrikaans.

Ouma never listens to Oupa. Ouma listens to no-one but herself, and her muttering and her thoughts are full of fuss and God. She talks to God all the time, but she is really talking to herself. That's why Oupa likes to talk to me when we are alone. He talks about all the things that annoy him about Ouma, but I can see that without him saying. Ouma fusses all the time. She fusses about me mostly. It makes me nervous.

She says she won't have me under her feet. But that is so silly because I never go under her feet. She says it's not natural having me about. I am this autistic thing; she keeps saying it. She says not natural every time she looks at me. She watches all the time and I watch her sometimes, but her colours are grey and dull and not worth looking at. Mama must take me outside when Ouma is busy. And what makes her maddest is when I wet the bed. Mama hides the sheets and washes them herself. Sometimes I scream and Ouma says she just won't have it, and I must be taken outside at once when I start. When Mama is with me, I never scream.

I have always seen people with colours around them. From the start, everything about Ouma has been grey: her hair, her face, and the colours that jump around her. Oupa is orange and sometimes pink, and he has a smile in his face most of the time. I love the sounds that come from Oupa. Oupa never worries that I don't speak. He does not try to make me like Ouma does.

Mama's colours are light and bright and change often. When she is afraid they go very dark, but here there is nothing to frighten her.

Most of all, I like being outside. I love to be with Kethla who works in the garden. I love Kethla's black, black face that has more colours around it than anyone I have ever seen, even way back remembering. Kethla never speaks. He listens to my thoughts and I can hear his thoughts. He has such beautiful thinking. He understands the trees and the plants, and the dogs too. He shows me the light in every plant, and how they grow into real living things that also think. I love most being with Kethla. Everyone thinks I am an idiot. But not Kethla. He sees me just the same as him.

Then there is Cousin Eric. Cousin Eric spends a lot of time here on Oupa's farm. Cousin Eric is Mama's sister's only child. Cousin Eric loves to tease me and hurt me when no one is looking, like Papa. He even has some of those dark shades of colour around him, like Papa has when he is being mean - then you know to stay out of his way. Cousin Eric just does not know. He knows so little. We are the same age... only I was born just a few months before Cousin Eric. Because he is much taller and fatter than me, he thinks he is must be bigger in his mind and better than me. When you are six years old and things don't match up they become like monsters in your mind. Cousin Eric thinks I am a monster.

Mama and her sister go out together quite a bit. If Cousin Eric is there, I stay close to Kethla outside, or go and stay in his hut. It's dark in the hut because of no windows, only a small door, but it is a friendly dark with light colours in it.

I have been thinking a lot about all the people here lately and how happy I am feeling. The black ladies in the kitchen and those that work outside and the dogs and the family - but I know it is not going to last. Not like this. I have this feeling.

Chapter Four

I know Papa is here. I can feel him here, and I am frightened.

Now I can hear talking inside, and I am listening. Ouma's voice is saying If you want her back, you must speak to her. Papa's voice says, I do. Of course I do, Betty, that's why I'm here. I am the only one that can manage David. He needs me for constant assessment with his condition. Suki must come back with me.

Ouma's voice says, Go, then. She says she won't speak with you, but you will find her hiding in the garden, down the bottom there near that big pot. She must go back with you. I can't take the child any longer - I'm not young any more.

Papa's voice says, Thank you Betty, well, I will do my best... you know I love the girl and will do anything for her...she has to come back with me. Ouma's voice: Go – go – go on outside, you will find her. Papa's voice: I won't forget this, Betty. I am so afraid that Mama will go back; she always goes back.

I follow, a little behind so that they won't see me and tell me to go back inside. I stand behind the old Flame tree that was struck by lightning, where Kethla has started clearing away the dead branches. I can see Mama hiding behind that big pot Ouma has just bought to grow petunias in. Papa finds her right away, and pulls her away.

No, Stephan, no.

Darling Suki. I have missed you so much. Dearest one...Papa's voice is full of tears, and he is trying to hold her tight.

It's no use, Stephan; things just don't change when you are around. Leave me alone, Steph. Just stop... you should not have come.

I can hear Papa's voice shouting now. You won't answer my calls, you little wretch - what else can I do? I have had to come all this way from England - and at a time when I have so much work on!

Mama's voice says, I want to stay here now, Stephan. I can't come back, not this time.

Look, Suki, we need to talk about this thing.

Nothing to talk about, Stephan. My mind is made up.

I am waiting and waiting for Mama to tell him to go, but... they have had these rows before. Mama was always saying she had had enough, but Papa always fetched her back. It is always the same argument, the same words, the same hitting and kicking, and it always ends the same way. She goes back to him. Now she is turning from him, and about to go back to the house.

Don't you dare walk away from me while I am talking to you! Do you hear me, Suki? I have come all this way to see you to work things out. The least you can do is hear me out.

Why, why should I hear you out? I have done nothing but hear you out for the last seven years, and when I appeal to you about something you walk away from me and shut me out. You only come to me when it suits you to come to me. We have come to the end of the line, Stephan.

You don't mean that - say you don't mean that.

This time, I really do. That's why I have come here.

You can't leave me, not now - we will come through this. We always do.

Not this time.

Why - why? You will learn to adapt to me. I will learn to adapt to you.

No, you will never learn that. You will always be the teacher, and I will always be your pupil, never quite reaching the right mark of perfection for you. You say so often that I must learn more, that I need to learn to meditate more, that I am not educated or intelligent enough - implying my lack of culture and sophistication. Leaving you is the most intelligent thing I have ever done.

But I can't live without you. Can't you see? I am nothing without you.

I have heard it all before. You are nothing without me till you have me, then I am the one who becomes nothing. You don't event acknowledge your own child.

Well, look at him - is there any wonder?

It's your treatment of him that I hate most.

Look - leave the child here, then. Let your parents cope with him for a time.

What on earth are you saying? That I must leave my child and endure life alone with you? Never! Never!

I am saying that the child is disturbed... autistic. You can't possibly manage him, and I need you.

My God, you are something else, aren't you! It is always just about you.

Well - look at him! He can't even hear what we are saying, let alone reply.

He could talk once, when he was small. You know that; you have beaten that out of him. You have done something to him. I know you have.

I have done nothing. The child was born an imbecile, only you have refused to see it and let someone better qualified take care of it.

17

I won't come back. Not this time. Things have just gone too far. I will never leave my child - and he does hear. He hears me. Mama is crying so hard her breath breaks between her words as she speaks.

Well, I won't let you go!

Papa has his really mean angry voice, with the threatening sounds he makes when he throws me into the dark space.

Leave me alone, you are hurting me! Mama's crying is frightened.

If I can't have you, no-one else will.

Leave me alone. For God's sake, leave me - you are hurting me. Please, Stephan, please...Mama is making choking sounds.

Scream as much as you like, you little bitch, but I will stop you from doing this to me. You won't do this to me. No one does this to me.

Please, please, Stephan! Oh God, help, help, someone...

I stand and stare but if I move, if I scream, Papa will hurt me too. Mama is making gurgling sounds in her throat.

It's no use going for Ouma. When Mama asked her this morning for her help, she said Mama had made her bed, and she must lie in it and cope.

Mama is coping.

Suddenly everything is quiet.

Suki, my darling, I am so sorry...please. Oh my God. Please. What...what have I done?

Davie - run! Quick, come with me. He will come after you if you don't.

Mama is standing beside me. She looks different. She is light, and she is floating in front of me.

Run - quick, Davie, run!

I am chasing after Mama, trying hard to catch up. Papa is still howling and holding onto what looks like Mama. We stop a way off, and watch. Papa is dragging that floppy thing like a sack to the great big Alibaba pot. He throws the limp sack thing into the pot, and looks around. Mama is calling me again to run.

We come to the staff compound, and Mama stops outside old Kethla's hut.

Kethla will help you to hide, Davie. I have a safe and good feeling about old Kethla.

Kethla is standing at the door of his hut, smoking a rolled paper with strange-smelling leaves inside. Kethla is looking very old and very black today, and his eyes are like a snake that watches and says nothing. He does not look at Mama - I don't think he sees her - but he seems to know that he must hide me. He takes some old sacks which are used for carrying mealie stalks. Mama goes to a dark corner and crouches there. I go with her to crouch next to her, and Kethla covers me with the sacks. There is no talking - only doing.

We are there a long time. I know about waiting, and how to stay still in one silent dark place for hours and hours.

Now I hear Papa calling my name – oh so gently, like he wants to find me, like he used to when Mama was not around. But Papa does not know this place as he does his own house.

The darkness becomes like the dark in the space in the wall that Papa locked me in to make me quiet. Mama keeps telling me to be still, but I already know how to be still and quiet. I know just how not to make a sound. I learned that a long time ago. They say I can't talk and I scream because I am the autistic thing, but I only scream when the things in my head become too much. I have no need to scream now. I feel safe here, in the dark under the sacks in Kethla's hut. I am with Mama. I am always safe when I am with Mama.

There are sounds of footsteps right outside. My heart begins to beat very fast.

The young boy. It is Papa's hard voice speaking to Kethla who is still standing at the door smoking. Have you seen the young master here?

I can feel Kethla smoking hard at his rolled up weeds, and he does not answer.

Do you understand, you old fool?

Understand good. No boy here. That is Kethla's slow, careful, gruffy old man voice.

I will give you this money if you help me to find him. There is a spitting sound, followed by a rough noisy cough.

How much money you give?

Here, fifty Rands.

Fifty Rands pay for boy, ja?

Yes, Fifty Rands, even one hundred, if you find boy right away.

No boy here.

Here, blast you - take the money and help me to look, at once!

No look. Go find boy in big house. Boy in kitchen maybe with Oupa. Oupa like boy too much.

Blast you, you lazy swine! What's that filthy weed you are smoking? Of course, marijuana - I'll get no sense here.

Silence.

Steps move away. Kethla coughs and spits. No sounds of moving about.

Nhliziyombi! Kethla says that to himself. He says he thinks Papa is bad.

I stay a long time in Kethla's hut, not moving under the sacks. I fall asleep there. When Kethla wakes me, it is dark outside. Mama's light is still there, but she is quiet. Kethla takes away the sacks from me and puts them to one side. He does not speak. He knows what I am thinking, and I know what the he is thinking. Kethla has gone lovely shades of violet and gold.

Kethla hands me a tin mug with tea in it. It is very sweet, the way Beauty the house maid does tea. I drink fast because I am thirsty and hungry, now.

Kethla shares his dinner with me. It is samp and stewed beans. We eat from the same plate, sitting by the fire. After Kethla has eaten enough, he smokes the dried weeds rolled in newspaper. I am so hungry I scrape the plate after with my spoon, and lick it like the dogs do. Kethla's funny smoke makes me sleepy. Mama's light has gone when I feel my eyes shut themselves.

Morning sounds come with the noisy African's roosters. They wake up all the early people who start the day when it is still not light enough to see properly. Then, schree schree go the Hadedas flying above. They always do that in the morning, going about their own business. Schree shree, gark, gark.

Kethla is getting ready to go to work in the garden for Ouma. Before he leaves, he takes no chances leaving me there alone, and once again he covers me up behind the sacks. He puts a finger to his lips to show I must stay still.

Mama is back. It is best to stay hiding today, my darling.

She speaks just as I do all the time, without speaking words, and my mind knows what she is saying. I smile, knowing.

They will come to look for you. If they find you now, they will send you to Papa. It is alright. Don't be afraid. Papa has left already for England. His plane left last night; I saw him go. No, you will not have to go back with him, just so long as you stay here hidden for a few days. Oupa will see to it that you stay.

We stay all morning under the sacks, Mama and me. I remember the Wind in the Willows story, and Mama is pleased.

I am thinking of the time Toad is trying to get home...Baffled and full of despair, he wandered blindly down the platform where the train was standing, and tears trickled down each side of his nose. It was hard, he thought, to be within sight of safety and almost of home...

I knew you had a good thinking side, Davie. I guessed all along that you are clever, and now I know, says Mama, when I have finished the story to the end.

From time to time, we hear the calling of my name. No-one thinks to look into Kethla's hut. After two days, there is no more calling. Then, on the third morning, Mama says it is time to leave.

Kethla gives me tea before I leave. Then he opens the door and bows to me, and I put my arms around the old man and hold him for a while, then he goes out to the garden. I walk back slowly to the farmhouse.

Oupa is on the veranda reading the paper when I climb the red-painted cement steps up to him.

In God's name, child! Where on earth have you been? Betty, come here, quick - just look who is here.

Ouma comes out to the veranda. She has got a basket of hen's eggs in one hand, and a tin bowl of kitchen scraps in the other.

Where on earth has he been all this time? He is filthy, and stinks like a Pondo fowl.

Where have you been all this time, lad? Your parents have left for England already, Oupa says, in a soft voice.

What's the use in talking to him? says Ouma. He can't understand a word you are saying. It was quite plain to me that his father did not want him, anyway. I'm most surprised that Suki left without him - and without a please or thank you for leaving him!

Cousin Eric comes out to see what is happening. Oh no, Spazzo is back. I thought they'd taken him with them.

Don't be unkind, lad, Oupa is saying. No, well...we thought they had taken him, too.

Not a word from Suki. Not one single word. She just walks off without a by-your-leave or thank you, and leaves that wretched man to sort out her clothes and pick up the boy.

Well, he clearly did not pick him up. He has been hiding somewhere all this time for some reason. Poor little chap. I don't like that man of Suki's I can tell you. He is far too old for her, and has a callous attitude towards the child. The boy is clearly frightened of him. Come, boy, come with your Oupa. I will take you to get cleaned up. Oupa takes my hand, and leads me to the bathroom.

I have to wear some of Cousin Eric's clothes as it seems that Papa has taken all mine. He told them he was taking me with him.

Now, why did you run off, boy? I'm most surprised at your Mother going off without you, and without a word about it, or even coming in to say goodbye. Most strange, most strange...Oupa is speaking more to himself than to me.

Why - she never let you leave her side. I just don't understand it.

Mama is standing right next to Oupa while he speaks. He doesn't seem to see her. I keep my eyes on her, staring; but she is not talking, just watching, like she can't reach them.

What is it you are staring at, boy? Why do you not look at me when I speak to you? Is it from this autism that they say is wrong with you? Poor old chap. Poor old chap. Well, I don't know...this is a real to-do. All the time Oupa talks, he is sponging me all over with soapy water in the bath-tub.

Cousin Eric comes into the bathroom. Aw no, Oupa, not those trousers - please!

Well, find me a pair that you like less. Go on. I can't put those filthy clothes back on him. I will buy more tomorrow.

Well, I don't want anything back that the Spazzo has worn. Oupa - he still wets his bed at night. Oh no - not that T-shirt, Oupa!

With all that has happened and is happening it all just feels too much for me, and now Cousin Eric giving me more problems. I feel a scream coming on. My thoughts are so full, and all this strange playing, as if they are pretending that they don't see Mama! But they see nothing, and what is worse, they know nothing - and I can't tell them.

The pain inside me builds up with all the non-understandings they have, and I begin to rock backwards and forwards, as the feelings and their expecting something from me and their stupid not-knowing begins to grow and puff up like an over-filled balloon that will burst any second, and Oupa becomes more anxious, making me more anxious...

Oupa shouts at Cousin Eric. Get out of the room! At once! Can't you see you are upsetting him? Out... leave us alone. Out, I said, you young pampoen!

With Cousin Eric out of the room we both become calm, and Oupa finishes dressing me in Cousin Eric's clothes.

Every day now I go to find Kethla, and every day the old man is waiting for me. He has a plant he wishes to put into the tall Alibaba pot. We can both see that Papa has already filled the pot up to the top with earth, and we know that it was to cover Mama's old body. No one can cover her new one - it is too full of light.

Paw Paw tree. Kethla says it out loud, so I really know it. Plant Paw Paw tree for Mama.

I know what he is doing; I can feel it. There is a purpose behind this planting. I have already learnt from him that the Paw Paw tree grows very fast, with strong deep roots that will grow through things.

Every morning now, I climb up onto that old wooden box while Kethla is doing something to the garden somewhere else, and I water the Paw Paw tree, willing it to grow. Kethla watches me from the side of his eyes, and Mama is always there. She also knows.

Chapter Five

There are always things to do on the farm. Animals need feeding, cows milking, sheep dipping, crops to be sown and harvested, eggs collected, and each has its sounds and its place in the order of things. I have been here nearly two years now. The Paw Paw tree has grown larger than a man, two men on top of each other. I never forget it. Each morning, I take it water and watch it grow.

Kethla shares the task of the evening milking and I go with him, watching and stroking the cows' wet spongy noses as they stand, patiently waiting their turn. The sigh and suck and hiccup of the milking machine makes them calm and dreamy while they feast on the shredded grain and straw set before them.

I am happy here, happy while I am with Kethla and the other servants, who treat me kindly and carefully, as if they know that I know things. There is little outside the farm that I know or see, and this becomes a world all of my own.

All the time I watch and feel myself grow, inside as well as outside of me. And all the time I carry deep inside me a knowing of a past. The memories creep dangerously into the present, without being able as yet to know properly. There is just that coal-black darkness I left behind at Papa's house. The memory of it is like swallowing a lump of black coal, until I become the darkness itself. It soaks me up into its shadows, and fills me with confusion about that thinking place.

Then I think of that light. The thought of it stays with me all the time, that brilliant light standing over me. It is as if that thought won't leave me. The memory of it follows me about some days, trying to reach me so hard that I have to recite The Wind in The Willows over and over. It's just that I do not like to think about some things, just as I do not like being spoken to.

People talk to me and I won't listen. I am beyond listening. I do not talk. I can't talk, nor do I wish to talk. They try to make me talk, mouthing words in front of me, trying to get me to make sounds. Talk, when they talk. It's all futile stuff.

I am where I am meant to be, but I can't figure out why.

Mama comforts me. She is always with me; I can feel her. She protects me and tells me not to be afraid, and I am not. She looks the same, just as she was on that last day, when...

Chapter Six

I turned seven in June. June the seventh is my birthday. There is something special about that number, I guess because it's my birthday number. I like numbers. I understand them, and what they stand for. No one has taught me. I just know. My birthday was always a special day. That is, before Mama…

Ouma has made a sponge-cake for me, but no presents.

What about a small gift for the little lad, Betty? Oupa asks.

Presents are a waste of money on him. He would not understand them, Ouma answers.

But I do understand them. I would like to be given a book. I understand books. I was very small when Mama gave me my special book.

It was always my favourite story when I was little, she told me.

Why are you wasting your time with books for him? Papa had said. The boy can't talk or understand what is being said to him - he is not ever likely to be able to read, or know what you are reading to him.

You can't see the potential in him. I can read it to him, and I know he absorbs every word I say, Mama had answered.

The Willows book was always kept next to my bed for when Mama read it to me - every single night. These days I carry it about with me - out into the garden, to the milking shed, to the compound, reciting the story over in my head every day. It helps to forget the nightmares. I know all the words by heart, and now I am able to follow the words in the book so well that I have taught myself to read.

After breakfast this morning I have come to sit here on the veranda steps in the bright sunshine. I follow the lines of the book with my finger, and mouth the words to myself. I don't make a sound, just the mouth movements.

What's this, Spazzo? Oh dear - Cousin Eric has come to pounce on me from nowhere. I should have known not to be here when he is staying. He snatches up my precious book, ready to taunt me.

'Spazzo' has become his nickname for me. It's short for 'spastic' - because you are one, he is always telling me. He may be Mama's sister's boy, even a close cousin, but we have nothing but age and a family connection in common. Eric likes to play football and collect stamps. He often has friends to come over to play, but they take little notice of me but for those bored moments when I make such an easy target for mockery - mostly, of course, when no one is watching.

He stands with legs astride, like a victor over the already beaten, opens the book and attempts to read the first line, making suitable lip actions for each sound he tries to figure out.

The M-ole had been w-or-king very hard all the m-or-ning... He stammers out the words he can't really put together, and he is seven.

This is crap...silly book... and you are too thick to read it like me, Spaz.

I begin thinking right away: The Mole had been working very hard all the morning, spring-cleaning his little home. First with brooms, then with dusters; then on ladders and steps and chairs, with a brush and a pail of whitewash; until he had dust in his throat and eyes, and splashes of whitewash all over his black fur, and an aching back and weary arms. Spring was moving in the earth below and around him, penetrating even his dark and lowly little house with its spirit of divine discontent and longing...

I have to break from the story thinking, because Eric's kicking is getting harder and harder to bear. He wants me to cry, but I don't. I learnt not to cry from the days when Papa hurt me. I rock instead. I can feel a scream building up inside me.

What are you doing to the poor lad? Why do have to torment him so? Out, go on outside. Here, David, that's enough of that. Come sit here by your Oupa. Oupa leads me to a chair next to him on the veranda.

...it was small wonder, then , that he suddenly flung down his brush on the floor, said 'Bother!' and 'Oh blow!' and also 'Hang spring-cleaning!' and bolted out of the house, without even waiting to put his coat on...

What is he doing in here?
Eric was bullying him again.
Well, we can't have him hanging about the house all day because of a bit of boyish play. His mother should never have left him. When was the last time you phoned to find out when they will have him back?
You know yourself it's been well over a year now, and that number no longer exists, the exchange says.
They are very likely having a wonderful life of ease, quite happy that we have been left with the responsibility - there you go, there is the car just pulled up.
Are we expecting anyone?

I told you this morning that Jess is coming today to fetch Eric. He is back at school tomorrow.

Not before time. The boy is a handful.

They are both handfuls, if you ask me. Two daughters with problems, and children they can't cope with. I'm being tested – that's what – I'm being tested!

I am back on my own while they make noises at the front door, talking to Aunty Jess.

Something up above was calling him imperiously, and he made for the steep little tunnel which answered in his case to the gravelled carriage-drive owned by animals whose residences are nearer to the sun and air. So he scraped and scratched and...

Hello, David. What's this I hear about Suki still not coming for you? I never thought that sister of mine would ever let you out of her sight - but there is no knowing folk, even your own family.

Aunty Jess looks so like Mama. I stare at her. Her colours are different, though. She has a lot of red about her colour.

Its no good, he's spastic. Can't read or nothing.

That's enough, Eric. Go pack your things. You are coming home with me tonight, and back to boarding school tomorrow - where you will learn a few manners, I hope.

She spoke to Oupa. Mother, I just don't believe that Suki has left David behind. You say he was missing for three days when they left without him? I just think it's so strange. Stephan comes out here, does not even stop overnight, and Suki just vanishes with him the same day he arrives? Something has happened...I swear it. Suki confided some terrible things when I last saw her. She was desperately unhappy with the man. I mean, they weren't even married, for God's sake.

Not the Lord's name in vain, if you don't mind. Well, she has left him. There is the proof before you. You know, yourself, that Suki has parted from the man before, but she always goes back. And as for the child's disappearance – that happens as regularly as clockwork - he spends days at a time at the compound. He seems to have an affinity with the old garden boy. Now the child plays around that large pot I bought. The gardener has filled it with earth and planted a Paw Paw tree in it, and the boy seems to talk to it.

I thought he was unable to talk.

Well he looks as if he is talking to it. I want to have him put into a home, but your Pa will not hear of it.

But Mom, don't you think it odd that Suki has not made any contact with you? Not one phone call to see how her beloved David is getting on? I think he has taken her out of the country and imprisoned her somewhere. Maybe even…

Really, Jess, you and your sister have quite vivid imaginations…agh, man, the stories she was telling your Pa about that house they live in…you have to be mad to believe the half of it…

Well, you must admit…

I have the church praying for us. The ladies from Bible study are confident that the Lord has it under control.

… and then he scrooged again and scrabbled and scratched and scraped, working busily with his little paws and muttering to himself, 'Up we go! Up we go!'…

Why is he rocking like that?

His way of shutting us out.

…until at last, pop! His snout came out into the sunlight, and he found himself rolling in the warm grass of a great meadow…

Chapter Seven

Kethla has a new puppy. Its tummy is like a blown ball, tight and hollow. It is a feasting ground for large black fleas. The puppy romps clumsily behind the old man, with its floppy legs like webs in the wind. He calls 'Inja' to it, and it comes right away. Inja means 'dog' but that dog thinks that is his name, and that is what he is called now - Inja.

Inja has no thought of what you should be or not be. He just allows you to be what you are, and loves you all the same just for being. This is a special kind of love. It is good. I took some of the worming pills out of the larder for Inja that Oupa gives his dogs. I mixed it first with some meat, the way Oupa does so that Inja will eat it. Now he looks much more comfortable. The worms were making him quite ill, I could see. Inja sees it too, and he knows that I am caring.

I feel stronger these days, like I have been growing up very fast and learning all about this life around me, and I am happy. Well, happy is lots of things. Happy when I am lost in my favourite story. Happy when things are quiet and peaceful, and there is no Eric around to make life miserable. Happy when Kethla is with me and we are doing things in the garden, watching plants grow and understanding. Happy when I find a book left somewhere, and I can read it and learn more. Happy that Mama – Mother is still here, though she does not talk any more. Happy…the remembering makes me sad, but with the remembering I also know things. I can't even put words to them in my thinking; they just stay as thinking, a kind of thinking.

I know very well by now not to allow myself to be caught unaware when Cousin Eric is spending his school holidays here. Like Ouma, he carries his failings about in a dark cloud above his head. Just like her, he tries to make every living being do what he thinks they should be doing. These days, he comes back from his school full of his own importance. He has found other children there to push around, and now he has become an expert. He sees himself as the superior boy in the family and enjoys nothing more than to find me and torment me.

I have become more secretive, and more able to lose myself. I am learning, and I am remembering. I can see them all now, and know them all for whom and what they are in the order of things.

Mother was the only one who did not believe in my autism. She knew I was different, but not in the way of autistic difference, and she used to worry. She still worries - not for my childhood, but about my future, and how I will cope with an imperfect world. I feel sometimes that all this, this life of mine, is like pieces of a complex machine that has been taken apart, never quite fitting back together again. Now that I am alone and without her - without her as a human any more, that is - I feel I am learning the art of being, and behaving as I am expected to in order to keep hold of my inner silences.

I have this pocket of stored memory covered over with layers and layers of more recent memories, until they become a tangle of thoughts. The remembering comes to me, like a warning of something similar that is going to happen. I feel that now. It feels like something of my past is coming back to me, as a kind of force.

Eric is back from school. His holidays - sigh. He has a schoolfriend who is staying with him for a few days.

I water my Paw Paw tree extra early when Eric is here. If he sees me he might want to kill the tree, break its brittle branches just to show me. Mama, help me.

A favourite place to be on my own is here, where the silver twisting stream carries cold mountain water over large boulders and yellow sand. This is the far end of the farm. I can sit here all alone and no one...unexpected voices! Oh no. It's happening too quickly for me to take cover and hide.

Hey, there's someone here, look, over there - by that tree!

That's a daft Spazzo who lives with the Afs.

But he's white. Why doesn't he live with his parents?

Left him. Didn't want him.

Why do you speak like this in front of him...can't he hear?

No, they say he's autistic. That means nothing goes into his brain or comes out of it. Watch this! Eric picks up some stones for ammunition.

All the same...I think we should leave him alone.

The stone misses and I stand perfectly still, unmoving. I know he will miss. He has no ability to throw straight. I have watched him trying to stone the chickens. He is unable to use his mind when he does things.

Come on Eric, man, leave him be.

No, let's have some throwing practice. He never tells anyone - too daft and too dumb to tell on you.

The friend sets up a tin can. He is trying to distract Eric from using me as target practice. They begin to aim at the can, but neither have much luck. They step closer, to get a clearer chance of reaching their target.

I pick up a small stone that lies at my feet and from where I am standing, a greater distance than they, I spin the stone, the way I have seen Kethla doing it. My stone hits the can and sets it flying. It is time to show Eric.

I thought you said he was dumb?

Gee – man! Do that again, Spaz.

I pick up a second stone as the friend replaces the can on the rock. I aim, and again send the can flying. They are rushing to replace the can, calling out and shouting how far it has been thrown. I take my chance to get away. By the time I have lost myself, they are calling out. They won't find me now.

The simple act of striking a tin can at a distance is not a complex issue. I have been aware for some time that I have been able to do anything I set my mind to, ever since that time…it's just that I have served for long enough his motivation for antagonism and bullying. It has been too easy for him, and it must stop - or he will become this persecutor, which is not his true nature. The can was simply the tool that was there to show him.

Chapter Eight

Things are much better here. I am free to do as I please. I can go where I like and do what I like, which is mostly following Kethla and Inja about the garden and sitting by the old man's fire in his hut when he cooks his food in the evening. Still, no-one sees me water my tree; only Mother.

I know that things like this do not last. They can never last in life. Life is for a short time, and things move with suddenness that comes when you least expect it. But I am happy, I suppose – happier than I have ever been.

Kethla does not mix with the other servants. Their housing is further off - a row of rooms built into the bank where they sit together, talking and having their meals. It suits him not to have to listen to their idle chatter. Between us, there is a shared understanding without words.

A simple creature, like this dog Inja, for example, has an intelligence that few humans have - and yet dogs, like humans, are trapped by their instincts. I take these thoughts to Kethla. He does not know words like instinct. Those you find in books if you read. No – Kethla's mind explains it in different ways. These are the ways of growth, and life-forming happenings that you need to survive in a life on this earth. Only Kethla does not – exactly - use these words in his thinking. It's hard to put together words for these thoughts. I need to read more, to find more books. Anyway, I have to think now of the troubles around Inja.

Inja has a problem with the compound fowls. He likes to chase them, and from time to time he catches one. The hens make plenty of noise, which calls up the angry African women, who are ready to beat Inja, to throw something at him or do him serious harm.

A large black rooster, the personal pride of Bongie from the kitchen, has legs as long as a spider and a blade-sharp beak below which hang two orange-red lobes, that are like the farm-worker's ears, stretched to take large pieces of metal which dangle from them. Above the rooster's beak is a pair of eyes that come from the very devil. Ouma is an authority on devils. She says that rooster has eyes like the very devil himself.

Anyone with any sense would know to stay away from this bird. You need that same kind of sense to keep out of Cousin Eric's way. Not Inja. There is something about the bold, jerky stride of the rooster's long, scrawny legs and the forward, thrusting movement of its head that terrifies the hens. They lie down instantly when he passes by. It has an opposite affect on a dog like Inja. It winds him up into an urgent need to go right out after it.

Coming round a corner, with his heart bent on a sense of fun, Inja sees the old rooster rounding up a couple of hens and making a good deal of noise about it. To Inja's eyes there is fun written in clear writing into the morning sun. This is a game being played out before him, and anyone can join in. Inja does just that. He is wild with excitement and he is not ready to give up and come away, despite all the screams and shouting going on around him. Inja means to kill or be killed. Such is often the way in life.

I have known for as long as I can remember that when something bad is about to happen I must close myself off. There is nothing you can do. I watch the attack with that same old cold feeling when father was about to do something to hurt, to destroy….

Inja charges in, full tilt, barking furiously while taking brave steps towards the flapping bird, getting closer and closer. The rooster, fearless of any enemy, whatever size, fluffs up his feathers - making himself larger than he is - and rises into the air, landing on Inja's back in one rapid pincer movement against the enemy's position, (I read this kind of army talk in a history book). His long fierce talons are deployed with military precision into Inja's back, while his razor-sharp incisor beak goes for Inja's eyes. Inja is now yelping in pain as the rooster's claws rip at his skin. Something inside me switched on the light, that brilliant light…it is as if a distant energy that has been sleeping inside me until this moment has come to life. It comes, like the scream that bubbles out of me without wanting it. The feeling becomes hot and clear. I raise my hands as if raising the rooster in my mind, and as I do so the rooster looses its grip on Inja's back and starts to lift up in the air.

Inja, who knows how to yelp in four different languages all at once, runs for cover. It all happens so fast - from beginning to end. Bongie is there, watching to see what is happening to her precious bird and as she watches she does not move. Her hands cover her face, and then she is exclaiming loudly over and over, Aw o Sangoma impela! (Oh, he is indeed a witch-doctor!)

Kethla is standing behind me. I had not noticed him. He takes down my hands, and the bird drops to the ground, making much noise. Kethla takes my hand and, soundless, leads me back to his hut, silent and knowing.

Chapter Nine

Turning eight makes a difference when you are a boy trying to be a man in a world that only sees you as a child, an imbecile child. You are like a fledgling bird that, once it flies the nest, no longer has a place there.

I have these private prayers with God that He will grant me anything I want, and only a period of time will fulfil the secret contracts. There are times when I feel like a king of all that happens around me. There is an eternity in a single moment, a continuity of the pleasantness of this life - when I am left to myself, that is. I have only to wait while God takes his time. Disappointment is only a time slip. Everything will be put right in time. Hiding and obedience are things in the past, not the present.

Eric is no longer a threat. Not since that time I hit the can with the stone and sent it flying. He sees me now as something different, even exceptional rather than dull, that has just not been noticed by all the adults in the family. He comes to look for me, more surprised by my elusiveness, which never before had occurred to him to think about. I will throw stones at tin cans to show him. I will bend metal things to impress him. I do these things mostly so that he will respect my privacy, and leave me alone. David, David, I hear, never Spazzo anymore. =I still pretend not to hear him. I use the calls as a chance to hide from him.

I only need to set my mind to something and I am able to accomplish anything I set out to do. I practice these powers, and even surprise myself some days.

Oupa calls out to me on occasions, to take me out into the fields in his jeep with him.

Still silent, old chap? I can't believe there is much wrong with you. Would you like to go to school with your cousin?

I keep my face pointed before me, blank and not reacting, to show that I have not heard what has been said. I would hate to go to school with my cousin.

You know, your Ouma is giving me stick about you. She says "School or institution!" but then she was never one for understanding much other than her Bible, and she has so much to say about that. I tell you, lad, you are better off in your silent world. There is always so much opinion about this and opinion about that. Your Ouma now believes she has a divine involvement with God's plans and punishments. Your mother and your aunt also…hmm, yes. They have their strange beliefs. I tell you, I can't catch up with it all. They always had so much to say about what they believed in, or did not believe in. For me… I believe in myself. I have no need to follow what they believe. All this claptrap at the church and all the Bible study in the world don't answer enough questions for me. Ouma says God has the answers, and you will only know them when you have passed on. Let me tell you, lad, there is no such thing as God, and when you are dead – man, you are dead. And all of this drivel about spirits your aunt Jess speaks of? You can take my word for it, I know it. Rubbish! As for prayer, a waste of time. No-one is listening on the other end.

He looks at me to see if I have taken in any of what he has been saying, and I am looking at the road ahead and trying to recite The Willows. It never matters much to Oupa that what he is saying might not reach me, but Oupa likes to talk to himself as much as anything. He needs to give vent to his thoughts, and I am a visual audience who will not object to his opinion. Oupa has lived too long with the irritation of scruples and regrets, that he has stored up after years of a cold marriage. I wonder if and when there had ever been any warmth from the woman he married. It's hard to imagine.

I wonder about love.

Oi, there, what are you men up to? Is this a holiday today? Where is the Induna here? He addresses these words in Zulu to the men working in the field.

Boss, we are waiting.

What are you waiting for now?

The engine is turned off. Oupa climbs out of the Land rover towards the group of planters, and I lose myself in my own world, unmolested by trivia.

…The Toad was so anxious not to be left out that he took up the inferior position assigned to him without a murmur, and the animals set off. The Badger led them along by the river for a little way, and then suddenly swung himself over the edge into a hole in the river bank, a little above the water. The Mole and the Rat followed silently, swinging themselves successfully into the hole as they had seen the Badger do; but when it came to Toad's turn, of course he managed to slip and fall into the water with a loud splash and a squeal of alarm…

My mind has entered Toad's world. I am travelling around secret passages, and going on an expedition with Toad. These days, I can picture the story so much more. Sometimes I forget certain passages that once I remembered so well, but my mind is beginning to feel more. I can concentrate less on one single thing, but can turn my mind in many directions at once. It is when I start to think like this that pieces of memory from those days start to come back. I feel the fear once again and I wonder at its return, again and again.

Come on lad, come on, stop day-dreaming, we are home at last; there is your Ouma, ready to lecture us about being so late.

Chapter Ten

The dream comes again and again. It's more a remembering than a dream. It is of when I was small and Mama has gone to London for her meditation class. In the dream, father has locked me into that hole in the wall.

It is dark. The whispering starts, and the musty air comes through the crack in the floor. He is standing over me, telling me that I will stay in the hole forever. One word, only one world is all it takes. I wet my bed after these dreams; there is no helping it. Only thinking the Toad's story helps me forget.

I wonder when I will be free of those memories. I can't think why I need them here. Nothing like that can happen here. Ouma nags and fusses, but she never smacks me. I just know she does not like me, and that is alright by me. Why do the memories keep on coming back, as if to remind me?

I sit with the Grandparents for supper these days.

About time you learnt to eat at the table, David. You could do with some table manners.

Let the lad alone, he doesn't do too badly - do you, David lad?

Well, if schools won't take him, he is starting with Sunday School this Sunday. It is high time he learnt to sit in church with us, now.

Oupa looks at me to give me an encouraging wink, but I am too busy looking at the colours around Ouma's head; they have gone a rusty shade of orange. Ouma is on a mission, as Oupa says - behind her back, of course.

Sunday School has begun. This is my second Sunday here and my mind wanders away, from boredom. The Sunday-school teacher is middle aged. Her name is Mrs. Martins and she has being doing this for a long time - much to the good opinion of the parishioners, who see her as a budding saint for her loyalty to the job. She has little to interest young people who notice - colourless clothing, and a voice that comes from nowhere and goes nowhere. She puts a lot of white powder on her face which falls into her eyebrows and lashes, weighing them down like white hoods over her eyes. I wonder if the other children also notice the deep grey that surrounds her head.

The story of the loaves and fishes: Which of you children know this story? Nearly all the hands go up.

And who would like to begin the lesson? My mind is slipping...

...Spellbound and quivering with excitement, the Water Rat followed the Adventurer league by league - over stormy bays, through crowded road-steads, across harbour bars on a racing tide, up winding rivers that hid their busy little towns round a sudden turn, and left him with a regretful sight planted at his dull inland farm, about which he desired to hear nothing...

Ouma is tugging at my shirt.
 Come on, come on. Time to go.
 Really, Mrs Van der Walt, I think this is perhaps a waste of time. He is taking none of it in. He is in a world of his own.

...Then suddenly they hear, far away as it might be, and yet apparently nearly over their heads, a confused murmur of sound, as if people were shouting and cheering and stamping on the floor and hammering on tables. The Toad's nervous terrors all returned, but the Badger only remarked placidly, 'They are going it, the weasels!'...

Come on, dozy, we are home - out you get. Have you heard anything I have been saying to you this past half hour?
 I am just pleased to be home. I need to find Kethla and Inja. They are near Mama's Alibaba pot. The Paw Paw tree has grown much taller; it is much more than two Oupa lengths now and its roots are reaching down, down into the soil. I can feel Mama close when I am here. I can talk to her in my mind and sometimes she answers, but less and less as I am getting older.

Chapter Eleven

Mrs. Martens made no difference to Ouma's decision about sending me to Sunday-school. Despite what she said about me not being able to absorb anything at the Sunday-school, it has made Ouma quite set that I must attend. So each Sunday I sit, unmoving and silent amidst other noisy and fidgeting children, who seem to ignore the fact that I am even there. Some Sundays I sit next to Ouma in the church and listen absentmindedly to the prayers and the droning responses that have little conviction, and even less meaning. Oupa is found to be so busy on Sundays that he seldom comes with us, till Ouma's stony scolding forces him to obey.

Ouma has taken to leaving a Bible next to my bed. She does not believe that I can read or understand it but the very power of the book matters to her, like it is some kind of living thing. I open it. There are pages with a list under 'Contents'. Page One. Genesis. The story of creation. In the beginning God created the heavens and the earth; the earth was waste and void; darkness covered the abyss, and the spirit of God was stirring about the waters...

It takes me days and days and days to read. Sometimes I have to go back and read something again. It makes little sense of what they were talking about in church, or Sunday School for that matter, for there are hidden meanings here that Sunday School and the parson in church has not noticed.

This question of God...I find it hard to understand why it is necessary to teach an idea of God as a means of discovering God. Sunday School would have God as the figure of a white-bearded old man sitting on a glowing throne, with bearded Jesus all healed up from his wounds sitting on his right, whilst the smoky holy-ghost drifts in and out on the left. Much like Father Christmas. Eric used to talk a lot about Father Christmas's visits. Of course, he never came to me. I was the autistic one that everyone forgot - Father Christmas, God and His Holy spirits.

Anyway, whatever pictures were planted in my mind from Eric or Sunday School were only dream images that begin to fade, as soon as I read theBible.There is a knowing already in my head. It does not come through what Sunday School wishes to impress upon me or those prayers of appeal recited by Ouma out of a sense of duty - without thinking. Words. Words are becoming important to me. I read everything I can find to read and sometimes some of the things I read stop me in my tracks - that's a nice expression, I picked it up from one of Ouma's library books. Words, words, words, expressions and words.

...The Holy Gospel of Jesus Christ According to St. John. In the beginning was the Word and the Word was with God; and the Word was God. He was in the beginning with God. All things were made through him, and without him was made nothing that has been made. In him was life, and the life was the light of men. And the light shines in the darkness; and the darkness grasped it not...

I just love all of that passage - how it describes words. Words are becoming significant. Though I never use words in talking, they fill me with awe. The sounds that those words the Kingdom - the Power - the Glory make when they go through my head are sounds whose purpose can only be imagined. Even feeling that I have known them before; they echo in my senses. Blasphemy - damnation – hell are words Ouma uses often, and they seem to be part of her. They appear in the Bible often, and in Sunday School also. Like so many words they can mean so many things to different people.

I read Ouma'sBible, following the words carefully, trying to make sense of it all. There are phrases and descriptions so contrasting and conflicting that can only become puzzles to invent interpretations for. Some of the words are so disturbing that the images they make are often in conflict with the soul of what it describes. I will break thee with a rod of iron, God said. I dare not think about it. It is too like father. There is more than all this. I read and understand - there has to be more - but it all seems so far out of my reach just yet, and that empty space that is soul fills me with sadness.

Ouma's friends join together in a tight social net after the Sunday-service, drinking tea and swapping tea-cakes and biscuits they have brought. They take turns in making cakes for this tea-bake, and also take turns for the honour of doing the church flowers each week. When it is Ouma's turn she spends hours making sure her cakes are the best, while criticizing the way others have baked before her.

There is a lot of gossip and speculation of each other's shortcomings. They find texts from the Bible to offer each other as lessons regarding these short-comings. Areas in Ouma's Bible are marked with brown kitchen paper, and underlined in pencil she can rub out later. She always has someone's name written on the brown paper. They are the offending friends who need the lessons this week. I read them when she is not there, and wonder why Mevrou Grobbler or Mevrou Swart needs to learn from this or that.

Sundays come around all too quickly these days. I sit still in the church. I look at the shades of colour about people's heads, and all those *why* questions come to my mind. It is so hard to tune off in that dreary after-church-tea- party conversation. I am like a tethered dog that must be taken out but must learn to be still and silent and obedient.

Betty, what are you going to do about the boy now? You can't keep him indefinitely. Have you still heard nothing from Suki?

Not a single word. I simply can't understand it. It is as if she has just abandoned him and left him for Harold and me to care for.

It's not right, Betty. I always said that when she turned to her funny beliefs and ideas of Spiritualism that no good would come of it. The Lord said thou shalt have no other God but me, *and you know what those people believe in!*

Yes, well, there is nothing you can do when your children turn from you. Suki was always trouble. She liked to mix with the strangest of people who were not part of the church. But I tell you, as soon as I get word from her, back he goes to her. I can't keep this up forever. I have told Harold.

Hello Betty, Kath…

Mumbles…Hello…hello…your turn for flowers next week.

Yes…have all my hydrangeas already soaking. Not talking of Suki still, are you? Poor girl. She was always my favourite. So helpful and kind.

Well, there are other sides, Ginny. Sides you don't know about.

What…because she left her child with Granny?

A snorting sound from Ouma. Without a single word. I call that selfish and cruel.

Well, there must be a reason. Have you tried to make contact with her? Surely she is still at the same address the man-friend lived in. They must still be living there?

No answers to letters. Telephone number has been cancelled.

What about going out there and seeing for yourselves?

As a matter of fact, Jess was out there a year ago. She visited the house. Stephan Tyndal was there, all right. Did not even invite her in. Huge place, she said, built some time in the fifteenth century. Must have some money, I say - and not a penny sent for his child!

And? Did she see Suki?

No, he told her Suki was away. She had left him shortly after they got back. Said he wanted nothing to do with the family or the boy.

I'll bet. What a selfish swine. I thought he was supposed to be so brilliant - a psychiatrist, isn't he? Jess told us that Suki said he was once nominated for some medical award.

I really don't know. Suki said his friends called him a genius.

Shame his son didn't inherit his brain.

Oh, you are being unkind. Look at the little chap. He has been sitting there on that stool all the time while we are talking. How do you know he does not understand what we are saying?

David! David, can you hear me? See, not a word.

But he does follow you when you are ready to go, Bet. I've watched him.

Well, I have a good mind to just pack him off back to England to his father, whether he likes it or not. I mean, we can't keep him with us forever.

What does Harold say?

Makes such a fuss when I suggest it, but he is not thinking responsibly. Hmm...here he comes now.

Ready for home, ladies? Hello David - coming with Oupa, are you?

Oupa takes my hand and walks back to the jeep with me, while Ouma is saying goodbye to her friends.

Had a good time, lad? Pretty boring I expect...poor chap. You were looking pretty fed up sitting there.

Chapter Twelve

I am nine.

Eric is staying for his holidays. He has a new cricket bat that he has been given for his ninth birthday. Everyone talks of how big he is these days. I think it's because we are the same age, and he is already a head and shoulders taller and wider than me. I don't seem to grow.

Oi, David, come here. There's no time to escape! He is climbing out of his mother's car and they have seen me.

I have to admit that I am curious to see the birthday gifts he has with him, - they are always interesting, and these days Eric is becoming more interesting to be around. He has books which he never reads, and schoolbooks he never opens, which he has a habit of leaving behind when he leaves. He is supposed to bring all his books home in the holidays to catch up with schoolwork. There is little else to read here, so I take them to my room and read.

Look, a cricket bat - know what this is? You have to throw this ball to me and I hit it, see?

Of course I know. I go with Oupa sometimes when he watches the local cricket team play. I copy the action I have seen, and pitch the heavy ball to him. Eric is not much good at hitting the ball. It takes hours and hours for him to get it right and after a few days he manages to strike the ball several times. Eric is really pleased.

He does not want it be known that we play together; the thought would shame him.

I've gotten into the cricket team since you started to throw the ball for me Spaz -um, David. Doing so great! We won't tell anyone you have been helping me. They will think I am ace at cricket all on my own.

Keeping secrets with Cousin Eric is rewarded by being allowed into his room to look at his school books. *History – Geography – Math* - printed in Eric's untidy writing over brown-paper protection-covers. I find a large book titled 'The Concise Oxford Dictionary'.

It's for looking up words, dumbo. If you unno a word, you look it up in here and it explains it to you.

Wonderful, so many words I do not understand.

Are you trying to read, Spaz?

I pretend I have not heard.

It is easy to keep back some of Eric's books from time to time. Eric never knows where he has left his schoolbooks or if he has simply left them at school. I read them all when he has gone and Aunt Jess complains about having to buy more books because of the lost ones. I get to keep 'The Concise Oxford Dictionary.' In case the books are taken away, I learn them all by heart. Learning is easy. I read them through carefully once, sometimes twice, and then I can visualize each page later when I want to think about them. There are old school books here that once belonged to Mama and Aunt Jess. I keep them in my room, somewhere no one will see, so that I can read them and remember them.

...The conflict between the Catholic Church and its adversaries took quite a different form from what friend or foe could possibly have foreseen in the sixteenth century...Page 73...

Now that is interesting.
I sometimes think you really do know what people are saying to you, you know. You can definitely understand me, I know it now. What's wrong with you? Are you just trying to get out of school? Huh? Do you like being a spaz?
I stare back, and leave the room.

Chapter Thirteen

Kethla is packing his few possessions into an old sack. I stare at him while he tidies his hut.

I must go away. There will be much trouble in a few days. They will find the young Inkosazana, *your Mother, and they will think it is I who has put her where they find her. They will send you away also.*

I am thinking that the reason we planted the Paw Paw tree was so that they *would* find her. Mama is standing right there as he speaks. It is some time since I last saw her light. A hot feeling creeps over me. It is that feeling of certainty. I get that feeling when I know what is going to happen, soon. The feeling rests uncomfortably in that empty echoing place of my mind.

Davey...this is the right time, Mama tells me. *You must see clearly now why things must happen as they do. Things must never happen in a hurry. People need time to value things and make slow judgments, so they can learn from them. Yes, Kethla is right - they will judge him wrongly - but that happens so often in a life. I know you worry about your Papa. It is right that soon you will join him. I have begun to realize so much, and you will too. I understand him now. You will be in control this time, Davey. Just watch and see how things happen.*

Kethla has gone.

There is an uneasy feeling of incompleteness about the mornings now. I try to fill my mind.

Toad shed bitter tears, and abandoned himself to dark despair...The medieval feudal state dissolved into the centralized modern state which at that time demanded primarily power and since then has...When Job answered, and said: Hear, I beseech you, my words, and do penance. Suffer me, and I will speak, and after, if you please, laugh at my words...history...geography...

Nothing remains solid in my mind. Abstractions, eliminations. My mind is a hollow and muddled place. *David, David, where are you?* Oupa calls. This is the time. I *must* concentrate, centre my mind...

...When Toad found himself immured in a dank and noisome dungeon, and knew that all the grim darkness of a medieval fortress lay between him and the outer world of sunshine and well-metalled high

rods where he had lately been so happy, disporting himself as if he had bought up every road in England, he flung himself at full length on the floor, and...

Come outside, David. No more of that staring mindlessly into space you do. Come on, my lad. I am going to do a bit of watering. How about that old Paw Paw tree that has burst from its pot? You haven't watered it for a long time now, have you?

There is a shrinking longing to go away and hide but it is mixed with dreaded curiosity. I follow, watchful and hesitant. This is where it starts. Or does it end? Mama had once said that all endings are new beginnings, and they are both worrisome.

Oupa is hosing the sand that is caked around the roots of the tree. Mama's light-presence is here, silently watching also but from a little distance, and my gaze shifts between the Paw Paw tree and at her.

How the roots of the Paw Paw tree have curled around the sides of the pot, as if trying to escape. Where the roots have reached the earth-stained lime below, a strange tangle of white bones lie like prisoners between the intertwined root-strands.

It is easier to look at Mama's light than this ghoulish residue of her. She is so still.

Oupa is calling out to Ouma. He is running. Ouma is coming...

To my mind, observed the Chairman of the Bench of Magistrates cheerfully, *the only difficulty that presents itself in this, otherwise very clear case, is how we can possibly make it sufficiently hot for the incorrigible rogue and hardened ruffian whom we see cowering in the dock before us. Let me see: he has been found guilty, on the clearest secondly evidence, first, of stealing a valuable motor car, of driving to the public danger, and, thirdly, of gross impertinence to the rural police. Mr. Clerk, will you tell us, please - what is the very stiffest penalty we can impose for each of these offences?*

Voices, persistent voices. I don't want to hear what they are saying. Someone shakes me, and I start to rock and remember pages and pages of Toad in my head.

Four large policemen are standing with Ouma. Three of them are African, one is white, and they are staring at me.

No need to be so rough on the boy, ma'am, you can see he is disturbed by all of this.

He is not disturbed - that is what I have been trying to tell you. He is autistic...he has no feelings.

The boy looks upset to me, ma'am.

He knows something, Betty. I tell you he has known about this pot for a long time; just as I have been trying to explain to you at the house.

You say he follows the old gardener about and together they have been tending to the plants?

Yes, yes.

I would like to see this chap, ma'am...where can we find him? I would say there is something very suspicious about him.

There is a murmur of accord from all the policemen standing there.

Oupa is coming towards me. I feel comforted at the sight of Oupa. *Come,* Boytjie, *you have had enough for the day. Sorry, Gentlemen. As you can see, questioning the boy will not help you, as I have already said.*

He gives Ouma a stern look, and leads me to the house.

Chapter Fourteen

There is a funeral service for Mama. Her bones have been put into a large coffin, much too big for those small bones. They say she will be cremated. I look it up. She will be reduced to ashes. Funny to think of her as a pile of ash when she is standing there watching us, looking sad. Everyone seems to be there, and everyone is whispering. Everyone is making guesses as to how Mama got inside the pot.

Days go by, and people still come visiting. It seems everyone is curious and everyone wants answers to satisfy this interest they have in Mama now she is dead. While she was alive, no-one seemed to care.

She used to be Ouma's child who disappeared to England and went to live in sin with a much older man. The odd girl, with the strange ways about her. Now she is no longer odd, just that poor child who has had such wrong put upon her.

And what of the child? You can't keep the child forever, Betty. What of the father? He ought to be told.

Kethla was right; no one seems to suspect Papa. They are not even adding up the information they have. Kethla said it was because he was white. They haven't suspected him because he was so good at lying about where Mama had gone. They really want it to be Kethla that has done this.

And there goes Ouma, making arrangements and doing a lot of talking when Oupa is not listening.

She writes letters secretly, and posts them secretly. *Yes, I will get him to the airport myself. Yes, he will need special provision and watching on the plane. You must realizes, he is not normal, and there is no need to communicate with him in any way - or he becomes very disturbed. Yes, he will be met the other end. Yes, I am sure of that.* Ouma is not taking any chances that she will be left with any unnecessary burden on her hands.

Chapter Fifteen

It is freezing. The air bites into any part of me that has no cover, like a thousand nettles leaving a sting which stuns all senses. It attacked me even before I got off the plane. Walking along the long tunnelled passageway, my legs go numb in my summer shorts and my face and hands burn from the cold. A smoky mist breathes out from my nose and mouth like a dragon's breath. I read about dragons in one of Eric's books.

South Africa was hot when we left. I think about it being winter here when it is summertime there, and hot. Then a cold sweat of fear comes over me for thinking about my father. I have no choices. I have no say. I have no way of avoiding what is before me.

It is nearly four years since I last saw him, and...those buried thoughts have come back to remind me. All those memories I have tried to lose.

My breathing comes short and shallow. I don't want to move, but I am pushed and pulled this way and that against my will. Sometimes Mama appears and tells me it will be alright, but...

My travelling escort – attendant - what can I call her? She is young and looks a little afraid of me and makes no attempt to communicate with me. In fact, she has said nothing at all, for which I am greatly relieved.

She pushes me about. She strapped me into my seat in the plane. She brought food to me, unwrapping food parcels and placing plastic spoons into my hands like a small child. She un-buckled the seat-belt to show me the toilet; closed the door on me and opened it when she thought I should come out. She has been told that I am deaf and dumb, and there is little point in talking. Anyway, I hate it when people try to talk to me - especially strangers. They pretend to be nice because they don't know what else to do, and all the time they are feeling awkward about it.

Our cases have been collected, and we stand outside now. Large, black, square cars called taxis are lined up on a very busy road. So many people walking about - some shout, some are talking, most are quiet with concentration on their faces. Because no one speaks to me I can spend time taking things in: the buildings, the hundreds and thousands of people. How I long to let go and float away so no-one will see me, and I will see no-one.

> *...We others, who have long lost the more subtle of the physical senses, have not even proper terms to express an animal's intercommunications with his surroundings, living or otherwise. We have only the word 'smell', for instance, to include the whole range of delicate thrills which murmur in the nose of the animals night and day, summoning, warning, inciting, repelling. It was one of those mysterious fairy calls from out the void that suddenly reached Mole in the darkness, making him tingle through and through with its very familiar appeal, even while as yet he could not clearly remember what it was. He stopped dead in his tracks, his nose searching hither and thither in its efforts to recapture the fine filament, the telegraphic current that had so strongly moved him. A moment, and he had caught it again; and with it this time came recollection in fullest flood. Home! That was what they meant...*

I seem to have thought up half the book and still I am waiting and hoping that he has forgotten me, and I will be made to go back to Africa and the warm sun. My companion has still not said a word to me. She looks at her watch often and says damn a few times. I think she is fed up with waiting. He is late.

He has not forgotten. Suddenly, he is here, large and threatening, come to collect his burden. He is walking towards us with a silly grin on his face saying he has been delayed, can't be helped...that face, that look, none of it changed but bearing down on me like the Assyrian who came down like a wolf on the fold – (Eric's poetry book, page sixty three). He reaches out to those edges of my memory where the shadows still fall in dark pools about him, and there...a slow, dark awakening in my mind. A look, a glance, a flicker, in those heavy eyes, and it all catches fire in my mind like Kethla blowing into life a small spark into the dry wood in his hut.

Of course that time there in the sun has all been a false sense of well-being and safekeeping, not to last. Of course!

What is it that pricks my mind like sharp needles waiting to come to the top of my memory? As I watch his every move and expression and those vivid colours that blaze about his head, I get this same old odd feeling that I must try to remember. It is as if there is something that is wedged somewhere between the nightmares and seeing him now.

Does he really think what he did to my mother has been forgotten? Was Ouma so keen to be rid of me that she truly confirmed his belief in his own innocence? She certainly believed in his diagnosis of autism. It did not matter to her that by handing me over to him they both would soon be rid of what was unwanted Spazzo rubbish. For reasons of his own he wants to – he needs to - really believe in this autistic-thing, and he has convinced everyone about it. I can be made to forget what happened if I am autistic. If he sees that I have remembered anything at all, no one would believe me. Would they? But I remember it all very clearly, and there have been more than that one violent act. I am beginning to remember.

Things happen with grown-ups which a child accepts, and bears with resignation as a thing done and no longer worth arguing about. What's the point in complaining about something you can do nothing about or find any way out of? What is in father's mind and the reasons for his actions are not yet clear to me. Yet I feel somehow I am some kind of...something, an instrument, a catalyst, perhaps, in his past.

He does not say my name or look at me. He walks up to my chaperone, introducing himself. There are few words between them as he cuts short any conversation by saying he is in a hurry, and just come to collect the passenger. I am the passenger.

He makes no sign to the passenger to follow, he simply knows that the passenger will have to follow - autistic or not. There is no connection between us. There is no leave-taking from my travel companion. He expects she has been made mindful of my condition, as every safety measure has been taken to impress this autism on her as on everyone. I have learned to play the symptoms they talk of so often in front of me - *He is unable to communicate in any way - he is liable to fits of rage - he has no control over his thinking or his motor actions.* Of course the condition has isolated me. I am used to isolation. I like it. It makes me feel safe.

He takes up the small suitcase that Ouma has packed. It's the old broken one she found in the shed. It had to be tied with binder-twine from the cow-shed straw to keep it closed. I keep my eyes on it as he moves ahead – fast. I need to pee, but I run to catch up. I am a fraction of his size; it is as if he really wants to lose me now. The suitcase is my last connection with security, with Oupa and Kethla and Inja. For that reason alone I cannot let it out of my sight. I am out of breath, but the running makes me warm.

The car journey is filled with strange outside images. Everything merges with the thoughts of Mama and her absence right now. I can hardly visualize her any more in any kind of living form. I feel her now as part of those many memories that are sometimes so real, and sometimes seem like just a dream with no real side to them. As I look out of the window onto this cold countryside, I long for her so much that there is no room right now even for the comfort of repeating to myself any part of Toad's story.

I know I am very small for my age but I feel old at nine - well, I suppose I will be ten quite soon and that is old. I have always felt old. That is, older than all those who have been in authority over me, especially Eric. There was always that state of not knowing about them, wondering each moment about what to do next, what to say and how to say it and how they need someone else to tell them. They all thought I didn't know what was being said, but all the time I have been able to read their thoughts, even before they put them into words. And those words they mismanaged never accurately expressed their thinking.

People seem to need to unburden all those petty hurts that are stored within them without letting it go from inside, but then, people never really listen. Kethla listened. I am listening to my thoughts. They are all so muddled. Muddled thoughts on a muddled journey.

Chapter Sixteen

It seems so long since Ouma pushed me into that taxi and told me go with the nice lady. Was it only yesterday? I seem to have dozed off. My legs are stiff. I want to pee.

This road seems faintly familiar. I am frightened now. I need to shut my mind out...

...Now, no more talking. Business! Use your nose, and give your mind to it. They moved on in silence for some little way when suddenly the Rat was conscious, through his arm that was linked in Mole's, of a faint sort of electric thrill that was passing down that animal's body. Instantly he disengaged himself, fell back a pace, and waited, all attention. The signals were coming through! Mole stood a moment, rigid, while his uplifted nose, quivering slightly, felt the air...

Here are broken gates with wide-winged flacons on top of the posts staring at me like before, daring and threatening. Winding path - bumpy road. I know it. There are the fields. Just the same.

He drives the car right up to the front steps, and stops. He pushes his hand down hard on the horn like he is irritated. It is as if the car too is irritated. The noise of the horn blast screams for attention until a large old woman, wearing a blue house-coat over thick woollen clothing, comes to open the front door. Her white and grey hair sticks out untidily about her face. She has a wide smile. The smile opens up her lips and shows her brown-stained teeth, with many gaps in between where teeth are missing.

Take care of him and his luggage, will you? Don't waste time trying to get through to him. Just show him his room and shut him in.

Hello David, remember me? She opens the back door of the car releasing me - the passenger from the journey. I don't remember her. I suppose I don't want to remember her. It is something about her I don't want to remember. I try to ignore her but I can't help noticing the glow of colours that come from her. She is gentle, and her colours are soft pinks and orange. His colours are hard.

I told you. Don't bother trying to talk to him. Nothing goes through, you will find. He is autistic, as I have already explained. He was like this before his mother took him away, you will remember. Now I have to fly off back to London for the week. I will try to sort something out when I get back at the weekends. If he shows any sign of difficulty, sedate him with those pills I have left for you and lock him securely into his room; he could be dangerous.

After lots of instructions, he marches quickly up the stairs to collect a briefcase and a small hold-all, and goes as fast as he arrived. I follow the old woman up the stairs. Only when he has left the house and we hear the car on the gravel outside does she begin to speak to me.

I am Lydia. I'm sure you do remember me, David. You was such a nipper when you and your Mum left - you have grown some since then! You know I have been housekeeper here forever...such a long time now. I've seen people come and go with your father, and for some better reason than I can think of, I am still here. I was ever so fond of your Mum. See, you are watching me while I talk to you. It's nonsense that you are autistic. I said as much before she went away with you. I have an autistic nephew, he was born that way. I know what has happened to you, David. Poor boy. But mind, as I say, you have grown some since I last saw you. But you are still a mite - small for your age, mind. You was always with your Mum as I remember, never left her side. Now I hear she has passed away these last few years. My, but you must have missed her!

I open the kitchen door, which leads to a back garden I remember. I pee on the stones outside, then I come back into the warm kitchen.

See, there, you ain't forgotten where that door goes. Should have said you needed the toilet. Remember where it is? Course, you can't say...Here, a glass of warm milk, expect you must be hungry.

She hands me a large slice of sponge cake. I carry it to the kitchen table and begin to eat. I am hungry. It tastes nice.

See, nothing wrong I say. Nothing wrong with that.

Bit by bit the puzzle pieces begin to fit: her voice, the way she does not pronounce h in 'her' - her large bum that moves slowly about the kitchen. The dark gloom of the kitchen and its big heavy table in the centre, the old fireplace with its metal hinges for holding pots, and the large Aga stove that takes up a good deal of the space in the kitchen.

She is lonely, this old woman. I notice that by the way she talks all the time of this and that and nothing much. I watch her as she moves about the kitchen preparing an evening meal, and I feel a certain comfort in her presence.

I have stowed away so many memories hinged on fear and anxiety and now they are creeping back, like spiders inching to the centre of their web once more. I am beginning to sense things here that my mind has not dealt with before. Those old hidden shades are coming back. They are just starting to show themselves in wraith-like wisps of smoky haze, watching me out of their darkness, trying to make me to look at them and find them out. This is their place. It is as if they have never left and have come back here after death, where they have always lived. The place is buzzing with a strange tone of things that live in nothingness. I feel a kind of dread. It is all a kind of knowing and yet not knowing. I am thinking and all the time this woman's voice is going on and on, I can't help but listen to it…

…when my old man died, I said no more - never again, I said. Quite happy to be on me own, but for those times when I ain't coping too well on me own - but I like a bit of company now and then…

Her voice drones on and on, like a bee Eric has caught in a jar. The room has begun to swim round and round me in a kind of whirlpool of words and memories. I…I…can't…breathe… I…am suffocating from it all…there is a tightness in my chest and in my head.

…so when he said David is coming back, I says to meself, 'I'll bet there's summat wrong there. And I know as 'ow he treated you when you was little and your Mum, God rest her soul…

Faces are appearing in front of me out of the mist; hundreds of faces smiling, frowning and crying faces. My knees, my knees are buckling like heat crackled twigs. They won't hold me up. I…am… falling…

Oh there, there, come - poor Davie.

Chapter Seventeen

I wake up in a strange bed. It's so cold in here. I know this room. This is where I used to sleep, a long time ago. Mama should be here. Oh no; it's that old woman, Lydia.

You alright, my duck? Had a queer turn. You just rest in here and I will bring your supper up to you.

Up? - Up? Were there stairs? Yes, of course, of course! It's all coming back, but those strange faces downstairs in the kitchen - where did they come from? How my head aches. It feels so strange. Nothing will ever be the same again. I know it. How tired I feel. I need to sleep.

A filtered, grey, half-light becomes the morning. No lovely hot sun streaming in through the window or the sound of dogs barking and African voices calling to one another; instead, the unusual song of a thrush-bird outside the window and beyond that, a bleak and cold morning. The solution to lying here and thinking and feeling cold is to dress as fast as possible to get to the kitchen and warmth and breakfast. Lydia has put away my clothes in a small chest of drawers. Oh dear – sigh. I'm cross that darned old Ouma has packed so few of my things, and she has left out all my personal treasures and the books I had kept hidden, I don't mind so much those which I took from Cousin Eric - I know them all from memory, for what they were worth. Of no use to him, I can hear her say. But she has packed the wretched Bible. I wonder who she thinks she might impress with that. Certainly not Lydia – no. Nor father, for that matter. He wouldn't allow me to have anything - let alone a book - even if it was a Bible, if he can help it. Just watch and see. Oh damn! Well, that's what Eric would say.

The dark-stained oak passages outside my bedroom add to the gloom. Floorboards creak at the lightest step. They are the only sounds that break the stillness. I pass vaguely familiar doors and corridors and cautiously creep down the heavily carved, grand staircase to the large wide hall below. I stare at the swords and shields attached to the dark wood panelling. They have a new significance to me now. I expect it's because I am older. All the same, I feel uncomfortable here. It is a strange…ominous…feeling. Like at any moment someone may appear from one of those closed doorways. They are waiting for me in that living silence. It is all kept alive by the heart-beat of the tall grandfather clock spilling its life-noise into the emptiness. I remember those long windows high up there, one on each side of the front door. Like a prison, studded, heavy, closed, bolted – to keep me in or to shut others out? Trapped, shut in.

The door to a large living room has been left open. I step inside the huge stone fireplace - *Inglenook*, I remember someone saying. I imagine the fires that burned in there. A sudden sweep of images crosses my mind. All the furniture seems to be as old as the house. It is a ghost house, a place where ghosts of the past have never left - like the furniture - keeping it an unchanging place of eternal time.

I explore further rooms down the corridor that have their doors closed. That last door at the end is hidden slightly from the rest, and it is open just a crack. Its heavy old oak beams are joined together with three solid steel bars, with jutting bolts driven through to give a medieval look, like something in one of those school history books. Maybe once it was a dungeon's entrance. There is something about this door that fills me with dread and the lost memory skewers me like one of Cousin Eric's trapped butterflies pinned to a board. I do not move for the black darkness of fear that oozes from some sleeping memory behind this door.

A voice behind me says *David*, and I shriek in fright.

Oh, ever so sorry to have startled you my lovely, but your breakfast is waiting for you and I heard you walking about and thought you must be hungry. Remember your way about, do you? Well, come on then, duck. No need to worry yourself about what happened in there. You just come along with your old Lydia, and she will give you a good breakfast. It's building up, is what you needs. Still so skinny, ain't you, and so small for your age? Now if I remember right, it was sausages that you liked. Your Mum was always starving herself with nowt much to eat, and you and your father could eat for England.

A comparison of with my father! How strange it sounds. I had never been told before that there were any similarities; so, eating meets the similarity. After a breakfast as full of chatter as of sausages and eggs, I am left to wonder about the garden.

Round the back of the house, I am certain that there was a large black pond I used to go to with Mama to feed the ducks. Ah - there they are, all still there as well as a few noisy geese. It is as if they have stepped from yesterday into today and there was never any different. They begin to shriek wildly at a stranger come to see them.

A menacing, wing-splashing gander swims up to the bank. Of course, he is protecting those two females swimming so gracefully around the small island in the pond's centre. The old nests are bare but a newly-made one has three large white eggs in it. It is still early spring-time here, Lydia said. They can't be quite ready to sit and incubate while there is a frost around. The male is hissing as he comes at me - surely I am no match for him? He seems so much larger than me. He thinks I come to intrude on their otherwise unmolested existence. Its wings swell out to a flailing wave of white feathers; his long neck is thrust forward, like a sword point aimed its target.

He charges at me. It all happens so fast; I am too close to get away fast enough. His serrated open beak snatches a firm hold of my jacket then twists his body in to me, his enemy. All the while he is ferociously flapping his powerful wings. The first blow catches me across the chest, winding me. There is no fear. There is something almost beautiful in the moment, and the words from Eric's poetry book, page one hundred and three, come to me -

> *In what distant deeps or skies*
> *Burnt the fire of thine eyes?*
> *On what wings dare he aspire?*
> *What the hand dare seize the fire?*
> *And what shoulder and what art*
> *Could twist the sinews of thy heart?*
> *And, when thy heart began to beat,*
> *What dread hand and what dread feet?*

And the strangest part is that I know I have much more power within me than this wild, hot-headed creature. I raise my hands forward and send a command down my arms the way I controlled the vicious rooster, the way I sometimes dealt with Eric. I don't hear Lydia's shouts as she comes round from the kitchen. She has a large stick in her hands and rushes at the goose, but there is no need. The goose has already loosed its hold and huddles itself down into the ground. It is quiet now.

I should have warned you about that wretched bird. Go, shoo! There is no letting go once he has a hold. Lucky, it is, that I came round the corner when I did.

Long before she reaches the bird she notices that it has folded away its wings and crouches down onto the ground, and is perfectly still.

Well, I never. Now how on earth did you do that? How did you make him do that?

Even if I could talk I could never explain that there are many inexplicable things I can do, ever since that day, that day when...

I step away from the bird who shuffles off back to the water, while Lydia keeps muttering to herself.

Well, I'll be blowed! Never have thought it! Just like the other little lad...

Tired of the garden, I turn back to the house. Lydia is outside near a high-walled kitchen garden, talking to the man who I think is the gardener. His name was Jake Cross, I think. It's such a long time ago...I think that was his name. Mama used to call out *Jake!* to him. Yes, it's Jake Cross. He seems so very, very old, even older than Kethla. His face is like a furrowed field, dry and brown from the sun, inset with beads for eyes, dark as deep wells. I want to walk away before he finds it necessary to speak to me.

I want to explore the house more in detail, perhaps find some books to look at. I remember that along with my treasures, Ouma omitted to pack my much battered 'Wind in the Willows'. Even though the story is in my mind, I like to have the book near me, with its old leather cover. Mama had written my name inside it. The story is more than real life; it is more alive. The animals are more than human and everything in their world turns out so well. They care for each other so, unlike humans.It is a world where everything is proportional. Rat is equal in size to Badger and Mole and Toad and they live in such friendly harmony with one another, sharing each other's pleasures, food and resting places.

Mama told me, since she has been in light, that we are all the same when we die. We get born in disproportionate sizes and needs so that while we are alive we are dissimilar, unequal and varying. Mama speaks a lot about such things. How I love to think about Mama...it makes me feel safe and comfortable inside, like Mole finding his house again.

...The weary Mole also was glad to turn in without delay, and soon had his head on his pillow, in great joy and contentment. But ere he closed his eyes he let them wander round his old room, mellow in the glow of the firelight that played or rested on familiar and friendly things which had long been unconsciously a part of him, and now smilingly received him back, without rancour...

Chapter Eighteen

I have found the library. I knew it was here. It is a dark and dusty room filled with books from floor to ceiling. It is on the second floor of the house, just above the room below guarded by the medieval door. The door is closed but not locked. It is heavy and I don't think it has been used much, because it makes a fierce rasping growl at being opened.

This room holds secrets. I know them, yet the memory of them is dust filled in my mind. This was the room that Mama was made to sit in to learn how to meditate.I remember how he used to tell her she *must* learn to meditate. He used to say that her mind was too scattered. He himself meditated every single day - for hours - in his study-room, behind the fearful door. Mornings and evenings he would sit, straight-backed upon his leather bound arm chair. Hands on his knees, his eyes shut blocking out the world around him. If he caught you watching him, you would get a thrashing when Mama was not about, he would say. Was it action or non-action that meditation was meant to be? I forget what they said. All those words that meant nothing to me, and not much to poor Mama. The word meditation still makes me think of punishment. There is so much that I have lost in my memory. But those words: sit still, be silent, be...locked away...frightened, darkness...I can't think of them anymore.

Each time Mama went out anywhere, it happened. I can see myself now, being dragged to that dark hole and locked in there. *You will stay there forever if you speak of it...don't speak...you will never speak again...you are slow and silent.*

I am slow and silent. Mama fretted when I stopped talking and became still and silent; she questioned Lydia. Lydia said she had no idea what Mama was talking about, but Lydia knew what was happening. I saw her watching when he put me there, and she said nothing to Mama...still! Enough memory! I want to still my mind...

...Then the brutal minions of the law fell upon the hapless Toad. They loaded him with chains, and dragged him from the Court House, shrieking, praying, protesting; across the market-place, where the playful populace, always as severe upon detected crime as they are sympathetic and helpful when one is merely 'wanted', assailed him with jeers, carrots and popular catchwords...

I am being silly, I am cutting out my mind over things that have passed. I so easily lapse into being a frightened baby. I won't allow it. I must make myself go forward. This is only the old library, the friendly library. It is much as I saw it last. Dark wood-panels, shadows, rows and rows of ancient bound books stand like Eric's tin soldiers waiting to be arranged and rearranged. Mama said some of the books were as old as the house, and were not to be touched.

I go from shelf to shelf, reading titles and trying to recognize authors I have heard mentioned. It is a problematical choice, as no one reads much where I have just come from. Short of Ouma's Bibles, old school books, odd story books, Eric's school books, there had been so little to read. On a dusty shelf in the living room, held together by some shady looking stone saints, was an old collection of books called 'Johnson's Works' which had belonged somewhere in Ouma's family past. I would often look at them and wonder where and how Johnson worked. Ouma totally forbade any touching. *Don't touch, there's a good boy - no good to you anyway you will never be able to read anything, let alone that collection of old rubbish.* And here is Johnson again, leather bound. His name Samuel Johnson embossed in gold lettering. I am fascinated.

Once a fortnight, Ouma would go to the local library and take out a couple of books - most often never even opened, but it was something people did. They were left, mostly unopened, at her bedside. Well she might have read them when she went to bed. I was not allowed into their room so I wouldn't know, but I would creep in there sometimes when she was out and read the odd library book. They were silly love stories, boring mostly, with silly conversations. Oupa got daily papers and poured over them, leaving them in untidy piles about the house for Ouma to complain about. Otherwise all my knowledge is verbally gained, and very little gleaned from books.

In this wonderful old library I spend hours looking, opening books, choosing. I come across a collection of books whose covers are just like my Wind in The Willows. There is a space where a book is missing. It is the same size space as my book. This is where it must have come from. I take out others around it; Robinson Crusoe, The Water Babies, Alice in Wonderland...

I have also found a dictionary. This one is massive, much bigger than the one Eric had from school. Now I need to look something up...

...Toad is busily arraying himself in those singularly hideous habiliments so dear to him, which transform him from a

(comparatively) good-looking Toad into an object which throws any decent-minded animal that comes across it into a violent fit...

Mama had no idea what habiliments were.

Habiliment, n. attire (esp. in pl.). – adjs. habilable (Carlyle), capable of being clothed: habilatory, of clothes or dressing. (Fr. habiller, to dress – L. habilis, fit, ready – habere.) Ah, yes, of course it is. I know what it means now, but I am even more confused with all those full stops and half words. I take the dictionary with me and the books I have chosen back to my room, and begin to read.

Lydia calls me downstairs for meals and talks all the while I am eating. I turn to my memory as I used to in the past so that I don't have to listen, but my mind jumps back to what I have been reading so that they become...

...'I suppose you go great voyages,' said the Water Rat with growing interest. 'Months and months out of sight of land, and provisions running short... Mr. Stanley, I presume!' was the work of a moment. But, alas! He had gone from my gaze – like a Cook's Tourist (jeu de mot, made in diary, even under the most trying circumstances); and once more I am all alone in the Great Desert... 'I can't explain myself, I'm afraid, sir,' said Alice, 'because I'm not myself, you see.' 'I don't see, said the Caterpillar...it happened one day, about noon, going towards my boat, I was exceedingly surprised with the print of a man's naked foot on the shore, which was very plain to be seen in the sand...

There you go, there you go now - you need to get outside, my lad. Up in that room all day...it's not right.

I can tell that there is a certain conflict between her duties towards me and her obligations to my Father, and she discusses it with me as a means of conciliation.

I know as your Pa says you must be locked in, but a young lad like you needs fresh air and running about in the garden. Nowt wrong with you, as I said. I was saying this morning to Jake that you is a normal lad needing normal things, not needing shut in. He says, I can see that Lydie - only to look at the lad, he needs fresh air. Shutting yourself in to your room all day, don't seem right. I for one won't tell your Pa if you is to go out. 'Ere, what about that meat pie; eat it afore it gets cold now! Put that there book down for a moment and eat, lad...now, when you've eaten, Jake says as 'e will take you up to top field with him this afternoon and you can see the new lambs arriving...

The thought of seeing new lambs has an appeal, but I feel less inclined to be in the company of Jake Cross. Though Jake is well-meaning and says as little as Lydia says too much, I miss Kethla. I miss Inja.

My eyes water at the brightness of the sun. This is different from the African sun, which beams hot gold down onto you every day. This sun is luminous. It wants to be recognized as a privilege to you for its being there, and eyes that have been in shade sting.

There is growing warmth in the air and I feel a sense of release as we walk up to the top fields to see the lambs. The lively abandonment of new-found life uplifts me and gives me that resolve to live and know. I have never felt it before.

I hold out my hands to the lovable small creatures and they come forward bold, unafraid and full of curiosity.

My word, you 'av a knack there. How they come to you. They seem drawn. They seem to know as you mean no 'arm.

Jake is being kind. I think he likes me.

Chapter Nineteen

This morning, Lydia brought me an exercise book with a pen.

If you can read my lad, you should be as able as to write. 'Ere, take this pen and make your name, there.

I take the pen carefully in my hand as I have seen others write. Mama used to help me to write. She would hold her hand over mine and make pictures that she said I had made. I never did much more than scribble, and then when I stopped speaking I found I could no longer make letters for words on the paper any more. I have thought often of trying to write, but I have never been given pen and paper.

I make a first mark on the white page and then draw the letter D as I know from print, then follows A and so on, until I see my name printed.

Good - now p'raps we are getting somewhere, see? You can practice with 'yes' and 'no' and when you want to answer me. You can do that, see?

I spend all afternoon filling those pages and all the day after that. I wrote out Toad's story till I ran out of paper.

Well, I never! You gone and written yourself a whole story. That's ever so good. Do you know joined up writing now? Print takes time, see. Ever so nice written though, I grant you. Well, I will 'av to buy more paper for you see. You used up the big pile there. How long that take you? Days, I shouldn't wonder. Nowt wrong with you, lad. Lydia gives me a lovely smile.

I feel so content, and the happiest I have been since Kethla has been gone. There are no considerations about Ouma wanting me to be under her eye all the time. There are no thoughts of trying to escape Cousin Eric or wishing for Kethla to return or willing Mother to appear somewhere, anywhere, just to feel her presence. I have freedom and as many books to read as I want.

Your Dad will be 'ome tonight, David. Its Friday, he comes home of a Friday - well, most Fridays, `cept the last two, he does. As well you stay in your room lad and I fetch you up your dinner, all right?

I don't need to be told. I like being there. The stories fill my life; they make my life.

At around seven in the evening, the dark-green car drives in and stops. I hear car doors shut and from below the stairs I hear him talking to Lydia. It is more accurate to say I hear Lydia talking to him. Her voice is always loud, and carries up the stairs.

He's been as good as gold. No trouble at all and he likes to read, sir. My word, he likes to read.

What nonsense, he has no reading ability. He is pretending to read. Where on earth did he find anything to read? Don't tell me you have allowed him into the library.

Well sir, can't stop him now, can I, and if it gives him pleasure…?

I am thinking; please Lydia, please don't tell him anymore. My heart makes a skip as I think how foolish she is.

Doors slam. He has gone into his study. I close my door. I don't wish to hear any more.

I have a feeling that I will be ostracized for taking books. I gather all the books I have finished with, then creep out to the library. I replace those and take a couple more that I can secrete into my room somewhere, before the door is locked from me.

Chapter Twenty

It was just as I thought. Early this morning he went out for a walk and came back for breakfast an hour or so later. Sure enough the keys were found, and the library door has been securely locked. I know I must keep to my room all the time he is here. Keep out of his way.

At lunch time Lydia brings me a tray of food. *Oh, I am ever so sorry, Davie lad. I told 'im you was reading and he has locked up the library. What a shame. I won't tell 'im no more what you is doing. I promise, lad. He just 'as a bee in is bonnet over you, lad. He was like it with 'is other son.*

Other son - what other son? I am thinking. Anyway, what a relief that I am not expected to have my meals with him.

Shortly after lunch, another car drives up into the courtyard. It is a white Cortina. I recognize it. Aunt Jess has one. From my bedroom window, I see a young woman step out of the car. My Father is already there to greet her. She must be at least twenty years younger than him but she seems happy enough to be folded in his arms, and taken indoors with a small hold-all from her boot. That is an indication that she will stay the night. Please, please don't let them want to see me.

I am safely left alone all weekend - in my room, undisturbed and relieved to be so. This new-found reading takes all my concentration and effort and is so rewarding to my understanding of everything.

Sunday evening, the young woman's car leaves and my Father retires to his study again. Meditating, maybe? Monday morning, very early, he has gone and with him goes that tight choking feeling that binds my mind to those ghosts that breathe fear about the house.

The subject of the key is no matter to me, but I don't tell Lydia. I see I can't trust her to keep her mouth shut. I learned the trick of opening doors that had been locked way back in Ouma's home when she wished to lock something away, especially from me. I simply go to the door and hold my hands there, concentrating until I hear the lock turn and I am able to open the door. I make sure to do this when Lydia is not around. I do not want her reporting what I am up to. I also make sure not to take books into the kitchen at mealtimes any more, for her to watch me and report back to Father. There is so much I am learning.

I read. Reading is all I do.

Going out into the garden I feel unsafe, so I read. If Lydia can let me down, so can Jake.

Reading has become my life. I am able to escape into a new world with these books, and each book changes me a little more. Each day I am changed more.

The young woman comes most weekends. I watch her arrive from the top floor but I can't see much of her, only that she is young and has long hair. I can't see her colours from up here, but she looks nice. They go out a lot. Walking, I think, and they talk when they come back in. Then they disappear into one of the reception rooms or Father's study. I tend not to notice. I am just relieved their activities don't include me. Well, of course not.

During the week, now, I spend a shared time between Jake Cross in the garden and Lydia in the kitchen, who keeps me up to date with her opinions of this and that, which are well tinted with colourful expressions. Jake, I have discovered, is very knowledgeable about the garden - perhaps not so well acquainted with the spirits of the plants as Kethla, but he works hard and likes my help, so I find him agreeable to be with. He does not talk – even more agreeable.

There has been no word from either of my grandparents. How could there be? I realize that if they had sent messages, I would never hear of them for belief that I would not understand them. I don't care anyway.

Weeks and weeks go by and with them the veiled weekends, keeping out of the way, especially weekends when the young woman does not visit - but this never changes the circumstances of my Father's routine, and his long sessions in his study when he is meditating, no doubt, and he leaves me alone. It seems he has no interest in me. It must be the circumstances of his friend.My comfort lies in not remembering too much or reawakening those fears that are still dark patches in my dreams, but I am still aware that nothing lasts forever, for life is predestined for change. I learnt that this morning.

It is Saturday, bedroom-reading time. I am happy enough with that, though now the warm weather has nudged its way into the countryside, I resent not getting out at all. I settle myself down to read, when the door opens without a single warning knock. I suppose I am used to everyone thinking I am the idiot who has no need for private space.

He stands there, staring at me.

Up until this moment I have not before taken in the details of his appearance. He has always been the presence that must be avoided or obeyed. He is tall. I suppose he must have been good-looking when he was younger. He just looks old to me. Not quite as old as Oupa; much thinner though, and thinner hair.

I notice mostly his eyes. They are a dark shade of green and have an angry look about them, just like I remember them. He radiates a mixture of colours about him, some greys, along with some vibrant violets. I am finding it difficult to assess him and he is clearly finding it troublesome assessing me. He imposes an air of blessedness about himself, as if he is almighty - superior and way above anything futile and worthless. This is the side of him that I expect he wishes people to see, but never to be described as arrogance.

David.

I can see he is finding it hard to know what to say to me, so he repeats my name again.

David. I do not make eye contact and wish I had had time to lose the book, but there it is - unmistakable and culpable. His eyes drop down to see what I was reading. He picks it up from my hands.

My, a rather obtuse literary taste. How much of this have you read? If, indeed, you can read. How much have you absorbed? A savant? Is that what we will call you? I expect Lydia forgot to keep the library door locked. I shall have to speak to her.

He takes a pause between each sentence, not quite sure how to go on. He is self-conscious. I choose at that moment to look back at him. I don't avert my eyes any more. I want to know what he will do. He is looking shifty. I know that he is fully aware of my own alertness and approachability but he is never going to acknowledge my abilities; he has made a professional diagnosis, and there it will remain. He has reasons of his own. I also know that I will never come under the scrutiny of any other professionals who might dispute his assessment. I am unsure what he will do next, and I feel uneasy about it.

Will I always be left to read as I please and do what I like? He knows that I am getting to an independent age. I am nearly ten years old. What if I leave on my own? What if I disclose the knowledge that is locked within me?

You will come down and join me for dinner tonight, David. Understood?

He leaves the room and takes my book with him. It is a strategy of power, I can see that.

The young lady is not here this weekend, and he is feeling out of sorts. I have the feeling that he will take the irritation out on me, as I go to the dining room when Lydia calls me to go. There is a sense of pure dread. I feel like those fish that Eric used to net at the stream, just so he could watch as they squirmed and slowly suffocated out of water.

Lydia leaves the meal on the table and goes out. She is looking worried. They have had words, and she too doesn't know where this is leading.

He watches every move I make during the meal, without comment and without conversation. I know that his mind is full of reservation and uncertainty. He would like to know how much I had seen and taken in the day he strangled Mother and thrown her body into the Alibaba pot. He wants to know if I have told anyone. But he is unable to put any of these things to words without incriminating himself. He has so many unspoken things buried in his thoughts. And I can read his mind.

A great shame that the old gardener disposed of your Mother as he did.

He has broken the silence at last. I know what he is trying to do.

Your Grandmother filled me in with all the details. Of course I had come back here, expecting her to join me.

He is testing me. I can see right through him. I am beginning to learn now how he is, what he is and where he has come from, and for some odd reason I feel pity for him. I look up at him and challenge him with my eyes.

He stops talking at once, and looks down at his plate. He is unable to continue. He is aware that I know. He is only uncertain how much I am able, or willing, to do about it.

Of course, now that you are here you will have to obey the rules of the house, do as you are told. You remember the meditation practice? It will have to be resumed. Mental discipline, David. Mental discipline, remember!

A silence.

Do you understand? Answer me at once. Don't you pretend you still are not able to talk. I can see the intelligence behind those eyes. You can't fool me, boy.

His fist comes down like a felled tree onto the table. The force of his anger releases those guarded and vicious soul-steeped traits. The colours that arrange themselves about his head turn a violent red.

I begin to remember. Remembering makes me vulnerable. I stand up. I am ashamed that I have lost control, and peed in my pants.

Lydia has come into the room to see why he is shouting. She sees the wet floor about my feet and the damp patch on my trousers, and I am embarrassed.

What's he done now? She speaks with her voice like a clucking hen, scratching at the turf to find fresh worms for its young. Behind her voice I see that she too understands him, and she too feels sorry for him.

Come on, David, don't stop here now. Upstairs with you, lad, and change out of them wet things. Don't think as he is up to eating at table sir, like you said - autistic children 'ave no control. I know at once that she too knows something, and she knows about me.

He has to comply. He is in a dangerous position. He slams out of the room. Lydia hurries me up the stairs, talking all the way like the mother-hen she is, pretending nothing has happened.

We are, the three of us, caught up in a kind of inescapable web. I am the fly that has become stuck, who does not struggle, but waits. Father thinks he is the spider, but he is just another fly struggling to get out. He has been challenged and no-one, nothing, challenges Father; that much I remember clearly.

Chapter Twenty One

I am ten, and I know that I have a mature brain. My birthday came and went with no recognition, even if it had been remembered. I have more self-assurance and ability to judge things for myself, and I feel that I am learning more and more daily.

I am beginning to see that I am in a certain position of power over my Father. I also know that everything has its limits, but I will not allow myself to be fearful again – and, of course, that will take time and practice. I must keep reading. I learn so much more through the books.

When Father returns to London I feel free, but all the while I know deep down that it is a freedom that lies sleeping. I realize that I need now to begin to face my old fears and come to terms with what lies before me. I reduce the word *fear* to harmless words as in the dictionary - *a painful emotion, apprehension of danger* - and tell myself that I can control the affect it has on my senses. But I know that fear is like a tight coiled snake that sleeps – harmless, but once disturbed from its sleep it springs out, dangerous and deadly with the implication of what has caused it. I know there is something behind that intimidating study door that divides me from those painful memories. I used to be locked up in there. Now he locks me out. Opening locked doors is an interesting challenge. The more I use this ability, the easier it becomes.

The room is as I remember it. A gloomy light is all the latticed window allows. The great dark reddish-brown mahogany desk stands there, almost threatening me. It has an owner who hates me and would never allow me near it.

Nothing had changed. His leather armchair waits for him, severe and basic. The ancient suit-of-armour in a darkened corner, a leather chaise-lounge arranged pertinently at one side, and sundry chairs opposite the desk suggest sometime visits from patients. On the walls hang typecast portraits of unappealing old men, whose distinguished lives advise them to frown down at anyone who looks up at them. There is a large bookcase filled with medical books on his subject; the detailed exploration of the brain and how to reach the mind. He uses his knowledge to twist minds and make them do the things he wants them to do. He has chosen a profession that really suits that inner purpose of his life.

Those heavy metal discs hanging there…ah, yes! I remember now. Mama said they were some ancient warrior's shields, but I know their double purpose. One of those warrior's shields moves. I remember that. Something triggered the movement. Behind it, my terror lay.

Now it starts again inside me, the beating of my heart. What is it? Why am I so frightened? All I can do is remember the arrangement of the room and its contents, but what is the forgotten thing that instils such fear in me and has become a block in my mind?

I stand there and call out to Mama, but she no longer comes to me. I can no longer hear her voice. I begin to shake. Something has been eradicated from my mind, and I cannot reach beyond what is suffocating me.

...The voice died away and ceased, as an insect's tiny trumpet dwindles swiftly into silence; and the Water Rat, paralysed and staring, saw at last but a distant speck on the white surface of the road. Mechanically he rose and proceeded to repack the luncheon-basket, carefully and without haste. Mechanically he returned home, gathered together a few small necessaries...

What an earth are you doing in here, Davie lad? Cor, would your Dad go mad if he knew you was in his office! Come on, come on now. No, don't just stand there looking vacant - 'ere, take my hand. Yes, out we go, out we go...careful, now.

Lydia says I must spend the rest of the week in the garden with Jake. She is certain that I am not well because I have been indoors too long. I am often ill. There is a weakness in my chest but she doesn't know about it - she just says *are you feeling alright, David?* and lets me be. I was always ill when I was in Ouma's house. I would stay in bed all day thinking of the story. Here, when I am ill I hide in the library, the door locked behind me, and pretend I do not hear Lydia call.

Jake has been clipping away at a briar rose that has taken over a large part of the wall on the East Wing of the house. There is a pile of thorny tendrils that I must pick up and take away in the barrow. I am pricked and punctured all over my arms and hands. Jake looks at me, and silently throws an oversized pair of gardening gloves to me. He says little. I like that.

Near the base of the bush there is a small door, rusted over. It must have led into the cellar of the house at some time. I want to know what it is and look at Jake, stupid in my dumb state, and he stares back at me, looks at the door, and shakes his head.

That door ain't bin used in many years, lad. Curious, are you? Suppose nowt wrong with curiosity. Like most lads I 'spect. That there old cellar below also boarded in, long 'fore my time, and I bin 'ere long enough to know.

Still, my imagination has started to grow. I want to know more about the house. How old it is, who owned it before? How long has Father had it, and why does he live here?

No-one ever comes here except his girlfriend. I don't even know if he has other family. If he does, they never visit him. I seem to remember that he had a funny sister who visited a long time ago. Perhaps they see him when he is up in London. Anyway, that is something I don't need to think about - they never come here.

Chapter Twenty Two

I am sitting in the library. I sit here often; I feel it is my own place. As I familiarize myself with the room and its contents, I feel a belonging here. It is part of me and I have once been part of it. Slowly, something seeps into my consciousness. A whole past reawakens in me of another way of thinking. It is affirmed after I have been reading Boswell's Life of Johnson; its interest only lies in those old leather-bound volumes in Ouma's living room. I stopped at a passage in volume I on page forty six:

The rod produces an effect which terminates in itself. A child is afraid of being whipped, and gets his task, and there's an end on't; whereas, by exciting emulation and comparisons of superiority, you lay the foundation of lasting mischief; you make brothers and sisters hate each other...

Has thinking and behaviour changed much, I ask myself?
Nothing much has changed here in centuries. Even the old furniture is heavy and uncomfortable. The wood has fossilized to a steel resistance which could in that state endure endless time. It has that musty smell of damp, fixed in with furniture wax so deep it has gone solid with the wood.

Besides a set of encyclopaedias, there is so much in the library to read about the origins of this property. In a large, heavy, locked cupboard are pile of old manuscripts - whole volumes of typed essays, articles, dissertations, compositions whatever you will call them. Many by E.L. Tyndal or A.T. Tyndal, whom I have discovered were my grandparents. I have yet to read those. Now I make a start to find the answers to all my questions about the house that I want to know.

Chapter Twenty Three

I have learned that the house is perhaps fifteenth-century, and even older in its original size. A certain Carthusian Abbot bought it and converted it as a place of refuge for the persecuted monks, and it remained as such for a long time before a betrayal.

In 1535, when Henry VIII made Thomas Cromwell his Vicar-General and gave him the power to visit any monastery in England, he drew up fictitious reports to condemn any monastery he wished to, without evidence, accepting bribes and helping himself to anything of value he so wished. The smaller monasteries fell first – then, with more violent measures, there was wholesale destruction of the greater monasteries.

The said Abbot had foreseen this destruction and taken matters in his own hands long before, by creating the façade of a private home into an underground monastery for his most devout monks. After the discovery that a few Carthusian monks were inhabiting this last small bastion of a banished order, the property was claimed and turned over to the crown.

While the aristocracy and gentry were busy buying up the monastic land sold off after the Dissolution of the Monasteries there were no immediate takers for this old property, as it was said to be inhabited by demonic ghosts, and anyone with an interest to purchase died some horrible death. Thus it remained closed up and un-tenanted for some long time.

The chronicles and articles written about the house are not very well-documented. I think many of them are deductions made by much later occupiers who had followed the stories of local gossip, but I enjoy them. They seemed to have a ring of truth about them, something that occurred in some distant dream, perhaps.

The table I sit at is called Jacobean, says Lydia, I have looked it up - it certainly fits the dates I have learned of the house. There are fluted scrolls and solemn faces carved into the thick wooden legs, and the tall back chairs have smaller sculptures of lesser sprites and angels. They seem to creep out of the wood and stare at me.

Behind me is a tall thin cupboard between the shelves. I have looked inside and seen old ink-wells there. What was once ink has dried to a black stain now, but there are also remnants of something that might have once been a quill or two, and scrolls of paper which crumble into feathery dust when I touch them.

I am actually surprised so much has been left intact, after the place had been ransacked by the invading iconoclasts and purifiers of the new religious order under crown and state. There is so much written about that time here. I am trying to absorb it all.

I see that the big stone carved eagle above the library door is the old Christian symbol of St. John. I like the idea of St. John - guardian of the books. The symbol for Saint Mark, a winged lion, stands above the living room. The Ox is for Saint Luke and it is perched appropriately before the kitchen. Saint Matthews's angel guards Father's study - some kind of irony there. I look around at all that this place represents, and I have this feeling of eternity here; a place where time stands still.

Lydia says that the library has been locked up ever since its holy occupiers had been put to death there. I think she told me as a means of keeping me out of it. I have the notion that not only was locking it up a deliberate act by those hidden priests for its preservation, and protection for the secrets that it held, but that it kept anyone at bay who might discover that there were still occupants in the subterranean passages. It has certainly been used in the last century by my grandparents, who have left to it all their research papers and their own books, which they simply put in front of old ones. Well, it helps to protect them...

I have tentatively tried to rediscover the dark tunnel that I came through into the library when I was small. I wonder if I had dreamt it. I remember that I came out from behind a bookcase.

I have pushed each bookcase in turn and nothing happens. I know that something in the room moves it, but I don't know what it is. Something in my mind tells me that the opening has something to do with the marble heads by the window.

I go to the least intimidating of the heads. He is a bald priest whose mantle covers his neck to his armless torso. I pull at him, trying to turn his head, but nothing happens. The next marble bust is a bearded saint. It also will not move. The third is a saint with plump, round cheeks.I feel a strange familiarity with this face as I turn it one way, then find that it moves quite easily the other way. At the same moment that I move his head, I hear a grinding noise, and one of the book cases moves very slowly inward into the room.

I go over and stare down into a dark cavity. It is a priest hole, just like the one in Father's study. No, too many horrors of being locked in there. I turn the head back into position and the book-shelf slides back into place, leaving no trace of its movement.

The next head seems to have no effect, but the one after it does. Out of the sad face, sightless eyes look upwards towards heaven, and at its base are written the words: *lux ex tenebris invictus*. I know at once, as if by instinct, the meaning. *Out of the darkness, the light of an invincible*.

Something about those words attaches itself to the edge of memory. What was it? Why do they seem significant to me? Another bookcase slides inwards, and there are the steps I remember from those years ago when I escaped.

Lydia keeps a torch in her pantry. I can walk about without losing my way. I go at once to find it, but now that I am on the way I am beset by a thousand doubts. What if I go down and can't come back up? What if the passages have caved in since I was last there?

Lydia is outside, talking to the man who delivers the milk twice a week. Good, that means she will be occupied for some time. I take the torch from its position on the shelf and test the batteries. Good. Back in the library I re-open the aperture, and begin to climb down the steep stairs. They are not as steep as I remember, but then my legs were much shorter.

There is a small reed of light that telescopes down from way above, now the torchlight fixes all that the darkness hid before. I want to see the boy's skeleton once more. Once I am there I doubt that this was the spot, but it is quite clear now that the skeleton of the small boy has gone. There is not a single trace of him anymore. I expect someone has been down here and removed him.

I remember Father's angry looks when he took the toy engine from me. It must have been him. But whatever the story behind that will have to wait. It will undoubtedly be revealed by one of Lydia's indiscretions, some day. Still, the image of the boy remains imprinted behind my eyes. It was something disturbing, terrifying, and the questions return again to my mind. I remember the blinding light and the high-pitched sounds that swept through my body and drowned me, and I remember the light figure and then fainting and waking up cold and damp in the dark, and after that...after that, I began to know.

In front of me is the tunnel I remember being spooked by. This time I use the challenging light of the torch, and go along it. It forks into two directions at one point so I follow the left hand fork, but there has at some stage been a fall of stones in front of me blocking the way. Someone, at some time has become trapped there. A lady's high-heeled shoe is just visible from under the stones. It's not old-fashioned in the old, old sense but it is a shoe that Mother would have worn, perhaps even Ouma. Someone has died here quite recently.

A cold feeling creeps over me. These walls are lined with traps triggered by a lever that will release a fall of rock on anyone in pursuit. They are traps designed to protect the pursued from invaders. The wearer of those shoes was crushed deliberately by someone lying in wait for her. I know it. I know the victim, and I know her killer. I shudder. I don't want to explore that likelihood any more. I retrace my steps to the fork and take the alternative direction. The tunnel has come to a sudden end. A flight of stone steps leads downwards.

The steps are steep like the ones in the wall, but there is an old iron rail that I grip to stop myself from falling forward. The darkness smothers me. The damp and clinging black is filled with swirling creatures.

Why have I come here? That fear thing has come back to frighten me. Where is the figure of light I saw that time? It flashes constantly across my mind. I must go on. I must find it again. I have to re-discover it. I need to know what it was. Have I been drawn back here by the strange sounds I heard before? I don't know. I don't know. There is nothing strange happening this time. Did I imagine it? Surely not! It was so real.

I feel the presence of invisible beings wrapping themselves around me. They are as curious to see me as I am to see them. Now the whispering starts. I remember the whispering. It is like a chant. There is no definite recognition of words, only a whispering, like lost souls calling out to me.

I flash the torch about. It pierces the darkness, catching here and there a wall, a door, a further tunnel. The remnants of rusty torch brackets line the damp walls. It stinks of rotten damp here. Strange bulbous fungi like wild mushrooms grow in corners.

I walk a little way ahead. The passage takes a left angle, and opens here into a kind of chamber. A heap of mouldy cloth and wood indicates the remains of some furniture. Leading off from this room are a series of small cells, each with the remains of what must have been rusted iron beds. Otherwise, the place is bare.Though the place is dark and damp from long neglect and non-use, there is a strong trace of air which comes through from ducts in the wall. These rooms must have an outside wall that faces daylight somewhere, perhaps a hill-side or a cliff. Certainly no places I have visited outside.

Anything here that was of any value has now gone. Austere lives - monastic solitude - stark necessities. These are their footprints.

I see the old priests living here. Long lives, long times cut shorter for the cold, damp darkness.That price of martyrdom for a supposed place in heaven. What heaven? Was it worth the heartache, the discomfort, the agonies? How did they perceive the betrayal of their hopes with just another life to learn by? What if? What if heaven were much further away than this sacrifice suffered for their faith? What if heaven could only be reached by learning more than just being a sacrificial lamb, this once? I sigh. I move on.

I follow the passage for a further distance. Here is another chamber, larger than the last. It has a heavy table of solid wood, or it could even be stone. One or two wooden benches remain; the rest have rotted and fallen to the ground. When I shine the light onto the walls, I see a cross with Christ in his eternal state of suffering pinioned to it. I have seen the cross before. I am certain of it. There is something about it that mesmerises me. It is some time before I can tear myself away.

The passageway outside ends in a doorway…it is locked. It opens only when I hold my hands to it, to make it open, as I do with locked doors. The lock moves and the hinges groan as I push the heavy door open. It seems to be a kind of cellar, or storage place where more modern things have been stored. A rusty old bike with rotted tires leans against the wall. There is an old push-along lawn mower and some crates. The door in front must lead outside, for light cracks through a small crevice at the side.

I hear a voice. It's Jake's voice talking to Lydia.

This must be the cellar that Jake told me was boarded up. Well, there are no boards. It has simply rusted and it has recently been locked. I see the floor is earth, and someone has dug a hole here, relatively recently. They have buried something. The earth is heaped up slightly.

I think of the boy's skeleton and know what is under that earth.

I hear Lydia telling Jake she must call me down to supper. I must have been down here for much longer than I thought. I retrace my steps and hurry back to the library, where the bookcase is still ajar. My keen mind feeds on all that I have seen.

There is some strange mystery here and I have been part of it. I am part of it. I know it now. It comes to me from all those lost dreams.

I push the bookcase back into position and go to the kitchen, silent and secret in my knowing.

Chapter Twenty Four

She has come unexpectedly early, even before Father. This is unusual.

I have been watching her come and go in all the months since I have been here. I don't believe she knows a single thing about my existence. About as little as I know about her, or their relationship.

I look out for her each week.I watch her climb out of her car and see how pleased Father always is to greet her. I notice the pretty dresses she wears, and how she does her hair. She reminds me so much of my Mama.

I am in the vegetable garden with Jake.He has set me to the boring job of weeding around the new asparagus shoots, explaining very carefully which is weed and which is a plant. He is never too sure that I have understood him and so he has to demonstrate, while I look out for small mole hills that I try to disguise from him. I hate him catching moles. They are such pretty creatures. I identify them with Mr. Mole from my story.

Jake always keeps conversation strictly to matters concerning the garden, the sheep in the top fields and the state of the weather, otherwise we work side by side not speaking. I know nothing about his life or family, unlike Lydia who enjoys unburdening herself to any ear. I expect she imagines I am incapable of judgement and will never disclose her secrets, and in all likelihood will not understand any of what she is saying. Jake regards me as a simpleton who is only capable of assisting in the more tiresome aspects of gardening, like weeding.

There is a need to keep them rows clear of all weeds or the young stems get tangled, see? Its raspberries, strawberries and asparagus as all comes in one go, see? The rest of the year is spent yearning for those things, and they all come at once – look, you.

Hello there. Her clear soft voice comes from the driveway. I see her for the first time close up. She is the most beautiful vision I have ever seen. Her skin is smooth and clear and her lovely soft blue eyes are so bright and pure, and her golden hair is loose about her shoulders. The colours that bubble around her head are light and blue like her eyes, and I am instantly in love with her.

Jake - it is Jake, isn't it?

Oh, 'ar. You come a day early, miss. I don't know as Lydia is expectin' you, is she, miss?

No, no one is. I have been in the area on business, and thought I'd surprise Mr.Tyndal with a visit a day early. Hello - and who are you? She is looking in my direction.
This 'ere is young David. Mr.Tyndal's son.
Good gracious! I had no idea he had a son. I only heard that he lost his wife and a child, some twenty years ago. You can't possibly be that child, she said, again addressing me. *How old are you?*
No good as you talking to 'im, Miss - he can't speak. Has not spoken since he were three years old, Miss. The Master says he be autistic, see.
Gosh! I can't think why he has never told me.
'E never tells no-one, Miss. The lad has been with grandparents in Africa since he were a nipper. Lydia takes care of 'im now, see. 'Is own Mother passed away just afore he came as I bin told, and he bin 'ere ever since.

The new information has somehow taken her by surprise. She stands looking awkward and restless, twisting her car keys in her fingers. I am something she had not anticipated.
Well, I will go in and ask Lydia to make some tea. Would you like to join me, David? My name is Josephine - people call me Jo.

I would like very much to join her. There is something fresh and new about this woman that people called Jo. She is so like Mama - Mother. I follow her into the house and sit down on a stool in the front living room, where she indicates with her hand for me to sit. Then she goes to the kitchen and I hear her talking to Lydia there. I only catch pieces of what they are saying, but it is obvious that they are speaking about me. They return to the room together.I have not moved an inch since she left.

Lydia carries the silver tea-tray and places it down on one of the low tables. She has put a plate of her own special biscuits on the tray.
Davie, I see as you 'ave met Miss Armstrong. See, he listens to what I say. Don't you, David? Well, I find him as good as gold, I do. No trouble. Are you, David? My proper little friend and companion. Helps a good mite, too. Then he spends most of 'is time reading. Can't think that he gets much out of the books he reads, but he gives 'em enough attention, he does.
Where does he find books that he can read?
Oh, he takes 'em from the library, he does.
I thought the library was kept locked all the time. Stephan said there were valuable books in there that must be kept under lock and key.
Maybe they is, but he gets 'em alright - don't you, David, my lad? I was just saying to Jake the other day - Jake, I says, that boy has some rum talents. Can get in wherever he wants to go. He mightn't talk, but

he knows 'ow to get around like as others can't, he does! Don't you, lad? Well, there you go. I'll leave you with him so as you can get acquainted.

He's not dangerous in any way, is he?

Course not; whatever would give you the idea?

Well, his father has kept him hidden from me all this time, I just thought...

No, don't you go worritin' yourself. If you would rather he not be 'ere I'll call him away. All right, David? See he has poured the tea for you both. It's just as he can't talk, see.

Why, thank you, David. How kind. No, don't put sugar in for me. I don't take it.

Lydia leaves the room, and at once the young woman has become unnerved at my presence. I raise my hands and send my colours towards her.

How did you do that? How strange I feel suddenly. What an extraordinary boy you are, David!

She is staring at me. She is totally uncertain how to deal with me. I lift my cup and drink my tea while she stares. Then I take two biscuits and eat them, rather fast. It's a habit I have left over from Ouma days when Eric would never allow me more than one biscuit after Ouma had left the room, and he would scoff the rest - quickly.

What is that book you have? I show it to her.

Tolstoy? Anna Karenina is a bit heavy for a boy of your age. Is this your taste?

I raise my shoulders. I have no taste in what I read. I read because I enjoy the words that form the sentences and fold into wonderful stories and that they require no responses from me.

Can you write, David? Perhaps you can write an answer for me? She takes a pen from her bag and an old envelope and hands them to me. I nod.

Do you like poetry?

I write: *I only knew one poet in my life:*
And this, or something like, was his way.
You saw go up and down Valladolid,
A man of mark, to know next time you saw.
His very serviceable suit of black
Was courtly once and conscientious still.

That is Browning. You have memorised it, she says.

I stop writing.

How well you memorise it! Remarkable. Do you know the rest? I enjoy reading poetry, David. How, how old are you? Seven, eight?

I write: *I will be eleven on 7th June.*

People don't like to make a fuss when my birthday comes around; they think I get confused about it. Only I know when it is. Anyway I don't think anyone remembers my birthdays. Not like they did other members of the family, or the fuss they made of Eric's birthdays. They always thought I had no idea of the days or what day I was born, but I do. I remember everything - almost everything. I don't write all that down for her…I just think it.

Ten? You are small for your age, David. Do you go to school nearby?

No.

Where is your school? Far away, I expect.

I have never been to school.

She looks bewildered, and for a while she does not speak.

Wait for me while I go to my car and find a book for you. She seems excited at the prospect of sharing something with me.

She returns shortly with a smallish book – 'John Keats', I read on the cover. She begins to read to me:

Season of mists and mellow fruitfulness,
Close bosom-friend of the maturing sun;
Conspiring with him how to load and bless
With fruit the vines that round the thatch-eaves run…

I watch her carefully while she reads and I mouth the words, for I know this poem already. I remember finding it and thinking how well it spoke of what is inside me. It is as if my Mother is here with me, reading again. Her voice, the words and the sounds she gives them, bringing to life each syllable.

My dream is broken by the sound of a car arriving outside. Father.

I begin at once to shake involuntarily. My subconscious nerves so irritate me.

Jo, Jo, where are you? We hear him calling out and she looks at me, watching again, and she looks concerned.

What is it, David? What is it? I take up the pages that I have written and scrunch them into my pocket.

You don't want him to know, do you? Don't worry. Our conversation is our own secret. Here, take your book - all right, give it to me. I will say I was reading it. I understand David. I will find you later.

Father has come into the room. *I wasn't expecting you till tomorrow.*

He looks pleased to see her. Among his redeeming features is a large widening smile that brings him to life. I have seen little of this aspect of him, but here it is in the presence of Jo. I try to slip towards the door but he has noticed me, and the smile goes in an instant.

Lydia, for God's sake! Lydia! What on earth is the child doing down here? For God's sake - come at once, and put him away.

No, Stephan, please leave him. He has done nothing but be my companion this last hour or so.

You have no idea what you are doing, talking to him.

Don't be utterly ridiculous, Steph - he is a bright boy!

I am halfway out of the door when he picks up the copy of Anna Karenina and flings it in my direction. It catches my head and sends me sprawling across the floor, where it reaches its second target on the open door. I am knocked senseless.

Lydia is putting a wet cloth to my head and mopping a stream of blood that has coursed its way down my face into my neck. Jo and my Father are arguing.

No, you listen to me! You have no idea what you are saying. I am telling you, the boy is a psychopath!

What! First autistic, with few of the predominant symptoms, and now psychopath?

Well, if you must know, he murdered his own mother - and his grandparents sent him out here for me to treat him!

I have risen to my feet. Lydia is taking me through to the kitchen. I hear no more but the words that he has left me with. How sad and confused he must be.

I lie still on my bed for hours, just thinking. I bring the image of Jo before me, and I remember. And I remember something about her essence that resonates far, far back...that she is here is no mere coincidence.

JO

Chapter One

I met Stephan Tyndal when I was in my second year at university. He was a colleague of Father's who happened to come to one of those annual cocktail parties Mother gave. Mother always had this crazy notion that she ought to socialize with her husband's workmates. Perhaps she saw it as her contribution to the family income. It was an unacknowledged gesture, as no one was quite certain as to why she should feel the necessity.

We all hated those evenings with stiffly formal individuals we had nothing in common with. They, in turn, tarnished a perfect good evening with formally strained conversation, flipping directly into work jargon with one another when we had moved on with our polite social food and drink offerings. My brother Brent was good at that sort of thing. He would always know the perfectly correct things to say. There was none of that wavering confusion his sister had about any current topic or news item.

Mother has always had that air of quiet sophistication and grace that could sooth a stress-worn academic into fervent confessions over a latest malady. Father was so different. I think you could say he was mentally smart, razor-sharp, verbally incisive and challenging, with little regard for trivia. My brother Brent is just like him in so many ways, utterly brilliant. He excelled in absolutely everything, besides being disgustingly attractive. Needless to say, he was and is the pride of the family. As for me, I was one of those uninspired pragmatists. I found it far easier being the insensible idiot in the family. There is not one competitive bone in my body that would dare to compete with Brent on any level.

When I finally surfaced from rebellious childhood to compliant adolescence, I began to recognize the need to earn myself a living and move beyond the security of the family nest. Our parents boasted of their rise from lower-middle-class insignificance to respected professionals of consequence by dint of hard work and mental discipline, which I had been told often enough I was lacking. I was actually keen to travel rather than study - funded by Father, of course. In order to do so, I needed to please him, trading with the idea that the moment I had dispatched some end results as efficiently as I could manage, there would be no reason why I should not be rewarded with a year out to see the world.

I chose to study Philosophy and Psychology, subjects I thought might impress Father. I also thought they might put me on a better level with him intellectually. Well, I hoped they would. There had never been much conversation between us beyond schoolgirl chitchat about school's eternal snags, to which he would always reply, "Go and tell your Mother, she is far more cognizant with these things."

I also began the study of Metaphysics, which impressed Father even less, but I wished to unravel all those mystical questions that pose themselves during that romantic period of adolescence. I was eager to explore all those 'extra-sensory' claims that obstinately refused to measure with logic and ethics. Of course, it was a subject readily dismissed as imagined nonsense by Father, who regarded me as an impractical dreamer. I had sadly lacked that genetic material that he could connect with. All the same, I did try my best to steer a course with a practical eye, making a good show of openly denouncing the quixotic, yet secretly intrigued all the same.

Brent had completed a degree in Neuroscience and was already well advanced towards his MS and Ph.D. in Human Genetics and all that seriously clever stuff, well before I embarked on a university education which may or may not have put me on any kind of footing with him. Despite all my shallow efforts I never caught up with him, or Father for that matter, and always remained a mediocre explorer into what they saw as useless information.

Mother had given up a medical career to marry Father, who qualified as a pathologist at a precociously early age and already bore the title of DMedSc after his name when they met. She might have been bowled over by him as a person of superior and enlightened intellect, you might say, but I had little in common with him.

Sadly, my subject choices were in vain; for both Father and Brent derided my interest in a science which investigated the first principles of nature and thought. They irreverently regarded with embarrassment and distrust any study of the supernatural, as abstract as its field of study, and felt such matters should be relegated to the psychosomatic conditions of the physical brain. I was therefore fascinated to learn that Dr. Stephan Tyndal had been invited to their annual soiree. I had attended a couple of fascinating lectures he had given on the subconscious mind and his approach to hypnosis. He had talked of past-lives and such subjects that Father had outwardly expressed distaste for, and had consequently not been invited before.

I dreaded that duty-bound evening. They were always as rousing as a firework in a bucket of water. They began with the obligatory passing round of her delicate little canapés to the murmuring buzz of chat amongst the gathering of egg-heads.

I was wearing 'a little black number' as Mother called that necessary wardrobe item of clothing. "One always needs a conservative little black dress for social evenings, Jo." Neckline not too low, string of contrasting white beads or borrowed pearls from Mother, and of course black high heels - not too high. Hair swept up into chignon - none of that loose hair to the shoulders that may be good enough for untidy students, but not for this evening, if you please - a touch of lipstick and a smattering of rouge, and the tiniest suggestion of Chanel No 5 behind each ear. Any more would be quite wrong! I was picture-perfect.

I cast myself about, making polite and as smart conversation as I could manage. I drank far too much sherry than was good for me and lunged in to the affray without much sense of what I was saying, or hoping to say. Now and then I caught myself slurring words, without a single hand-brake to put an end to my drivel. I managed to find myself with some highly-strung professor of something or other who insisted on knowing the details of what I was studying, and dismissively enlightening me that Stephen Hawkins had wrapped-up all those questions efficiently enough. Each remark was punctuated with an offensive laugh which seemed to come from the back of his throat, blasting peanuts at me like undirected missiles.

After that I was confidently able to approach my challenge; the tall and handsome Dr. Tyndal, who (like all the others) politely inquired about my fresh pitch into university education. I happened to mention that I had also started Meditation classes to fix my mind in some way into striving after the ideal through the incorporeal, etc. My words tumbled out, alcohol-inspired, into a tangle of nonsense. However, the subject of meditation sparked a camaraderie which put him more at ease with me, as it appeared he was a doyenne in this field at some illustrious school of meditation in London.

He rambled on about the exploration of what is *a priori* in human knowledge through meditation. We talked of that which is vague and illusive in philosophy, the Puritan prejudices, how philosophy should be based on psychology etc, etc - but I became lost somewhere between 'humdrum orthodoxy, old fashioned metaphysics and the materialistic philistinism of R.W. Emerson.' By the time that I mentioned to him that I had been impressed by his lectures on the subconscious, I could see that I was now totally sanctioned by him. However, I had consumed several more dainty glasses of Mother's sweet sherry and I am ashamed to say, particularly as the man was almost Father's age, that Dr.

Tyndal's eyes had begun to lure me beyond the intellectual, to a basic primal sexual allure. His hypnotic influence had snared me, once and for all. After a gallon or so of Mother's sweet sherry, I found that Dr. Tyndal had immense sex appeal. And, after a passionate embrace in the garden on the way to his car, I knew instinctively that sparks of pure physical lust had ignited a fire in him, also.

That night, my head spun out of control into a full-blown cyclone as it hit the pillow, and a compelling interest began to sow its seed, as what was left of thought went over each nuance and expression there may or may not have been. What we had talked about was unimportant - it had made little sense even at the time - but I had the feeling that I would definitely see more of Dr. Tyndal.

Ridiculous, I told myself. *He is far too old, and Father would never approve - of course not!*

I suppose I could have been excused as naïve and easily influenced by this disproportionate attraction. After all, I was only a couple of years out of school (an all girl's school at that), and being positively bombarded by that surfeit of rampant, overly-forward young male flesh newly released into abandoned university life. Someone older, excessively intelligent, sophisticated, refined and charming was an extremely palatable option.

Chapter Two

"I see you got into some deep discussion with Tyndal last night?" Father began almost immediately after I appeared at breakfast, and rather too speculatively for my over-sensitive and guilt-ridden conscience.

I sat down with a piece of charcoal-toast that I had inadvertently cooked twice. "Your toast is burnt," observed my brother. "Lost your concentration?"

"He is into Meditation," I answered, rather matter-of-factly.

"Odd chap. Keeps himself to himself, mostly. One of those brilliant boffins in his field. Of course you would find him interesting, with your course."

"Yes, he was. He came alone, I see."

"It is rumoured that he was married years ago, early twenties; he had a child that went missing and I gather the wife left him. That's all I know."

"Surely you are not interested in the old chap?" my brother broke in rather loutishly. "You seemed all wrapped up in one another last night."

"Oh, for God's sake, Brent," I snapped, spilling a streak of guilt across my flushed cheek. I got up and went to the sink to scrape the black off my toast, making as much noise as I could about it, while the family scorched furtive glances into my back.

"He has a rather exceptional home," Mother continued along the same track. "I believe it goes way back to the days of Cromwell's dissolution of the monasteries and has all sorts of interesting secret passages, and what have you. Remember, Charles, when we were invited there years ago and he had that strange little South African girl living with him? He seems to like younger women." She allowed a discreet pause before she discharged her dart. "I should be so careful, my dear. You never know with these Svengali types."

"I don't believe it! Why should I be warned about the man? I only spoke to him. I am never likely to ever see him again," I stormed in response, defeating my claim to innocence. No one dared mention the man's name again all weekend.

On Monday I returned to my grubby digs near the University - shared by four other females of the similarly seriously untidy sort. I had gathered my wits about me, cleared my head of any kind of weak female-type brooding and ploughed myself into the lectures of the day, whilst casually looking up my next appointment to the Meditation class.

That evening, there was a phone message left with Penelope Kramer, the only flat-mate with an air of distinction about her, having come from one of those rather posh public schools.

"A message for you, Jo, from a Stephan Tyndal. He says he will call at six with something he wants to deliver to you. Sounds a lot better than some of those football fiends knocking about here. He asked for 'Josephine'. I had to think for a moment who *Josephine* was - sounded quite nice, actually."

"Sounds pretty boring to me," my best mate Tess replied for me. "God, anyone calling me by my full name would get something from me..."

"Undoubtedly. I expect they would get it without..." Penelope mumbled, as her voice trailed inaudibly after her through the door. She could be rather cutting - or was it humour? Conversation in the flat generally riveted around what to expect or not to expect from men, and never moved much beyond that.

While Tess gave riveting advice on how to deal with the message, I was experiencing a distinct thrill of triumph. He had gone to the trouble of finding out where I was living. I was certain I had not told him, nor had he asked. Pure pleasure rippled through every part of my body. He was interested.

By six o'clock, I had showered and dressed. I decided on a long denim skirt. *Go a bit old fashioned to suit his age*, I thought. Then a low-cut red sweater not to lead him right off course. Masses of scent and hair left swishing about the shoulders, just to contradict Mother. Then I went downstairs to wait, far too eager and restless for my own good. God, I had only known the man one evening. I was calling myself insane and quite ridiculous when, pronto, on the dot of six, a voice behind me called out, "Josephine?"

I visibly jumped, at the same time attempting to look as detached as was unattainably possible.

"Ah, oh, Dr. Tyndal. I got your message."

"Please, not Dr. Tyndal...surely we are on more familiar terms than that?" he smiled, almost sardonically.

"I er, I wasn't expecting to see you again. I thought...you know...father's colleague and all that. Well, I mean...formal. You know?"

What was I saying? It was blatantly obvious I was going to see him, and here he was all perfectly controlled, and he had found me without any suggestion of where I was or how I was to be met again. There was enticement in that very fact. His cool, proprietorial reserve somehow presented an exciting challenge.

"I have some books I wanted to show you. They are in my car. Just round the corner. Would you like to come and have a drink with me? Any nice pubs in the area not too frequented by noisy students?"

He had that disarming kind of shy, remote smile that inclines females to want to reassure and comfort. My varied emotions were disturbingly new to me. I had never felt this way before. I had never been so - so out of control.

"Well, I don't really know the area that well, but I am sure that if you have your car handy you can drive to somewhere that you know, far from the madding crowd - that is, if you know what I mean…ah."

I was tongue-tied and ill at ease. What was I doing here with this much older man, way out of my depth? It really was too bad. Why was I like this? What made me so?

He took my hand, quite casually and confidently, and led the way while I turned somersaults within, wondering about intent and inclination.

His car was one of the latest, expensive-looking Mercedes sports models. I noted that the roof was on, not off - a tad wasted on the old. No chap I had been out with owned anything near this, unless it had been borrowed from a parent. He opened the door for me and I slid in, awkwardly fumbling with the safety-belt, but before it was even buckled he had jumped in beside me and had an armful of my surprised flesh and was kissing me passionately. The kiss was startling and unforeseen because it came without any indication of fondness or terms of endearment, let alone any keen declaration that he had been longing to see me again, but there was no mistaking the wild passion. I tried ineffectively to respond as if these things had happened to me on a daily basis.

The evening led on to a drink in a large and snobby-looking private club, then on to an equally snotty meal, the sort Father would take Mother to for some celebration or other, and from which both my brother and I would steer clear. Trying to assume an air of sophistication, while completely out of my comfort zone, was unnerving - to say the least. We stared at one another across the starched-white table-linen and hungered not for the meal, but a repetition of the touching. It was a peculiar lesson in restraint. Repressing any intimation of that wild sensation that flew between us was like stabling recently captured wild horses. There was not one single word or gesture to express those wild and vibrant energies that ricocheted between us. It was as if we were performing some formal ordeal to appease an unknown, unseen referee.

It was clear that Stephan was a person of few words, unless he was spouting forth on the subjects he was conversant with. That evening those subjects were not broached. Instead, we touched on pure trivia: my parents, university life, and my likes and dislikes. He casually steered the conversation towards me with an abstracted indifference, and I found myself talking volubly about myself, whilst aware that he disclosed nothing about himself or his feelings. He managed to turn every question into an interrogation of his own. It felt like some superior stratagem to strip me bare of any cover up. I felt exposed and vulnerable, without recourse to salvage any sophistication or self-confidence.

After the meal he simply announced that we would go back to his small flat for coffee, and I submitted unhesitatingly. He stayed at the flat during the week when he was working, he said; then went to his home in Sussex at the weekend. We did not touch when we got back into the car.

I began to wonder at all the artless, guileless immature things I had done or said. Had he seen through my naiveté? Had he tired of me so soon? It must have been something that I had said; perhaps my table manners? Mother had often commented on them being sloppy and unhealthy. I, too, became silent. I had rebounded like a yo-yo from one extreme of perplexing emotions to another, and like an insect trapped in a web, I was ensnared so fixedly that release was not an option.

It was a large, sparsely furnished flat whose décor would be described these days as minimalist. I suppose it complied with the simple needs of a single man whose requirements lay solely in the direction of the books that were haphazardly scattered everywhere; they spilled off the book shelves to become heaps of loosely piled pillars on either side.

He routinely threw his keys onto a side table as if he was still alone in his habitual function, and unceremoniously led me, with assumed expectation, into a large, stark bedroom whose built-in cupboards similarly minimized the necessity for furniture.

It was a large bed with one single side-table with a reading lamp upon it. That was all there was. I was awkward, incompetent, inadequate and struggling to know how I should feel about it all. Is this what older people did? Had he seen me merely as an adolescent cocotte, a *fille de joie* begging to be taken at will? If I had anticipated some enticement, some restrained and shy finesse, I was to be disappointed. There was none. The absence of any tender, amorous ritual took me by storm, giving me hardly time to react to the unexpected suddenness of his attack. He ripped at my clothing with the fury of a lost traveller crawling in from the desert in search of water.It was a kind of sexual act I had never before experienced. None of that fumbling with excuses for inexperience, this was a well practiced engagement in sexual-warfare. It was thrilling, exciting, ground-breaking and wild.

Well - that was how I felt at the time.

The evening continued like an electric storm, unabated, untamed and exciting. Then I must have fallen asleep, as he roused me from a deep and fathomless state, the sort that when woken, all memory has evaporated. There was never a past and a future was something vague and obscure, for it could come from anywhere. As he and the unfamiliar surroundings took shape and reached some distant cognisance, I registered that he was to take me home, which he did in silence. He had an early start in the morning.

When full consciousness was restored, I was left with a seedy aftertaste of pensive brooding, as a sense of shame lurked somewhere in my conscience. The evening had lacked something fine and good, but at that time I was unable to grasp what it was. I decided to put it all down to inexperience and not to be repeated. By the next evening I kept reassuring myself that I was in no way going to see him again - I would be cold and aloof when he rang.

He did not ring.

Three days went by, and then a whole weekend. I imagined him going to his country home.

He may phone on Monday, I told myself, and I would be prepared. He did not.

I found myself trying to think of reasons why I should phone him. I had not thanked him for the evening. I needed to return the books he had left me. I went to the phone several times, and a cold sweat would break over me as I rehearsed my nonchalant, "Hello, Stephan - I have your books with me, shall I post them to you?" or "Stephan, I have been so busy with my studies that I have not had time to phone to say…" or "Stephan…"

The phone rang. I jumped a good seven inches from the telephone stool.

"Hello, Mother…no, of course I am not disappointed to hear your voice, just frantic over some papers I need to study…yes, been frantically busy with all sorts of things going on here…no, I have had no messages to say that you rang," I lied. "Yes I may have time this weekend - I will let you know. What did you say the family is doing?" etc, etc. Dear Mother, and her arrangements.

I put the phone down with a sigh and turned to look at my diary, with its empty dates. The phone rang once more.

"Mother, I told you I would phone and let you know - I have only just found my diary…oh, Stephan, it's you - so sorry - been rather caught up in family affairs." Good start. "No, of course I would love to come…what time? Same as last? Okay. Yes, I will wait outside the building for you. Stephan! Please call me Jo, no-one uses Josephine. Well, if you insist, but you may find no response sometimes."

He was at the same place at the same time, and as punctual as before. I was busy kicking myself that I had allowed it all to be repeated. What was I doing! Casual, that's it. I found a very casual old sweater to go with faded jeans and scuffed boots. Absolutely no make-up and no scent. Hair, moderately – no I cannot lie – hair well-groomed.

I knew what to expect this time. I would not be pounced upon unexpectedly. I saw him coming and tried to suppress the butterflies that fluttered around my middle.

"Stephan."

"Josephine."

"Dr Tyndal, then."

"Well, have your way, Jo." He had succumbed with a fleeting smile. I had at last managed a small command of the relationship.

The evening was different, somehow. He had prepared a meal at his flat, informal and relaxed. Being caught off guard and addressing him as 'Mother' had done it for me. It gave everything a much more casual edge somehow, and the result was that I felt less threatened and far more at ease. I caught him glancing at me throughout the evening trying to work out just what I was all about. I felt elated and more confident. I withdrew from one of his quick snatching embraces and I saw that it had left him crushed. Good!

We talked more, we laughed more, and when we ended up in his bedroom it was all quite different. It was as if he had conquered me and had no more to demand of me. Once the obstruction of rampant sex was out of the way, conversation became less inquisitional and cavalier than that first evening and more on mutually shared subjects of interest, and so much more than mere physical attraction.

Love-making after that became more affectionate, more considered and much more appealing. Eating out at some formal restaurant was no longer an option or the prize. Instead he would invite me to informal evenings at his flat with the pretence of lending me books on the subject matters of my course. And there I was, guilty graduate of sexual emancipation and blotting paper, to the romantic notion of the older man taking charge.

Chapter Three

Behind all that hormonal stuff, I had arrived at a contemplative stage in my life. Life-values and the importance attributed to them were under rigorous interrogation in my mind. The concept of 'Religion' had come seriously under scrutiny, and my childhood belief in a personalised God had reached a crisis of faith. I told myself that it was that metaphysical aspect of Stephan's mind that I had been primarily drawn to. I guessed it was those subjects raised that first evening, and his responses to them, that initially bound me to him.I was in search of spiritual reality and needed answers to a void that was growing within. I needed to exonerate those creeping doubts, and Stephan seemed to have all the answers that made sense.

Talks with Stephan were so insightful, so enlightening of what a clever mind had perceived. We had this revealing conversation that got as close to his beliefs and researches as I could ever go.

He had asked me, "Why Metaphysics?" and I answered "I thought it would resolve the God question. Where do you start in a search for God?"

"When God spoke through Jeremiah, he said, *You will seek me and find me when you seek me with all your heart. I will be found by you.*"

"And do you believe that?" I asked.

"Why not Theology?" he asked, evading my question with one of his own. "You might have reached your answers more directly that way."

"Do you think so, or would I only have become bogged down in a mire of religious contention?"

"You would be just as bogged-down, as you put it, by the equations and arguments of logic and philosophical debate - and in the end, you are only left with opinion."

"Well, I suppose what I mean to do is to investigate spiritual reality, whichever way it might be obtained."

"From the pagan to the cathedral?"

"No. I need more than the search amongst religious beliefs. I am more interested in the claims of the Spiritualists who profess to speak to the dead."

"Then why not study the conditions of Schizophrenia and Psychosis, and drug-induced hallucinations?"

"I intend to, and to ferret out the illusions from the reality. I also mean to explore the claims of transcendental meditation and their claims of eternal bliss - whatever that means."

"Have you tried? I mean, *really* tried?"

"Meditation?"

"Yes, as a matter of fact I have. I discussed that with you that first evening I met you," I replied indignantly, as if he thought my approach too casual. "The initiation was all a bit too ritualistic for me. I mean, it smacked of Pentecostal fervour, which put me off."

"That is about discipline…discipline of the mind. The mind tends to become restless, impatient and needs a control. You must persevere."

"Somehow, I have begun to wonder if meditation is the submissive step you take to understand that God is not there, and if there are no answers it becomes the consolation prize of oblivion." I could hear myself challenging him to a dual line of reasoning. I wanted subjective idealism to win over a Hawkins wipe-out of any hope beyond the physical.

He was silent for a while. Sweeping statements uttered recklessly by the facetious and uninformed would not deter him, but something in his mind troubled him. Stephan was a man too controlled and self-opinionated to allow doubts or dispute to cloud his viewpoint. Nevertheless something bothered him, and his flash of insecurity remained in my mind for future reference.

"Man's existence becomes futile unless there is some infinite reference point," he continued. "Man has always been in search of God or a supreme power, and according to the Prophets of the Old Testament and the Apostles of the new; God is in search of man. Did God not send Jesus to find and save the lost souls? We are all lost, to some extent."

My own doubts and confusions outweighed sensible questions. I mean, all these little quotations from the Bible are so ill-defined – you can translate them any which way. Demanding answers, I ploughed on guilelessly, if only to get a rise from him.

"You see, the Bible is where I become unstuck," I emphasized ineptly. "The whole matter of salvation, judgement day, and the resurrection of man, back on this already overpopulated small planet. It does not wash."

Stephan seemed not to answer but to continue with a train of his own thinking. "No," he said speculatively. "So long as evil exists on the earth, man is bound to become contaminated by it, even after he is salvaged from Judgement Day."

"I take it you believe in the existence of evil, then? That is something I have never given much thought to. It all seems such nonsense, you know - the devil and all that. If as you say we are so easily contaminated by evil, then where are we headed if even the saved among us are predisposed towards it - even after their salvation?"

"Ultimate perfection – and that is attained only through rebirth."

"Is that what some Christian sects refer to as 'born-again', a second re-baptizing into the church? Or do you mean the soul's reincarnation as in Buddhism?" I asked, testing his ambiguous Christianity and hoping for an inspired answer.

"I mean the rebirth of the soul into a fresh new physical body. It has to be the answer," he said almost solemnly. "It is the answer," he emphasized.

"Tut, tut," I answered irreverently. "That coming from a man of your status and science, I find surprising."

"Why?"

"Father calls it mumbo-jumbo."

"And you? What do you call it?"

"An interesting hypothesis, but only an idea, after all. I have had no reference point from which to discuss it or to verify it."

"It is the balancing of good and evil. How else can we thoroughly rid ourselves of evil, beyond all temptation of it? Religion would naively describe good as all that comes from God, and all that is evil is the devil."

"Do you really believe there is such a thing as evil as in the Devil?" I asked, pushing the question a second time. "I mean, it all seems so bizarre, unreal - the monster in children's fabled stories. I simply find it ridiculous making a reality out of a horned half-man interfering with our lives, leading us to temptation, damnation and all that, just for the fun of it. I mean why, what on earth for?"

"I am as certain of evil as I am that there is also a direct opposite."

At that point the conversation came to an abrupt end, as he stood up and went out of the room. The content of it remained with me for long after. I think he felt he had said enough or had reached a point where he was reluctant to continue. The whole matter had become a problem to him. The issue of reincarnation was to re-appear much later, in some rather terrifying depth, but at that moment it was all a rather mystifying concept without evidence. It was as illusory as Moore's Utopia, even if it did answer questions.

Chapter Four

As the earlier part of our relationship was fixed in the physical, after some weeks it gradually developed into an assumed emotional rapport that bound us together into an attachment that was often bewildering, indecipherable and at times, remote.

Later, when I began to look further into the significance of our relationship, I found it debatable that there was ever any real deep emotional love-stuff between us. There was certainly plenty of feeling - sexual, as well as a strange magnetic hold he had over me - and I was undeniably hooked.

"How on earth did you know so little about the man after being with him for so long?" I was asked much later. It is strange, I agree, but even my brother, who had always been so close, knew nothing about my relationship. It was a sort of unspoken mutual agreement that our attachment was something we kept to ourselves. It was a relationship I did not wish to sully with the usual 'man-friend-talk' back in the flat with buddies who looked for legendary 'soul-mates', aspiring husband material or gratifying lovers. My relationship with Stephan was different. It was as if I had been lured to him by some mystical outside force. It was kind of sacrosanct.

His far superior intellect and his immense sexuality were enticing in a strangely compelling way, but I was tiring of his secrecy and I was curious about his country house where he disappeared each weekend.

"When do I get to see your remarkable house?" I asked.

"What have you heard about it?" he responded with his usual irritating question before answer.

"The parents have been there as you know and commented on its antiquity."

"Is that all?"

"More or less."

"Then you will have to find out for yourself," he answered wryly.

The very next weekend I visited his 'country retreat' for the first time.

Chapter Five

You came upon *Nasiarcuth Hall* through a series of sharp bends, with little excuse for the hidden pot-holes in the dust road leading to it. The primitive approach was a perfect camouflage for a house not wanting to be recognized. There was no tree-lined avenue-guarded driveway. No curving walls holding up those foliated-patterned, wrought-iron gates one expects to find on entering large estates. All there was left of a once grand entrance were the now dilapidated yet substantial pillars, with broken falcons perched above. At some time a stout wall had joined it. Now only remnants of it remained, and instead a barbed wire fence stopped short of a cattle grid.

The driveway seemed designed only to avoid the mass of rock that abounded there. It led right through an embankment of mountainous grey rock, cloven in two to allow vehicles to pass through in single file, after which one is surprised to find it opening out onto a large greystone Manor House. Its distance and concealment from the road and its unobtrusive entrance all suggested, at the very least, a place of concealment. *How appropriate for Stephan*, I thought.

Its mere size was a total surprise to me. I had expected nothing like this. The building was rectangular with wings built on to the east and west of it, as if added at a later date to extend it for some purpose other than a modest country residence. I assumed at first that it was Elizabethan, but it was clear that the original building had been added to at least twice and could be any age, for the chimney stacks on the external walls were evidence of there being a much earlier building. The gables were overgrown with ivy, covering any detail in the brickwork.

I would never have described it as a 'country house' from my limited experience of what families might or might not own as a second home. The families and people I knew had caravans at the seaside, or perhaps a holiday flat in some European resort. Establishments like this belonged in Austin novels.

I stared up at the wide framed, mullioned windows and gables which seemed of an earlier, perhaps pre-Elizabethan homestead, with well-proportioned cornices to the eaves. The windows were arranged in three groups - three together in the centre and a couple on each side of the first floor, and above that, smaller dormer windows perched on a hipped roof of leaded tiles. The ground floor was arranged with similar windows separated by massive steps of grey cut-stone, leading up to an imposing entrance.

The door had lost an original hood and framework, but there remained the brick pilasters with moulded capitals and bases flanking the entrance. Engraved on a plaque of wood, way above the door was its name: *Nasiarcuth Hall* - not so much to name it, but to indicate its presence.

The whole gave a feeling of a carefully contrived home rather than that of a large manor house. It lacked architectural formality by being less decorous than most houses of its age, aiming at propriety and necessity. I learned that it had been some sort of spiritual retreat and the residence of a defrocked Abbot, who was allowed to retain this, at least, when his Abbey had been destroyed at the time of Cromwell's dissolution of the monasteries.

I half-expected a footman in uniform to appear. Instead, a rotund, red-faced woman opened the door and started talking without cessation the moment we entered the large, open entrance hall. While she talked and Stephan listened, I looked around at the dark-panelled walls leading up to a massive stair case.

Tapestries hung from the walls, and here and there polished armour, swords and helmets hung with cautionary austerity. A large grandfather of all grandfather clocks solidly marked off the seconds that held all the time in the world, encapsulated there in that dark sombreness.

With my attention absorbed in the single direction of make-believe, and aware that the woman was still talking, I followed the direction of my eyes up the staircase, which reached the first floor in three flights. A broad-moulded handrail with short stout balusters and tuned bases shaped like ancient urns followed along the sides of the steps. The entrance and stair case halls were paved with diagonally laid marble squares, unbroken even though time had aged and worn them. Beyond was a panelled passage, which was screened from the landing by a range of arches, standing on panelled piers with moulded bases.

I tip-toed along the passages as if to go about undetected, examining wall hangings and objects. All the while, Stephan listened distractedly to the woman's persistence of all that had transpired since she had last seen him; from the mundane, to the positively monotonous humdrum of plants growing. I noticed that many of the internal features must have been remnants of the older house which must have been added to, or built over. Decorative fittings had been re-fixed, to be left undisturbed by any elements of an earlier character.

The house was simply wonderful. You could see at a glance that he had obviously come from money. Being a successful psychiatrist was one thing, but this house spoke of more than a professional salary. The interior was bedecked extravagantly in furnishings going back to the Ark, so it seemed to my limited knowledge. I assumed that either a previous wife had chosen some of the furniture, or he had inherited it all and a 'she' had decorated. Well, judging by his uninspiring flat, he clearly had little aptitude in that direction.

"Where are you wandering to?" Stephan's harsh voice broke the silence as he appeared rather abruptly at my side. The woman had retired into a large kitchen the other end of the passage.

"Just looking - just admiring. It's all quite out of this world, Stephan. I had no idea quite how…"

"Inherited," he answered. "It all belonged to a great-grandfather somewhere along the line. It is of little importance."

He was trivialising and dismissive about the house, whilst I caught the air of someone extremely proud of what he owned - but I knew that he liked to pose as non-materialistic, non-acquisitive. It suited his Transcendental Meditation practices of self-denial, attainment of the humble and all that rubbish.

"I don't buy that for a minute," I said. This place is of great importance to you, or you would have sold it long ago."

"I never engage in conversation over money or possessions…it is a contemptuous subject."

"How absurd! Money and possessions are the unavoidable necessities of life."

I was not fooled for a moment with those idealistic principles - all part of that posturing that went with the Meditation School ideals, all so unrealistically pretentious. It was that very superior sort of piety that jarred with me. If his assumed principles had formed the disciplined exterior of the man, it had not jelled with what lay beneath. His curt reaction had made me respond petulantly, and besides which, I was still reeling in stunned awe.

"If possessions are truly unimportant, why do you drive such an expensive car?" I challenged. "Why should you retain such a large house, purely for yourself?"

"Sometimes Josephine, you are such a child," he parried with such derision that I was forced to move on from my protest. It had created a bad start to the weekend, and I so wanted to be shown more of the house and hear more of its history.

That first weekend seemed shrouded in mystery and a kind of suspense that I could not unravel. Stephan was haughty and cavalier and strode before me up the stairs.

"Put your things in here, this is where you will be sleeping." He opened the door onto a large, panelled bedroom, which heralded an enormous four-poster bed with all those heavy drapes that garland the four points. It was like something from a film set, or a closely shielded room that is on exhibition for the tourists to view only from a roped-off distance. I made no comment but put my bags down upon a tapestried chaise-lounge, pretending not to be over-impressed, and casually said, "And where will you be sleeping?" It broke the ice that glazed the distance between us, as he lunged towards me.

I carry the memory of that first weekend, with that revered kind of nostalgia, as romantic and exciting. Experiencing something quite out of the ordinary for the first time has a way of obscuring anything negatively curious. I had had no time to wonder about the mystery of it all, not then. I simply accepted that I had fallen into some mysterious spell-binding relationship that carried with it all the enchantment a young mind can fantasize over.

I only vaguely recollect the hurried introduction to the housekeeper 'Lydia' as something like, "...and Lydia, this is my friend Josephine, who will be staying this weekend." It was as if the arrangement were temporary and only thought of at the last minute. I can't recall my first impression of the woman, except for her size and her jolly nature. These days, she has faded into an obscure background of so many details that were all extraordinary to me.

Mother had a cleaner who came twice a week. She said little and smiled even less. She would lose herself in her chores the moment she arrived until the moment she left. Thinking of her now, it is clear that she had wanted little to do with the family, as we had little time to embrace her into our lives. I can't feel a shame for that indifferent neglect; it was simply the way she wanted it. Not Lydia. Again, that was something I was to slowly acknowledge at a later date, but that first weekend was all about being awestruck.

Aside from the delicious moments spent as the maid-of-the-moment in the large medieval bed, there was so much to take in. Meals were brought to us in a small sunroom – well - small compared with the rest of the house. A glance at the formal, dark-panelled dining-room with its massive heavy table and formal chairs, lent a relief that we were not dining there. Then there were the wonderful walks around the estate, whose details I took in more and more with each proceeding visit.

Chapter Six

I attempt to reconstruct myself as I was then in a way that makes sense to me now, but I battle with how little I held certain of where I was going, or how little I understood what was happening to me. I can only recognise now that it was a compulsive attraction from which I could not disconnect. I suppose that at the age of twenty, one is convinced of one's invincibility, and that one knows everything. Recalling it all now, I see that the course of my whole life has been affected or influenced by that one evening when I met Stephan Tyndal.

I egotistically told myself at the time that I had gone to him hesitantly and I was drawn towards him out of boredom, but on reflection, it seems that Stephan was meant to cross my path, as it were, and I was drawn to him by some innate purpose. Those mystical words: 'Kismet', 'pre-ordination', 'fate', 'pre-destination' come to mind, and I wonder at how much we are in control of our lives.

Of course, his quite extraordinary house had immense attraction. Who would not be fascinated by it! But there was something else about Stephan which I still cannot name. Part of it was that aspect of him that was never disclosed. Whilst I was inwardly aware that it was dangerous and dark it was that very essence of him that drew me in some inexplicable way and made me want to shield him, though God knows what from.

As for love; I can't remember a single time that the word was ever mentioned, either by him or me. I have always believed that there is something sacred about the term 'love', something deep and stirring, and there were none of those feelings that I can remember. But then again, I have become so confused about that relationship with Stephan that nothing about it could be attached to an expression or an emotion. I have searched my feelings to find that which could be seen as sacred in Stephan. I am sure that there was something, way below there, somewhere in his psyche; deeply embedded by the demonic. Perhaps we did love one another - it's hard to say. I still battle with those immediate terms of endearment, careless of meaning.

I have never forgotten him. He still lays siege to those quiet moments when I have that silent yearning to revise the past - so many years in abeyance.

I got to know him more and more over those next several months. He would phone every day, sometimes several times, with nothing particular to say other than checking up on me. As time went on I realised that he had become obsessed with me, and that I found hardest to cope with. I enjoyed it at first - it gave me a sense of influence over him, and there was little else I could exceed above him. He was so smart, so illustrious and authoritative, it seemed. His discussions on the matter of Metaphysics opened a whole new dimension of thought. He could quote from Plato, Quarles, Herbert, Donne and Traherne, and I would listen in rapt admiration at his prodigious memory, always intending to read a bit more to improve myself, and never quite finding the time. I was the doting and focused student, while Stephan was this erudite doyen full of virtuous ideals and hypotheses of his own, which he managed to convey with conviction.

It was only much later that I saw he was the direct antithesis of all that he preached.

Chapter Seven

Stephan had made a lifetime study of aggressive behaviour, and had published a number of papers and books which I only got round to reading much, much later. At that time I was so involved in the literature of my own studies that I failed to regard, or really recognise, the impact of what he had to say.

The most interesting aspect of his research was his use of hypnosis as a basis of his investigations. He had delved into the subconscious mind, taking people back into pasts which had no bearing on their current lives. Then he would try to substantiate their claims by researching what they had 'remembered'. His parents had initiated the interest in him with their own research, using him as a subject on many occasions. However, he talked haltingly on that issue, as if it were a sensitive matter he did not wish to share.

He believed that many behavioural and medical problems, fears and anxieties were related to some distant past, a past he would refer to as his concept of 'original sin', which the Catholics believe we are born with. The subject of 'past-lives' was not taken seriously by his colleagues, who expressed contempt at the idea, requiring a more rational, radical, scientific basis for explanations of behaviour. Besides which, it could be proven in many cases, they said, that the subjects under investigation had been fed with information beforehand.

Conversations would often lead into those tenuous issues of existence outside space and time. He talked of the powers that we possess that we do not even suspect we have, and how we need to strive to free ourselves from those habitual assumptions our senses project upon us. He believed in self-examination, private prayer and meditation, a negation of the ego and the importance of the soul.

There was something about *Nasiarcuth Hall* that was a fundamental part of Stephan himself. He was intrigued with those devotional and mystical exercises that absorbed a monk's life, and recognised that there came with them the difficulties, the complexities and the pitfalls that so many were unable to withstand - but Stephan saw himself beyond those weaknesses. He liked to see his life akin to Christian's journey in Pilgrim's Progress, only he felt he had won the battle and the rest of the world was full of half-hearted attempts.He was full of scorn over the lofty assumptions of those incomprehensibly abstract, pragmatic and idealist Philosophers who dismissed God by rationalizing that anything that can't be seen or reasoned is illusion, and insisted upon their postulation as vigorously as each schism of Christianity professes its own incomparable pre-eminence.

Whilst I was currently being baffled by Descartes' dubious proposition that 'by thinking we are', John Locke's 'experience makes us what we are', David Hume's materialism and no more, George Turnbull's claim that 'ideas are faded impressions of sense', Immanuel Kant's suggestion that the mind was the creator of reality by compartmentalizing all that we see and hear and Fiche's 'ordinary me and the me who is behind the scenes creating the world out there' - Stephan appeared so comprehensible, so sane and so in control of that higher knowledge, that wider dimension that governs us all.

I had Father in mind when I was sometimes facetiously tempted to ask questions like "What have you to say of August Comte who denounced superstition - by which he included God and religion and metaphysics - saying that man will never be free until he learns to live by logic and reason alone?"

"Needless to say the fool went insane and attempted suicide," he replied, condensing emphatic statements made by scientists into pointless trivia to be dismissed out of hand. "One has only to regard Kierkegaard. He declared 'Truth is subjectivity', then spent most of his life in a state of mental depression. There is more in what Bertrand Russell meant when he said 'to know something merely with the mind is hardly to know it at all.'

All those subjects that I had chosen idealistically were being swept away by logic and its finalizing deductions that all truth is relative, and everything is only explicable through concrete sciences. There seemed to be no way of including God or universal meaning if one was to listen to the philosophers, other than the odd idealist ones who would like to sparingly include him. But as the study of philosophy snuffed the light on all my early concepts of God and metaphysical veracity, Stephan's beliefs kept me buoyant. "The real problem with all those clever philosophers are their subjective methods to explain everything, while dismissing anything which is out of reach. As Kierkegaard said – 'it leaves me and my free will out of account.'"

All these years later I revisit those wonderful moments with him where all his answers were encapsulated in simple understandings. I am still able to go over those conversations we had, and remember all that drew me towards Stephan, despite the misgivings that arose later about his state of sanity.

It was not until things began to happen in a far more bizarre way that my mind brimmed with phenomena that I could not come to terms with. I have spent my life since then deliberating over what was hallucination and what was reality, and what I could have learned from it all.

Why is it that those significant and remarkable ad hoc times with outstanding and extraordinary people come at a time when one is unqualified and ill-equipped to deal with them? It is only much, much later, with a more mature deliberation, that one is able to re-examine them objectively - and then it is all too late. Everything becomes itemized and torn apart by debate as to whether what happened was real. Did it really happen that way, or was it emergent imagination?

Chapter Eight

Nasiarcuth was an unequivocal mystery to me. It was wonderful; it was a part of history past and in motion. It seethed in a silent, secret life that whispered from every corner. It spoke of undisclosed secrets, hidden somewhere, of some inconceivably hideous past. Mother had mentioned secret passages, but Stephan was emphatic that he did not know where any of the secret passages were or even if the priest-holes still existed after the modern conversions of the house – the term 'modern' to be taken loosely.

Accordingly to the doughty, information-to-be-relied-upon Lydia, *Nasiarcuth* was last 'modernised' at the turn of the nineteenth into twentieth century, and later, plumbing and electricity brought up to scratch perhaps about twenty or so years before I came on the scene. It was Lydia who provided me with most of the information about the house. It came in small episodes of information when I spent weekends there. Stephan was always at hand to draw me away just as she began to get interesting. He would have somewhere to take me, something else to show me, and conversation was drawn to an abrupt close.

I did not mind at first, but after a time, I began to tire of all the underhand secretiveness, his reticence to talk of his past. I became irritated by his obsessive phone calls at regular intervals, particularly if I could not make the weekend for reasons of exams and what have you. My time was split uncomfortably between family, university and Stephan, and I have to admit to withholding the information as to where I was and what I was doing from all three areas. Of course, my parents would insist that I put a look-in from time to time and wanted to know all sorts of things about my comings and goings; but it was all becoming a bit too fraught.

Stephan insisted that I did not tell my parents about our affair. He said it would hinder his professional association with Father, and others who would not understand. I was happy to comply as I was well aware how the relationship would be reacted to. However, I felt I was being kept in deliberate ignorance of his own life and his own whereabouts and it was beginning to get on my nerves, particularly when he was so insistent upon knowing exactly what I was doing and who I was doing it with every minute of my day.

Over the weekends he would often be in deep discussion with Lydia about something - something he was clearly keeping from me. The whole situation was becoming an out-of-reach itch I could not scratch, and I was tired of it all. Besides which, I was young and needed to be with people of my own age some of the time; perhaps lacking in those superlatives in education and sophistication, but enjoying the bliss of their ignorance nonetheless.

I had no function in the house or the garden. The house was well managed; food was prepared by the more than capable housekeeper, and the garden was attended likewise by the gardener. Weekend visits from the owner were most likely seen as an interruption in their daily lives. As for the visits from their employer's young girlfriend, that must have been seen as an imposition.

We spent a good deal of each weekend taking long walks, talking, meditating, and often sailing. He had an old gaff-rigged cutter at a nearby harbour, and he spent hours at an end seeing to it. The thing was an original from Noah himself. It was heavy to handle and slow to manoeuvre but there was certain pleasure in sailing in it - well, more for Stephan than for me. I believe it was a boat that had belonged somewhere in his childhood; I presumed that was where his development had arrested.

Housekeeper Lydia lived in the house somewhere, in her own apartment. I never got to see it. She was one of those ceaselessly busy women who toss life about in perpetual toil without more attention to what they are doing than frog spawn proliferating pond weed. She was like cog in an outmoded wheel that had overextended its purpose. All the time she fiddled away at something she was polishing or attending to, she talked with as much determined dexterity as a dog getting at an unreachable flea. She had a fund of obsolete phrases said in mock-imitation of someone who might once have been famous, but they were all way beyond my humour and time, and I could only smile weakly while she roared with laughter at her own jokes.

I only knew her as Lydia. I did not get to know her surname then. Without any more knowledge of her than that, I felt I had known her all my life and, I have to admit, I grew rather fond of her. She was so open and honest and ready to confide even that which was entrusted to secrecy. When I knew what it was that I wanted to know she was more than willing to whisper the answer, as if whispering wiped out betrayal.

After a year of covert weekends and secret liaisons I began to wonder what went on in that house during the week that was so mysteriously whispered about between Stephan and Lydia.Would I find a demented wife ferreted in an attic a la Wuthering Heights, and would Stephan turn out to be a passionate Mr Rochester being burnt alive one ill-fated weekend, because I had trespassed too far beyond the restriction of rooms he allowed me to? I could never quite understand why he should keep such a large house with two full-time servants to run it when there was no family to share it with, nor any likelihood of one. Stephan was not the marrying type, and how long he intended to keep me as his Affaire de Coeur was a perfect mystery.

As time went on he seemed to become even more fanatically fixated on me, not less, and I was beginning to feel increasingly uneasy and trapped; I mean, wonderful sex and a truly magnificent house is one thing, but an over-obsessive partner, another. I guess I must have had reasonably strong feelings for the man to put up with it all. A kind of committed affection, I think you might say. But, as always, I snagged at that charmed amatorial word 'love'.

The whole question of the relationship and where it was going was becoming an enigma. There were far too many unanswered questions, and the more thought I gave to it, the more determined Pandora was to inhabit my soul.

I decided to pay a visit to the house when I knew he would not be there. There was not much on at university, the parents had gone away somewhere abroad on their annual holiday, and Stephan had mentioned that he was going to be particularly busy in London that week. Ideal, I thought. I will go and see what happens there when I am not expected.

What I did unearth was way beyond anything I had anticipated.

Chapter Nine

I rolled up one Friday, shortly after lunch time. There was no one about but I heard the gardener, whom Lydia had introduced me to as Jake Cross, talking to someone, and so I pitched myself around the corner and peeped at them.

It was a young boy; I put him at about seven. He was wearing baggy jeans, an over-large, plain grey tee-shirt, and black Wellington boots that came above his knees. At first I did not see his face. It was shrouded by a mass of unruly, unkempt hair, which wizened his youth. As he turned around, I was taken aback by a remarkable face, as if subdued by some great wisdom.He stopped and looked up at me. He might have been an old man standing there, waif-like and almost ghostly. There was no charge of life about him that children usually have. He was more like a street urchin or a stray cat uncertain of its welcome. I was surprised at how like Stephan he looked, but for his eyes. His eyes were quite different. They were like two dark pebbles that shone out of his pale face with such intensity and intelligence, I was quite thrown by him. Then he looked away, as if by staring so long at me he had revealed a secret about himself.

Jake Cross explained that he was Stephan's son, and that he was mute. He was autistic he said, and was unable to comprehend what we were saying. I absorbed the information like brittle-dry earth rained heavily upon after drought. It was all so much to take in, and I found myself confused and stumbling. When I suggested we went indoors to have tea, I noticed him pick up a book he had resting upon a stone near where he was working in one of the vegetable rows and bring it carefully indoors with him.

Lydia did not seem too surprised to see that I had found him. Lydia, I found, took everything in her stride. She seemed genuinely fond of the child and spoke tenderly to him, as if addressing a pet animal. Whatever she thought of his condition she kept it to herself, but was nevertheless specific that I should be aware that he was not normal.

I did not know how to react. Should I be afraid? Why had he been kept secret for so long? Was he dangerous?All the questions piled in on me from among the accumulation of uncertainties and reservations I had kept to myself all this time. Then, just when I was feeling my most apprehensive about him, he raised two thin white hands towards me and stared. I felt an astonishing flow of intense energy coming from him, and at once I felt calm and at ease. It stopped me in my tracks. Was I imagining it? Had he done this to me? He seemed so normal, yet his muteness and his classification of autism were a mystery.

I did all the talking, and he responded to me - not in a spoken language, but by some astounding kind of telepathy. It was as if I could 'hear' his thoughts, and he seemed to read mine. He had even poured the tea that Lydia had brought in. autistic? I didn't think so. Never! Why had Stephan so diagnosed him?

He clearly could not talk. I asked if he could write replies, and he gave a brief nod, so I fetched a pen and paper from my car and handed it to him. I was interested to see quite how cognizant or limited he would be with his answers. I was about to be astonished.

"I see you are reading Anna Karenina," I said referring to the book he carried. "What is it that you enjoy about that?" I remember reading it as a recommended book at school and finding it tedious to the extreme.

'The conversation,' he wrote.

"The conversation? Do you enjoy conversation?" Silly question, I thought; how could he enjoy conversation when he was unable to speak himself?

"I mean," I hesitated, "I mean do you enjoy listening to conversation...I mean, reading conversation?" I was becoming more tongue-tied as my sentences progressed, but he was busy writing his reply as I muttered my words.

'I have had little experience of listening to conversation, but when writers such as Austin, Dickens and Tolstoy create conversation for their characters they are giving an insight to their own minds. It is interesting. Some authors like to bare their souls with endless descriptions; others like to create a story. They both reveal so much about themselves.'

My God! How old is this kid? I thought. I rather feebly continued the thought aloud. "How can someone of your age find an interest in such matters?' I said, sounding horrendously patronizing.

'What does age have to do with interest in any particular matter?' he wrote, leaving me feeling like the maiden aunt offering sexual advice to a well-versed adolescent.

When I asked him about poetry, he showed an interest, and was able to quote from Browning without a single error. I fetched a slender copy of John Keats from the car and read to him, - that much clichéd one, Season of Mists etc. When I looked up he was mouthing the words, as if he had memorized them also. His eyes burrowed into my face with such intensity I felt the blood race through my veins, as if for the first time in my life I had discovered something quite, quite extra-ordinary. A savant, perhaps? Perhaps not? I did not yet know enough on the subject. I only knew that I was drawn to him by some imperceptible enticement that had totally captivated me. I knew instinctively that here was a remarkable being. My whole body – essence - felt on fire just being in his presence.

At that moment a car drew up on the drive. It was Stephan. He must have guessed that I had arrived early. One of those determined-detective-fixation-moments, no doubt.

As I watched, David's face turned white. I touched him softly on his face, but from his body through to me came the corrosive shock of some intense dread from him. He shrank back and rose to his feet as if to preserve himself; it was a clear indication that all was not well between father and son. He was visibly agitated, and I tried to reassure him. Something terrible must have occurred between them. He was moving towards an exit as Stephan came in through another. Then Stephan saw him.

There was a reaction I had never seen before, let alone suspected of the man. For a few frozen moments we all remained in a state of chaos as the air was charged with an electrifying conjunction of forces, unified into a shadowy, silent rage. Seconds of time elapsed, and then came this desperate, loss of understanding and control.

I watched Stephan's face transform as it plunged into some kind of inner revolt that knew no bounds. His eyes were bright with a cold, unmoving hatred. Then he moved in a violent, wordless passion from some deep-seated loathing within him. It was a hot and bitter emotion that came from his soul, a dark inhuman thing caring for nothing. There was something about him and that place of his that I had not sensed before. It was something evil, something alien, as if he were not the person I had come to know, but some inhuman being who used up human life for unfeeling and wicked purposes. He had gone completely mad.

He threw the book that I had placed on a table at the boy. The book struck him in the face and knocked him to the floor, striking his head on the door as he fell and lay there, still and unmoving. Then he turned slowly with an almost deathly effort of volition, and stood before me. He could not look at me, but started to scream obscenities.

Lydia was there in seconds. It was the yelling between us that drew her. I was plunged into a deep frenzy and agony of uncertainly; none of this made any sense to me. I felt outraged and confused...there was so much that had happened all at once. I wanted to get away, to set him apart from me. I was in a blackness of outrage and frustration, and shocked that I had all this time been in total ignorance of all this.

Lydia removed the boy from the room very rapidly, and I was left with his deranged father, who was still making the most nonsensical accusations about the boy.

He was raving. It was as if he had emerged from the shadow of some dark, powerful secret which I did not want any part of. Like the opening of Pandora's Box, it cast such a shade of darkness everywhere. This revelation was nothing at all what I had expected. Then, as suddenly as it had all started, it ended as he fell to the floor in a convulsive fit - out for the count.

"Lydia!" I yelled frantically. She dispatched her first casualty, and rushed to attend to the second. For the first time in our rather bizarre relationship I was determined to break the unspoken circumstance of silence between us.

Lydia seemed quite au fait with the situation. This was evidently a regular occurrence, and there was evidently so much more to it.

When he had come round sufficiently he lay where he had fallen, his face hard and cold and unchanged. He had been brought back into that place of recognised unreality. He had been cast back into the sea to swim until he sank again, because those silent secrets were weighing down on him.

Jake had been summoned, and together he and Lydia managed to drag their master up the stairs to his bedroom. They shut themselves inside with him. I stood outside listening to the incoherent mumblings from within, feeling detached and separate from this aspect of it all and grateful that it was so. Then I went downstairs to the living room where the elaborate and out-of-place Twenties liquor cabinet stood and poured myself a whiskey, a large one. I wanted to drown out the stark and desperate reality of it all. How had we, two very separate and different beings, living two separate lives, become so united in this inexplicable way that was almost impossible to separate from? What was I doing there, anyway? The man was not only too old for me, but clearly off his rocker. And this situation with his own child? Why? It seemed as if everything I had ever known and believed in was shattered, all life spoiled, desolated - laid waste. I would go mad from being in his very presence again.

Like Pandora, I had wanted to find out something and I had, and its very revelation was like some strange underground thing, abstract and haunting, and - dare I say - evil.

Chapter Ten

How had Stephan so firmly become the foundation on which I stood? I decided I must take a stand against him. I must stop depending on him, or allowing him to depend on me. Was I so caught up in this dark sea around him that I was trapped there, and would drown with him?I wanted to get back in my car and leave, but something stopped me. I could not go.

I must have been standing there for at least half an hour, staring into space. The sharp bite of undiluted alcohol burned my throat and numbed my brain in fractions. I was trying to make up my mind as to what I should do, when Lydia came back downstairs to the kitchen and nonchalantly put the kettle on as if nothing had happened.

"How is David?" I asked, following her into the room that smelled of fresh herbs and something she was baking.

"He is fine - in his room reading, already. I took the book back upstairs what 'ad been thrown at 'im, and that pleased 'imself enough. Mr.Tyndal 'as taken bad. though. He gets like that sometimes but 'as 'ad 'is medication and is sleeping deep enough. I hope you don't mind but I 'ave taken the precaution of ringing 'is sister. She knows what to do in these circumstances."

"His sister? I didn't even know he had a sister, let alone a son. Lydia, I have been a perfect fool...I have allowed myself to become involved with a man I hardly know."

"Well, he 'as taken to you, Miss. It 'as been something of a relief 'aving you around, I can tell you. Look, don't leave just now - p'raps a talk with 'is sister will put you right, I daresay. It's all a mite complicated for me to explain."

Yes, I thought. *What other little surprises may be lurking around the corner that I have not been told about, for the sake of keeping peace?*

"I have known Mr. Tyndal for a year now and I haven't seen anything like this before. Why does he so dislike his son? He said the boy had killed his mother and he has been sent here to be taken care of."

"He told me none of that, Miss. The boy and 'is mum were inseparable, Jake can tell you that. It was she as protected 'im from 'is father. She ran away from 'im, she did - when David were around five, I think it was. Took the boy and left, she did. Mr. Tyndal went 'arf mad when he knew she were gone. 'What's it to you sir?' I said. 'You was always punishing the boy, now he's out the way you can get on with your life.' He didn't 'arf turn on me! I says to 'im, 'Look, you raise a hand to me and I walk out, and there ain't another will put up with your ways.' Next thing he was gone out the door, gone to Africa to fetch her back. Then a few days later he came back, white as a sheet, without 'er or the boy. Not a word about it. Next I hear about 'er is four years later and he says the boy's gotten worse, 'is mother is dead, and he is going to fetch 'im from the airport. He says to lock 'im up when he gets ere. Why the lad's family sent 'im here after 'is Ma died, Lord only knows. Cruel, I call it. Anyway, since you are on the scene, Miss, things 'ave been ever so quiet. You seem to be good for 'im. No more rages - nothing. Even the boy don't trouble 'im so much. Mind, I keep the boy well away when he's 'ome, I don't mind telling you. The boy knows to stay away also. He's ever so bright, Miss. Sometimes I wonder about 'im."

"Then why is he not in school?" I asked.

"Why he is not in a school, Miss? Well, the fact he can't talk shows there's summat the matter. Mind, when he were little he used to sing nursery rhymes and talk to 'is mum all the time. Oh yes, he weren't always like this. The little lad's noise drove Mr. Tyndal mad, I can tell you. Jealous, he was. Couldn't bear the boy near 'is ma. When his Dad was 'ome I used to take the little lad out with me, but he were always crying for 'is mum. Mr. Tyndal used to beat him something terrible when he cried. Then he would lock 'im up somewhere in 'is study. Then one day something happened...not sure what. Mr. Tyndal, he used to send Miss Suki - that's the boy's mum - to classes, meditation of some sort, in London. She would be gone for the day. David was locked up somewhere in that time and when 'is ma came 'ome, he was all quiet. From then on, he just stopped talking. Then Suki comes to me one day and says, 'I'm leaving', she says. She waits until he 'as gone to London, and she packs 'er bags and she is gone. She says, 'I'll write when I get there, Lydia,' but I never 'erd from 'er from that day to this - not a word."

Lydia was still talking when a small, violet-coloured Morris Minor rolled up outside and a large, portly woman emerged, like tooth-paste being squeezed from a tube. A mass of untidy grey hair was wrapped around her head and impaled there by a chop stick or two. She was wearing a long dress to the ground like Joseph's multi-coloured dream-coat and about her neck was a festoon of gaudy beads, some of which reached to her knees.

The adjectives *rages - cruel - jealous - mad* tumbled about my head, as I watched the strange woman open the boot of her car and remove a substantial wicker basket. She then marched towards the front door which Lydia had already laid open for her, and there a flourishing and demonstrative embrace took place between the two ladies.

"Aha!" she said, on seeing me at the back. "You are the wonderful being who has kept my brother sane all these months. Welcome, welcome!"

A bright pink lipstick had misfired onto her front teeth but she was not deterred from planting a smacking kiss upon my cheek, and printing a good deal of it there. She introduced herself as Bethany Tyndal, never married - it figured. She seemed already to know my name. It was a bit like Alice through the looking-glass with the absurdity of it all. Everyone knew about me, and I knew nothing of them, or what was happening

Bethany was attractive in a wild sort of way. It was easy to imagine her a lot younger and a great deal thinner as very lovely. That unrestrained bubbling personality would go down a treat at parties, especially the dull ones my parents gave - she could be quite indispensable there. She enthused about everything, making light of the distressing afternoon cited by Lydia, offering to each detail of the plight of young David a series of reassuring *ahs* and *ohs*. However, I was in no mood for soothing charm or a long chat about her brother. After the disturbing revelations and prospect of even more to come, I was more in mind of a quick retreat. Despite my agitated state at the turn of events and my determination to remain aloof, we were soon discussing our private lives as if we had known each other for years. Age gap – what age gap?

Lydia joined us, as we drank coffee laced with something severely alcoholic Bethany had taken from her basket. That, with what I had already plied myself, unleashed the wronged woman in me, ready to avenge my gender and allowing Lydia plenty of scope to add her own vilifications.

"And why was I not informed that my nephew had been returned?"

I too wondered why Lydia, with all her swift-to-reveal-all chat, had failed to disclose David's whereabouts to anyone - particularly to me. Her long-winded explanation led nowhere but to leave one surmising that she was a lonely old woman who wanted to keep the boy to herself for company, with full authorization from his father. For some reason he wanted his son out of the way, and Lydia was only too willing to comply.

While the explanations and missing information was becoming more and more convoluted, I asked Lydia where David's room was.

"End one, on the top floor," she said, "but he won't come down…not now. He will stay up there now until 'is Dad as gone."

I was already making my way up the stairs as she spoke. Naturally, he would be placed there - it was as far away from his father's room as you could get. I tapped on the door and was surprised when the boy opened it and stood there, looking at me as if he had anticipated my visit. He had a large blue lump on the side of his head and his eyes were full of wonder and expectation.

"My poor David," I said, and put my arms around him. To my surprise the boy clung to me, and began to weep pitifully. He was trying to speak, but no words came from him.

"Don't worry, David; I am here to help you. I will make sure no harm comes to you ever again."

It was as if something inside him was yearning to come out, something far off, lost to him. I felt that I could not speak to him as one would to a child; he seemed so much more than that in years. His tears were tears of some deep sadness, and not of fear or anxiety. He had evidently suffered, and there he was, locked into the confinement of defenceless childhood: done away with, and subjugated to a bad and destructive will.

"Look, David, you father has been sedated. He won't wake, not for a long while. Your Aunt is here and she would like to see you. Why don't you come down with me and we can all have something to eat? I am sure it must be well past your supper time."

He followed me meekly down the stairs, tip-toeing as if not to make a sound, a practice he was clearly versed in. Once in the kitchen I took the precaution of closing the door quietly behind us to make sure sound would not carry up the stairs.

Aunt Bethany was gentle and kind to her nephew. He did not appear to acknowledge her. No doubt her visits to the house had been limited over the years. She invited him to sit next to her, which he did, after giving me a glance to see where I would be sitting. The conversation remained quiet, controlled and without any mention of the person lying above stairs - in a state of insensibility, I hoped.

Bethany's coffee additive had the desired effect of inebriating us all, with the exception of David who sat mute, as to be expected, and ate little of the cottage pie that was administered in large helpings to us all.

When the meal was over, David rose from the table, came round, and formally put his hand out to me, then to Bethany, and left the room.

"For a child who is purportedly autistic, I find him unusually alert," said Bethany. "I last saw him when he was four, only briefly. Stephan was adamant that he should be left undisturbed and that poor girl Suki seemed to be in a world of her own. There was obviously something going on and Stephan was behaving like he did as a teenager. I thought it best to stay out of the way, as you know, Lydia, but I am now lost for words. Why is the boy not in school, or at least a specialised school? Why have you not told me before about his condition?"

Both women started talking at once, so I announced that it was time I left for London.

"Nonsense girl, you can't go all that way back now - it's dark, and there are plenty of rooms you can sleep in."

When Lydia had departed to make up beds, Bethany had the chance to speak to me. It was clear that she had a lot to say on the subject of her brother. I was curious to understand what was going on. I needed resolutions to all those unanswered questions; that is, if I knew how to ask them, or indeed what to ask.

I made some limp remark about the mysteries of life and instantly wished that I had kept my intoxicated tongue in my head...God knows where I thought that might lead. I was in no mood for amateur philosophies, not now. I had been through the best with her brother, only to discover that those well-defined and educated opinions had turned out to be from an insane mind. Like her brother, she too had well versed viewpoints she was quick to run with in a direction that soon lost me, my own mind going in every which way.

"Why should one attribute some special mystery to life? It is simply that we none of us really understand life as we so little understand electricity or telegraphy, but that doesn't stop any old fool from saying that our lives are something special and distinct from everything else in the universe. Life is an interaction of physical and chemical actions: action and reaction. I don't see really, why we should imagine there is a special order of life or determine our actions on a vague past that no longer exists. It is all random." Her words continued on and on. I was finding it more and more difficult to follow what she was saying, when her voice faded on a note of puzzling uncertainty, indefinite and reflective. It was as if she was wrestling with something in her own mind that she had not come to terms with. Her brain was perhaps as befuddled as mine at that point, so she told me that I should visit her in London during the week and she would fill me in on the family history.

Chapter Eleven

I was up early the next morning, and found Stephan already in the kitchen. He was pleased to see me, making no mention of what had occurred the evening before, but the shocking fact of it tainted the usual ease between us and was supplanted by a pall of tense and recoiling distance. He spoke about the weather outside with an almost flippant air, and all the while an ominous and dismal sense of anguish poured out of his eyes like a strain of distant and discordant sound. It was as if he was wandering purposely towards an impending and inevitable abyss which lay ahead.

I had this inexplicable feeling of unease, as if I was receiving some troubled kind of warning from somewhere. It sank me into that sort of lethargy that takes breath from lungs and blunts the senses. When his sister entered the room several minutes later he greeted her enthusiastically, surprised even that she was there, and he proceeded to introduce us. It would seem in some way that the events of the evening before had been totally eradicated from his mind, creating a Mad-Hatter's Tea Party event.

We took the weekend in our stride and chatted about this and that in the garden, and the state of plant and animal growth. Meals were pleasant and copious as always, and Bethany saw to it that as much wine was consumed as was possible. Bethany's liquid requirement was an essential part of her well-being.

"Have you visited any of the secret passages yet?" she asked me, as casually as asking if I had tried Lydia's fig jam.

"No," I said, rather startled. "Stephan told me he had never seen them."

"Poop and nonsense." It was a note of derision aimed at something she was attempting to expose - maybe a fear, maybe another of the secrets that were beginning to pop a tight vest.

"What on earth did you tell her that for?"

Stephan, not to be cornered, wandered off down the garden. I gave Bethany a glance to advise her that I was not yet ready for a repetition of last night's performance, no matter how cathartic the revelation might be. With equally-badly applied tact she asked in a loud voice for him to hear why David had not appeared. When Stephan was out of earshot, I told her how he had been secreted away each weekend while his father was about.

"Well, I can see that matters have become as dramatic as they were years ago. Something must be done. Come and visit me in my house in London...we will talk and discuss arrangements. Here is a card with my number and address. Phone me when you are ready to talk."

Having determined on her final decision to take matters into her own hands, she departed, dangerously preoccupied with a set of plans she was mulling over to tackle her brother with. She was a beaver of meddlesome activity, ready to cut down logs with her bare teeth if she had to, to bridge that insurmountable predicament that was becoming more obdurate by the minute.

The remainder of the weekend was a strain but I felt the obligation - or was it an urge? - to remain there, silent witness to an undercurrent of some terrible and obscure darkness, in which Stephan himself was clearly trapped.

He was bound up in a kind of blind, dogged will about something, and it was patent that the something was to do with David. He had it in his power to destroy the boy, deliberately shaping him into a helpless mute and imposing upon him an imbecile character so that he would remain fixed under his will. It was a brute will, fixed by sheer force. And all the while there was Lydia, quite satisfied to live in a state of complacent self-deception about both her employer and his son.

I could have left them all well alone and gone away - right then. This mess was nothing to do with me. What could I do? If I reported what I had witnessed, who would believe me? The housekeeper would deny anything had happened. After all, the boy had been diagnosed and accepted as abnormal. Besides which, the boy was clearly strange, and mute into the bargain. How would one make a case against a highly professional father taking care of an allegedly-imbecile child, who had been rejected by his own grandparents? Then again...

David's look of appeal had struck a deep chord in me which was never to leave me. I had been instantly and profoundly affected by the extraordinary child...human. If I simply walked away, something might happen to him. I was compelled to stay and work it out, against all sensible reason.It was a conundrum that simply bewildered me. Here was an undeniably brilliant mind, eclipsed by insanity - but was it the father's evident insanity or the son's diagnosed abnormality that had caused it all? The very insight that this could be a life or death situation held me as surely as a moth trapped by light.

Stephan would never admit to anything. For him, everything was without limits, everything was within his reach, within his manipulative control - and I had been the unwitting captive ensnared by him all this time. And that is precisely how I saw it at that moment. I felt that I had been deceived, taken in by him - but for what purpose?

Conflicting emotions rearranged themselves constantly in my mind. I was confused, mystified, bewildered. Anything, everything I had felt for him and about him up to that moment was under cross-examination.

I did my best to adjust to the situation and turned to a feigned familiarity of our relationship as it had been. But it was never to be the same again, as it had taken on a macabre and dilatory tone. We talked on mundane subjects while the crisis that had occurred was masked like a snake that hides in the shadows of long grass. All the while, I wondered how I was going to tackle the situation. How was I going to be able to see David again? How could I save him from his father without being thrown out before I could do anything?

My mind at variance with my emotions made no sense of how I was feeling at each moment that passed. I wanted very much to go and speak with Lydia to ask about David, but there was never a single moment alone. David was out of bounds and all I wanted to do was go and find him, to speak with him again. At the same time I had this deep-rooted urge to leave, to clear out and not to have to understand any of it. Yet I stayed put. Waiting and hoping for that right moment.

I left early the next day, with the excuse that I had some reading to catch up with. By then Stephan seemed almost relieved to see me go. The tension was palpable, but neither of us was able to discuss it. We both had our reasons.

I drove back to my parent's home, and for once decided to divulge all the details of my clandestine affair. There had been enough secrets.

I was taken-aback, shocked even, to discover that they had been fully cognizant of my affair all along.

I always felt that I had a sort of distanced, formal even, relationship with my parents. It was as if they had had children as a conventional expectation to justify the status of their marriage. It was something people did. Our upbringing had been formalised to accommodate all the necessities required of parents. There was a 'them and us' sort of thing. It was our obligation to acknowledge respect and show gratitude, and they were there to acknowledge responsibility and guidance and cope with the inbuilt anxieties that went with parenting from time to time. It was about how to handle these un-launched humans to whom they had given life, with their attendant strange pubescent behaviour and attitudes that they never quite understood or could come to grips with. And there I was, burdened with the greatest quandary of my life so far, and totally unable to know how to unleash it upon them. I decided to launch straight in with a suitably innocent question.

"What do you know about Stephan Tyndal?"

They gave each other that knowing look which undercut any equality that might exist between us.

"Well, er," Father began, with loaded hesitation. "Of course, you know that he is connected to my forensic department, which is how I became acquainted with him."

I did not know, nor did I know anything about his professional life, but I was not ready to admit that. I was suddenly overcome with shame that I had never troubled to find out enough about him.

"He has published some interesting papers on profiling the criminally insane, and has worked extensively with the Criminal Investigative Analysis Program. As a pathologist, I have from time to time worked with that department and had a lot to do with his work. About his personal life...I would imagine by now that you know a good deal more than we do."

"Well," I began hesitatingly, "I have seen quite a bit of him, as you seem to have guessed."

I didn't demean myself by asking how they had guessed. It was all too awkward, so I let loose the situation of the secreted young son I had only just met who was allegedly autistic.

"He must have been that young South African girl's child by him. I don't think they married, did they, dear?" Mother asked rather piously, inclining her head towards Father.

"Yes, he is," I answered hastily, "I believe she died and the grandparents sent him back to his father from South Africa, where the boy and his mother had gone to live."

I avoided the surprising little details of how I had come upon him, followed by the pathological behaviour of his father on seeing him in my company. I enlarged rather on the tremendously inspiring aspects of the boy.

There were questions I needed to ask to validate those misgivings I had. Knowing the answers was not enough. I needed to purge myself of those feelings I had for a man I should now distrust. Added to which, I was battling now with the profound effect his child had on me. A boy I had known only for the briefest time, and for whom I had the greatest concern.

I snatched at a hundred variables. He was mentally affected by something that had happened to him; he was a chip off the old block sharing a genetic mental disorder with his father; he really was autistic with savant qualities; he was some incomparable being who had found himself…

"What has made you so interested in the boy? I mean, up to now, dear, you have not mentioned a word to us about your friendship with Stephan Tyndal - but you are ready to talk at great length about his son," Mother asked, rather suspiciously. "Are you worried that he might have inherited some genetic disorder from his father?" she added, with uncanny perceptiveness.

"A genetic disorder? What made you think Stephan Tyndal has a genetic disorder?" I protested.

"Aside from his muteness, did the boy display any other symptoms of disturbance?" Father asked.

"No, quite the contrary; I found him to be the most fascinating, quite extraordinary person I have ever met. He was exceptionally bright, especially for his age."

"A savant, perhaps?"

"No, a savant is usually brilliant in a single direction. No, there was something else…I just can't explain. It was as if he was reading my mind, and answering questions I had not even asked."

"I thought you said he was dumb, my dear?" said Mother with an infuriatingly innocent ruse at entrapment.

"Yes, he is." I responded, irritated that I had initiated this confidence out of a need for useful recommendation, only to find it going in the direction of cynicism. "He wrote the answers down but I felt that I could hear his answers in my head before he wrote them."

"Really, dear?"

Why did I have to mention that! Blast. I was digging myself in deeper and deeper and becoming thwarted with the need to confide.

"How was his father towards him?"

Trust Father to ask that question.

"I can't really tell you."

"Why? Did you not see them together?"

"Well, yes I did. They both seemed rather afraid of each other as a matter of fact."

I paused, knowing that soon I would have said too much. "I need more time with this situation before I can answer it." I added dismissively, all the while desperately needing advice on how I should proceed with the whole situation.

"Actually, Stephan had a sort of fit after a wild outburst with the boy." I decided to add, rather impulsively, as if to divest myself of the entanglement that had found a permanent foothold in my brain.

Father suggested that some severe childhood trauma might have occurred with the boy, or he *was* in fact autistic - nothing I had not worked out for myself - but Stephan's fit was a greater alarm to him. He had heard reports at the hospital that Stephan was subject to rages and epileptic-type seizures when he was angered.

"Do be careful, darling," said Mother, becoming infuriatingly maternal. "We haven't wanted to say anything about the relationship, as we were so afraid that it would become too serious by inhibiting it."

We were all silent for some agonizingly thoughtful moments, while each tried to prepare what to say next.

"I was strangely drawn towards him. He is so intelligent and conversations are so much more worthwhile with him than the students I mix with. I can't explain."

"Are you in love with him?" Mother asked.

"I have never been 'in love' with anyone," I answered. "It's hard to say how I feel. 'In love' sounds so intense and entangled. I can't say I feel that way but I feel bound to him in a strange sort of way, almost like I am responsible for him."

Again the brittle silence spiked the keen atmosphere, wedging that old dissatisfaction uncomfortably between us. Had I gained much useful advice by speaking to them? I don't think so. It was a wild and rather stupid idea. Cathartic? – definitely not! I had only landed myself in another constrained situation. Mother's covert re-arrangement of my life came with so little encouragement - and there I was, opening myself out to her little suggestions and delicately structured arrangements.

"Well we have the Gregsons coming here next weekend. Why don't you join us for a change? Remember Jeremy, their son? He will be down from Oxford for the weekend and may be joining them. Remember how fond you were of him, dear?"

"No, I have no such memories of fondness for Jeremy whatsoever. I found him dull and irritatingly inquisitive about a particular friend of mine he had met over one summer holiday. Remember Rita? It was Rita."

"Yes, a rather lovely-looking girl;" said Father.

"Well Rita disliked him on the spot. She said he was creepy, and he insisted on tailing her."

On first contact with Jeremy, one might well think him attractive in a sort of flashy, pretentious way - but Jeremy was so fixated upon his own sense of priority in all things that anything attractive about him paled under his own approval of himself. He had that supercilious air of his own supreme importance, in which he regarded everyone else as inferior. He would incline his head inward as if an answer to a question would grate upon his superior intellect, a habit he practiced most when I was about. I remembered his jokes, his awful jokes which left everyone silent as he filled the room with his own raucous laughter at his own appreciation of them. Then he would attempt to explain them to those un-amused among us, and deride those who would persistently not understand as humourless. I remembered, with aggravation at myself, that I had a huge problem trying to dissuade him from contacting Rita, to prevent him being spurned by her.

Rita was one of those exotically beautiful women with a glut of devoted admirers about her, whom she was constrained to swat back like irksome flies round a jam-pot; she was well known for her talent at reducing even the feistiest suitors to naked worms. Not Jeremy. He was totally oblivious to all her sarcasm and went right on following her about. I seem to remember that at some stage she even slapped him, without effect.

I could think of nothing less exciting than a weekend with the Gregsons with their insufferable son. But I accepted. It would provide me with a legitimate excuse to give to Stephan for not turning up for the weekend. I needed time to think.

The David situation would have to wait. Before I returned to *Nasiarcuth* again I needed to speak with Bethany, whom I hoped would put things into perspective for me. She would fill me in with all those missing details I had been shielded from for so long. I arranged to have dinner with her in the middle of the week.

Chapter Twelve

Bethany's apartment - I could hardly call it a flat, the category 'flat' would not do justice to its size - was part of one of those massive houses that overlook Hyde Park.

Most of the furniture was larger than life. She had those dreadful robust, kind of all-enveloping sofas and chairs, which swallow you instantly into a feathered entombment. In direct contrast, the casual tables that nestled the sides were impractically delicate, for much use as antiquity had made them fragile. Every inch of floor space was filled with antiques and relics of the past and *objet d'art* upon every table top, in diametric contrast to Stephan's London flat.

She talked of the wonderful furniture that had been handed on over the generations, stroking pieces of Chippendale, Robert Adam, Hepplewhite and Sheraton as if they were alive. But amongst the preserved splendour of extinct furniture was a living state of littered chaos. One would never guess that she had a cleaner to 'do' for her, as she put it. The place looked as if it had been ransacked by thieves looking for buried treasure.Discarded clothing, moribund flowers in stagnant water, dirty plates scattered about, pots of oil paint and unfinished paintings leaned up against the furniture, often spreading their still wet paint onto the fabric, and everywhere had the aroma of enclosed animals.

I don't think I ever saw Bethany modestly clothed. That day she had out-done her adornment, but it was hard to draw ones' eyes from the substantial brassiere straps that peeked out where her long silk caftan seductively slipped off the shoulder. The caftan was festooned with bright red dragons on a peacock blue background. Across her temple, 1920's style, she wore a velvet band into which were set a dozen bright blue feathers. A long ivory cigarette-holder projected a blue cigarette that spilled ash as she went about, haloed in a nimbus of smoke. The infusion of tobacco, incense and doggie smell was joined by an even stronger smell of garlic wafting from the kitchen. I dreaded the thought of the meal that was to come. I have never had the best of digestive systems.

My hand was soon amply supplied with a massive glass of red wine and I was directed to one of the large, more than accommodating arm-chairs that gulped me into its core, making a movement as awkward as an insect caught in a Venus-fly-trap.

Bethany Tyndal had inherited those eccentric genes from both her parents, along with her large London house. Stephan had inherited a wealth of neurosis and the country house. She had subdivided the house into three flats, one for each floor. She occupied the basement, ground floor, and garden. The rent, I imagine, afforded her the luxury of living there and buying expensive canvasses. Those she filled with rather peculiar portraits of people she must have pulled in from dark corners to paint.

Bethany was living proof of a life of alcohol, rooms of tobacco smog, and as many strange and challenging people about her than you could shake a stick to. However, a lifestyle of indiscriminate taste and indiscretion did not deny her a perceptive, well-meaning and sweet nature, and an eternal youthfulness which glowed behind a face as creased as an old road map pulled from a crumpled handbag.

Three small fluffy white dogs, beautifully groomed and bejewelled with sparkling collars, waited patiently for her to be seated before leaping up onto her lap. She crashed her weight down into her chair, knocking off a pair of extremely grubby moccasins, and wriggled her recently restricted scarlet toenails.

"Come on Chaps, that's enough of that. You will all have your turn on Mummy's lap!" Regardless of the promise, they all vied for the best position on Mummy's ample lap, sneezing copiously when too much smoke had entered their tiny lungs from Mummy's permanently combustible cigarette. Unlike her brother she asked no questions about me, but launched at once into the enlightenment of her own, rather unusual, background.

She described their parents as wild eccentrics, and coming from her, I imagined a pair of extreme radicals, unconventional intellectuals straight off the shelf of the Bloomsbury Group. They had met each other at Cambridge and, being like-minded, they soon fell captive to analytic philosophers akin to Bertrand Russell, Moore and the like, and joined the philosophical revolution of their time.

Their attitudes towards perception of external nature, the ultimate separateness of individuals, truth, love and beauty etc, etc and all things indefinable, led them on towards The Golden Dawn Society, an offshoot of that eerie sect that called themselves the Rosicrucians, who involved themselves with secret rituals straight out of some ancient archive. It all smacked to me of those primitive ancestors who daubed themselves in woad and danced naked at midnight around a pyre of wild bush.

"Didn't Yeats have something to do with The Golden Dawn?" I asked, clumsily spilling my ignorance about.

"Yes - there were a good many intelligent people influenced by all those links with alchemy, the occult and those out-of-reach subjects. Of course, those were topics that no one in a reserved, socially-straight-jacketed kind of mind would associate with; not publicly anyway. The late nineteenth century founded wonderfully captivating societies with inspiring names like the 'Society of Inner Light' and our parents were keen on indulging in them all, despite social stigma. No different from today...no one wants to be seen as an oddball. Those with any interest in metaphysics are often in conflict with religious groups and modern science, and those societies opened doors to other dimensions otherwise neglected."

"Yes, I have noticed that," I said, with some experience of reaction from Father. "I could go along with all that those societies present - but all those old rituals? Come on!"

"Well they lent a kind of mystic intensity to the aficionados. No, it was not that; it was the mind involvement that our parents were interested in."

"I see," I said, but didn't.

"Our parents were interested in anything odd that leaned towards mystery and stimulated the imagination. They were also serious psychologists and pursued personality disorders which cause havoc in so many lives, particularly obsessive-compulsive traits which start from an early age. I suppose you could say Stephan gave them that incentive. His obsessions over trivia led them to look more closely as to why he displayed such neurosis at such a young age. Their research led them to regressive hypnosis, which they had dabbled in mildly whilst still in university. They studied anything from Mesmer and his magnetic wands to Freud reaching into the subconscious, to Hermann Ebbinghaus' hypnosis as anaesthetic to calm nerves. All those cathartic techniques..."

"Jung, too I believe..." I interrupted, trying to show willing and also to push her on a mite. She was not too pleased at an interruption, as her eyes glazed momentarily.

"Stephan," she continued, eclipsing me. "Stephan happened to be an exceptional subject, and it appeared that he had had many past-life links with *Nasiarcuth Hall*. *Nasiarcuth* has been in father's family for a few generations now, and the family were always interested in its history, of course. Most of its history had never been documented - or was perhaps destroyed. All that was known about it were the passed-down legends of the locals. It was known to be a religious sanctuary for a long period. It became a safe haven for the much persecuted Carthusian monks, but was invaded at some stage with undue pertinacity by an official inquirer of Cromwell's Inquisition tribunal. Appalling atrocities were said to have been committed within the house, in the name of righteous religious cleansing.

Apparently, a servant leaked the word that the house was harbouring banned Carthusians. Every soul on the property was butchered, but for some reason the invaders left the building untouched, perhaps waiting for it to be gifted to one of Cromwell's followers. However, the house remained unoccupied for over a hundred years. It was thought to be haunted by some powerful soul that would protect it and its concealment in perpetuity. Many years later it became a lunatic asylum, which ran for several years until it was closed down, for some reason or other. No one had dared to live there until great-grandfather saw its worth and bought it to modernise - but he never came to live in it, and so it was passed down. I believe even our grandpapa never really lived there. He visited the place from time to time, but lived mostly in London - here, as a matter of fact - and then passed it on to Daddy, who loved it. He and Mummy revelled in its antiquity, its priest holes, sliding panels and secret tunnels, many of which had long since caved in."

"Stephan never talked about the underground passages or priest-holes. I did not even know they existed, until you mentioned them last week."

"Well Stephan has a kind of morbid attachment to all that side. He has always been secretive and I suppose it was part of his wanting that to be separate from the real world. Our parents were quite different. They loved to talk about it, to fantasise about it, if you will. The place was an inspirational fantasy for quixotic visionaries with an off-balanced sense of the mythological. They probed and ferreted for information about the past inhabitants. Some of the reports came from patients who had been institutionalised there when the house was a mental institution. They talked of bizarre haunting, of re-enactments of disembowelled priests, but so much of that could be discredited from whence it came. Those locals who had worked there at the time of the institution were by then pretty old themselves and could report nothing but hearsay of the extra-sensory or remarkable, other than difficult patients and authoritarian medical staff. From time to time the patients would 'see' visions, but mental patients were expected to see visions - it was part and parcel of their complaints."

I could imagine Stephan withdrawing from the hype of it all and I wanted to question this aspect of him, but Bethany was in full throttle and I could see she wanted to talk. I let her go on, uninterrupted by cross-examination.

"I was twelve years old when our parents inherited the property. In those days, one seldom sold property...it was passed down. Stephen was born a year or so after they had moved in to *Nasiarcuth*. There was a large age difference between us, and of course I was away at boarding school by the time they started having problems with him. We had nannies. They were silent, subservient and obliging creatures then, seldom complaining about a difficult child. Our parents were often up in London, attending lectures and working."

"I take it that they were both psychologists?" I asked.

"Yes, and you know how psychologists are; hovering on the brink of freshly constructed deductions taken from a collection of findings, and making hypothesis on other people's assumptions with a smattering of observable fact."

"It is a subject I am currently studying at university," I apologised.

"Well then, my dear, you will soon get to discover that psychologists have a tendency to anthropomorphize by identifying with the object of study and projecting their own ideas, even when sober evidence may be lacking. They redefine old words to give scientific jargon a meaning and impress the layman. - sometimes re-inventing a simple malady and turning it into a serious maladjustment, with a name which separates the person into a category of abnormality."

I wondered if she was referring to her brother's diagnosis of his own son, or reacting in opposition to her own parents. Anyway, I was unable to ask much as she had drawn herself up into a fever pitch, intoxicated by her own voice, listening to her own words and liking them. This was well rehearsed rhetoric and needed to be quenched before it developed any further on a detour of self-assertion, losing the point of what she was going to tell me. I was not particularly interested in what psychologists did or did not believe in. I had had a surfeit of that in my studies, and was as bored to distraction with my career choice already as I was becoming increasingly drained by her erudite jargon. I interrupted her flow.

"Is all this leading to the point of telling me Stephan, or your parents, were maladjusted or abnormal in some way?"

"No, quite the contrary. I am leading to the point of their ambiguous interpretation of Stephan's problem, my dear. Our parents sincerely believed in another dimension beyond this world. They held séances from time to time, dabbling in the extrasensory and the supernatural - the most of which was hypothesis and conjecture, but they took it all in."

"I take it that you were never grabbed by their beliefs?"

"The supernatural is not something that can be turned on by an investigator making a scientific documentation. It is sporadic and random and requires someone of extraordinary abilities and powers to bring about."

"Now you are suggesting some supernatural power that has a hold of him."

"No, not that either. Though I think as children we were both stirred up by the tide of sensational speculations. But even children nurtured by families with strong religious or arbitrary beliefs will have doubts cast at them from outside information…unless, of course, you have parents who live in sterile circumstances, where their children do not come into any contamination of other ideas."

She was rambling again, so I got up and filled our glasses with wine, and fidgeted.

"They would involve us in their experiments and discussions. Stephan came to believe that he was the reincarnation of an Abbot trapped in an underground space leading from a tunnel, and that he had returned to earth to seek retribution for his terrible death there."

I flinched. "Who on earth is he going to find to punish? What rubbish! I mean, how will he know when he has met the poor sod who has clearly forgotten all, assuming the culprit has come back at the same time? I really can't believe this. Steph is so…well, he is…oh, to hell… I suppose I don't know what he is."

I was overwhelmed with distrust, feeling ridiculous that I was asking questions, as though the discussion was at all probable. It was just too damn much. I was beginning to feel extremely uncomfortable, like discussing Father Christmas with a four year old who was in fact a mature woman. I couldn't even think about it anymore. I had exceeded my cut-off point of liberal-mindedness.

"Our parents believed that one could return in one incarnation as a victim and the next as a perpetrator, but that from time to time one soul will follow another for some specific reason."

"Well who is to say that the converse may also be true - that he was the perpetrator, and he now needs to seek redemption for the terrible deaths that he might have incurred. Wow…just think of all the possibilities!"

The subject was as bizarre as those who still hold to the belief that we who have descended from Adam will one day return to the earth after millenniums of confinement in suspended animation, whereupon an uninformed medieval saint can rub shoulders with a futuristic intellectual hippie in some blissful Utopia where we are all at peace with one another.

"Where on earth is all the proof of this stuff?" I asked ungraciously. "I mean, it all sounds very interesting as theory but, well, damnit - one needs some sort of direction about this stuff. The Christians at least have their Bible. The Mohammedans have their Koran, the Atheists have Darwin. I mean - what do the Spiritualists have?"

"They used hypnosis to expand their investigations, - nothing to do with Spiritualism," she continued, ignoring my outburst as no more than a trifling interruption for her to gain breath.

"They documented and sometimes recorded the voices of those subjects who went back into past lives, describing how they lived and died. Of course, recordings in those days were difficult to achieve, for the instruments of recording were still nowhere near as sophisticated or available as they are now. Often their recording machines would not pick up very clearly what was being said, so they would also write down all the communications they had with their subjects under hypnosis. Then they would try, where possible, to research the information they obtained to corroborate events and circumstances."

"What proof did they have that the subjects didn't already have a subconscious store of information that they were using, like a distorted dream state, as an imagined past life?"

"None. That is what makes the whole scientific process one that is hard to corroborate. But for the fact that they found some subjects would speak fluently in another language, where they had had no connection with that language before, perhaps they would not have continued with the concept."

"I have to admit, I have always seen Stephan as a rather practical, unimaginative sort of chap. I find it difficult to believe that he could be influenced by their beliefs, even as a child. I imagine one has to be a little imaginative to dwell in a past life, whether it existed or not." The cynicism in my voice was hard to disguise. "How about you Bethany...were you ever persuaded to go under and describe yourself as a maiden of good or bad virtue, or whatever?"

I realised that I was sounding pathetically patronizing, but I was beginning to feel so ill at ease about the subject. I had gone there to find out more about Stephan and his child on a more accessible level, and here we were, discussing the intangible aspects of existence. Whilst the romantic in me has always been secretly fascinated in such subjects, suddenly confronted by it and applied to someone I was intimately involved with was beyond my comfort zone.

"It is easy to be flippant about anything which arises out of an unexplored, incalculable field...but I have to say that, despite my own reservations, I must acknowledge that there is a lot of evidence to persuade me of its validity," she said very pointedly, crushing the final sparks of light from her completed cigarette into an ashtray, to the tempo of her last five words.

"No, I was never hypnotised. They maintained that only eight percent of people make exceptional subjects. They were unable to reach my subconscious - *too full of clutter*, Daddy would say. I tried, they tried, but not a single memory or occasion of inducement could get me there. It is hard to understand why some people make good hypnosis subjects and others are impervious to any hypnotic influence." She paused to light another cigarette, blowing clouds of unhealthy grey cumulus into the air above her head.

I was silent. I was thoroughly insecure about where all this was leading to.

"Their investigations into past lives actually began in much more depth when they had found such a worthy instrument in Stephan." She looked at me, as if to challenge my artlessness once again.

"When Stephan was small he would talk of another Mother, another time, and he would have the most terrible nightmares. He believed himself released in this lifetime from an earth-bound bondage in a cell beneath the house, where he said his bones remain lying. He would have fits of uncontrolled terror from which the nannies would try to comfort him. But Daddy, when he was there to witness the fits, would keep him in the moment, making him explain what it was he saw and felt...I suppose, in a way, feeding his fallibility."

"It is in my experience that all children have vivid imaginations." I responded insensitively with that ill-ease at the absurd or unfamiliar, as one does when one sees a severe deformity for the first time.

"Yes, that is undeniable, but my parents were just beginning to put together the theory that children had previous memories from which they built their imaginations. I suppose like original sin mentioned in the Bible - where does it come from? They believed that children were closer in time to their past memories and were able to restore them to memory more easily."

"Did you ever have any such experiences or memories?"

"No, as I said, I can't say that I ever did. I painted from an early age. In fact I would draw all over the bedroom wall and Daddy said I must have been a Michelangelo in a past life and did nothing to deter my artistic license, much to our grandparent's horror at the sight of expensive wall-paper with childish scribbles all over it. Our parents were very liberal in our upbringing. One could never blame a horrific experience in Stephan's current life for his nightmares."

"No, quite clearly not," I said, trying to imagine two uncontrolled infants with a mind to destructive expression. Bethany's mind had certainly not lost its course in the matter of time.

"Might you have been some famous artist in a past life?" I asked, with a desire to tease the theory.

"No - if I was an artist at all, I would have been one of those street artists who have pennies thrown at them for chalking the pavement. I was never hypnotised, as I said and Stephan was far too good a subject to let up and go looking elsewhere."

We stopped the conversation at that point to eat a rather burnt meal, which was highly-flavoured with garlic, ginger and hot spices to disguise any error in its cooking. The wine was good though, and with several gulps at a time the food became more digestible.

After the meal, good Queen Bethany (as she now became to my slurred mind) gave me a tour of her apartment, leading me to a room full of her paintings. She did herself a disservice by measuring up to a street painter. Some of her pictures were remarkably good. Her portraits were weird and wonderful, but then the subjects she had chosen were unusual, to say the least. Perhaps a copious supply of red wine helped to make them really rather remarkable, but I would have to review them when I was more sober. She had done her stint at the Slade from which she said she had barely passed from one year to the next, but I was fast learning that dear Bethany was no trumpet-blower. At least she was honestly accurate about her cooking skills.

"Tell me about Stephan's first wife. I believe he was married with a son over twenty years ago?"

"Yes, pretty girl. Her name was Miranda. It suited her, like Prospero's daughter, you know? Dreamy, adorable, and enthusiastic. I don't know if it was a love match. Perhaps his large and exciting house had attracted her. I don't know; I will never know, now." She paused a while, as if trying to recollect the details of something that had happened and been forgotten.

"He had an extraordinary fixation over her. I can't say it had anything to do with love - he saw her as a sort of possession. He hated for her to be out of his sight for a moment. They got married shortly after their child was born. Mummy insisted upon it. She and Daddy were very involved in all their societies and were living in London most of the time when Stephan married, and he and Miranda moved from Stephan's London flat to *Nasiarcuth Hall*. They both stayed in London during the week, much as he does now and came home at the weekends. Once the baby was born she remained in the country, which

Stephan did not like one bit - but he hated the sound of the baby crying, so it became a tolerable compromise.

Edgar was a fine little baby, with bright red hair. His mother always called him Neddie after some fond uncle she remembered. She chose the name Edgar just to shorten it to Ned or Neddie. Another thing to drive Steph wild. He loathes abbreviations.

He never took to the child. He was cruel to it, and banished it to the nursery whenever he could. Lydia was with us back then and she took on the job of nanny - she adored the child. Lydia came to us when we were still at school; her mother had worked for our grandparents as a sort of housekeeper-guardian of the property when they were not there. I seem to remember that she had even been around a generation or so before, working for the institution when it was going, and she is unaccountably attached to the place.

When the boy was about four he would wonder off on his own sometimes and Miranda would become frantic, but he always returned, grubby but cheerful. He had imaginary friends that he said he spoke to. Of course, as you can imagine, his grandparents wanted to know all about them. I am certain that the experiments with past-life regressions would have been practiced on dear young Neddie if they had all been around long enough. But both Neddie and his grandparents died before he had turned six." She drew in a long breath of tobacco smoke, releasing it into the air above her head.

I was silent, uncomfortable with it all, but silent. She was about to discharge some heart-rending memory, and she had come full circle with her saga to someone who was making enough distrustful remarks that would deter most.

"Our parents were killed in a car accident, and with them went all their convictions and conclusion from experiments. Though they had written masses of papers on the subject of regression, there was little scientific credence paid to any of it at the time.

Then tragedy stuck when Neddie was five. He wondered off one morning and simply never came home. Stephan did little to console Miranda, and Miranda blamed Stephan for Neddie's disappearance, because she said the child was always hiding somewhere to get away from him. They suspected that Neddie might have gone into a derelict tunnel and become trapped beneath caving earth. But there were no plans of existing or obsolete tunnels, and after dozens of exploratory holes had been excavated, nothing was found.

After several months, Miranda too disappeared. She made no farewells...she simply went. I think she had grandparents living in Ireland. Her parents had died when she was little. I never knew her grandparents' name, so there was no means of getting hold of her. I had just suffered the break-up of a long-standing relationship and was too involved in my own emotions to look to my brother or his vanished wife. Stephan was on his own for a long time. He never went out or socialised and then one day, years later, Suki turned up. I think she was working at the hospital. She wasn't a nurse. A nurse-aid, I think.

Stephan had been initiated into Transcendental Meditation a few years before he met her. He said that the meditation classes had balanced his mind, and for the first time he was able to cope with his 'life-problems'. Stephan's 'life-problems' were something we were all affected by, so I blessed the society of Transcendental Meditation and all those who sailed in her."

"What do you think of Meditation? Were you persuaded to try?" I had in mind Stephan's fanatical belief in Meditation as the solution to everything.

"No, it was something I had found wanting in stimulation. Transcendental...what a word! I looked it up; the dictionary says it is to rise above, superior or supreme in excellence, or something or other." She took a dictionary from the shelf and found the place she was looking for.

"'Transcendentalism, the investigation of what is a priori in human knowledge or independent of experience; that which is vague and illusive in philosophy, the American reaction against puritan prejudices, humdrum orthodoxy old fashioned metaphysics, materialistic philistinism and materialism, best associated with the name of R.W. Emerson.' I am still not sure what that all means except for the bit that said it was vague and illusive." She slammed the book closed and replaced it, while keeping a grip on the cigarette holder in her teeth as the smoke seethed into her screwed eyes.

"T.M - the new-age fad that everyone in the sixties was rushing about to try out. It went with magic mushrooms and purple-hearts and LSD, to waft one into an unreal world. That seemed to sum up our youth: a manic immersion in neurosis. They spoon-fed it to us and it enthralled Stephan, who broke from ordinary medicine to turn to Psychiatry."

"Well, after all that plundering of the brain, Psychiatry must have been a dire need. Do you think Stephan came to a better understanding of his psychological issues by his studies and his meditation?"

"No, I don't. I think it has been no more than band-aid on an infected wound. He is no better now than he ever was. I think my brother has dangerous psychotic tendencies, with a strong dose of that obsessive-compulsion disorder. When I saw young David last week, lost in a world of his own, I knew that Stephan had something to do with it. I believe Stephan has damaged him in some way."

"Bethany, I found the boy to be exceptional, quite out of the ordinary. Whatever you think Stephan might have done to him, inwardly the boy is a kind of miracle."

"Well, what about his muteness? He is clearly not deaf. I went to visit him yesterday. As Stephan was not there, I felt that I could try to communicate with the child more easily. He was reading some of the science journals he had found in the library. He hardly paid me any attention at all. He has a way of looking at the air around you with very little eye contact, but when our eyes did meet there was a penetrating stare - and then back to the space above my head. I asked him if he understood what he was reading and he gave a short slight nod, as if I was wasting his time. Lydia, of course, had a lot to say.

I told her that I was intending to arrange for schooling for the boy and for the first time, he came up and stood before me. I had this strange feeling that this was something he did not want to do. I said that I would discuss it with Stephan and suddenly I was beginning to feel quite ill, as if someone had drawn all the oxygen out of the air. Something is wrong, Jo. There is definitely something wrong with the boy."

She spoke with a tone of anguish I had not yet noticed from her otherwise placid nature. "It all reminds me of Stephan at that age, but without the rages."

"Is he like Stephan at that age?" I asked, wondering about the heredity-genetic factor.

"No, I can't say he is. He is quite different. No, David just seems to gain control with a kind of inner calm. It is hard to say."

"I understand exactly what you are saying. I too spent a little time with him. I found him quite exceptional. It was as if I was communicating with an old man of great wisdom, not a child, an underdeveloped child at that. What I find quite extraordinary is that he has never been to school but he reads really sophisticated books, and understands what he is reading. But he does sense fear. I watched his face when Stephan appeared. They seem to be afraid of each other, for some strange reason."

"That is what I was hoping to learn from you. Have you seen this happen before?" she asked.

"No...that is the most peculiar part of it all. I have been seeing Stephan for well over a year now and going to the house most weekends. There was never a sign of David, and Stephan never mentioned him, I had no idea he even had a son. Even Lydia was silent about him. There was no trace of him about the place. No talk of going to see him, or finding him anywhere around the property when we went for walks. It was pure chance that I came upon him in the garden."

"Yes, it is most strange. Lydia seems to be in some kind of conspiracy with Steph, and I really can't think why. Did he ever mention me or his past?"

"I had no idea he even had any siblings whatsoever, and I never thought to ask. He was so - so sort of secretive."

"That is how he has always been, even as a child, but why Lydia chose to be silent is a mystery. I have stayed away over the last year or so because he has been so aggressive, but I met with him in London a month or so back and he seemed so happy, so relaxed. I should have guessed he had someone new in his life."

"Did you know David's mother? What was she like?"

"Quiet little thing, pretty - like yourself, but different. I never saw what it was they saw in one another. She was gentle and sweet." She stopped and stared ahead, as if trying to recreate an image in her mind. "He kept her very much to himself, as if he wanted to control her. I have no idea what happened between them before Suki went away to her home in South Africa."

"Lydia says she just decided one day that she had had enough, packed her bags, and was gone while Stephan was in London. And from what you say, it is a repeat of what happened to his first wife. Does it not make you wonder just a little about it all? Where is his first wife? You say she simply disappeared. I think I would like to speak with her and find out what he did with his first child to frighten it so, and now David."

"Well, it is a subject that is quite unapproachable. Stephan refuses to discuss her or tell me what her name was before they were married, so I have found it impossible to trace her family in Ireland. Stephan and I have never had much in common with one another. It has always been hard to get him to talk or discuss his emotions, even when he was distressed about Suki just going off and leaving him."

"What do you know about Suki and her family in South Africa?"

"Suki was one of those innocent girls come to a strange country from an isolated country's small town to massive London, which had beguiled and astonished her, I suppose as much as *Nasiarcuth* did. She had shy, unsullied, childlike looks with pale blue eyes, silky blond hair down to her waist and sylphlike proportions…yes, she was lovely. You had the feeling that she was plagued by family shortcomings. She once told me that she had escaped a rigid, rather religious background in South Africa. I wondered if she might even have been one of Stephan's patients, but that was never mentioned. When I met with them on those rare occasions, she would disappear with her child, leaving me to talk with Stephan. We only talked when Steph was not around. He made her go to London to take meditation classes. He said they would help her.

Personally, I was not surprised when she just up and left. The mystery was that she did not stay around with her family but disappeared from there also, leaving David with them. I learnt that when her sister came over here a year later to ask where she was, as they had not heard from her. Stephan told her that she must still be somewhere in South Africa because she had not returned with him. She came to find me in London as she was not happy with the answers, but I could not help, Stephan had confided nothing to me. Then the biggest surprise of all is that they had actually sent David out here after they discovered she had been dead all along, murdered by one of their servants. Well you must know all this; Lydia was the one who told me."

"As I said, I knew nothing of David's presence there until the day you were called in. Have you tried to discuss David's situation with Stephan?"

"Yes, of course; I tried phoning him as soon as I got home. He told me to mind my own business and put the phone down on me."

"Well, as he is the legal guardian of the boy, he has a right to decide what to do for his child. If the boy has been diagnosed as abnormal, and by a father who is professionally qualified to do so, there is little one can do in getting outside help, I suppose."

"As the boy's Aunt, I feel an obligation to try."

"Have you anything in mind?" I was curious to know just how she would go about it.

"Oh, I have people I can talk to in that field," she answered secretively.

"Before you incur Stephan's wrath, would you mind if I go to the house myself without Stephan knowing, and see if I can approach David just one more time? I may be able to learn from him what he wants for himself."

"I am sure there is no more information that you can get from the child that I have not tried for myself;" she replied indignantly.

"All the same, I would like to try, and I will come back and tell you what I have learned. Please?"

"Well, all right, but I warn you that Stephan has something up his sleeve. I know him well. A second disappearance of a child that can never be explained will be on your head."

"Are you suggesting that Stephan did away with his first son? And then if he did, what about the missing wife? It all sounds a bit dramatic, don't you think?"

"Oh there is a lot more about Stephan that I have still not mentioned, but I feel I have bored you enough for one night about subjects that you have found hard to come to terms with."

By now Bethany was tired, I could see that, and she was irritable. My scepticism had irritated her and she wanted now to be rid of me. She thought she was best able to deal with a situation which she had more command over, but David's reaction to her was explicit enough. He saw her as an interfering aunt whom he had less control over than Lydia, whom he was able to command by a mere thought. I had the strongest suspicion that his father too was under his control, and perhaps Lydia's silence was something he himself had engineered. Or was it?

Chapter Thirteen

There was nothing wrong with Bethany. She was a good soul, and she meant well. She was the upshot of a Bohemian and avant-garde upbringing and she had, after all, spent a lifetime questioning it. I, on the other hand, was the product of a staid and morally conscientious upbringing and was battling to get beyond the barriers of fixated thought by trying to grasp this reincarnation thing as a reality. I was brought up to believe that it belonged in the realm of fantasy, along with all those beliefs in the vague and ethereal. I guessed we were both still immersed in the remnants of those trends we were born into, and upbringing dies hard. While I balked at bizarre assertions, finding it hard to differentiate between reality and the surreal, there was a part of me at that time and place of inexperience that was, deep down, blotting paper to new ideas.

Behind those questionable beliefs that had shaped Stephan and his sister's thinking lay the product of a damaged child. I could understand Bethany trying desperately to do the right thing for her nephew. Even if, in one way of looking at it, this was his karma, as Bethany herself would say. I was so unsure of everything but at the same time I had this uncanny feeling that David was orchestrating me in the direction of assisting him in a future he had already planned to happen.

I felt a need for space before I returned to *Nasiarcuth Hall. Ridiculous name, ridiculous place, ridiculous situation,* I chided myself.

Chapter Fourteen

My mind was restless, waiting for something to happen, like a flea that has lost its dog. Then the phone rang. It was Stephan asking me when I would be 'home', he called it - Friday night or Saturday? He was sounding casual but I detected a certain nervous hesitancy in his voice, and I was reminded of his obsessive interactions with the other women in his life.

"I thought I told you, I won't be there this weekend. I am expected at home...*my* home," I stressed.

There was a slight pause before he answered. "*Your* home," he emphasised. "What is so special about *your* home this weekend? You are not trying to ignore me, are you?"

"Why should I try and ignore you?" I answered, giving him a taste of his own medicine in pretending that his behaviour had not happened.

"Oh, I don't know...just that I am missing you, and really want you with me this weekend."

I petulantly repeated his question to me; "What is so special about this weekend?" I was, of course, driving at how irritatingly obtuse his conduct had been towards me.

"Oh the games that people do play;" he said offhandedly.

"Perhaps the games are the only access to an eluded issue." I said testily.

"What are you on about, girl?" He had instantly brought me down to size and made me feel like a neurotic patient. He had done this so often that even then I found myself recoiling. I mean, who likes to be seen as a childishly irrational neurotic?

Before I could find a suitably mature answer, which was excessively hard to invoke in a moment of self-righteous justification, he had put the phone down. I felt vexed and rejected and lacking in the maturity that was always seen to be lacking in the relationship. All I wanted to do at that point was phone back and say I would be there, but my sensible self stopped me. Perhaps I was maturing, after all.

Chapter Fifteen

The weekend at home with the parents and the insufferable Gregsons was excruciating, to say the least. Wretched Jeremy was insisting to one and all that I had once determined to win him over from my friend, with whom he already formed a liaison. God, how immensely conceited some men are. I allowed him the accorded conceit and sat silently, listening to his bragging. My non-reaction was an excellent sign, I assured myself, that I was learning the art of mature behaviour. I began to long for Stephan and agonised that he might now throw me over.

Shortly after Sunday lunch I excused myself, saying that I had much work to get on with back at the student digs. Jeremy called out, impressively loudly so that both sets of parents could be in no doubt of his generosity of spirit as I was leaving, "Do give me a ring sometime, old girl, and perhaps we can catch up a bit more."

How magnanimous, how pompous he sounded, how humble and worthless it made me look. What was it about men that could so easily squash me like a beetle underfoot?

"Yes, yes," I replied, "sometime - perhaps." *Sometime not ever*, I muttered to myself, as my car threw up gravel on the drive in my haste to leave.

No, I would *not* phone Stephan when I got in, I resolved. Mother had asked if I was in love with him. How absurd! What a curious syllogism: to be in love! Really! Being in love suggesting a hedonistic conditioning, gratifying, wild, pleasure-seeking: no, it was none of those things. He was simply an interesting companion who was rather exciting in bed.

The first thing I did when I put my bags down on my bed was to phone Stephan. He was not there. Lydia said he had not come home for the weekend. I was in agony.

"How is David?" I asked casually.

"Doing ever such strange numbers and things on every piece of paper he can find. He writes E and an equal sign, then MC with a two above it. It seems to be bothering him."

"Let him be. He is discovering the algebraic world."

Wow! I told myself, when I put the phone down. *How old is this kid?* I felt at once that I must not; definitely not let this relationship slip away.

Stephan was not answering his mobile or his land-line, house or apartment. I would have to wait for Monday when he would have to be available at the hospital. Sunday evening lasted for an eternity.

Chapter Sixteen

"May I speak with Dr. Tyndal?"

"Is this to make an appointment? Dr. Tyndal is extremely busy right now...I can take appointments?"

"No, it's personal - um, a private call."

"Who shall I say was calling?"

"Josephine Armstrong."

"Are you a relative?"

"No, I am *not* a relative."

"Can you leave a telephone number?"

"He knows my telephone number."

"Dr. Tyndal does not like to be given arbitrary names without telephone numbers."

"Damnit - can you please just tell him I called!"

I put the phone down, well and truly rattled. Then I phoned Lydia. She started on one of her long conversations which vexed me more than I could manage right then.

"Look Lydia, if Stephan is not there, can I come over this afternoon and visit?"

I didn't want to give any indication that it was David I wished to see, so I made up this utterly inane intimation that I missed her lovely afternoon cakes. God forbid! The idea delighted her, and she said she was off to bake right away.

Part of me wanted Stephan to be there so I could make up for the last rather flawed occasion; another part hoped he would not so that I could talk to David, unhampered. But there was no other car in the driveway, and I noted that the garages were empty.

David was waiting outside. He knew I was coming...perhaps Lydia had told him. He had the most delightful smile on his little face. His pleasure at seeing me made up for all the snubs I had received from his father.

Lydia was at the front door in minutes and already she had made up for the chatter that was absent from David, but I felt an immense pressure of thought coming from him, and at once I turned to him and said;

"David I would very much like to go to the library with you before tea - there are books I wish to see." The words just tumbled out, they had not reached my thoughts before they were spoken, and I had no intention of looking at any books. I had this strange feeling that David was in control of the afternoon.

Lydia had become silent and returned to the kitchen as we went up the stairs to the library. On the library table were notes on nuclear fission, divisions of atomic nuclei and pages and pages of equations as of Solar system – way beyond my brain power.

"Your aunt wants you to attend a special school, David. They will assess you, and you can build up to that knowledge."

David's words bounced back into my mind as if he were shouting them at me like a ventriloquist, but he wrote them out also, making no mistake that I should know them.

No. I called you here today; only you will understand. I can't waste time with schoolboy knowledge. I have already seen what is taught in school to boys of my age. A cousin in South Africa brought back books.

"Right...well, I will speak with someone from my university. Are you prepared to be interviewed by someone who will know how and where to begin to teach you?"

'Yes, if that is the only way to reach the right books.'

"I would suggest you learn to type, and then you can use a computer. Once you have established a link with a correspondence school a form of lectures can be arranged. Leave it to me. Have you no interest in being with others like you? Others of your own age, that is?"

'No.' The negative had already stung my senses before he had written it. I felt that the boy had spent so long on his own that to start trying now to integrate him in some social environment would only confuse him. At least, that is what I think he was implying to my thoughts.

You are like my Mother, he wrote, rather touchingly.

"I will try to be, David. I have heard that she was a very sweet person."

She was more than that. She was able to see things. She could hear my thoughts just as you do. We are closer in age. I feel you will always be my friend. Thank you. Again, I was able to receive what he had written even before he had written it.

"David, what has happened between you and your Father?" I ventured to ask.

He is a complex soul. He has incarnated many times in pursuit of atonement, only he is unable to attain contrition, as he imposes his own culpability upon others.

"The prisons are full of inmates who feel themselves wrongly convicted. Recognising guilt is the hardest thing."

Yes. It is an open wound that festers until acknowledged, as it pursues redemption with retribution.

"Who has spoken to you of reincarnation?"

There is plenty to read about it in the library. It seems my grandparents were campaigners for it. The thoughts of my father and my aunt are steeped in it. It is a subject hard to neglect. I wish soon to face the fears that have become hidden in my own subconscious and realise the truths behind the mysteries hidden in this house. There is something here that I have returned to that I soon need to resign myself to, and assume.

"Will you enlighten me when you have found them?"

You will be the first to know, as you will read them from my mind.

"Well, I had better be on my way then," I said, feeling as if the conversation had reached it purpose and he was dismissing me. "I have a lot to arrange. There is a lot to consider about education and instruction, David. I would like to help you, but there will have to be certain interaction with others in order to learn."

It had occurred to me for some time that Stephan had little or no appreciation of music, and there was none in this house. Whether there had been any in the past was questionable, but I had noticed that Bethany had an old hi-fi system. It was out of date but she must have used it once, if not infrequently.

"For some reason there is no music in this house - no piano, or even a means to play music to listen to. I want to bring music into your life, David." He looked at me for a while as if absorbing what I had said, then his thoughts came across to me as if he were responding to other issues.

Don't worry about my father's absence from you. He likes to play games.

As I walked away back to the car, I had this uncanny feeling that his thoughts followed me. How had he learnt to know all those thin, unsupported things that were on my mind?

Chapter Seventeen

Out of the blue, I had landed in an inconceivable world of fantastical issues. The conversation with Bethany was ever-present in my thinking. True, my attraction to her brother had been ignited by his intimated knowledge and apparent awareness of that 'something' always just out of reach. But was their strange belief any different than those from people who wear their religion on their sleeves, creating a kind of elitism with which they elevate themselves above people like me? I always seem to be the outsider of their convictions, leaving me feeling ill-disposed and out of reach, while diminishing my own faith in myself. I felt with Bethany and Stephan, likewise, that I was outside their insight and never quite able to understand what they were speaking about, just as the church's view of spiritual reality, the feasibility of God and allusions to Christ's goodness and demand for purity of thought and intention, had always put up barriers to find God for myself.

When I was very young, religion and belief was all so comfortingly tissue-wrapped. I was reassured by the simple exchange of a prayer that all would be taken care of. Bible texts could be given and received to cure a dire moment, like a remedy laced with honey. Then, as a mature sense emerged with age, I began to speculate where in all this the truth lay.

I now found myself confronted with a very different tenet that was being presented to me. The question of its veracity was turning me inside out with conjecture, misgivings and reservations, and it was tearing my imagination into shreds.

I did not speak to Stephan about David. There was no point. This was something deeper than I could reach out for, something I could not understand. I wanted to see for myself if I could help David, to find out what could be done for him. I knew that help in any way had to be done secretly, before doors were firmly bolted against me by his father. I knew that speaking any further to my family about helping David would only incur their disapproval. Father would say that I was interfering in matters that were not my concern.

I decided finally to discuss the matter with one of the professors at my college. I chose Professor Thompson, an expert in child psychology, who had done a lot of work on the subject of gifted children. I heard that he himself had been 'gifted' as a child and had numerous degrees behind his name, so David would be able to benefit from a wide range of subjects.

I told him that David had never received any formal or other education in his life for being wrongly diagnosed (in my opinion) with autism, and at the age of ten was reading advanced books and showing a sophisticated interest in quantum physics - omitting, of course, any mention of David's ability to telephathise.

He was intrigued and wanted to know whose child he was, and details of his mutism. I invented a long story about him being a relative, and managed to persuade him to see David and discuss what could be done for him to further his studies. We arranged a date and time and I felt a growing excitement at the idea of being able to do something positive for David.

Then I began to wonder about introducing David to music - not the pop stuff, but something beautiful and inspiring. I had taken violin lessons whilst at school but I had never amounted to much. I played with the second violins in the school orchestra, which was sufficient to make the parents proud. I fished out the old instrument and decided to give it to David with all the music books I had acquired over the years. I was curious to see what level his genius could aspire to in other fields. I had in mind those brilliantly gifted children who could hear a piece of music and imitate it with perfection.

Savantism was a subject I knew little about then, and of course it crossed my mind many times that this was what David was. I read that it was associated mostly with autism and had a ten percent possibility of occurring in autistic people. The information I gleaned suggested that savants had highly advanced intellectual gifts in only one area of cognitive functioning. David seemed to be more diverse in his brilliance, though of course the music side had yet to be tested. I recognised also that there was also a possibility of Aspergers disorder, in which there are severe difficulties in understanding how to interact socially, which could apply to David - and there also was a ten percent chance of Savantism occurring. Still, here was hoping...or speculating.

I found a second-hand laptop and decided on communication with David via that. I then telephoned Lydia and put up with a tediously long conversation with her, in order to ask her permission if I could take David out for a day. Without his father's knowledge, of course.

I was undecided how to play the following weekend. It was wise to be on amicable terms with Stephan. Was he going to remain uncommunicative and silently aggressive, or was he going to contact me? I decided to wait and see.

On Friday evening, I had a phone call from him. I tried to sound as nonchalant as possible, and the strain in his voice suggested that he was doing likewise.

"Are you spending the weekend with me, or that Jeremy Gregson friend?"

"What are you talking about, Stephan? Jeremy Gregson is the son of friends of my parents, and I have no interest in him what-so-ever. And how on earth did you arrive at his name, or even know that I had seen him lately?"

He responded with a brittle laugh, but I intuited an impression of relief that came with the laugh. I pursued the question. "How did you find out about Jeremy bloody Gregson?"

"Look, are you coming this weekend or not?" he asked petulantly, ignoring my question.

"Hard to know if you will be there," I answered contritely.

"I will be here and you will be welcome, but without the boyfriend."

I was itching to make an acidic reply, but sensibility stopped me, knowing it would only end in another weekend of scoring points and being excluded.

The question of how and when I could see David had not properly entered my mind until I got to *Nasiarcuth*. I had brought with me, in the boot of my car, the laptop computer and a dusty violin - but had no idea how I could get them to him, let alone show him how they worked.

Stephan was still playing the aloof prima donna, but was clearly pleased to see me. I had learnt to read him like an over-rehearsed script. He did not mention Jeremy, and neither did I. How he had acquired the information of Jeremy's minor and insignificant existence in my life remained an unwanted and un-dealt-with mystery.

I filled the hours of Saturday with gestures of aimless affection while Stephan carried his tiresome petulance around like the faded, poignant air of a sad rose losing its petals. Several glasses of wine and a good night of rampant sex brought us both to a reasonable state of sensibility, and I conceded to how agreeable some parts of the relationship were.

There had been no sign of David all the time I was there but a resonance of thought blew through me from moment to moment. He knew I was there as much as I was introspectively aware of his presence in the house. The knowledge seeped into my skin like a restrained and insinuating dart. The magnetic allure of it was beyond all logical logic.

On Sunday afternoon when Stephan had taken to his study to meditate, I took my old laptop up to the library with a computer manual and the old violin. It was one of those thick manuals that leave one more confused after attempting to read it but it was all I could offer until I was able to reach David later with details of the arrangements and to show him the elementary steps of typing and accessing e-mail. I slipped the book and the computer between a gap of large books on a back shelf. The violin I rested below. No one could possibly find them and they would have to remain there until I was able to tell David exactly where they were. Restored to my former eminence as tolerable and yielding lover, we parted on Sunday evening amicably reassured of one another.

I was busy all Monday, and by Tuesday I was ready to confirm arrangements with Lydia, hoping she would relay messages to David about the meeting with Professor Thompson on Thursday morning. I planned to take him out to lunch, followed by a concert at the University given by third-year music students. I seem to remember it was one of Haydn's Symphonies - I think No.104 in D - anyway, I worried that it was a little heavy for a start in music appreciation.

When I got through to Lydia it appeared that Bethany had already been in touch with her and was visiting David at that moment, and would I like to speak with her?

"No," I said, explaining that I could talk to her later. I only hoped she was not going to involve her brother. She phoned later to tell me that she had arranged an e-mail address for David and that he had already come to grips with the mechanism and operation of the laptop.

Later when I opened my laptop to attend to any incoming mail, there was one from David. I couldn't believe it.

This is David, accessing you from your e-mail address I found in your records. I found the book of instructions along with the machine, when I went to replace the books I had taken out. How easy it is to follow. Aunt Bethany has arranged a telephone connection. How good to have such an instant voice. Thank you.

I replied at once with all the details of the arrangements for the next day.

Chapter Eighteen

Professor Thompson was, at first, baffled by David. He found him hard to access. I suggested that I leave them together with the laptop, for David to make replies. I went off to do a bit of shopping, wondering all the while if I had made some dreadful mistake with David, and would return to an irate professor whose time I had wasted.

When I returned to Professor Thompson's study an hour or so later, they were still communicating in rapt deliberation on the scalar invariant curvatures of space time. Thompson was writing extraordinary equations on a blackboard, and David was silently correcting them. I was told that I could perhaps return a little later, so I suggested that in order not to miss the concert that we all three attend. I explained that David had never been introduced to classical music and wanted to see how he would react to it. I think old Thompson was as keen to see David's response to music as much as I was.

It was as if we had, between us, discovered some phenomenal creature that had appeared out of some blueprint like an alien creature from another planet. We were watching for reactions or what feedback it might provoke, and waiting for the consequence of some other brilliance that the evening might affect. If we had hoped for some enlightening response we were to be disappointed, but I was slowly learning David. David's responses were a separate thing, for he portrayed none at any time.

It was a recital given by students and, though not outstanding, it was good and the music was wonderful. The second half was Mozart's Symphony No. 31. When the audience applauded, David sat silently inert. Of course, this was his first concert, or his reaction might otherwise have followed the crowd I thought - but that, I was to discover, was never David's way. I was to learn that David was never swayed by the general public, nor did he respond to them in imitation of others. I did not enquire if he had enjoyed the session, or whether he would ever be interested in hearing more.

We left the hall and Professor Thompson said his farewells, promising that he would be in touch with me. He shook David's hand silently, and left.

I sensed a palpable revolution going on in David's mind as it heaped and churned with new and unexpressed ideas, formulating themselves into patterns of thought. His concentration bombarded me like a volcanic force erupting into the ether. It was as if he belonged in another world which existed with unseen things that hide from the sun, and our two worlds - light and dark (dare I say: his dark, our light?) - were separated from each other by fear that is born of lack of knowledge. I felt suddenly that I was trespassing in this world and there I would stumble, for it was not my world and I could not see my way. I had become the intruder into those unseen things that stare from their darkness and mocked me in my vulnerability in their world, for there I was - the mute, the blind and the fearful, and I was humbled by my own confusions.

Chapter Nineteen

We got back to *Nasiarcuth* to find Stephan's car there. Without a word to David, whose thoughts were at one with mine, I stopped the car just before the central drive, as he slipped out behind some bushes. Stephan had seen me arrive, and came storming up to the car.

"What do you mean by this?" he demanded. My mind was somehow calm; it was as if I had rehearsed an expectation of this.

"Am I not allowed to visit you on a Thursday? Did you not get a message from your uncommunicative secretary, who seems to be determined to exclude me from your engagements?"

"I know nothing about that, but my wretched sister has been interfering and saying you wanted to take David out - and I find him gone, Lydia confused, and you arriving at this hour. What is this all about?"

Blast and damn Bethany! I thought to myself.

"Have you checked David's bedroom?" I asked casually, as if the words had been spoken to me. We were standing in the hallway and Lydia was miming some idiotic parody behind Stephan's back at me.

"He is not in there!" shouted Stephan.

"Are you certain?" I asked, feeling doubtful that David could possibly have got back up the stairs in time, yet I probed the possibility.

"Look in his room," I ordered, from the suggestion that posed itself in my mind.

Stephan grabbed at my arm and marched me up the stairs. "Come and see for yourself! The boy is not there, and I want to know where you have taken him. My God...there is going to be hell to pay for this."

My heart leapt to my throat, and panic gripped me suddenly.

He came to David's bedroom door and kicked it wildly; it gave way to the shove and flew inward. David was sitting at a small desk, no sign of laptop or books. He was writing with an old broken pencil on a scrap of paper, small round figures in childlike writing, unlike the writing he had become skilled at. He stood up meekly and looked at the floor.

"Where were you when I came to check on you fifteen minutes ago?" he roared.

David pointed to the bathroom opposite his room.

Stephan looked sheepishly around the room, turned and closed the door angrily, which by now had lost its grip and remained ajar. Then, turning to Lydia, he barked at her. "Get Jake to come up here at once and re-fix this lock. We don't want any more trouble now, do we?"

"Well," I said, rubbing my arm where he had taken a vice-like hold, "I can see that I am not welcome. I will go - and I suggest you have this out with your secretary."

This was not the first time that this kind of manic violence about him had erupted with a strength I would not have thought possible.

"Come back, will you?" Stephan called, as I shakily made my way down the stairs. "Bethany told me that you had taken David out for the day…what was I to expect?"

"The child has obviously been here all along. How is it possible for him to get back to his room without you noticing if I had taken him?" I lied, not without a tremor of anxiety to my voice where anxiety could only be expected under the circumstances. I secretly wondered how on earth David had got up the stairs without being noticed. One glance at Lydia, and I realised she knew something.

"Please stay?" said Stephan, now contrite. "It's my sister. That is why I never mentioned to her that I had the boy living here. She is the eternal interferer."

"And me? You never thought to mention to me that you had a son living with you. Yet you can find it quite permissible to accuse me of a clandestine meeting with that ghastly Jeremy whatsit? Really, Stephan…I am not sure I can cope with this relationship anymore."

"You won't leave me. I won't let you!"

I sensed dangerous ground; a warning was coming to me from somewhere. "Well, Stephan it's about time you had more faith in me, and less secrets. What do you intend to do to persuade me to stay?"

I was battling to get back on a more secure footing without the feeling of entrapment beyond my own will, and at the same time giving myself an open door through which I could escape. Lydia was watching us both with a look of nervous concern, so I turned to her.

"Lydia…what about tea and some of your delicious cakes?"

"Oh, them cakes I made for you…"

I interrupted her as she was about to put her foot in it again. "Lydia, please, would you leave us alone now? We need time to be together, and we will have tea in the sun-lounge - don't you think, dear? It's so nice at this time of day with these lovely long summer evenings…"

I chatted on, while taking his hand and pulling him after me.

He was easily placated, especially in a wrangle over his sister, and I was in a rebellious mood ready to encourage him and condemn her myself, for reasons of my own. What were the words we bandied about her? Overbearing, meddling, opinioned, nasty, bitchy? Well, I suppose some of the adjectives were going a bit far. She was, after all, trying to do her bit for her nephew. Anyway, a good half-hour of collaborating with him and disposing of her to a proverbial dustbin had a suitably placating effect, and left him feeling he had an ally as we slipped into a closer, warmer, more tolerant accord with one another.

That night, in a tight and suffocating tangle of Stephan's arms, I began to feel seriously uncomfortable and vulnerable in the state the relationship had reached. How could I help David without access to him via my affair with his father? How would I be able to extract myself without endangering myself somehow? The man was clearly paranoid. Qualms about his past relationships were beginning to seep into my consciousness from somewhere beyond me. And I wondered what David knew about it.

The night hours crowded upon each other, trashing any rational thought as they tumbled upon one another until they became a bizarre warp of reality, creeping finally into deep recessive nightmare. What a relief is morning after a sleep-unhinged night!

Stephan had to leave particularly early in the morning for work. I told him I had a late lecture and wanted to sleep a little longer. I stayed in bed until I heard his car moving off. I needed some serious conversation with Lydia, and later a more aggravated one with Aunt Bethany.

Everyone seemed to be self-justified, to have their own motives and silent secrets, and I was party to none. How David crept up the stairs was not disclosed to me by that old cretin Lydia, but at least she was well aware of the importance of keeping things from his father -unlike that dim-witted, idiot of indiscretion, Bethany. I began thinking that there must be some deep very strong bond or attachment between Lydia and her employer. Theirs was more than a servant/master relationship.

I managed to have half an hour with David. Any longer I felt was being noted from somewhere, as I sensed invisible eyes watching me, and some not so invisible in the face of the overridingly vocal Lydia. I secured just enough time to show David the old violin, along with the old teaching music I had in the boot of my car. I gave a brief demonstration of how to hold the instrument and its bow, where to place fingers, and how to find music notes from the book. He appeared vaguely interested - but more than that, I felt him impress upon me that I must not hang about, but go as soon as possible.

I left without tea or breakfast to shorten my time, and as sure as God made little apples I spotted Stephan's car from my rear mirror, secreted behind an old stone wall down the drive. Ten minutes later it was following me onto the motorway.

He must think I am stupid, I thought to myself, as I chose to pretend I had not seen him.

Shortly after I settled myself in my room, I determined on a biting phone call to dear old Queen Beth, whom I began to charge at once with crass stupidity in disclosing all. Before I had lunged too far into accusations it appeared that she knew nothing about the call she had allegedly made to Stephan. Lydia had apparently told him that she had visited David, and the rest was ingenious deduction.

"He was like that as a child," she said. "He would spend hours spying on me, trying to trap me at something he felt needed reporting to someone - immensely childish, but a side of Stephan that he has never quite grown out of. I suspect that he has been watching me from the road outside somewhere and saw you come in and out, and he has made a few assumptions of his own."

"Don't you find it all rather disturbing, Bethany?"

"Well, I am used to Stephan. He has always been like this. You have only seen his good side as he was trying to win you over, and now you see his - shall I say - eccentric side?"

"Eccentricity is one thing; this behaviour is manic to say the least. What is he thinking? What is he planning? How had he assumed that I had taken David out for the day without being told? Do you think Lydia is party to this?"

"No, she is far too fond of David and his well-being, I am certain of that. But we must not forget that David is his son and he is entitled to do what he thinks is right for the boy."

"You can't mean that, Bethany - surely the way the boy is being unnaturally confined is wrong. I mean, the diagnosis of his autism is obviously incorrect...there is something so wrong with it all."

"I am well aware of all that, but I know my brother. If we do too much or interfere too hard the boy will simply disappear, as his other son did. There was no recrimination, no recourse, no proof, no substantial fact that could be used as evidence that he had harmed the child, and no one even thought to question him, yet...Well, he is my younger brother and I am fond of him, but I can't rid myself of those huge misgivings; it was all so hard to imagine, yet so perplexing. Miranda was going crazy with worry and wild accusations flew about, but there was nothing she could base her allegations on. Heaven knows, he himself led most of the investigations into trying to find the child, and no amount of finger-pointing from the boy's mother helped. Then she too disappeared and no one questioned her disappearance, as she was the one who was behaving insanely at that stage and had threatened several times to leave."

"Surely the police must have been involved by then? I mean, the disappearance of a small child must have caused a huge furore."

"Oh yes, it made headlines in the paper all right, and searches were made all over the grounds and in the villages nearby...but when Miranda herself disappeared after her threats to do so, the police began to think she had contrived the whole situation to get away with her child. I mean, it was known that Stephan had treated her badly and she had talked about it to anyone who would listen."

"Surely the police made investigations into her disappearance. What about air-line tickets out of the country, or attempting to trace her family? What did you do about it? Did you not think to tell the police of your own suspicions?" I could not believe that the situation was left to lie open without any further investigation.

"Remember, he is my brother. I nevertheless anonymously sent a message to the police suggesting that her body might be found somewhere around *Nasiarcuth*, and all hell was let loose. Stephan went completely wild over the allegations. He had receipts for a woman and child leaving the country which he said he had found, and they had been paid for with his own credit card. Other names had been used, of course, passports, and they have since become untraceable."

"Perhaps that is exactly what they did. They left the country and left a trail behind that made everyone suspicious? What about that?"

"Yes, that is possible and it could be that that is so. It is certainly what I would like to believe."

"Is it what you believe?"

"I really don't know what to believe with Stephan. As I said, he is after all my brother and yes, I would like to believe that he is innocent and does not have an extremely manipulative and criminal mind. But he is such an oddball. I have never been able to read him. He did such strange things as a child, and perhaps that is why Daddy thought to explore his inner mind through hypnosis. I only know that this time it all needs careful handling. Perhaps you should think seriously of separating yourself from him."

"I can't do that just now. I feel trapped somehow. I worry about David." I found myself playing devil's advocate, not quite understanding my opposing and divergent hopes. Had we imagined all this and were maligning Stephan wrongfully?

"That is what Suki kept saying," Bethany answered speculatively.

"Well, she did get away didn't she, and she took David with her. But I have this strong feeling that I need to rescue him, get him away again. I just can't understand why his grandparents sent him back."

"They had never really known Stephan and as you know he can be charming, plausible and compliant. It is only recently that they learned of Suki's death. Anything else about it can only be conjecture."

"Yes," I said, warming to a better reason. "I too feel that I can easily be swept along by imagining the worst."

Somehow I could not remove that wonderful image of the romantic and charming Stephan. I did not want to lose that and have it replaced by something that did not bear thinking about...how easily drawn I had been to him, how relaxed yet stimulating his company had been. I balanced all those unresolved issues with how our inflamed imaginations could feed so readily upon potential of the absurd. Then I drew up alongside the outbursts of strange behaviour and the violence with which he had erupted, and I was at a loss to know how to proceed. I reasoned that, perhaps in time, the David question would be quite simply sorted.

We both knew that to openly press forward with an involvement in David's plight might frustrate what could later become reasoned logic. Before any kind of intervention in his life, we needed first to know what direction and to what extent his intelligence in opposition to his disability lay. What if Stephan was right and we were trespassing upon dangerous ground for which we were not equipped to deal with?

We both agreed to keep in contact with David by email, to know that he was safe. I asked Bethany how she could keep the telephone account from Stephan, as he would soon notice that his son was now in possession of an email address. She explained that the phone line connection was made via Lydia's own private number. Stephan, wary of his housekeeper's need for substantial verbal exchanges, was by no means the open-handed altruist and had taken the precaution of allowing her own private line. Bethany offered to pay the entire bill in order to use a part of the line for David's use, which suited Lydia down to the ground.

The positive that arose from all this was that we were now both in contact with David without interruption from his parent. The negative was that I became positively aware that my life from now on was under constant surveillance from his father.

Chapter Twenty

A few weeks had lapsed, when I had a message from Prof. Thompson one afternoon saying that he would like to speak with me. I knew what he was going to ask, and I was more than ready to ask all those questions of my own that I had about David.

I met with him in his rooms at the university. He had been studying something on his desk, and after I knocked and stepped into his office it took a moment or two before he was aware that I had come in. Below his furrowed brow, dense eyebrows overran thick spectacles propped on an arched nose. They lifted up, exposing those deep eyes that now acknowledged me.

"Aha," he said, unfurling himself to the full extent of his surprisingly large, gaunt body. I had never observed him with much interest before. When he gave lectures, he had a way of shifting himself about behind the massive pile of books he always carried with him, transferring attention from himself to a slide-chart of examples of his expression. He appeared self-conscious that he was now the subject under scrutiny, as there was little else this day to draw attention away from himself. He made a sort of shuffle of his shoulders as if to rearrange the clumsy fall of his jacket, then he came forward and shook my hand warmly. It was an honoured act of familiarity reserved for the intellectually elite, I am sure - of which body I was not a part, but for my association with the incomparable David. I felt rather privileged, even if it was only second-hand approbation.

As I had guessed, he was anxious to make a contact with David's parents. He said that there were certain implications and investigations he and the university wished to make, but the boy was unwilling to disclose information about his family. I explained once again that the boy's father had diagnosed him as autistic, and that if he were to discover that we had gone behind his back the boy would be withdrawn entirely from any further educational contact or examination.

"I have made a few investigations of my own," muttered the old boffin, coughing slyly into his chest. He had of course already deduced that Stephan Tyndal was the boy's father. He agreed that we kept the correspondence undercover without pursuing any reasons or explanations, but I was left with a space in my head that asked why he had even entered into such a devious strategy to substantiate what was obvious to us both.

"Just had to make absolutely certain about all this, m'dear. I am aware that the chap has a tendency to fly off the handle somewhat. A serious business though. I, ah, assume you know the man reasonably well?"

Of course I knew him reasonably well. I had brought the son to his attention. Was our clandestine affair already such common knowledge that even his colleagues - and distant ones at that - were aware of the status quo of our relationship? I wondered how much more had been surmised about Stephan's past, and how it had been deduced. Bethany had said that Stephan's first son's disappearance had made headline news and the police had become involved, and I imagine the news had leaked about the disappearance of his wife also. I began to rebuke my own lack of perceptiveness. How was everyone able to assess Stephan's abnormalities and peculiarities when I had taken so long to see beyond those frilly bits of blandishments that had so attracted me, to never look beyond the immediate?

"Is there any sign of autism that you might have detected in David?" I asked.

"David portrays a definite anti-social pattern in his communications. One could say he has a bias towards Aspergers because of his difficulty in understanding how to interact socially; that is all. His inability to speak seems strange, but then I have not yet had the opportunity to investigate his condition more thoroughly. It could be deliberate, or it might be a psychological block or even some damage to the speech areas of the brain. These seem to be the only symptoms. Otherwise, he is more than lucid in his communications, and he shows phenomenal brilliance in all scientific areas. He has shown a prodigious intellectual understanding and interest in the questions of time and space, singularity, black holes etc."

"Could he be a savant?"

"Savantism is not a recognised medical diagnosis. It has been described as a rare condition in which people with developmental disorders have one or more areas of expertise, ability, or brilliance that are in contrast with the individual's overall limitations. It is a condition that can be genetic, but can also be acquired. Not all autistic people have the savant syndrome and not all people with a savant syndrome have an autistic disorder. The conclusions about this syndrome are hearsay mostly, uncorroborated by independent scrutiny. In some rare situations some savants have no apparent abnormalities other than their unique abilities. This does not mean that these abnormalities have not been generated by a brain dysfunction of some sort, but it does moderate the theory that all savants are disabled and that some sort of substitution is required."

"So, you *are* suggesting that David might be a savant?"

"No...there is more to his brilliance than mere savant. Something that almost all savants have in common is a special type of memory. They can recall a vast amount of information but have a hard time putting it to use. David not only has a prodigious memory but he is able to use information he has learned, and can advance his own findings on mathematical theories that are way in advance of highly skilled thinkers. It is believed that savants retrieve low-level, less-processed information that exists in all human brains which is not normally available to conscious awareness. This is not so with David, for he seeks out information for which he needs to further an idea of his own."

I explained David's extraordinary ability to project thought and physical sensation. I described the time he put me at ease when I first met him. The professor looked at me sideways, his head inclined and his hand cupping his chin as I was talking, absorbing the information as if it were being compiled into a dossier of his own mental notes on the David deduction, amongst which were now the amusing, superimposed embellishments of ignorant bystanders creating fiction out of the rare and extraordinary. I immediately regretted that I had allowed this information to pass my lips. I could only be regarded as some kind of foolish woman with fanciful ideas of the supernatural, that in his scientific world would not be given floor space. Instead of commenting on the verity of the information, he tried to give another explanation.

"Many autistic individuals have an enhanced perception or sensory hypersensitivity. Their acute attention to detail or hyper-systemising predisposes them to empathise with others by systemising facts about the external world..."

I felt that he had bypassed the real David and was looking at him purely as the phenomenon that had captivated his scientific imagination, without any definite conclusions of his own. I wondered if he had anything to say about David's reaction to music. Surely the music had stirred some deep emotion that could prove he was not an impassive hollow of emotion? However, that aspect of his brilliance had clearly been evaded, for on the few occasions I had briefly gone to visit him I noticed the violin untouched and the music was buried beneath a pile of geometric equations.

Before Thompson confused me any further with his theories, I asked if he then was able to positively affirm or deny that David was in fact autistic with a savant syndrome, and if so what about the music that we had introduced him to? Of course, in my naivety I had hoped that he might be one of those gifted children that learnt to play an instrument with no instruction. I had read about a particular case in some magazine somewhere. I realised of course that it was all an artful fantasy that must be shelved. My curiosity must lie in the direction of David's sanity and not those whimsical speculations of suddenly discovering a musical genius.

"Here," said Thompson, who rummaged through some papers first, then handed me several sheets of hand-written music. "When I asked David if he had understood the music he replied that he would mail his understanding to me, as he was unable to produce the notes on his computer. He has written out almost the entire music score of what he had listened to, from memory. Of course only the underlying theme and not the music score for each individual instrument - but none the less, quite remarkable."

I didn't know quite what to say. It was strange that he was unable to express what emotions the music had stirred within him, but then he had been asked specifically if he had understood it, not if he had been inspired by it. I had had no contact with genius of any kind in my life, other than rather bright parents and a far superior brother to myself.

"What do you want me to do about it?" I asked, too overwhelmed for words. "I assume you want my involvement in some way, or you would not have invited me here. I cannot intervene with his father, as I have already explained - not yet, anyway - and then I am uncertain how to deal with him or the situation, which is why I asked for your help. Not only to instruct David but to perhaps to find an answer, and to know if he is abnormal in any negative way, I guess."

"David has already given me the answers you need. He has told me that you would, in a short time, provide the solutions and clarification to everything. He has great confidence in you, and I thought to meet you and talk to you so we can see what is best for David."

"Well, if David predicts that I will resolve all the issues, there must be something that only he knows...because I don't. But I do believe that David has some kind of control over us all. I can't explain it. Of course I will remain in touch with you, Professor, but I feel strongly that I must wait for the right moment and only David can prompt that."

We talked for a while longer. Then, with pressing engagements elsewhere, we agreed to stay in touch over the extraordinary phenomenon that was Stephan's neglected son.

I guess each man constructs a truth or reality in a way that best suits his own perceptions, whether it is built on illusion or based upon learned theories. It is that very mystery of discovering for oneself where a reality behind something lies that becomes the purpose of life. I was about to discover more than I could place at the hands of anything I had learned, or tried to imagine, before.

Chapter Twenty One

I was in the midst of end-of-year final exams and had just cause to spend less time with Stephan, either in London or at *Nasiarcuth*. He remained in a strange distracted state, obsessing about where I was and what I was doing. He made no mention of his child, though he must have guessed that I was curious. It was as if he was dangling a carrot over my head in temptation of my interest. I, in turn, never mentioned David or the last encounter that we had together with all those incensed accusations.

While we were together he filled the hours with gestures of awkward charm, wandering from breakfast to evening carrying his wounded pride and world-weariness with him, like a cheerless dirge. I pretended to ignore his morose mood and kept my face hidden in a book that I insisted I was learning, though with all the tension building up from his veiled and furtive deliberation it was a difficult thing to do.

During the week when I was walking to and from my digs, I sensed I had seen his car go past several times and I would tell myself that I had perhaps just imagined it. I even felt he was spying on me from somewhere, but again, I dismissed the thoughts as paranoia.

David seldom emailed me but to say that he had seen Bethany or that he acknowledged a visit to the professor. It was as if we were all waiting for something to happen.

I spoke with Bethany occasionally. She had donated an old hi-fi system to David. It was difficult to imagine how and where they had installed it, or if Stephan was even aware of it. I wondered again if David listened to music, and if he did, what effect it might have on him.

I felt somehow that, as long as Stephan remained satisfied that his son's retarded mental state was as he had prescribed, he would continue to be moderately relaxed and contented. I could not withdraw myself from the relationship without losing sight and contact with David, who was becoming increasingly more important to me each day. *Strange, really*, I told myself. I had had so little contact with the boy, so little communication, and yet I felt him there with me in my thoughts all the time. There was at the same time this insightful feeling within that I was somehow not entirely in control. It was as if I had been drawn into an invisible vortex of enticement. I was compelled to examine my feelings and emotions all the time. Was it some trick of the situation, the time?

While I was finding myself strangely connected to David by some unimaginable emotion, for some reason I was unable to let go my thoughts of Stephan. Part of me wanted to relinquish all ties with him, yet I would go over and over all the recent events, comparing them with those first few months of knowing him. Overwhelming sensations began to arise in me that I had not felt before. It was as if those coloured fringes of my mind longed to hear from him, to be in touch with him when I knew that I should instead be withdrawing from him, especially now that I had become fully aware of all those issues that had never been addressed.I had no evidence of any of these things, yet I seemed to know them in my mind and the more I knew, the more I wanted to be with him to help him. At the same time, I was at a complete loss to understand that strange fixity in him, or the emotional hold that he still had over me. I could not make out what he wanted from me. His needs were so subversive. Why could he not tell me what he wanted? Was it something so terrible that it had turned him into this dark, arcane soul I no longer knew?

When I did see him, I was alarmingly conscious of the changes in him. One minute he would be kneeling before me, vulnerable and passive, and the next he would be clenching me with a fierce and morbid intensity of animal desire as if he wished to do me harm, leaving me bruised and bewildered. Then he would be pacing the floor, inaccessible and muttering wildly to himself, with habitual and compulsive jerks of his head.

And all the time I was inexplicably compelled to wait and see what would happen.

DAVID

Infant memories are abstract images, not concrete things. They come with the borrowed attitude of those in their guardianship, for opinion and belief are spoon-fed to an infant mind. Memories are not cohesive things; they are like remembered flavours twinned with an experience. It sometimes takes a mere cue to unlock a memory long past that has no significance with current life. The abstract sensations of fear, deprivation and suffering remain the most deeply embedded in the mind. I have begun to explore those hidden depths of memory, sifting those of intrinsic importance to the current. The memory bank is like a reference to which we are able to refer to. So much is missed in the translation when put into words.

Words: those inadequate renditions of thought that so often misrepresent the authentic concept that lies beneath. I had thought so much about the power of words. Now I see their destruction, their misuse.

Music: physical sounds arising from vibrations in the air, abstract concepts regarding whole numbers yet deeper, so moving transmission of thought; those poignant patterns of sounds contrived by some great master, rousing distant echoes within the soul, evoking memories to a surface of sadness.

This violin, an instrument of very inferior quality, made in speed and without the care that instruments were used to be made, unable to produce perfect sound as it is.

Love: that sensation of something I have known, so involved with pain, I dare not allow those emotions to stir my feelings once again. Love, on so many levels. Love that never dies with death but becomes that blissful light within…I see her hair, her face and it is just the same…I dare not think…

Experience: that harsh teacher without which little leaning reaches consciousness.

Fear: that perception of dread - where does it arise from? What is its purpose? Is it linked with memory?

Thoughts: the cobwebs of the mind. My thoughts jostle with ideas and concepts; savouring, trying, testing each experience, each memory.

I carry that childhood fear so deep within me that I wake with it in a sweat at night, blanking out all reminders of what it was but the base sense of fear itself. Is it only a childhood fear? I am beginning to feel another identity - or identities - that lie behind my current recognizable one. I am like a caterpillar crawling its way out of its chrysalis, and the pain of emergence is overwhelming. There is a knowledge that is within me and I am as yet unable to access it. Where do all these ideas come from? I wonder at this misleading accident of mind we call imagination. I have looked at these emotions from all angles.

Emotions: difficult and painful without any real conclusions, unlike mathematical equations that have instant answers just for looking at them.

Awareness: there is this complex and deep and inexplicable awareness. It comes to me like a kind of fear, not just with the first instant of the threat of injury or death, but the simple betrayal of a primal covenant with life. With that connection gone, anything at all is possible; a howling terror of the abyss, the black and limitless space that underlies all the hidden anxieties of the human condition. It inhabits that entrenched, un-sifted core within. I feel it has been buried for a lifetime – or perhaps, lifetimes? There are few things that call it out past the careful layers of self-preservation.

I have begun to be aware that I have within me a certain percipience that allows me to see into other's lives and past lives. It was only after my reawakening that I was able to dispel the fears that I had carried into my youth and reasoning, and see clearly into that infant time when my world fell apart. Dispelling early childhood fears comes with an understanding of how the fears arose, piecing together a sense of reality out of the chaos of infant myth.

Fear and hopelessness, trust and hope: they all begin with human emotions; a subject which gives me hours of complex scrutiny. Analysing other people's emotions can only be skewed, for there is no accounting for each person's taste in personal attraction and why two opposite characters remain together. I still wonder at the chemistry which draws and keeps disparate people together. I will never understand why my mother stayed with this father for as long as she did. She is a soft and gentle being whose only purpose was to exude love. Lydia says that he loved her, but all that I could see was a destructive, possessive love which alternated between passion and aggression as I became the other object of her love, and thus the target of his vicious jealousy.

It has taken a long time to read the multifaceted aspects of passion that humans have for one another. This father is so entangled and fixated with complexes that range way beyond his current life. His brain appears normal, but his soul is tormented and his thoughts are vagrant - when he is not consciously meditating. It is only very recently that I have begun to see from whence his impediments come, and what part I play in his redemption.

I am like Saul. I am locked behind a barrier unable to speak until I am released by an acknowledgment of something that is somehow locked within me and these walls: these mad-intimidating-imprinted-walls. My thirst for learning has been a kind of unlocking of knowledge I already have within - but there is more, more - and I can't access it yet, not yet.

Nasiarcuth has revealed a whole new dimension in my life. It has become a living thing in a sterile world of unanswered questions. I have read all there is written about the house and its past occupants. There is so much more, undocumented, untold, kept secret.

I know.

Nasiarcuth, the anagram for Carthusia; named, I imagine, by those it was meant to protect. On reading how most of the Carthusian monks were disembowelled and executed for treason when their houses were closed, I am never able to come to grips with how a church that is understood to represent the reverse of evil could perform such evil acts.

I question the concept of evil. What one century considered was righteous, the next saw as evil. I ask: is evil a reality, or a calumny? I used to think of evil as the architect of all wicked acts by some demonic force, recognised by cloven hooves, a horned, scarlet face, and forked tail.

The word Evil - there again, the use of a word to describe a manifold of things, contrary and contradictive and ambiguous - the word evil is drawn upon to describe the smallest misdemeanour of character, to the extremes of malicious wounding. I wonder. Where does personal culpability come in?

It appears that my grandparents have asked the same questions. They have left behind them many papers in the library. I found dissertations on the question of 'Psychopathy versus Evil', 'Past Life Weaknesses Visited on the Current', 'Sadism: an Inverted Fear of Evil', etc, etc...and all their probing poses more questions than answers. So many of their questions are cast into the air, undefined: *If psychopathy is simply a lack of discipline, are we all capable of it? What is evil beyond the malevolent act? What initiates it?* I have been obsessed with questions and the need for answers...immediate answers.

I have given as much attention to Darwin as I have the Bible. They both have their philosophies built on what evidence mere men had on the point of writing. The difference, as I see it, is that one script is a hundred years old, the other thousands of years old -but both speak with as much insight and intelligence as at the time of their writing.

Both had limited knowledge, modulating their equations to the dimensions from which each viewpoint stands. Then the quantum science point of view becomes, in the end, undistinguishable from reality. Reality as we know it.

After dealing with those tools of scientific knowledge, I am left with more questions than answers. I look at where I am, at this moment in time. I find myself in the centre of a world which requires no mathematics or science to know and understand it.

I have come to examine my innate scope of perception, to find that all the solutions lie at my feet, in this very house. I was born in it, escaped it and brought back to it; and it is here within these walls that the answers come, slowly, and sometimes with surprising speed.

Danger is imminent. Something is going to happen very soon. The very wind speaks of it and the air is dense with perceptibility. This father is in a state of irrational agitation over something locked in his memory that he has been compelled towards for so long. I need to prepare for this time.

A circumstance of existence is upon us. Those of happenstance that have no real involvement but for their propinquity are in danger. It is like a play that has to be performed.

Cognisance of risk and jeopardy is seldom evaded or forestalled. Awareness of it can warn, but not impede what is written. Fate will run its course, with or without warnings. Clotho, Lachesis and Atropos are said to have spoken.

I long to return to Africa.

I long for the simple souls absent of complex issues, yet profound in perception.

Every day my mind expands more and more to a wider and greater understanding.

STEPHAN

Tuesday

I stand firm in my resolution. Perseverance and determination are implanted in me from that time. I am sole privy to those secrets. I have always been so, since a boy.

Nasiarcuth is a place of secrets. I am steeped in its secrets. They have become a part of my soul for an eternity.

I am like an emerging dinosaur come from a distant past. I am trapped in an unhatched egg of vast proportions, waiting for my time of revelation and amnesty. I am from an ancient world brought forward into one of grown impotence and non-recognition. I have never been able to remove myself from this place, or that time when it was built.

I am the reincarnation of the Abbot who designed and changed this house from what it was to what it is. I am from a time in history when religion and faith counted for more than life itself. It was a time when the oppressor saw power as entitlement and authority, and the spiritually oppressed saw power as a sense of something magnificent within.

The house was chosen and designed as a secret spiritual retreat and a final refuge for safe worship and secret intelligence against a cruel and inexorable enemy - dare I say - evil? Until I write it all down I cannot move forward, to do what it is that I am destined to do.

It is my time.

Escape tunnels and subterranean spaces have been as cleverly contrived as is the cosmetic camouflage of the exterior. They are part of my plan. I know them from before.

When Cromwell offered pensions for all and fat ones for the abbots, in exchange for voluntary surrender of our churches and monasteries, or the threat of prosecution, some of us took our money and built retreats like this one, hiding our religions under-ground. In some places, according to the justice of the peace, the abbots were selling off land cheap. It was suggested that it was this money that paid for the costly underground spaces beneath this house. I know this to be so.

Places like *Nasiarcuth* were guardians, preservers of God's holy worship, intended – no, needed - to uphold the true faith. This place was a place of divine protection. There were so many secret commissioners around, sent in search of any illegal worship. They came, greedy for reward from that antichrist Cromwell, fighting for a king whose only thoughts were for himself and not for God.

None came here. We were far too inconspicuous, so clever was my design for concealment, and only those priests that I could trust came with me.

It was that fated day in December sixteen hundred and...before the hoar frost had fused with the dew and frozen the earth into a bitter raw anchorage for snow. Four commissioners came under another name – anonymously. We were unprepared. They had been given every detail of our concealment and the passages beneath the house. Everyone hiding here was put to death, burned in the bath-house beneath the chapel.Everyone - that is, everyone but me.

Those that came here from the village said that I had betrayed them. They said that I was but a cloistered madman too long secreted way below the light of day. None of them had ever identified me before, so they would not know an Abbot from a simple monk. They were simple peasants who made guesses from a lack of information. But I knew who it was that betrayed us and I know him still, and he comes to taunt me.

I, who hated more than I feared those who came on missions of religious compliance, would never have divulged the secrets of our cause; yet it was I whom the villagers took out and burned before the house, the house they said that I had betrayed.

Wednesday

I am feeling more positive today.

Jo phoned to say she is calling in this evening. My lovely Jo, Josephine, my beautiful Josephine. I will not allow my weakness for her to stand in my way. I still think of my vocation and undertaking destined for this life, but I think also of what I like most about this place. It is, after all, a part of me. I am its invention, its originator.

Nasiarcuth: the last bastion of the most persecuted Carthusian monks, hiding here in semi-darkness, our flowing white habits and long scapulars hanging before and behind. Our habits radiated a luminosity of whiteness from random torch-light, a ghostly contrast in the hollow dark. We look so different from the Benedictines in their plain black. Perhaps our very dress might have been seen as a double effrontery to rigid Cromwell, whose religious cleansing necessitated the worst punishment for the Carthusian. Oh God, what torment man is made to suffer...

I knew the solid and ancient original house that once existed beneath this substantial and grand Carthusian facade. It may have been as old as fourteenth century, by the reports from carbon dating - Father saw to that. Its ordinary household rooms served as a perfect smoke-screen for the religiously functional places way beneath. The original walls were wattle and mud daub. Much later this was covered over within and without the building by a covering stone wall, to give it extra stoutness to carry a floor above. This much I remember. These walls were conveniently wide enough to recast in sections, where the original wattle and mud had disintegrated, as secret openings down to the tunnels beneath, then disguised with dark panelling. The stone doorways on the ground floor and plain moulded fire places are original, but the carved oak staircase and most of the panelling, with their visible marks of the adze, have been part of the cleverly contrived extension created by monks a century or so earlier. I have all these details in my mind, as if they were written and memorized by me.

Embedded in a richly wooded landscape of the Sussex Weald, the property was chosen for its inaccessibility. It is that very remoteness from the outside world that I love about it. When it was surrounded by marsh and hidden behind large grey boulders that prohibited any approach by cart or wagon, it was totally private and protected, away from the noise of the village and the road.

At one time the property included a mill, and some three hundred acres of land. When the place became an asylum, the old mill house was converted into accommodation for staff. The mill-house and the water-mill have long since rotted - even the sluice gates have been washed away, to revert to the wider pond in the path of the stream. There, I have raised angry geese, to forbid intruders.

There are no records of dates or history. All that I know I have remembered. And it has remained incognito for all these centuries, after all trace of its religious owners had been disposed of. It has been lived in only by squatters and beggars until it was purchased from the crown by that London Benevolent Society, who wished to turn it into an asylum away from the world. There is still the plaque outside that reads: 'This building was acquired for the very ignorant heathen and insane that live in this parish.' Little did they know that it is, and always will be, reserved for the spirits of the dead.

The spirits saw to it that little was done to the house when it was acquired by the institute, but a driveway was hewn from the rock for access, and the surrounding land reclaimed from the mire. It has also retained the name *Nasiarcuth Hall* that is chiselled above the door, and the date 1602 beneath as its only record of when it was built – or should

I say *rebuilt*. It is a date unauthenticated and deliberately manufactured to distract from a time when we Carthusians were at the height of being persecuted.

And the Lord said, "If anyone wishes to come after me, let him deny himself, and take up his cross, and follow me. For he who would save his life will lose it; but he who loses his life for my sake and for the gospel's sake will save it..." Oh what a price, what a price...

During the time it was used as an asylum, the secret tunnels were forgotten and unused and entry to them remained secret. We saw to that. The locals and subsequent occupiers made no attempt to find the pathways to the crypts below, as they believed that it was still inhabited for many years after by priests that managed to escape, yes, yes indeed. And...and there were of course the legends of the hauntings that were said to occur there that kept intruders at bay...yes...yes...

I was a boy when I first discovered - or should I say, re-discovered - the world that existed beneath the house. It had been a place that had tormented my dreams and thoughts. You have suggested that some of the thoughts had been planted there by my quixotic parents too willing to believe in a non- existential state. Certainly, their investigations into the supernatural explored the subconscious states of the mind. They would explore my nightmares, engage upon them and investigate each thought I had until they became my reality. And that reality has taken root in my mind. I feel now those tormented days that I have lived before. Examined them and explored every avenue of their reality.

Of course, when I was at school and later university, there was no one I could talk to about that life. Had it not been for my parents, who opened the doors of my memory onto that time, I would for how many countless incarnations be battling with this inner conundrum of a past injustice that I have been unable to release myself from. It is a shame that there is little information about reincarnation, other than the inconsequential dabbling of someone wanting to find sensation out of a subject that cannot be explored scientifically.

When Father was young he was in the receipt of a single psychic experience. It so confused the issues of an inflexible religious background, and caused him to question his creed and doubt at the same time what he had seen. That is, until he met Mother at university. Mother knew people who talked of similar experiences. It opened up a whole new dimension of Father's life and led him to search for literature that could reveal to him more knowledge of this exciting new dimension. They were both aware that the subject appealed to a certain naïve curiosity, and effected derision from the erudite scientist. Because supernatural occurrence and manifestations - like magic, for want of a better word - are random and spontaneous, they cannot be contrived. There can be little or no scientific substantiation in its feasibility, and any reported experiences were therefore consigned to a neurosis. Scientists hold to the doctrine that a substantial reality underlies all phenomena, and all scientific data is easily observable by the physical senses. Those tangible elements which we are able to judge are governed by a separate law from those intangible ones, which can only be regarded by the scientist as bogus. Father and Mother thought otherwise.

Most of the books that Father found to read on the subject glowed with dynamic titles, all leading to long and attenuated jargon with little pith beneath that might indicate a valid and intrinsic valued truth somewhere. No matter how much he willed and wanted a repetition of his phenomenal experience, he was forever left with a vague feeling of self-doubt for what he had seen. The ridicule he had received on repeating his experience left him with an even deeper curiosity to investigate further. He realised that there would always be an abundance of sceptics, or those who would tell him that 'that' world was full of agents of the devil who were keen to entrap him. Though there seemed little purpose, and less evidence, of such an idea.

At first, he joined of one of those spiritual communes where the inmates incline themselves towards a charismatic leader with pious sermons on healthy living and good conduct with sensitive reactions; but he needed more than homilies and oration. He and Mother joined those societies of 'Inner Light'. Oh, how they droned on about their meetings and who said what to whom!

Through hypnosis they delved into the buried aspects of subconscious thought, and found amongst those subjects they investigated a whole new dimension beyond the physical. They used me as a subject but as I remembered nothing when I woke, it was of little interest to me. How they quizzed me, how they regarded me.

When we were very young they would explore and analyse our dreams. They believed that dreams often held the key to subconscious knowledge. My sister was one of those contented children who neither dreamt nor imagined anything beyond the space that existed around her, where dogs and cats might invade. Therefore our parent's delight came with me, when I saw and dreamt of things beyond this world. Thereupon I was used as a sort of guinea pig, I suppose, to verify their deductions on past lives. I guess I must have chosen them as parents – prebirth.

I remember hearing those voices as a small child, calling within my head: *Burn the papist traitors, use the heretics own images as fuel and* hear them scream.God would not strike out the fire.It is a sign, a sign that we are doing God's will...

I was born here, in *Nasiarcuth*. This is my fifth incarnation in this same place. Always here, trying to redeem my past, to discover those who betrayed me and to find my salvation here. I never lived for very long...weak parents. You need the right parents to live longer.

This would seem, to some, a figment of my imagination, but it is a state of reality that is so real, so vital; it is the very purpose of my incarnation. You ask: am I writing this to expiate myself? No, not at all. I have done nothing that is not worthy of what life has been ordered for me. I have committed no evil act nor any transgression that would blemish my soul, for I have acted as God would have me act.

I return each time for my absolution, but am met with endless betrayal. I long for my release from this eternal cycle of rebirth. I have each time been in search of my soul mate, lover, my Dulcinea, my goddess - only to learn that I am betrayed by my nemesis of that hidden past.

'For what does it profit a man, if he gain the whole world, but suffer the loss of his own soul? Or what will a man give in exchange for his soul?'

There is a corruption in the world that is hidden behind a wall of polite veneer. All is false, all is void. How do we rid ourselves of the evil that lurks behind every pretence?

Insanity – madness - psychosis? Now there is an issue that has always jerked at the very foundation of my thinking. Insanity is that place that people go when they have reached a saturation of those ills committed to them. It is a corruption of the brain. It is a behaviour that challenges life itself.

Dementias and distortion of reality; that's how we name those states, but have we an embargo on this assumed knowledge? I have begun to examine my own mental state. The more I am faced with it, the sooner I wish to escape it.

There is only one way forward: meditation. The power of the mind. From dreams and nightmares there is a discovering of memories...such memories.

I have this raging compulsion for action.

I hear voices whispering. They come out of the dark and take over my mind.

What will a man give in exchange for his soul...?

I know that I have lived before, perhaps many times, but this one significant time has moulded me, trapped me in this vortex of uncertainty. This time I am pursued by a child of my own loins who follows me, persistently, to torment me. He has incarnated twice in such short a time and prevails over me with an inexplicable, supernatural intelligence. He is the monster who betrayed us all. I know it. Disembowelled into screaming deaths; I have had nightmares of those executions, betrayed for the price of a jewelled cross. *What will a man give in exchange for his soul…?*

Thursday

She arrived in the afternoon and stayed the night. Her mind was elsewhere, and not with me. I felt I was making love to a stranger, to someone who would betray me. I know this feeling. I know what she is thinking, and I have it planned how I will deal with her.

Traitor, conspirator, turncoat. I will not let her go. How can I have such conflicting feelings for someone who will betray me? Yet I worship her, with this terrible intensity.

I wanted again that exchange of love and passion, such as we had when first I knew her, when we were at the highest intensity of our relationship. I have this relentless craving for that kind of love, as I did with the others. I want it again and it is not there, not any more.

I took her with a brutal and violent passion, kissing her until her lips bled and forcing myself upon her, hurting, wanting for her to suffer. I wanted to kill her right then and there, but I knew the time was not right. If I had done so, I would not be able to fulfil my contract with atonement. She groaned beneath me and would not complain. I know I frightened her, but she said nothing.

Her silence was to me a testimony of her deceit.

How I have struggled to prevail over this so diverse and dividing obstruction in my life! That is why I have so often been overcome by it. It has destroyed me. These thoughts attack me most when I am low. God give me the insight to know how to cope with this weakness within me, to recognise the enemy and know how I can vanquish this evil that has attacked me, again and again. Give me strength to overcome weakness at the moment that I must fight the enemy. I am that warrior of righteousness, Lord… I will destroy when the time comes. I do it in thy name's sake oh Lord. *Or what will a man give in exchange for his soul?*

Friday

She is not answering her phone when I call.

The days are so short now. The frost and ice, the eternal cold and damp, are twinned accessories of this house. That unparalleled cold, barren cold, bleak and dark; it haunts me.

I remember the dark and the cold.

I meditate, and I am resolved. I am strong again, even though the voices urge me on. I have returned to the library to contemplate what is to happen.

It was from this library that I began my first discoveries and investigation of what lay beneath the house. There was always a lingering fascinating with the library. since my early infancy. It was as if a map had been drawn for it. and I had learned it. I surprised my parents with my knowledge and ability to find my way about those secret dungeons and subterranean places beneath the house. It was that revelation that initiated their first interest in me. and fired their responses to my dreams and to that subconscious state that holds on to past memories.

It began with the busts of the four apostles captured in marble that stand on granite plinths either side of the library window. looking onto the garden. There are Matthew, Mark, Luke and John, the holy evocative icons; links with Christ, testaments of His knowledge. They stare from sightless eyes demonised by the blankness of marble, representing life that has passed by and yet still clings to it, like lichen on old rocks.

I used to watch them in snatches as a small child, knowing that there was something I had once known about them, and what I saw I retained within until I had remembered their secret purpose behind their marble façade.

I learnt all the secret passages, the ingenious trap-hatches that could be pulled, allowing rock to be caved in upon pursuers. Those underground routes were littered with them; many had already been released. Beneath a certain mound of heavy rock still lie the crushed remains of the traitor to our cause. While all the rest were disembowelled, their screams echoing beneath the domed ramparts, he had tried to get away, but he was found with the cross in his hands as he was. A fall of stones was released upon him and the cross taken from him. I have such a clear impression of him lying there, crushed by rock, unable to breathe as the life-force left him. Panic – fear – anger – Then I used those stones again…and she is still there. She took so long to die…calling and calling her child's name…I left him where he lay, so that she might discover him, and suffer as I have suffered.

The walls and tunnels are vaulted, producing an eerie echo, which bounces back without escaping to outside ears. Those cries of anguish and of anger were trapped there.

Those walls have given a lasting strength, to endure centuries without destruction or detection. These very secret passages and underground crypts and chapel have kept their secrets intact, long after others of its kind were destroyed and its inhabitants put to gruesome death. Religious deviance must be sought out and purged. Life is bargained for betrayal. *What will a man give in exchange…?*

The lasting survival here has depended upon the inspired designs for escape and non-detection. I will find my nemesis here. I have always known that.

I know that I carried that jewelled cross with me in that first life. It still haunts me. It is the most lasting of my memories. I know it is still down there somewhere, forgotten now. I have searched for it since I was a boy, but I never found it. It is the sacred cross of eternal beauty, embossed with rubies and precious stones. Ah yes…they say it is very valuable. It was mine. It *is* mine. It was given to me by some high-ranking order of the priesthood in Rome when I was made Abbot.

After our monastery was destroyed, it was I who constructed and designed *Nasiarcuth* for the secret and sacred use of the last of our diminished order.

I, above all, was betrayed. Those others beneath me were put to a cruel death. Disembowelment and burning by those who had been sent directly from Cromwell himself; those antichrist betrayers of the original word of God through Jesus. I was put to death by the common proletarian cretins that came from the near-by town - tatterdemalions come for boorish amusement.

Now, in this incarnation, it is my duty to absolve all those past deeds and release myself from the torment that is within me. I chose a psychiatrist's profession in order that I might best understand and come to terms with my - should I say - my *Karma*, as it has become.

Even this body of mine has become affected by my past. I have been subject to convulsions and fits since a child. It is all a throw over of my past life, and the memory of my experience of being betrayed and violently put to death in that fateful life.

When I was young my mind was so often disordered, uncontrolled – hysterical, even. I learned to meditate. Without meditation I would not have the powers I have, the power to use my mind and control thought.

I needed to learn to do those things that gifted yogis can attain. Meditation and mind-control will find me what I am seeking.

There is beneath the passages and crypts a secret inner temple. I know it is there. Somewhere; I have not yet been able to find it. It is lost somewhere within my memory, yet I am certain of its existence, for I have this yearning to find it. It is like a deep hunger that comes from a forgotten memory I cannot bring to life. I know only that it is a cavern beneath the crypts that was used in ancient times, long before any history that we know of.

I have this intense and fierce darkness in my head. My heart rages from time to time with frenzied persistence, speaking to me of what I must do. Yet there is something baulking me...suffer the loss of his own soul...

I want to smash through something. Suki and Miranda haunt me.

What is guilt?

Guilt gets in the way of any future action.

What is it that Nietsche says about good and evil? Where did I read it? Ah yes...towards a Genealogy of Morals...something about good being noble and evil being common, plebeian base. Hah! He was right. Man is prey to his bad conscience, as Nietsche says; man has founded a culture on an appalling inversion of all genuine and healthy values.

What am I trying to discover about myself? I think it is that supreme peace that was destroyed by suffering. Supreme peace moves beyond suffering, they say. Peace: the dictionary says it is ease of mind or conscience, freedom from contemplation. I don't wish to be free of contemplation...

Tranquillity, quiet, stillness. Silence, where harmless fish monastic silence keep - to be silent - passing from the imperative into the interjective – to be still, unmoving – to be at peace - the peace of God that passeth all understanding - on Sundays and on Holy days. And I will know her once again before she dies, yet I must not hurry, or I will miss something. I must enjoy every pleasure, one at a time, and the innumerable pleasures of her body, those little rapturous places. I spend all day waiting for her to arrive and when she is here I am caught, trapped by these doubts and feelings, and my obsessing over her turns to a madness.

She is mine. I know no one else will ever have her, for they must all go. I, too, will go. I long for that dark nameless emotion, the emotion of all great mysteries of passion.

Ave Maria, gratia plena, Dominus tecum, benedicta tu in mulieribus et benedictus fructus ventris tui Jesus. Santa Maria, Mater Dei, ora pro nobis peccastoribus, nunc et in hora mortis nostrai, Amen.

Saturday

My meddling sister has interfered with the boy's 'well-being', as she calls it. She thinks I do not know that she has given the boy music. Those sounds, those demonic associations of sounds…she knows how I reacted to them as a child. Music, concertos, any…any…sometimes lovely, but those sensations of frozen anticipation of dread. I have warned Lydia that if she also meddles in matters that she cannot understand, the boy will disappear, as he did in his other body.

The time is close. It will happen soon. The urge to do something is growing in me. The boy has to go. He has to see what it was he has done, and he must repent or I will be here for an eternity seeking my own absolution. All is dissolving. All is dissolution.

They must all go. I can see that. None can remain. The past is with the past, and there it must stay. I know that I have driven her away these past weeks, but she has promised that she will be here on Sunday. I know she will come. She comes for the boy. I know it.

Jo, my beloved Jo, I find it so hard to let her go. What would I do without her? She is the positive in my life. I remember that first evening I saw her, a swan among old geese.

It was her hair I saw at first. It was always a flame of life that bounced about her shoulders, a radiance of brilliant light, all fierce and rampant and beautiful, encompassing a softly glowing face of such infinite beauty. She stood out from all that erudite company, choosing superlatives and correctness in their pressed suits and elegant clothing, separate, exclusive, set in divisible bounds of intellectual elitism. I watched her slender willowy figure as she stood there on the edge of the dim-lit shades of the room and I waited, wondering how to approach her.

I walked across to her and converged upon those vibrant blue-grey eyes, gleaming with an intensity of light. A vibrancy of life only the young have. There was something wild and untamed about her. I knew through all my senses that I wanted her, as she glanced at me with an intoxicating, sensuousness that compelled me into her destiny. I had that irresistible compulsion to have her at all costs. I was obsessed. My blood beat up in waves of desire to touch her, to discover her and yield her up to me. Every part of me tensed and soared for wanting her, for making her want me, to desire me. For days I lived in a passion of sensual yearning for her. I had drawn her to me with my will. Something imploded within me. It was a wild and maddening passion, a contest, a battle of mind to have her want me again and again.

We did not speak of love. There were few words; only that maddening passion and the manifestation of intense wanting over and over, incomplete and searching for more and more of her - to own her - to possess her. She was so different, so unlike the others, yet I knew within that she must be the same. Miranda, Suki. You are known by other names. Yvette, temptress, my beloved. Rosamund, my enchanting Clara. All the names but all one. They were deceivers, all of them. The devil incarnate. Inhabitants of Pandemonium: Lucifer, Beelzebub, Belial, Mephistopheles, Mephisto, Abaddon, Apollyon, the Princesses of the Devil.

It was ordained that they had to go, but Jo? Such a sacrifice, I know. I need to meditate, to calm my mind, to still my peripatetic soul and bring me to this final moment when my own glory will be restored.*Emitte Spiritum tuum et creabuntur et renovabis faciem terrae.*

Pater noster, qui es in caelis,
Sanctificetur nomen tuum.
Adveniat regnum tuum.
Fiat voluntas tua, sicuit in caelo et in terra.
Panem nostrum quotidianuum da nobis hodie,
Et dimitte nobis debita nostra sicut et nos dimittimus debitoribus nostris.
Et ne nos inducas in tentationem,
Sed libera nos a malo.
Amen.

What is this frail frontier of existence?

It is strange how, as I have got older, I have become so close to those forgotten ghosts of the past. These days, they eclipse my thinking, and I find myself habituating them in ever increasing returns. It takes all my effort, some days, just to keep going.

All those dreams I had once, wedged between childish excitement and adolescent awkwardness. They have become a madness in my nightmares.

All those hopes and wishes have gone - where to? Is it age has swallowed them up, or loss of momentum? Where has it all gone? In their place is this nagging reiteration for forgiveness, an appeasement of guilt. I don't know. Only memories of something old, long gone, will not leave my mind.

This is the original sin that the Bible mentions. This is what it means. I know it. This is where it comes from. Past misdeeds - that's it. Karma, and I am Dharma, the righteousness that underlies the law.

All this pain I have inside me for redemption...or is it retribution? What does it really signify? *The loss of his own soul...*

I only know that I am urged to seek it out.

Tomorrow is the Sabbath. Tomorrow is the day that has been set aside for this final resolution of my soul.

JOSEPHINE

Chapter One

The days were closing in earlier and earlier. I dragged out all that winter cladding with a sigh for summer. Scarves, woollies and long socks, meant to keep the cold from penetrating into my bones, but it still seemed to get there. It seeped into my very soul, that year. With the cold came those sinister insinuations that I had unconsciously become collaborator to some dark force that crowded my mind, and disrupted my thinking.

Something had happened to Stephan. He was simply not the same. I truly believed he was going insane – or should I say, *had* gone insane. He had begun to talk to himself and watch me, with a wild look about him. He would mumble things to himself and sometimes called me by other names; strange names like Rosamond, or sometimes Miranda, and sometimes Suki.

Before his madness took hold, a sort of diffident hesitancy had begun to grow between us. The changes were so slow and gradual that I did not notice the shift in conditions and the expectations we had of each other. Familiarity had outweighed barriers and stretched boundaries that were before untenable. What was once a shy acceptance of each other had unexpectedly become painful dismissals, and what I once saw as a rejection of me in his secret world was becoming a slow acceptance of something quite bizarre. He was often violent towards me. Sex was no longer a pleasure, but a torment. I guessed we were moving into the next stage of the relationship, and it was a stage I was completely unprepared for. But I stayed on, like the Ancient Mariner. I felt trapped there. David was the reason, I kept telling myself.

Some days he appeared quite sad and sometimes quite terrifying in many ways, and yet it was kind of liberating in that I found myself more able to detach myself from that earlier binding intensity of emotions. I suppose I could say that I was getting closer to the truths that had been withheld from me.

It might be said that I should have walked away and that would be right, but for some reason I was mesmerised as a mouse becomes to a snake. I was immobilised. A recurring image of David plagued my thoughts. There was this inconceivable connection with him, and the need to protect him at all costs.

As for Stephan: well, I suppose I could say I felt obligated towards him, especially now that he was in this terrible state. I could not leave him - could I? Or so I kept telling myself.

I talked with his sister about his strange moods. She seemed detached – dismissive, even. Avoiding answers as if she was unwilling to let me know what was really on her mind. She said her brother had often become strange like that, in the past. She was much more interested in what Professor Thompson had to say about David.

David's intake of knowledge had been exceptional and eagerly sought out, but when Thompson began persisting that he be observed scientifically for his phenomenal intelligence, David himself cut off all connection with him and his learning ceased - that is, in connection with the university. He had, of course, access to a computer and certain information from that, but that was limited, and I wondered how he was coping now.

Thompson made several further contacts with me regarding David but he was also becoming more and more inquisitive over what he saw as a phenomenal prodigy, trying to compel me to coerce David to become part of his scientific 'investigations into the super-normal,' he called it. I told him that I must adhere to David's wishes not to be interfered with. But the importunate Professor would not leave it at that and contacted David's aunt over my head.

It was from that time on that Stephan's manner became more detached and strange. He began to withdraw into a world of his own, mumbling to himself and calling out to invisible discarnate beings. I have no doubt now that the wretched Professor had approached him, after all my warnings not to.

"What is it, Steph?" I asked one day. "Are you wanting me to leave? I really don't know what it is that I have done."

"You don't, do you? Well you and my sister have interfered very nicely over my son. He is none of your business. There are things you just don't know about."

"Well, why don't you tell me? Perhaps I can help."

"You have no idea at all about what is going on, and I have no intention of telling you. It's none of your business," he snapped back, like a petulant child.

"Well, I guess it is time for me to leave," I said, packing away several items into my holdall, but he was determined for me to stay. His first 'No' came as an aggressive protest, followed by a second kind of supplicating 'No.'

"No, please don't go, Jo. I need you. I need you more than you can possibly know. You have become the very purpose of my life. I need you now more than ever. It will all become clear to you soon, I promise. I will have you all here soon when I can show you, demonstrate to you, something so important."

"Has it something to do with David?"

"Yes, as a matter of fact...it is all to do with him."

"Please, Steph, don't tell me it has something to do with that past-life crap that you keep on about. Really, it simply doesn't wash with me."

"Well, why don't you humour me? It is only for a while. There is so much you can't possibly understand. Why should you? You need to see to believe. Derision before research and personal experience keeps man in eternal ignorance."

"Well, for a start, my parents did not go around hypnotizing me or others to learn some garbled imaginative stuff from their subconscious egos. I think - I really believe - your parents have affected you somehow. You know your sister goes on about it so it drives me insane. She has even disclosed some absolutely outrageous theory that they hypnotised both these servants of yours, and talks of links with mysterious pasts. I mean, Lydia...who in all hell could she have been? Don't tell me Queen Nephritides. And, and Jake! For God's sake, what twaddle! Come on, Stephan. I mean..."

"Jake was a good subject right from when he was a small boy. His grandparents worked here, you know, long before...."

"What! Are you telling me that they were inmates of the loony-bin here, and had little Jake who turned out to be the incarnation of some old priest in times gone by?"

"Jake was simply an excellent subject. He channelled the priests whose souls are trapped here."

"Sorry, Stephan, I simply can't believe that you of all people really believe this...your sister, yes. Why, she is as nutty as a fruitcake, but you, Steph? What has gone wrong with you? You used not to be like this."

"Saint Paul tells us, in 'Acts', that the Holy Spirit speaking through Isaias the prophet, said *With the ear you will hear and will not understand; and seeing you will see and will not perceive. For the heart of this people has been hard of hearing and their eyes they have closed...*'"

"Steph, my love," I cut him off; I had heard enough. "I have three final exams coming up this week for which I have not worked, and I must go."

"I will phone you when you get back to your digs."

"No, please don't. All this! All this is too much for me to take in. You never mentioned these things when I first started to visit. It has all come about since you suspected David of having more brains than a nutty mental retard. God, what *is* it with you?"

There was a wild look in his eyes. I had seen flashes of it before. Suddenly I felt David warning me to be silent. Was I going insane myself? Voices in my ear now - telepathy? It was all getting just a bit too much for me. Fascinated as I might have been in the past, I was growing seriously averse to it all. It was all so...off the wall. I mean, it was the way everyone was reacting to it, more than the singularity of it all.

"I will phone you when I get in," I said.

"And next weekend? Will you come next weekend? I need particularly to see you then, and after that there will be no more of these conversations. There will be no more secrecy over David. There will be nothing but peace. I promise you that."

I was in no mood to argue the situation. Something was going to happen. Something had to give. I had to get away. If next weekend would culminate in that end, there could only be a sense of relief. I walked to the car with him, and he kissed me lightly on the lips. It was a kiss full of real love and expectation of something more. Was I overreacting?

For the umpteenth time since I met the wretched man, I questioned what it was that drew me to him - what allure, what charisma, what power and why? We really had little in common and this garbage about past lives and guiding forces - dear God, what was I doing? It was as if his pragmatic, intellectual, scientific side had been blown off course and he had fallen among the very thorns of idealism. He was not what I had originally considered him to be! He had become this unknown, potent, dark force which I felt unable to deal with, and I was finding it more and more difficult to surrender to all his nonsense in going along with his strange fantasies and the quirky, unreal character that he imagined was the origin of his current behaviour.

I had made a quantum leap since those early months when I first knew him. I was well past that early bud of innocence that anticipated each new experience with him. That idyllic state of ignorance had been replaced with a sort of knowing, and reluctance to be drawn any more into an insane web of illusion. Yet, deep down, that keen enthusiasm of youth that absorbs and draws attention was still there, driving my curiosity and willing to see how things would turn out.

I turned my car in the drive. Stephan was standing there, staring at me as I left. As my car bumped along the potholed drive there was this heavy weight that burrowed into me, with the cold insinuating itself upon me as if it were a warning that it would transform me into an eternity of ice, soon; very soon.

Chapter Two

The weather was turning very cold, and winter dark had already shrouded the afternoon. My head-lights lit tiny diamonds of ice that sparkled from the frost-blown lawn. There were no commendations for this winter. It was soon to discharge its extremes upon the earth, along with a forewarning of something electrifying that was about to happen.

Next weekend? The potential of it somehow terrified me, yet intrigued me. Stephan had promised it to be the conclusion of the long-sought-after answers about David. I wondered if perhaps I might also learn something more about the house, and its secrets that he had been so eager to keep from me.

By the middle of the week I felt exhausted from study, exams and all those unspoken matters. Things had reached a dangerous state of disproportional unreality. David had made no contact with me in days and did not reply to my emails.The situation suddenly terrified me. It became awful and threatening. It was dangerous to a degree; giving myself up to the play-acting of a madman who was trying to conceal the outstanding genius of his son.

Why was I concerning myself so much about him? He was after all a stranger to me, inviolable and inaccessible, like his father and somewhat like his aunt. It occurred to me that they were all strangers to me and I must also be infinitely and essentially strange to them. They were like the other half of the world, the dark half of the moon. I began to feel isolated by it all. Who could I turn to about it? I had, after all, alienated my family from it and kept them uninformed for fear of unwanted judgement.

Was I the ignorant scapegoat, or fated catalyst in some family drama? I felt it so. Something was trying to tell me. Could it have been David? I was refusing to acknowledge that spurious stuff, for fear that I might become as mad as Stephan. I tried to remain calm, composed and unchallenged by the complications of those around me, whose lives had reached far beyond my grasp.

I went to call on the invasive, all-knowing Aunt Bethany. I needed answers - if not, reassurances.

Her elderly 'obligor' - as she called her daily cleaner - opened the door and nodded to the stairs.Bethany was in bed. It was a place that Bethany spent most of her time. Bed was a massive, generously proportioned, and curtained four-poster, looking more like a house within the house. The bed-clothes spilled out over the edges onto the floor, along with a littering of books and magazines, where doggie-bowls of dried uneaten food lay moulding and ashtrays overflowed grey ash and ends onto the carpet.

I was barked at from moving shapes that appeared from under the covers, and there she was, propped up against an embankment of small pillows, long since devoid of original whiteness or shape.

"It's the wretched tummy," she explained. She complained that the condition was always brought on by stress, to which her gastric responses created a deficiency of stomach acid, making her unable to digest her food. She was proud to report that Rasputin had suffered the condition which she called hypochlorhy...something-or-other. I admitted that I had not heard of it, as my eyes met the chocolate wrappers on the floor and the empty bottles of wine nearby.

"I have come about Stephan," I said at once, to thwart a long description of her ailment.

"Oh yes, he has asked me to join you both this coming weekend. He says he has things to show us. I have to say, Jo, dear, that I am extremely worried myself."

"Tell me, Bethany. Is there something about him that I ought to know? I mean, has he suffered mental problems in the past? You see, I thought his recent behaviour...well, it's....I thought with David being this exceptional genius, as Professor Thompson has called him, you know...genius and insanity - close parallels, I read somewhere..."

She was giving me this odd stare all the while. I was finding it hard to explain myself and she was not going to help me. She stopped me abruptly, mid-track. "Are you planning to have children together?" she asked, diplomacy gone to the wind.

No, not at all its, well it's just that..."

Then there is no need to concern yourself with the normality of our genealogy, is there?"

I had offended her. She was really put out and becomingly increasingly so. Giving a little consideration to her Rasputin condition, I made no attempt to take it further.

"Will you be there this next weekend?" she inquired abruptly.

"I just don't know," I answered. "I have a lot of work to do catching up with work I have not done. I...I don't know," I stammered, even more concerned and confused than before.

"Have you had any correspondence with David this last week?" I asked.

"Well, as a matter of fact I have. He emailed to say he thought I should stay in bed for a week or two rather than come to *Nasiarcuth* right now. But you know I won't. If my dear brother has summoned me, I feel I must go."

I had this uneasy feeling that David had been trying to warn me also to stay away. *Why?* I wondered. He was working through my mind and I could not explain that to anyone, let alone his daft old aunt who was as potty as her brother.

"Stephan excelled at most things at his public school, and at university afterwards," she started, by means of an explanation. "He was what our admiring parents proudly called a good 'all-rounder' while I, his older sister, was decidedly second grade. As the differences between us grew, he was never short of deriding remarks on my lack of scholastic excellence. I learned to distance myself from him, though I could only admire that certain brilliance he had."

I could go along with all that. I had only to think of Brent and I was there. Bethany paused in her narrative to light up a cigarette, puffing furiously at it to make sure it had been sufficiently lit.

"He was such a tormented soul, forever in search of something indefinable - whether it was the inner workings of some female in his life, or a particular subject he was researching."

"Was there anything that upset him in particular? The moods you referred to…what in particular would spark them off?" I asked.

"One could say that he had tremendous, almost violent reactions to what he found beautiful. Things that might stir his soul." She looked out into an invisible distance as if conjuring these injuries with her mind.

"Such as?" I was growing impatient with all this affectation.

"Listening to beautiful music, seeing a wonderful work of art. So sensitive, you see."

I did not see, but then I had not been programmed by a worshipping family who doted on the impeccable son. Why should any sentiment send him round the bend, I wondered? Had he so little control over his emotions?

"Stephan was a perfect candidate for one of those meditation and spiritual cleansing groups that preach perfection of the soul. He was driven towards them. You see, the old priest within him urged that aspect to come out. The group that he fell into were inveterate advocates for that pure Auristic Meditation. They believed that the only way to God was through the absolute purification of the soul. In some ways their strict rules suited him, and helped to modify his wild side; in other ways they were invasive and puritanical and demanding, but shrewd enough never to condemn any orthodox religion and in fact went in praise of attending church services regularly. They were subtly invasive over funds to afford attraction of their adherents, and with that came their own brand of stringent rules, rigid disciplines, mantras and rituals and conformities which were never to be broken; all for the purpose of cleansing the soul, and each member was honour-bound to remain within the bounds of its practices."

I knew exactly what she was describing. He had tried at first to get me to convert from the meditation classes I had gone to, to his. One session had convinced me that the whole caboodle was a counterfeit trap set by self-seeking egocentrics for the emotionally susceptible and the naively gullible.

"Yes," I said, recognizing the vulnerability of becoming bound to such a group that that I myself had tentatively considered. I remember that they required an initiation ceremony before one could embark on their gift of what they called 'knowledge', giving the word some mysterious significance other than its intrinsic denotation.

"Yes, I have noticed all that. They advertise free thinking, yet on a subtle level overwhelm all original insight with ideas of their own, making one feel that one is without any individual purity of thought without them there to urge it into being. But Stephan's association with his group cannot wholly explain his behaviour."

"Stephan is a dissociated being whose life has become blocked by an original sin before he was born. He is a brilliant soul, like David. You are reading too much into his aberrant behaviour."

"By 'original sin' I take it you are referring to something committed in a so-called past life, and not the biblical suggestion of taking on Adam's sin of disobedience. I'm afraid that I find them both hard to digest. Or you are suggesting his dissociation is guilt for something he has done within this life-time?"

Bethany's eyes did a quick reverse gear change which indicated that I had struck a sensitive chord, but I answered for her before she came up with another of her self-righteous justifications.

"I think it is more likely the result of the confusions of his mind, nourished a by an imagination fed and encouraged by your parents into a state of total unreality," I said with emphasis.

"Our parents were absurdly fanatical over their theories; I am the first to agree. They were caught up in the hype of their time when it was fashionable to be seen as avant-garde, and to come up with some new-fangled approach to unexplored dimensions, at a time when Quantum Physics had a note of mysterious anonymity about it. A bit like a mystery novel that excites anticipation with no real conclusion. It is only these days that every scientist is ready to challenge and invalidate any claim of psychical experience or past memory that has not been scientifically proven. But you see, proof is hard to establish with limited yardsticks."

"Yes, indeed," I said, drawing the lack of evidence into that vacant spot of my mind. "As the expression goes...it does seem though that we are dealing with a shit-load of fantasy with half a teaspoon of fact."

With all this talk of past-lives, my mind could not get beyond that insane picture I had on the Buddhist view of human souls reincarnating into other life forms as a sort of karmic justice. How did all this relate to Stephen's strange and secretive behaviour and his denial of his son's genius, condemning him to imbecility?

"Perhaps Stephan was a dog before and is leading a 'dog's life' now," I teased. Bethany did not smile.

Chapter Three

I went home, as pensive and as confused as ever, but perhaps less traumatised. Bethany had a way of diminishing reality and putting things into a crazy perspective. I was even rebuking myself for becoming disturbed over nothing. This little charade that Stephan was preparing was, after all, only going to be one of those family games the parents had conditioned him to in his youth. *Why be alarmed by it?* I asked myself. It might be quite entertaining, and certainly informative. Perhaps he would get to see how ridiculous it all was and come to his senses. Nonetheless, I was unable to concentrate on any further study. Exams would have to take the consequences of a highly-charged brain.

Despite all the negative insinuations from my mind, I wanted to be there the next weekend. My thoughts had been analytical and ponderous for too long over Stephan. I needed some kind of closure from it all. I needed to get to the bottom of his neurosis.

There is that optimism in youth of one's immunity; the feeling that one is in control. Decisions are based on emotions and emotions are so often unstable, and naïve ego gets so in the way. I saw myself then as exclusively dependable - only I could help a dangerous and explosive situation - when all the time I was out of my depth. I could not see that I was being lured by some mesmerising influence beyond my control. I think differently now. Time does that to you. It changes attitudes, alters perspectives, and makes you wish you could turn back the clock and could have seen it all then another way. It is easy now, after all these years, to be objective about the Stephan dilemma. I can make prudent and reasoned judgments now, like anyone else under no pressure of some emotional persuasion.

At his best, Stephan was loving and attentive, exuding sincere warmth. All the while, a silent, mysterious soul, full of a deep-rooted anger was playing out a manic role from some extraordinary manifestation of his mind - or was it memory?He had restricted his own child in a state of deprivation, in order to shape his behaviour into the concept he had assigned him. And, despite it all, he had been outwitted by the child who had foreseen every intention, every motive, every action. And I was brought in as witness; but for what reason, I shall never know.

Stephan was so different from his sister, whose depths bounced back from no further than beneath her bed-covers which contained her limited life's joys, in the shape of three small dogs. She conveyed no animosity but only goodwill towards everything that life had cast in her direction; and that was solely a negligent and anti-social brother locked into an imagined world, and an outstandingly gifted nephew. She regarded everything as it should be, as ordained by God, and anyone who did not see things as lightly as she did she pitied for their lack of perceptiveness.

Of course, at that time I saw things differently, naively. I had no way of knowing then that the future is seldom as it appears and the present blinks past us with a mind-numbing speed. I had no way of knowing that I was stepping straight into a trap, as one does in life, with the obscured knowledge of how it will be, but blindly going forth anyway with what limited life-skills-experience were available to that current state of mind. It took years to disentangle the veracity of it all. Even now I baulk at what I had witnessed as 'real' or the minds ability to amplify. It still hangs about in my mind as a thick soup of conflicting images, now blurred and out of reach from precise recall. But then, memory is what this was all about.

That fateful Sunday, I was full of misgivings which I argued against, finding first a reason not to go, and then a more persistent one insisting I go. I felt or 'heard' David's constant voice, if I can call it that, reminding me that he was there and needed help. I had no idea what it was that I would do to help him – but help him, I would.

I agreed to pick Bethany up on Sunday morning, and we would go together. There seemed to be some sort of mystic preparation for something that Stephan had promised us, and we agreed to come on Sunday, not Saturday. He would be busy the day before, he said. Some silly date thing – perhaps an astrological convergence of foolish triviality, I thought.

A thick grey mist blocked out the world beyond, and only the immediate part of the house and shrubs that bordered it could be seen, drawing them in to a feeling of closeness. There was a palpable corrosion of life about the place. I could feel David's presence about me, but there was no sign of him and no sign of Stephan come to greet us. The atmosphere had even silenced Bethany for once as she removed her bulk from the car, adjusted her many wrappings, and walked ahead to the front door.

I slammed the car door loudly to make a statement of sound, then stood a moment, trying to catch some sign, some indication that I must turn back. Yet I was still compelled to go forward. There was no schizophrenic voice in my head this time - nothing - only that buzz of silence you get when there is no other sound.

Chill stabbed every fibre of exposed flesh and breath condensed a pearl of mist around our heads. A prickly hoar-frost wrapped the ground but for the places that were shaded by some shrub or tree. Even the birds had vacated the area, allowing no interruption of that static silence but for our footsteps crunching the frost as we stepped towards the front door. The jagged anticipation of a presentiment of something terrible about to happen. We had become like resigned lemmings somehow cognizant of a certain presentiment of evil, yet willing participants awaiting the conclusion of some abstract and arbitrary importance.

Lydia was in the kitchen, preparing lunch. She greeted us cordially, offering a mug of tea she had just poured. Lydia was always hospitable and most usually always had plenty to say, but for once she was surprisingly quiet. She took the turn of listening to Bethany, who was sounding off about the weather, as if it were the one and only thing that mattered right then and there. No one mentioned the absence of our host.

Bethany busied herself with the removal of her many over-garments, then made a performance of dogged buoyancy, removing various bottles of wine and jams from her large basket as if she were determined to pay no attention to the atmosphere of pent-up emotion sweating from Lydia. It was all very disconcerting. I was not sure whether to be worried by Lydia's constrained anxiety or Bethany's affected joviality. She had come dressed like a butterfly to play her part in like-minded light-heartedness, in bright flowing robes that fluttered around her.

I do believe that Bethany saw herself as a malleable *Caryatid* pillar shoring up her demented brother, lost to reason but for the support she gave him. We others paled into insignificance behind her primary importance. She and Lydia talked with a light, feigned detachment, which was a clear indication that they had been here before attending to these insane bouts. I was wondering still how and why I had been roped into this charade, and why I had been so willing a lamb to slaughter; after all, this was nothing to do with me.

The two women suggested we remain seated in the kitchen, to await further directions from our host. Further directions! What was this? It was becoming more pretentious and wacky by the minute. Here we were pandering to the whims of an insane man - what for, and why should we be so curious? Why?

It occurred to me, much later, that I had suddenly become remarkably undaunted by it all. On the contrary, I felt a curious calm, as if it was all going to be taken care of by some impalpable being.

Then Lydia went to call for Jake. *Why Jake?* I wondered.

"Where is David?" I asked Bethany, who seemed to be carrying some heavy secret under her large wrappings. She pretended not to hear me as she busily uncorked a bottle of wine.

Lydia returned, looking white and strained. Stephan wished to put his plans in motion right away. We were ordered to follow.

"Where is David?" I asked Lydia. She did not answer.

I repeated the question to Bethany.

"That is why we are here my dear. Something has happened to him. He has been missing for days."

My mind began to swirl about all the options that could have happened, but somehow I felt reassured that David was quite capable of taking care of himself. Or was he?

We entered the back garden through the old Wicket Gate, and came to the walled vegetable garden where a maze of paths lead past the old mill pond, and there we found ourselves at the back of the house, where a briar rose had once blocked the entrance to the cellar.

The door was open. Jake took the lead, showing us to enter.

Jake was in some kind of subliminal trance. He was clearly not himself. He did everything with a self-assured, poised show of the hand and an inclination of the head, bidding us to do as he inclined. It was all so unlike Jake; humble Jake, who cowed when he was spoken to and avoided eye contact. This Jake seemed to be someone who was in complete control of the situation. This Jake's stature was expressively grand, with a somewhat pious air about it. He was no longer the humble servant, nor did he stoop or yield in deference to others, and the expression upon his face...it was quite different!

"This way, if you please," the voice said, and it was not Jake's voice but some other; more powerful and much more articulate.

I caught a glimpse of Bethany's expression. For the first time I noticed that it was white with anguish. A startled look crossed her face, but she said nothing. Lydia was pensively preoccupied with her own thoughts. It was evident that both ladies had witnessed these little foibles before. Quite bizarre!

We entered the dark gloom of an unlit and grubby cellar undermined by the weevil of old decay. Passing through the cellar we entered into what seemed a cavern of even deeper darkness, lit only by the torch which Jake carried with him. Before us stretched a labyrinth of well-built tunnels, each indicating a series of black channelled voids. These were more than escape tunnels for fleeing monks. They were more like those passages of underground tunnels from some old tin mines I had seen in Dartmouth on a school trip. They must have been prehistoric, as I had never heard of any record of tin-mining in that area. They had been shored up and reinforced at some much later date. I imagine it would have offered an excellent service to priests in flight from inquisitors.

Here and there bared veins of slate showed through, and in many places the sides of the tunnels had given way where heaps of fallen debris and rock blocked the path, then later cleared by someone gaining access again. Some were mingled with crumbling bones: the remains of some poor devil once trapped beneath. The whole feeling was of a barren, ageless existence, and the enduring evil intent of those who had at some time invaded those spaces.

Celts might have been there - Romans, Norsemen and Saxons, perhaps - though no traces remained, save the odd long-decayed bones left to rot, and scorch marks where torches might have been held by old iron frameworks from the sides. It was a place of rancid putrefaction. Any advancing life other than mould and fungus would be brushed away from time. Any inclination towards change would merely alter for a while, then shrink back to its origin in ironic irrelevance.

I was so awestruck by the whole of the arena that I neglected to feel anything more than pure curiosity. All this had existed beneath a house that I had been visiting for over a year, without having the slightest inkling about it.

I did not for a moment think of any physical danger, certainly not from Stephan. He was weird, that was all. I told myself firmly that there was no cause for alarm, this was something that Bethany and Lydia and no doubt Jake had taken in their stride many times in the past, and had been tutored to go along with it. No doubt, I told myself over and over, all part of the eccentricity of the peculiar parents. We were merely going to staunch this untamed harebrained scheme of his. We were going to insist on taking David away from this ridiculous false presentation of a presumed 'past-life' and the mad ramblings of his deranged psychiatrist father.

We followed blindly, in every sense of the word, for the darkness had silenced us and made us attentive to direction, less we trip over some invisible obstacle as we travelled like Alice in Wonderland, following her mysterious white rabbit.

The darkness took on a macabre life of its own. Out of the blackness, weird shapes seemed to float and stain the hollow eternity of non-vision. Now and then the torch-light projected long curved phantoms of our shadows against a tunnel wall, hovering above our heads, and everywhere was tainted by the musty smell of decay and damp.

It seemed we had been travelling downward for some way. I began to worry about the accumulation of gases that are said to exist in these deeper recesses, but all the while I was aware of a breeze that came from somewhere, allowing air into the passages, cleverly contrived by some ancient engineer, no doubt. We passed several openings from the tunnels into dark enclosures, but there was no time to stop and explore as Jake moved ahead with the light.

We came at last to a kind of crypt which could be vaguely detectable as a small chapel, though it was unburdened by any architectural design that might depict it as such. It was bare but for a large stone block in the front that could be taken as its altar. Above it hung a large marble or alabaster crucifix with its Christ suspended from flaccid, slumped limbs. I could take in no more detail for the light had halted at its centre, where Jake had come to a stop. Then the slow vision of Stephan appeared, coming out from the shadows behind the altar.

He was clothed in the white robes and scapular of a Carthusian monk. The sight was disconcertingly comical, but filled me with an uneasy and repugnant sense of obnoxious madness about it. Then, he spoke.

It was not Stephan's voice that spoke but another more unsteady, almost reed-like voice, that came from him.

"You have come today to witness an execution." The voice was flat and without expression. It was as if we had been invited to some sinister Punch and Judy show in which Punch had announced to his disparaging, derisive audience that he was going to kill Judy. What does one do at these pantomimes but roar out some equally inane answer - *Oh no you don't!* It seemed at first absurdly serio-comic but the atmosphere was menacing and preternatural, and there was an ill-omened sense of reality that froze us to the spot.

Engulfed in the shades of darkness upon the altar behind Stephan's ridiculous figure was the amorphous shape of a small thin boy, lying bound and helpless. I knew it was David.

No-one answered. We were thunderstruck, wondering why we had pandered so long to this delusional and dangerous act that could at any moment become a tragedy.

"Enough of this now, Sir", said Lydia, trying desperately to regain her composure.

"Jake - look here, Jake, you know what to do. His medication...have you got it with you, Jake?" There was no reply from Jake. He was in a deep trance.

I took a step towards the altar, where I could get a closer look at the motionless figure. Was he dead already?

"Stop there, temptress - Jezebel, Messalina, Aspasia, Lais!" He shouted at me with a mad semblance to his voice. He had a long sheath-knife in his hand, and had raised it above the boy.

"For God's sake Stephan, what is all this nonsense? If this is your idea of entertainment, I have had enough of it."

With his left hand he took hold of my arm and pulled me back. No one attempted to stop him.

"Why are you allowing him to do this?" I screamed at the two women. "What's wrong with you both? Lydia, stop him for God's sake! Help me to free David!" I imagined him dragging a resistant, struggling David through the cellar entrance, and no one had opposed him. Why?

His sister now advanced upon him, with Lydia at her side. He had a vice-like grip on my arm, twisting it with the vicious ferocity only a madman could have.

"Enough, enough now Stephan! You know we have been through this whole palaver before. We have allowed you this game to satisfy your old sense of retribution, but now you have gone too far. You know the truth of your incarnations. There is no-one to blame, Stephan, no-one." His sister was talking calmly to him as if trying to placate an ill-disciplined child. But Stephan had gone too far on this imagined role of the once-persecuted monk. It was all too bizarre to be true - and to think I had been taken in and fallen in love with this lunatic, and never suspected this side! How blind I had been, I reminded myself over and over.

"How dare you patronize me," he screamed back at his sister wrenching me to one side where I was powerless to move. With his other hand he flashed the knife; its blade caught the torchlight slicing the darkness with a mirrored flame.

"Hold her still," he ordered Jake, who came forward to bind my hands behind my back. I felt a wrench of pain as the bone in my forearm snapped with his vicious grasp. With superhuman strength he held at the ropes that bound my arms. I whimpered in agony but it was all so unexpected, so implausible, that the severity of the pain became secondary to absolute fear and astonishment. I had hardly time to think, when out the dark a small figure stepped from black shade into soft light.

It was David. The figure on the altar must have been a decoy.

"I thought you might appear when I had her in my grasp. And I tell you something else, I will think nothing of killing her. You know that."

A small thin voice came from the boy. It was a voice that drew upon vocal chords not used before. It had a purity to it, and a fearlessness that challenged and demanded attention.

"*Et dimitte nobis debita nostra sicut et nos dimittimus debitoribus nostris*…and forgive us our trespasses, as we forgive them that trespass against us. I forgive you, *Frater Petrus Trestissimus*, as I forgave you before."

"Forgive me! Forgive me! How dare you! It is I who should forgive you, and that I will never do. You bought our lives for my precious cross given to me from the highest place in Rome. A holy Christian relic exchanged for sacred lives!"

"Then you will remember where the cross remains hidden, as you profess to remember so much," came the calm incisive voice.

"How can I? It was snatched from me, and given to the inquisitors."

"No, it was never taken from here. How much do you really remember? How much do you really think you remember? How much have you imagined you would like to remember that will leave you guiltless and above suspicion?"

"You lie. You are twisting facts. Once a pariah, always a pariah. Now you think you can play the master of wisdom, but I see through you."

"I will show you where the cross is if you let her go."

"Liar - you have nothing to show. This one must die, just as the others died!"

David, or whoever it was that had impersonated him or taken on his body or whatever other ridiculous exhibition they had devised, raised his hands. As he did so, Stephan's grasp relaxed and I fell to the floor. The thin rope that had bound my arms behind my back came loose and my tortured limbs fell limply at my side, painfully restoring the flow of blood to nerve endings, and a voracious pain burrowed into my whole being, severing me from my immediate surroundings.

Thoughts rushed violently through my head. I would soon be disposed of, tidied away as briefly as death is allowed to interfere with life. A hospital mortuary, perhaps a doctor may be called, the pathologists table, the undertakers embalming room, enclosed in a dark coffin awaiting cremation! This was a badly-written script written by theatrical amateurs; it was all so pseudo-comic and insane. How had I inadvertently come to take part in it all? If it wasn't for that excruciating and desperate state of physical pain, I would have dismissed it for what it was. But this was real, stark madness.

Impelled into this world of blood and pain, I had never given much attention to that time that I would leave it. The thoughts of dying violently and without dignity were things I had not made allowances for but it was that moment of inevitable fatality, that closeness to a final exit that I was not prepared for. Death is that inevitable anguish that happens to others, but when the imminence of your own death stares you in the face it comes as a shock, a sudden reckoning of the frailty of life.

I was busy with my urgent whispered prayers to a hopefully-listening God, when David came to me and put his hand on me. At once I felt a drowsy state of calm, and the intensity of the pain abated. In a single moment I had moved from terror to composure, as I was engulfed by that sense of not quite belonging to the present. I was caught in the ebb tide of some peculiar occurrence that had nothing to do with me, and these players here were mere copies of those people I had come to know. Was this counterfeit Stephan really Stephan or was this an alter-ego, a schizophrenic episode of multiple personality or some demonic possession – if there were such thing? Where had all that anger stemmed from? Surely not from someone who had so often said that the world is a dangerous and cruel place from which he would shield me.

Had I been singled out - snared into this drama from no choice of my own, but by some imperceptible source? By chance I was a hapless victim, vulnerable, powerless and infirm. I felt as if I were a falling leaf, blown about in the wind without direction.

That sudden and unexpected imminence of death necessitates all that strength of self-discipline, courage and will can impart. In that frozen moment I was equipped with none of these things, or if I had them I was unable to use them. I had, until then, not taken anything seriously enough. I had not properly examined reasons behind all the abnormal and unusual behaviour. I suppose I could argue that at that stage in my life I had not had much experience of it.

Stephan had attained a demonic power over us. He was compelled by a sense of self-justification over something which had long since lost its significance, but it had been so long sustained that it had fixed a personality disorder and its very circumstance had become intrinsic to his soul. At that moment, it was all so stark and real and confusing.

I look back at that weird pageant now and it is as if I had imagined it. It is as if it had all occurred to someone else, to some distant dream that had no substance. It seems so strange that I can recall it now with such unaffected indifference, as if I doubt my own memory. A funny thing about reminiscence is that as time passes, the reality of it all becomes second-hand and dubious to one's reasoning.

When I try to imagine now how it was then, I have arguments for myself about how we allowed ourselves to be drawn there. Why were we so ready to watch him play out his mad fantasy of a remembered nightmare, instead of going back for help at once? But it was as if we were under some kind of spell.

Things seemed to happen in slow motion as the delicate figure of this mere boy, now in complete control, went over to the suspended alabaster Christ and raised his hands; whereupon the figure shifted slightly to one side, as if driven by some invisible force. He stretched up and reached into a fissure in the wall, and from it he removed a curious green object. When the light caught it a thousand prisms of dancing light bounced from it, and flickered across the darkness. It was not a Christian cross as Stephan had suggested, but an old Latin Cross. A ring surrounding an intersecting cross, not a cross as symbolized by Christ's crucifix, but what the Irish call *Cros Cheilteach*; a Celtic cross twined with scrolls of gold. Five large emeralds took the centre of the cross and the four points of intersection, and the circle was studded with large rubies. It was certainly magnificent, the sort of thing one might see in a Faberge catalogue or a Medici collection.

"This is where your guilt lies," said David as he held the object up into the light that shone towards him, and as he did so its very magnificence sparkled into life. "This trinket has trapped you here and brought you back many times, with all these conflicts and confusions in your mind. You will never rest until you have acknowledged your own guilt and come to terms with it."

I looked at Stephan who was standing, transfixed by the cross, as if an old identification had returned to haunt him.

"I have been sent to release you, and you have tried to stop me. Perhaps now, with the cross, you will remember. Jewelled icons and symbols of a revered past have no connection with the present; they are mere replications of fevered thinking. This cross has come from a distant past, way before the time of Our Lord Jesus on the earth. This place has its roots in a distant millennium that has few lasting remnants and it is easy to be trapped by this."

Stephan took a step towards the cross and David placed it gently in his outstretched hand. Stephan did not speak. He was not listening. His mind and thoughts were caught somewhere else, ensnared by some deep significances and telekinetic transference from the object he was holding.

"All is dissolving, *Frater Petrus*, all is dissolution," came the voice from Jake, who seemed less conspicuous than before and less oppressive.

"Dissolution now is a closure of the past, of that worn out and forgotten past. You have made seven incarnations since the time, by which you have been ensnared, and you have learnt nothing about your soul. You have been caught in an evil cycle of killing and wounding and it is time for you to move on, for deep down yours is a good and intelligent soul. There is, in this life, a remembering and a forgetting. Forgetting is the balm God gives us. It is a consolation that better allows the present to liberate the past. Remembering bargains with retribution and absolution. The present is all we really have. Looking back so often fills us with regret for those things we could have done another way. The soul is a living thing, forever moving and growing and developing; it delights in evolving spirals in the direction of its evolution towards increasing rationality, but once it is trapped by evil, the evil will attract other evil and perpetuate itself *ad infinitum*, until it is broken only by your own individual will. Vengeance without forgiveness is the rot that binds the endless cycles of suffering, for vengeance devours concord. Life and death and life are about forgiveness and forgetting; *dimittimus debitoribus nostris...*" David's voice trailed into a hushed murmur, and as it came to the end there was silence that no one responded to. No one moved.

The light from a candle that had been placed upon the altar began to flicker as its wick burned to its end. The torch also began to fade, and the outline of faces and figures were beginning to recede.

Stephan's old voice returned; he looked about him, startled and afraid.

"What have I done? Bethany, Lydia, why did you not stop me? Oh my God, what have I done? Jo..."

David's voice came back tranquil and serene. "*Suscipe, Domine, universam meam libertatem, Accipe memoriam, intellectum atque voluntatem omem.*"

Then, once again, silence penetrated the darkness.

"Come," David's voice said.

We followed with no light to guide us, but the sound of David's footsteps going from one corridor to another. The journey seemed endless. The dark took on a formless chasm of space which swallowed us up, and lent urgency to escape. I wanted to call out *go faster, please go faster*, as our feet clattered on stone flagstones underfoot. Now and then I scraped in contact with a passage wall. It was damp and fetid with some noxious morbific life-force that flourished within, recording all past deaths that had occurred there. Faint sounds of whispering hissed warnings that were drowned out by our hurried footsteps. At last, we reached stone steps that led sharply upwards, going into lighter and lighter space until we climbed through a narrow opening, and daylight burst like an expression of pure ecstasy upon us.

We found ourselves, quite miraculously, in the library. This room was perennially cold like most of the house, even in the summer, but now it seemed invitingly warm and welcoming after those subterranean passages.

I felt I had escaped death and reached a kind of acquittal. I shook within from relief, or perhaps a realisation of how closely death follows life and how tenuous each moment is. I marvelled at how I had always blindly accepted what I saw as reality. And no one spoke.

It was as if David and his father had set up this incredible simulation for us, and we had become mesmerised by it all. Slow awareness of my pain, sentient of ancient tortures, had begun to throb with an intensity that masked all fantasy.

We returned to the kitchen and I turned to Bethany and asked her to get me to a doctor; my arm was swelling up. The bone seemed to be snapped in half, and it had protruded through bleeding flesh.

"Oh my, I am so sorry my dear - oh my! Look, just look at your poor arm. I never thought he would go this far," said Bethany.

"I warned you, didn't I, when little Ned went missing. I warned," said Lydia. "And now, where is Jake? He's not come along with us, nor 'as hisself. Still down there, and they 'ave that there cross thingamajig between them. How will they ever forget now?"

"Those were all things of the past and in the past they are meant to remain. In the pursuit of redemption the present has been neglected," said Bethany, a belated judiciousness come too late.

The fact that Stephan and Jake had not joined us was neglected by the pressing circumstances of the moment. All that stuff of absolution, only in renunciation of an obsessed-over past. Or had this all been insinuated by over-enthused and presumptive parents? I did not care. Not then. I simply wanted to go, to get away.

Lydia found a cloth in the kitchen and bound my arm. "What strength, what blooming strength 'e must 'ave 'ad to do this! Ever so sorry, girl, every so sorry. You see, 'is Mum and Dad made me promise to see to 'im and pander to 'im. Guilt, I `spect they felt, for awakening all those old thoughts."

"It's called schizophrenia in my language," I said, between clenched teeth.

"We must get to a doctor," said Bethany. "I will drive your car. David, I would like you to come with us, please."

"I will wait 'ere for hisself to appear," said Lydia.

"No," said Bethany, taking charge. "You will come too, until we have decided what to do about Stephan. He is still not in a right frame of mind and could still be dangerous."

I remember very little after that. What with pain-killers and rather a lot of alcohol given by Bethany, everything was beginning to lose significance in my mind. I remember only that we all climbed into the car, taking little care of cold, and left *Nasiarcuth* hastily and as sensitively anxious as we had arrived.

As the car circled round the drive, I turned and looked back one last time. A cold mist had shrouded most of the building like the ghosts that had wrapped themselves around it, defensive and defiant, casting out the last of the intruders so that they could return to their own silence.

Chapter Four

I suppose that in most people's lives there are fearful and frenzied occasions that remain forever ensnared in horror - like an unexpected accident or death, or some incident which can never be removed from the memory. They hang like a dark cloud above one's head, fetid with the rotten repulsion that they once were.

I have tried to piece together what actually happened that day, but I find myself lost somewhere between a nightmare and a fantasy that I may have imagined. But for the scars on my arm and the ongoing pain I have had from the pins holding bone together, I would have dismissed it in time, I suppose. But then again, all those images and people involved still revisit my dreams and preoccupy solitary moments with tormented speculation.

Then again, I find that when repeating any arbitrary experience, no matter how simple or how complex, after a time the experience becomes an absurd story that takes on a humorous quality, inviting scorn or doubt, perhaps even derisive humour. Or it may stir up a sense of awe in those who like to be aroused by the sensational. Discounting the experience, or suppressing even the thought of it, it becomes a festering doubt of one's sanity as if infected by the lunacy of it.

For me, that whole experience was so extraordinary that I was totally unable to talk of it for a long time - certainly not to parents whose vision was strapped firmly to *terra firma* and what could only be logically concluded. I guess the main reason I never spoke of it was the fear of ridicule. I did not wish to be seen holding on to an inexplicable, outlandish and impossible experience, and I did not wish to be cross-examined about the logicality of it. It made me dig myself in tighter to the illusion of it all. It was easier to follow the system of allowing myself to be blindly led by those who are said to 'know' and convince us in this frail line of existence of that which is necessary, and simple to understand and dismiss that which is indefinite.

I began to doubt everything; Stephan's intriguing historical house, with all its secret tunnels and passages that had been kept from common knowledge. I questioned my imagination. Had I distorted a simple event into a hologram of mind? It took me years to peel away the doubts and face the images once again. I found it easier to write about it, and so started at the beginning, when I first met Stephan. The after-effects are harder to write about. I sit here at my typewriter and battle to put it together.

It was Lydia who stayed with me at Accident and Emergency, but she was not there when I came round from the anaesthetic. Someone had called my parents and mother was standing over me with one of her cheerful-at-all-costs looks when I opened my eyes.

"Poor girl...I believe you had a ghastly fall," she said.

"A compound fracture," Father explained from behind her. "You will need to come home until it is mended."

"Is Lydia still here?" I asked.

"Who is that, dear, one of your university friends?" asked Mother.

"No, she is Stephan's housekeeper."

"Why should she have been here, dear? You had your fall just outside the university. Have you forgotten?"

"Who told you?"

"The ward nurse, dear. She said you came in an ambulance."

There was a feeling of madness about it all and everyone was a co-conspirator to make it seem so. Could I have imagined everything, I mean – everything? When had it happened? *Yesterday*, Mother was saying. Yesterday - was it so recent? Time seemed to have jumped eons, and yet remained fixed in that unbelievable world of sudden change. I was in no mood to argue the circumstances, or to add anything to them that would prize open a hornet's nest of alarm and superfluous comment.

I was only in hospital overnight, but I was unable to do much while my arm was bound and plastered. Metal pins and several stitches for my right arm, as luck would have it, prevented me from driving about for some time, which left me in the care of parents who thought I was suffering from the shock of my fall.

As soon as I was able, I tried to phone Stephan, but there was no reply from him and none from the hospital. I was told that he had taken leave weeks before and had not kept in touch since. Likewise, Bethany did not answer her phone. I imagined her making all kinds of unsolicited arrangements for David against his will, which left me feeling useless.

Those convalescent days of immobility and distraction were like an implosive tornado of unstable and tense emotions. Mother was being irritatingly attentive and Father obliquely wise and counselling. We had that kind of strained and conventional affinity. Affection was tacit, even remote in some way, but radical none the less. There had always been a gentle evasion of discord and a misdeed could churn out icy and silent clashes. No one spoke of the how and why of the accident. No one commented on the accompanying bruised fingerprints up my arm. The idea that I had fallen at university and taken to hospital in a fitting ambulance suited their approval.

Chapter Five

My parents were sticklers for convention, and habit was inbred. Mother had her sewing circle and Father had his career. Mother made those undeniably beautiful patchwork quilts from a random collection of hoarded material, turning them into works of art with intricately woven stitches. Father became lost in an anonymous world of work. Together, they had their circle of friends, who enjoyed discussions from the disparities between the gospels, to the *faux pas* of politicians, to interest in complex plays insinuating the futility of life. Going to church was a social necessity but discussing religion was imprudent, and any thought that might imply an otherwise controversial belief system would be disregarded with scorn.

I could not for a moment imagine how they would have treated Stephan's belief and re-enactment of past lives! I had just moved from the nonsensical to the commonsensical and could not pull them apart from their hidden agendas.

Father had managed to gather my books from college. I learned to write with my left hand, wrenching my brain from the singular to the plural.

A week went by before Bethany called me to tell me my car was still outside her house. *Illegally parked and awaiting clamping, no doubt*, I thought, but at last some recognition that I had not been dreaming and that we had experienced something together. She made no mention of the theatrical ordeal we had gone through, and I was in no mood to prompt it.

"Is David with you?" I wanted to know.

"No. I believe his grandfather in Africa has been asking for him for some time, according to Lydia, so I thought it best to return him there - but your Professor has been making a nuisance of himself with inquiries. Seemed to think David should be an acquisition of the university. I put him straight. It is not what David wants."

"Did David say so?"

"Of course not - what a thing to say! David is mute, we all know that. No, he went off quite happily to South Africa, I can assure you." She sounded flippant, aloof - dismissive even, as if she were dealing with an encumbrance that was forestalling something more important in her life.

"When did he go?" I asked lamely.

"Yesterday," she answered, without enlarging on the subject.

I felt once more that I might be going a little insane myself. Had I dreamt it all? Had I imagined David? Had I seen something so special that no one else had noticed? Had I imagined that he had wanted my help and understanding? Had he not spoken in reply to Stephan's charade in that subterranean crypt? Had he not found the cross when Stephan had no idea where it was? I was beginning to doubt myself over everything: Stephan's wild anger, his violent wrenching of my arm with a deliberate intention of breaking it and wounding with intent to… to what? I could barely bring myself to imagine it.

I tried to raise that last image of him, made visible for a moment in my mind. The disturbingly comic/tragic figure of insanity, frayed with some old fantasy worn like a discarded coat, bearing with it an assumed entitlement to pre-eminence and domination. And who would lay claim to him and his madness now?

I wanted to ask Bethany about him, whether she had seen him, but she cut me short, saying she was in a fearful hurry about something. She asked no questions about my own condition or how I felt. She was intent only on drawing the conversation to a close, sounding uneasy yet polite.

"Must go," she said. "I have an enormous amount of things to sort out. I will be in touch." She simply put the phone down.

I was stunned. I felt isolated, abandoned in a disquieting memory of something impenetrably bewildering. Who else could I speak to of Stephan or of David, or of those things that were revealed in that stark episode of transit from illusion to insanity to reality?

That evening Father assumed a somewhat solemn manner, and I knew he had something to tell me that he had mulled over with Mother, in their usual mutual and succinct way.

"We have something to tell you;" he began slowly, then launched straight in to the heart of the matter. "We have heard that Stephan Tyndal has been burned to death, along with a man-servant in his house."

It was only a few words, blunt and to the point. A simple piece of evidence of no particular importance - just factual and final. Whether or not he and Mother had any idea of the intensity or involvedness of my connection with Stephan, they were clearly keen to circumvent any further involvement in it. I was stunned, pained, lost, and emptied. Stephan had been dead a whole week, and they had not informed me until now.

It was a disclosure presented as an amputation to any further discussion. I imagined it was a relief to them that I could now marry someone sensible and get on with a more prudent and socially acceptable life, but I was beyond caring about family responses. It was Bethany's reaction I did not understand. Why had she not said anything when I spoke to her that afternoon? She had been so evasive and abrupt. Why had she wanted her brother's death to be kept from me?

Father had learnt about it from colleagues at work. For some reason, very little had been reported in the papers. The press indicated, 'according to a family member', that the cause of the fire was faulty wiring, as the house was old and the electrics had been neglected for some time.

They said the fire had started in the early hours of the morning when no-one would have spotted smoke at a distance, and it appeared that the house had burned pretty well down to the ground before an alarm was made to call the fire-brigade.

I wanted to get away, to go there, to see the place and hold it in my mind. His death, this whole matter, this circumstance was such a secret thing; as was his life. It was all so unreal, so hushed up, so folded upon silence. As leaf folds upon leaf and silence upon the root and the flower, hushing up the secrets of all between its parts, as it moves into life from the death from which it appeared.

I wanted to cry, to call out, but there was only smothered silence in my heart. I lived through that day numbed with the expectation of emptiness ahead. I went through the motions of dressing and brushing my hair, with the detached movements of my body. I noted when I looked into the mirror that I was worn-down; my cheeks were hollowed and there were dark circles under my eyes. I had hardly slept for so long, but overtiredness separated and distanced me from the world and insulated me from tears. It put a further unreality to my role in the last act of madness by... I could not think his name any more.

I thought of the life into which he had been born. I thought of the immortality he believed it involved. I thought of all the lives and deaths gone by and the ones he would embrace again. I thought of this 'rebirth' thing. I thought of that process – dying – living again, like the darkness before germination - full of potential and so full of pitfalls. I thought of this new transition of his life.

I lay on my bed, and thought. I thought for days - trapped in helpless infirmity because of my arm. Instead of action, I thought. I thought of those last hours with his menacing behaviour. I thought of all those issues that had surrounded him. I thought of the spurious circumstances of his death and the burning of *Nasiarcuth*. And the thoughts were all locked up in that web that had woven itself inside my head. And the thoughts stuck to me like burrs to clothing.

Had he had caused the fire himself, or had his sister returned to the house after we had left, while I was indisposed, unconscious and immersed in my own injuries?

It was as if I had been deliberately removed from it all and become blind to it. But had that not been the circumstance of our relationship, right from the start? I became certain that I had been the scapegoat or catalyst; or was I merely some tool of distraction, an incidental bystander to this charade? Had I been mesmerized into a kind of stupor to it all? I had always assumed myself to be receptive, aware of my surroundings, but here, I had not. Is that what love is? A blind acceptance, a tolerance of that which would otherwise be detected as unconscionable?

Neither the living nor the dead could claim him now, I thought. He was, in his death, as he was in life - mystifying, furtive, potent, dark. He was the one and the other, inviolable, inaccessibly himself.

Then I began to think of the imponderable. Where was his complex soul now? Was his life – his soul – finalised, ended, 'to die, to sleep no more'? Or was it ready to begin again in an eternal quest for absolution? Had he finally resolved those issues of his past before he died? What if his awareness of 'that something other' continued on to that other next life after death?

I was beginning to think like him. I gave fresh thought to all those things he had laid claim to - past memory, a continuation of the soul's evolution - but what for, if the soul did not learn but continued to make the same misapprehensions over and over? I tried to 'see' those psychic visions that clairvoyants claim to see. I willed, desperately willed, some sort of sign, any sort of indication that a spirit-world existed. If spirits existed in that other world, why would they not appear, just once in mine?

Nothing happened. There was no great awakening, no life altering sign, not a single indication that anything beyond the mundane, the visual and audible existed. All I had experienced with David had been in my mind, after all. It had been there because I wanted it to be there, just as I wanted God to be there.

It is only when those incontestable belief systems one is brought up with are seen to be flawed that one challenges those solipsistic certainties. But then, what of the alternatives? If God is where reality is found, what is reality? How does one verify the conviction of any belief when man so readily enslaves the idea of God as a tool for himself alone, like a Genie corked into a bottle? The small harnessing the mighty! We all seem to be on this habitual quest to uncork God for ourselves, and then - this unreachable 'salvation' thing. I was so full of confusions and wanting answers, yet I was unable, either physically or mentally, to move beyond the confines of where I was, to find answers.

My arm seemed to take an endless age to heal, and the substitute of study books was neither consolation nor remedy.

Months of tormented thoughts elapsed before I was able to drive again, and regain my independence. At least I was amongst fellow students with whom I could wallow in idle chatter once more. But by then, everything had moved on and was way beyond my reach.

As soon as I could, I went round to Bethany's house, and was relieved to find it was not empty. The housekeeper, Mrs. Timmons, came to the door. She told me that she was house-sitting and dog-caring while her employer was away on a world tour on one of those vast ocean-liners. She had taken a Mrs. Lydia Hunter with her - a woman who was known by the family, she explained carefully.

Mrs. Timmons was a small bird-like creature, middle-aged perhaps, with a neat perm and bravely balanced spectacles perched on a delicately small nose. She spoke hesitatingly and precisely, as if she were slicing into a rare and delicate cheese that must be dealt with sparingly. There was none of the familiar chatter that came with Lydia. She one of those people who had hit a mediocre stream in life which not only suited her best, but in which she held a sense of self-esteem - and there she remained, crystallized in a cocoon of precise actions and articulate answers, especially to someone like me, probing into what she saw as classified privacy. She was nowhere near as informative as Lydia and gave away only what was absolutely necessary about her employer's whereabouts. I could see that there was no point in pressing her for any further information, for I had the feeling that she would not divulge anything; even if she knew.

I drove from London out into the country, to retrace my steps to *Nasiarcuth*. It was strange going along the ramshackle driveway, knowing that at the end of it there would be nothing and no one there. Nothing, however, would have prepared me for the shock of what lay ahead.

The house, or what was left of it, had shrunken into the earth and seemed to have become, once and for all, lost to view. One would never for a moment even imagine a large manor house had once existed there. It was as if the caverns and secret tunnels had finally succumbed to the weight above and had drawn down into its depths all the fallen debris. All that was left was a pit of broken masonry and blackened beams that had smouldered to a dry black crust, like the forensic-police's black body-bag over a murdered cadaver.

I wondered about the progression of those souls that had died there, leaving their bones permanently interred somewhere beneath that heap of stone. Had they stagnated like Stephan, caught in a memory that had become unreal?

Someone said that history was an endless, meaningless progression which never got anywhere, but I had begun to believe that as it changes episodically it progresses, also. I started then to think of how we improve ourselves with each new life we begin. Slowly, it was dawning on me that reincarnation made sense.

The worst of the winter was over and brave, tiny buds were breaking through parched bare branches. The nearest shrubs had been burnt away and from where I stood I could see through to the mill-pond where the geese had returned and were busy there, unperturbed, as if nature's prior entitlement was resuming its residence once more, undisturbed by man's transitory tenancy there. The voices, the subterranean tunnels, the ghosts - the past - had been eradicated. It was as if they had never been.

I walked around the circumference of the ruin as if I was encircling a dead thing, waiting for its final entombment. All the while I had this curious feeling that invisible eyes followed me; watching, waiting for me to go, so that they could resume their eternal watch over what once was. Perhaps this vicinity of some rare and special occurrence would be forever a sacred sanctuary to the lonely ghosts that inhabited it.

I went back to my waiting car with a weight in my heart, and my eyes burning with tears. I was grieving for someone and something I could not bury. Someone who had been consigned to that other world along with all his old demons, just as all those others had been dispatched into the bowels of that ruined and fated house.

Had there been a funeral service? I wondered. Without a funeral there would be no closure, only a long extended period of stifled grief. *How could anyone be lost and forgotten so easily?*

There had been no further mention of him in the press, nor was there any information about him from his work number. I felt lost and broken within. He, David, Lydia and Bethany - even Jake - were all gone in one fell swoop, and I was left like the Ancient Mariner, as...*a thousand slimy things lived on, and so did I.*

Chapter Six

I decided to make an appointment to speak with Professor Thompson. He was the last and only connection I had with the family, and though it was a very slender and questionable link, it was all I had. He seemed almost reluctant to see me, at first. He knew little about Stephan's unaccountable death and had been told even less about David, except that Bethany had written to him and told him that David had been returned to grandparents in South Africa.

I had no idea how to broach the subject of what had occurred with Stephan in his madness. All the ends had been so neatly tied as to how I had broken my arm, how the house had been inadvertently burnt to the ground, and David's rapid removal to South Africa. That was common knowledge by now. No doubt whatever Bethany had said had put him off the idea of any further communication. I decided not to discuss the incident, but to launch straight into the subject of reincarnation through hypnotic regression.

His answers were more obtuse than any of my other investigations. I had an underlying suspicion that he had a very good idea about Stephan's fixation over the subject, if you can call it that, for he was evasive, almost dismissive about the subject.

"The psycho-analytical contention; that all the divagations of the subconscious carry a deep passionate significance and cannot be made to fit the facts." He began with a dilatory air of one about to give a lecture to the ignorant.

"One has only to observe oneself and others to discover that we are more or less exclusively the servants of our passions and our biological urges and, I may stress – imaginations. We are, it is agreed, creatures possessed of a very complicated psycho-physiological machine which grinds away incessantly, and in the course of its grinding throws up into consciousness selections from an indefinite number of mental permutations and combinations, that stretch out in the course of its random functioning…"

I felt that he was reciting an old lecture from a catalogue of common thought which had long since become part of a repertoire he could bring out and dust down.

"What about the memory that some people have of something they have had no experience of in this lifetime?" I interrupted, trying to divert him back to simple terms which I could possibly understand.

His reply was a long analytical explanation of the amigdala: "...an almond-shaped cluster of interconnected structures perched above the brainstem, near the bottom of the limbic ring..." I cut him short, saying that I was already cognizant of all the functions of the brain.

"Then you will remember that the amigdala is the storehouse of emotional memory. Without it, the life is stripped of personal means..."

"But what of deep-rooted memory?" I again intercepted, feeling now frustrated with unnecessary information.

"All memory has a basis in emotion," he continued, as if ignoring me. "People come up with debatable memories that are purported to have emotionally affected their lives in some way. I put it down to a learned response to something they have once read, and transferred to a current problem." He was clearly dismissive of any suggestion that a past life was a possibility.

I was silent. I had come to the wrong person to find answers. I thought that as someone who had such deep communications with David, some of the insight might have rubbed off. David had been a pretty convincing player.

Well, who *was* the right person? It could certainly never be someone connected to a confining religion with clear-cut ideas and ideals about salvation and judgement day. I had mistakenly thought a professor of psychology, with his experience in mind and thought-processes...oh well.

I was feeling somewhat let down, and wished that I had found out more from Stephan before his propulsion into the actual character he thought he had been.

"I have not been able to give you the answers you would have liked," Thompson answered dryly, as if reading my thoughts. "You were expecting another kind of answer where inspiration plays a part. Inspiration or mere faith does not provide infallibility or guarantees; it merely gives a reassurance that the existence of God is truly delivered. We must suffer our conception of inspiration to be moulded by the facts as they appear, and be cognizant that they may be tempered unrealistically by the imagination. I am a man of science and, as such, I am trained to concentrate upon the events of the world of space and time, though it has come to my notice in the past that scientists, when they do turn to God, appear to revert to that primitive kind of religion in which 'miracles' play an important part." He was soliloquising once more, going onto the same track of worn-out lectures...or was he inadvertently referring to Stephan?

"One is always reminded of St. Paul's own conversion, which was purportedly due to an appearance in the heavens of the glorified Christ.

Similarly, these people involve themselves with external signs, like the occultism and mysticism which is present in all historical religions.'

"Did you ever have this kind of conversation with David?" I asked,

"Well, no, as a matter of fact. However, I have to say that I found that after communicating with him my own mind seemed directed towards the inspirational..." He tailed off the conversation as if trying to recollect something for which he could not find the words, words that he was able to put into scientific jargon.

"I once studied the *Upanishads* when I was a student; eighth century Indo scriptures, you know. A metaphysical theory of the universe and of man's relation to it summarized in the phrase *tat tvam asi – thou art that*. Ultimate reality is at once transcendent and imminent. God is the creator and sustainer of the world; yet they believe the kingdom of God is also within us. As a mode of consciousness underlying, so to speak, the ordinary individualized consciousness of everyday life, but incommensurable with it. Different in kind, and yet realisable by anyone who is prepared to 'lose his life in order to save it.'"

The conversation had reached saturation and I had the urge to move away, move on, and wonder if I could make any sense at all in what he had been saying.

Chapter Seven

I never saw Bethany or Lydia again. I watched and waited for their world tour to come to an end, and each time I returned to her house I was greeted by the bird-like Mrs. Timmons, only to be told they had not returned and she had no idea when they would. I don't think they ever returned, for I saw a 'For Sale' sign one day outside the house, and Mrs. Timmons no longer answered the door when I knocked. The sale-sign wasn't there for long before builders had moved in, and I was told new owners were having it redecorated. It must have needed a massive alteration, as they seemed to be at it for ages.

I wondered about her little dogs; had she sent for them? She was so devoted to them. I could not imagine what could have happened, and now there was no one to ask.

Revisiting *Nasiarcuth* was much the same. One day the blackened remains were there, away from time, always outside of time, eternal - yet so soon to vanish completely out of sight. Another day and the land had been levelled flat; the 'before' and 'after' were folded together, and all was contained in oneness.

I was told that last time I went there, that I was trespassing; I assumed, by venturing on newly acquired land. I turned around to walk away and find my way back to where I had come from, without answers, wondering about the geese and what they would do about the mill pond.

The whole place had moved forward into daylight like a seed that has burst from dark earth into bright and promising sunlight. All its experiences, its spiritual fulfilment, its obligations to the divine - its disappointments and tragedies - would forget the darkness after death, and would somehow find new life and hope. Like a reincarnation, I imagine.

The habitual loneliness of the survivor crept into my bones, and stayed there.

Chapter Eight

Five years went by from that formidable time. I had progressed to the position of novice clinical psychologist after a mind-numbing degree, still convinced that I was in the wrong career. I had felt that I had become a machine of logical deductions. I was no longer the participator of action, but its nameless bystander, listening but inoperative, with futile nods at acquiescence. Few wanted truth or could establish what the truth was, for what they believed in had already shaped the whole mind.

Everyone wants answers that only they can find from within. It seems our whole being is somehow involved in true knowing. I began to discover that the greatest mystery of life is who and what we truly are and where we have come from, but it is seldom looked at squarely in the face. I began to see that to know something merely within the mind is to know that it is beyond intellectual knowing.

My mind had gone into a kind of reverse gear since the last time I walked away from *Nasiarcuth*. It was as if I had involuntarily changed the way I saw things. As if some remnant of *Nasiarcuth*'s past had adhered to me as a smell lingers on clothing, long after it was impregnated there. I had to release that intellectual charge of knowing to find a truth behind that learned knowledge.

I began to find beauty in simple things, things I had not noticed before: evening light on a garden of flowers when it transforms them into a deeper colour, the gnarled bark on old trees, or the smile on the face of a stranger in the street. That sudden significance of those simple things took my breath away with a conviction that there is more than this life. It's not that those things I noticed were important in any way, but for me they became for that moment perfect and unique. It was as if I was living a different life now, but a life that was going nowhere in particular. I felt myself reaching out to find something beyond me, and I wondered about David over and over.

David had never ceased to haunt my mind. Ever since the last time I saw him, I had the image of him impressing itself upon the retina of my inner eye. There was something unexplained, indefinable that had affected me, and the old emptiness that I felt before rattled about inside me like a tin can blown about the streets in a wind. Although I had become more compliant with life, I felt an entrapment between all those currently reported problems and those unresolved ones. And where the past and present met, there was this mingling of distorted ideas.

I had this dream. It would come again and again when I felt the emptiness return. I had passed back through millenniums of time to a raw inevitability of life, which bore with it its own hardships and joys; yet a simplicity that did not deprive each person of their own instinctive thought, but allowed a process of thinking that understood and respected that which was in nature around him. Then there came a split from the old form of living to a leap into a future of intensified expansion, engineering evolution, and with it instructions on how and when man must think - so that all thought became contaminated and controlled and more often than not erratic, flawed, ambiguous. It seemed that, overnight, man became dissociated from all that was around him. He was living in disharmony with his planet with attitudes of selfishness, separating himself from other creatures, despising and ridiculing ancient wisdoms. Man had become technological experts living with death, based on commodities, without any real view to a future. There was a feeling of suffocation, extinction and stagnation. I saw Stephan urging for another life, another chance on the endless circle, without any progress in his spiritual development, but an eternal need for destruction just as the world was about to cease being. He had still not relinquished his need for vengeance for something that had never happened the way he saw it.

At that point I would wake up, feeling as though I had been harnessed by a group of Greenpeace supporters wading in on my greed and determination to suffocate the planet with my car fuel.

I continued to explore the question of reincarnation as opposed to religious contentions, and on the other hand, scientifically stereotyped conclusions. There seemed to be so few who could speak logically about true possibilities without eliminating a truth right from its concept, either with an over-inflamed sense of history or by over-reaching fanciful ideas and principles with little proof, and deriding those who did not share a belief.

I went to the library and did a research on the dissolution of the Monasteries. It seems there had always been a raging dispute between the Catholic and the Protestant people. From the fourteenth century on there was the wholesale execution of Catholics, especially in the time of King James, the Plantagenets, the Stuarts and the Tudors, aside from the notorious Cromwell - despite his 'Declaration of Indulgence'. There must have been many houses like *Nasiarcuth* that had opened silent doors to hide priests and holy men, providing them with their secret tunnels for rapid escape, and underground crypts beneath their houses in which to worship. Why Stephan had become stuck in this time God only knows, but of course, the converse may also be valid - that he was born in a house steeped in the history of that time, with parents willing to indulge any imagination that would excite a young boy.

I researched all the information I could find about ancient tunnels and subterranean crypts that the Christian refugees must have made use of, as was suggested at *Nasiarcuth*. Long before Stephan's alleged time upon the earth, priest-scientists from Delos had come to Britain on a voyage of exploration that had been organized by the church of Apollo, the Greek-born god of healing and of the arts and sciences. As far back as then underground caves and natural places well below ground were said to be made use of, but whatever buildings and places were made at that time, all traces of their existence has long since gone, and we have lost sight and knowledge of them. Perhaps they have been built over, or simply disintegrated from time; or restored at some time, to be used again for later purposes, as had happened to *Nasiarcuth*.

An ancient, highly intelligent, people lived in the old Briton, unlike the barbarians that were later encountered there. The freemasonry that had existed among the priesthoods since the Old Stone Age was adopted by the newcomers of the cults, who also acknowledged the priests of the Egyptian sun god for the men of science that they were. A friendly rapport was agreed between the ancient Britons and the visiting Egyptian priests. It is said that gifts were exchanged and arrangements were made for future collaboration. Even the Delians were impressed with the Britons knowledge of medicine, which, thanks to generations of patient research, was far in advance of their own. Nor were they slow to recognise the advantages of having at their disposal a scientific research station far removed from the prying eyes of the inquisitive fell-countrymen, where natures secrets could be prized open privily, and put to service for the glorification and enrichment of their god.

Where are those brilliant souls now? I wondered. *If they have reincarnated, who are they now, or who have they become again? Someone perhaps like David?*

There are so many things kept secret, unrevealed, unrecorded in history. Most lives are full of private secrets, private moments and private thoughts that are seldom aired; and for the price of that repression, a lifetime is lost. I had been living in a vortex of those private places, unresolved issues, trapped there by secrets, by other people's motivations for unknown actions they wished to suppress from me - and their silences had prevailed.

I began to feel that life was closing in tight about me. It seemed an eternity since I had arrived at this stagnant space around me, and it seeped in on me, stifling me and giving me no peace. I tried to select some significant moments from those fragments of experience and conversations that had impressed me about Stephan, and those memories brought back that implication of what had occurred, and renewed my investigation into his belief of a past life.

Stephan had had profound convictions that were in conflict, yet above and beyond his scientific persuasions, so it did strike me at the time as ironic that he, as a scientist in opposition to the idealism that religion posed, had gone with me into a church - had even advised me how to get solace from religion, without having the faintest idea I was in need of it..

It was much later, after he had gone from my life, that I sat in an empty church one day and stared at the altar with its brasses, altar cloth and crucifixes, and tried to find meaning in it all. I stared at the fresh flower arrangements, trying to find inspiration in something that was living in that lifeless place. The flowers had that formal set look that altar flowers have. Everything was still, sombre, reserved, solitary, and I felt no comfort at all. Then I remembered Stephan's voice saying *be still, and listen*.

I sat rigidly motionless, until all I could hear was my own breathing. My thoughts turned to prayers, as they do when in a church; they were those mandatory prayers that lose their meaning for the chanting of them. I remembered that innocence of praying as a child, that as I got older became contaminated by doubts and conflicting ideas of what it is all about, and I found myself in discord with my intentions. I returned my concentration to the silence, so that even distant birds became a centre of attention. But I had become so cut off from the significance of a church that I became restless again and after a minute or so the enclosed silence began to press in on me, but I continued to wait, expecting, hoping for something to happen.

Stephan had said something about knowing God from deep inside with all ones senses. I tried to intuit that sense of God for whatever that might mean, but I was only made aware of the mustiness of the church, the wood-polish on the pews, the faint smell of flowers. There was nothing more. The dull shadows gathered into a gloom about me. *Where is God in here?* I wondered. Then I remembered a poem by Henry Vaughan:

There is in God – some say –
A deep, but dazzling darkness; as men here
Say it is late and dusky, because they
See not all clear.
O for that Night! Where I in Him

Might live invisible and dim!

What was it that I was missing? What did I lack that I remained the mere observer, just outside the limits of this spiritual realization others wrote about? I looked around the empty, sombre church, with nothing but its silence that denied everything I had hoped to witness only a moment before. *The church is dead...long live the church*! I thought resentfully. *Long may we remember those that have suffered under it and - I suppose - those who have been exulted by it.* History leaves us in no doubt how much the Christian church has suffered from the arrogance, ambiguousness and hypocrisy of great ecclesiastics.

I used to expect religious people to have the answers of what it's all about, but I have found that they are no closer than the rest of us, despite eager pontificating interpretations of the Bible. Yet to some it is all so certain that there is something more that awaits them. They are the ones who are always so positive, so secure in themselves, even when the world is falling apart about their heads. I wished I were one of them.

I started at that time to really search for meaning. I thought perhaps I would find it in the answers from all the questions I had been asking myself. I knew that finding and solving an enigma like Stephan, or more so, like David, was something I must do alone, without trying to find explanations from someone who has only read accounts of them. I started praying every night, though I think my prayers were not much more than wishing on the moon - yet I prayed, just in case.

My time with Stephan had made the time in progress seem less real and insignificant, despite the apparent lack of reality that he had emerged from. I was trying to find significance in day to day life, asking those eternal questions; where are we going, and what purpose do we have on this planet? Everything seemed so pointless. I felt I was just killing time. What an expression - killing time! Time must be alive to be killed. Is it alive? Time is inexhaustible, eternal.It is and yet it is not when it is past. I began to resent that unbearable clash of time, when spending it in fruitless quest of the polite expectations. Why, I asked, did so many people lead such dreary lives? Was a dreary life self perpetuating? Would it be lived like that again in proceeding lives had it been lived like that in lives before, and for what purpose? I felt I was missing something, and it was something within me.

I needed some sort of corroboration for this past life thing. There simply had to be some evidence to substantiate that last crazy pageant with David and his father. There was little evidence that it had been based on some actual event that had occurred – what, four hundred years ago? - but for the appearance of the cross. But that, I argued, could have been something they both had discovered from the archives, and David had discovered its presence. I was finding it challenging.

Inwardly, I needed that there was an element of sanity in David, or what I had seen in him was really some lunacy after all. I longed to be in touch with him again, but how? I had no idea where he was living or where his grandparents lived, other than he was in a distant country which I knew nothing about. All I knew was this place was called Natal, in South Africa, and I had no idea what the surname of the family was. The maps showed me that Natal is a province bordering the South East coast of the country. "On the way to India," my brother had offered helpfully, when I asked him if he knew of it.

Chapter Nine

My dilemma came to an end when one day I received something in the post that restored my lost hopes.

It was addressed to my parent's home, and arrived by registered mail. Mother phoned to tell me there was a mysterious parcel that had been posted to me from abroad somewhere.

"Lots of jolly looking stamps with birds on it," Mother offered, "and on the back it says that it has been sent by a Mrs. Lydia Hunter. Shall I open it, dear?"

I knew to open it in private, despite the curiosity of enthusiastic parents, so I ignored the offer.

"Who on earth is Lydia Hunter, dear?" Mother asked.

"An old friend; a very old friend," I replied wistfully, trying desperately to contain my pleasure.

"Shall I open it for you, dear?" Mother repeated. She was never one to suppress her patience or curiosity.

"No, please don't," I said. "It may contain private and personal information that she would not like me to divulge, even to a curious parent. I will come this afternoon and get it from you."

Mother was even more intrigued that I had responded as quickly as I did. I was known to procrastinate over any other of her recommendations, which generally inclined towards something I did not want to do or be included in - most often in finding me a suitable mate from amongst her friends' offspring.

Mother was holding the parcel up to the light and rattling it at her ear when I turned up, even earlier than I had arranged. Fortunately, it was effectively bound up with a mass of brown paper, and enough tape to restrain a reluctant hostage.

I took the package from her hands, dropped it into a shopping-bag, and grudgingly accepted a cup of tea, saying I was in a hurry to get back to a patient. Of course I had nothing of the sort, having cancelled all my appointments for the afternoon. I went directly back to my small flat to open the parcel.

I uncovered a shoe-box that had been filled with Styrofoam pieces packed around a smaller parcel, and on top was a large white envelope with what seemed to be a manuscript inside, stuck down with the message: *To be opened only by Miss Josephine Armstrong*. She must have had some inkling about Mother's curiosity. The letter was carefully written in a shaky, simple, rounded lettering, and from its date I saw that it was a year old.

Dear Jo,

By the time you get this, I will have passed on. I will give this to my solicitor to post on to you when I am gone, and not before. It has been a hard five years since I last saw you and, as you know, I am getting on now. I will be 82 this September and I am creaking and rattling like one of them old doors at the Hall. There is things that I believe in fairness have to be confessed to you, as you need to know. Being silent to you is not fair but it would have not been wise to tell you before, in case you had done the right thing and went to the police and all.

Mr. Tyndal, Stephan to you and me, was a sick man, as you could see. He had been like that since a boy. Troubled he was, troubled with his past if you know what I mean, and not with the past with Mr. and Mrs. Tyndal. No, they was the very best parents any child could wish for, but they too were worried about Stephan. He was ever such a clever lad when he was little. Like David I suppose, in a way, but David had that autism thing and with it some right peculiar powers. When things got really bad with Stephan there was no stopping his mind going on about his fancies. He thought people was working behind his back and all.

Jake and me tried to help as much as we could but when the young lad went missing - that is, his first son, and then his mother - we knew what he had done, and we did our best. I was never acquainted with them passages under the house but Jake was, and they spooked him really bad I can tell you, but Jake did his best.

We had no control, finally. Jake specially was under his spell, kind of. Something I can't explain. Anyway Bethany, Miss Tyndal that is, she said "we can't let this go on, Lydia and we can't let him go in a home. They will find out things," she says "and they will take David away." That day I left you in the hospital I was real shook up, I was, but I left you and I then got a taxi back to the Hall. Bethany was already there and Stephan - he was going mad, calling for you and asking forgiveness - but we couldn't trust him, see. I thought Bethany, she must have left David behind in her flat. He was not there and there was no time to ask. Jake, he was still like as in a cloud, like he was someone else. (Stephan done that to him many times, so did old Mr. Tyndal, they called it hypnosis stuff).

Jake came and took Bethany and made her sit down, and Bethany was frightened. I didn't know what was said before I got there but she was saying, "This has got to stop, Stephan, don't you realize what you have been doing? I have found what you have written and I know what you have done, Steph. For God's sake, this has gone too far. Heaven knows what you have done with Miranda and Ned. I think you know don't you," she was saying. Stephan's face was white and he was pacing and wringing his hands. I had never known him like that. He said he needed something from his study and he must be alone for a few minutes.

We wait out in the corridor and Bethany was asking what she must do now. He was gone some time and we thought he was meditating. "Good," said Bethany, "he will be calm." Without Stephan there Jake comes to, and he asks what is going on. He went to fetch Stephan's medication and we tried the door but he didn't answer. "I have your medication here," said Bethany and Stephan came out from his study and then closed the door behind him. "No," he said – "no – no more of that – I need to think; I need to be conscious for once. I am going to the library," he said, and we followed.

"Come with me, brother," he said to Jake - Jake was Jake then, but he still went with him. He said he didn't want us there with him and we must leave at once - he was shouting "I am going back down into the crypt - Bethany, please go." Then he turned to me and he gaves me this here parcel I am sending you. "Give this to Jo," he said. "Tell her I loved her." he said, and he went into the library and he shut himself in with Jake and we knew he was going back down into that tunnel. That's when we smelled something and somewhere was a fire, downstairs somewhere.

"I think it's from his study," shouted Bethany. We tried to push the library door but he had locked it and the fire was coming on leaps and bound. We rushed back to the stairs but that fire had reached us first and it was already flaming itself up the stairs and there was no way down. Next thing there was David, out of the blue.

"Come," he said, "come this way," and we ran after him, trusting, though later I couldn't think why we were trusting, he is just a boy. But at the end of the passage was an old stone wall, like it sticks out a bit. I never thought of it before, just part of the building I thought, but he knew to push it and it moved ever so slow and the fire was coming up a storm behind us and the smoke was so thick as you couldn't see. Bethany was screaming "we are trapped!" and David, he raised his hands and she and me were quiet somehow. We got behind that wall somehow and David he pushed it back, and the flames were beginning to creep up on the floor and above the ceiling behind it and we heard timber cracking and caving in – there was a small stone stairway that curls round and down below. Bethany said it must have been part of the old house and we were going fast as we could as the smoke crept in behind, and before weknew it we were in the garden to the side of the house, near the drive would you believe it. Hidden by bushes it was. I been born and raised in that place and never saw it before.

Bethany ran out onto the lawn and shouted that we must go and get help - we must go – but we didn't move, none of us, we were just watching from the lawn. It was dark now by now, late at night, and that fire burned itself into the black sky. Above was stars, and they and we are all that saw that fire, and we stood there and we stared as the building goes up in flames. There was something about the Hall that we know was trapping people to it. We felt, the both of us, that it was best to let it burn down.

If we called the fire-brigade they would have stopped the fire - we all knew it and we didn't say, we just stood and watched and knew and we were crying. David was quiet as we watched that big building collapse and fall in piece by piece, and it seemed that it would keep falling, and we were not talking, none of us.

It was early morning and the light was breaking through, and we had to go before we were seen. There was a problem with Bethany's car, for it was parked close to the front door and the tyres was melted from the heat of that blaze but for some reason it never caught, but it couldn't be moved. "I will think about what to tell them," said Bethany, and she started the car that was your car, that was way down the drive. No knowing how it got there, look, but was thinking - what if David?

We drove back to her place and she said no-one must ever know. What about Jo? I asked. "No, not Jo", said Bethany. She had it all arranged that we would go back to David's mother's home in South Africa with him. Bethany told you on the phone that he had already gone, but we decided we wanted to see for ourselves that the lad was settled.

David's grandfather was so happy to see the lad - he made a big fuss and thanked Bethany over and over - but the grandmother was not pleased to see us. She is a sour old puss that, I can tell you. She said quite clear she didn't want the boy back - she couldn't cope, she said. "But you wrote to his father," Bethany said, and the grandmother she said "That mad fool of a husband of mine wrote to him. We know the father is a bad lot, but that is not my problem."

The grandfather, he found a place for us to rent somewhere nearby, and David stayed with us. "What do you think we should do?" Bethany asked." We can't leave the chap here. They don't want him."

David says he can be left to care for himself now, in his new voice. It sounded ever so strange to hear him speak and he don't talk when the grandparents are around, which don't help because they think he is not right in the head. He goes outside and looks to be talking to a tree in the garden they call Paw Paw, and they say he is still autistic.

Bethany is missing her dogs and she is not well, her stomach problem - I can see that - but we must stay because she says she don't know what else to do and they will be asking questions about her car being left at the Hall and not reporting and all. It's a fine bother, I can tell you. Then one evening when Bethany said she was feeling really poorly David stood near her, stroking her head. She was ever so fond of David, was Bethany.

Anyway, that night we sent Bethany into the hospital and they said she had a stroke. She is too ill to be moved or to go back to England so we have to stay, no other way. David sits with Bethany most of the time and they are sort of talking to each other though neither says a word. David just knows what she is thinking and what she is wanting, and he gets it for her.

One day David said he must go somewhere to see a friend of his called Kethla. He said Kethla is sick and needs him. He just went - no car, nothing. He walked out. There was no stopping him. When the grandfather visited I told him and he looked worried, but no one knew where to look to find him. He was gone for nearly four weeks when one day he turned up, walking back, happy as Larry, and he had an old dog with him. He said it was Kethla's old dog, and Kethla had gone.

That old dog, he follows David everywhere. That old dog is smelly enough and old enough as he is, and ugly too, but there is a bond between them. Bethany is getting weaker and weaker and in her way I know she is missing her own dogs, so we arrange they be sent out to her. Cost a pretty packet, I shouldn't think, but there you have it - her dogs are with us and they don't like that old dog of David's. But enough about dogs. I'm getting sort of used to the place, you know - different birds and animals about and them darkies, ever so kind and helpful in the house, and David seems so happy. He works in the garden a good deal and then he reads, but reading is not so much of an interest for him now. It's outside and being with them darkies he likes most.

One morning I went in to Bethany and she was asleep, and as usual David was by her bed. "She has gone." he said - just like that, real calm. I was in a state, I tell you, but David put his hand on my shoulder and I knew that Bethany was at peace.

I started then at that point to writing this letter to you, Jo. I feel David and you would like to see each other again and it could only be after Bethany had passed away, and now I feel an ache in my side and I know deep down that I too will soon be gone. I need to give this *message to you from Stephan, for I think he really loved you best. He was at heart a good man. I have known him since a small lad and something got mixed up with his memory and that, but he was keen you should have this parcel and you should know how it was. I don't think he ever meant to harm you as he did and what might have happened did not happen, so there is an end to it. I liked you best Jo - you was always so cheerful and clever like him - and I hope your life is more happy than as his or Bethany's was. All the best, Jo.*

P.S. David's name these days is David Van Der Walt, his mother's name and this place is Dassiedorp in a province called Natal. I can say no more than that because David may not even be here by the time you get this. I don't think he will want to stay, but it is as much as I can do to help you. Goodbye, Jo. Lydia.

I put the letter down and thought a while. It must have taken her days to write, for it took up several pages after crossing out parts and errors corrected, and then she had folded it away and pressed it into its large envelope.

I looked at the parcel and picked it up. It was heavy. It was a smaller cardboard box wrapped in brown paper, and tied with string. What was inside was wrapped carefully in one of Stephan's handkerchiefs. I knew what was inside before I even opened it. The emeralds sparked in the light and the rubies seemed to bleed colour from the centre. It was quite captivatingly beautiful close up. I had never held anything so exquisite or so incredibly valuable before. I stared at it and wondered about all the lives it had cost, and what hideous history ran past it in its keeping or manufacture. I simply did not know what to do with it. I did not want to keep it, such a thing of beauty but so steeped in evil and suffering. It was something that was far too valuable to leave in my flat or carry around with me. I had to think.

Chapter Ten

When Brent and I were small, holidays abroad meant somewhere in Europe. It was usually one of those over-crowded beaches of over-populated Spanish or French resorts. The beaches would keep us occupied, while our parents sipped the wine and sat in interesting little bistros. As we grew older, our parents would attempt educational journeys - to Russia from Saint Petersburg to Novgorod, or Italy, from Rome to the Vatican to Verona, or perhaps France, from Tuscany to La Rochelle. Going East or to one of those 'other' continents was just far too hazardous to contemplate. I had always dreamed of back-packing around the world and seeing places I had read about, but somehow it never happened. Certainly not while I was a student, and later, when I started working, my mind had become too crammed with other agenda.

South Africa to me conjured up pictures of wild bush with lions, elephants, rhinos and giraffe peeping through long dry grass, and little else apart from Mr. Nelson Mandela, who had become a kind of saint for having something to do with the end of apartheid in the country. Strange word, 'apartheid'. It became sort of analogous with South Africa, and meant little to outsiders like myself.

I had always wanted to travel but with a sense of naïve uninformed curiosity, not necessarily to recognise some accredited interest in the place. You could say that I was not an avid news follower. I had paid little attention to all the colonial countries' affairs after the obligatory spoon-fed school histories - probably why I shied clear of those intellectual parties of my parents, where the buzz of what was current 'over there' left me cold. South Africa was foreign in the extreme. Now I was faced with travel, much further than I had planned for, and the thought of going there to find David filled me with awe, but I determined to go. I suppose I knew as much as Lydia and Bethany when they embarked on the journey, which ultimately swallowed up their remaining years.

I was at a defining moment in my life. I was floundering like a fish that had outgrown the bowl it had been bred in. Life that had once contained an infinite number of possibilities had become limited and undefined. I was tired; not the tiredness of over-action but of the lack of it, and the lack of stimulus. It seemed that everything was closing in on me. Freedom of choice had become an illusion. Life had in fact become a lead weight, waiting for something to happen that never happened. I guess I had been repressing my emotions and thoughts for so long that I was unsure of anything anymore but the uncertainty of life. I needed a break. Then Lydia's letter came out of the blue, and my life was abundant once more.

Over the gap of years since I had seen him, I reasoned that David had had plenty of opportunity to write to me, to email me, but I had heard nothing. I had no idea where he was or any idea of how to find him, and now that I did, I stopped to consider if finding him would be the right thing to do. What if I simply turned up one day, unannounced, and said I wanted to see David? What if I had gone all that way and he was no longer living there, or the grandparents, for that matter? It was, after all, several months since the date on the letter from Lydia, and I had no indication of when or even if she had died. She must have died, I reasoned. If her information was true, the letter would have been forwarded by her solicitors after her death.

All that Sunday I sat alone, debating every moment of my life and wondering how or what I would do. All that intensity with Stephan had left a gap and those short, but overwhelming, concentrated, moments with David had electrified some distant, dormant chord that was in me.

I took the Celtic cross from the white handkerchief that sheathed it. As I stared at it I became mesmerised by its magnificent brilliance, its perfect artistry. There was a vibrancy of something old and mystical about it, a sort of distant consciousness like eternity receding in time, and I came drifting in to take up a place in its history. I felt suddenly impelled by a force within it. Was this the force that had driven men mad to lose their souls to possess it? It was as if it intended to be itself; but what self? Had it adopted the projected images of those who had been in possession of it like a kind of fetish?

My mind moved to another dimension in which I saw the world shimmering strangely with an intense light, like the nucleus of a creature under a microscope, and in that moment I shifted into an intense awareness of realisation; a kind of extreme level of consciousness I had never known before. I suppose you might call it a kind of epiphany. I only knew that it was not some degree of involuntary impulse I had wished for or imagined to expect from such an item, for the mere purpose of self-assertion.

True, I had expected something of this sort from being in the church or some sacred place, but it had not happened, not then. No - this was pure energy, an illumination, an indescribable power, a feeling of infinite life. As I opened myself out to its purifying and transforming radiance it was like a supreme triumph over infinity. It was as if my soul was in suspense, yet infinitely busy in this extraordinary new world. Gradually, the sensation lifted, and little by little I felt my mind easing and unfurling once more to the day.

I had read about the phenomenon of psychometry, where some people are able to divine the properties of inanimate things by mere contact. Perhaps I was tapping in to some past relevance that had been placed upon this icon, I don't know. I only know that after the experience - which was never repeated, I might add - I felt myself submitting to something that was happening to me on some sort of subliminal level. I was entering a new dimension of life, releasing my will to an alternative bidding like a creature evolving into a new birth, and shortly after I was hearing David's voice in my mind again. Nothing specific - nothing I could put words to - and the urge to see him again was unshakable.

Chapter Eleven

My job had been put on hold, my flight booked, and a hasty explanation to the family had left me in the centre of a tornado. The only other preparation I made was to write to the address that Lydia had sent me, asking for my letter to be forwarded to David and hoping he would receive it. I then went to a travel agent to find out how to get there, and how to find accommodation when I arrived. After that, I had to wait patiently for the date of flight, in order to escape the questions and looks of consternation.

It was a long and tedious journey with a change in Johannesburg, where I was to transfer to a domestic flight for Durban. When I got there, exhausted but enthusiastic, the humid air engulfed me. I was reminded glaringly that I had surfaced in humid sub-tropical temperatures. No one seemed certain where I was to go to catch a train. Communications and transport facilities were non-existent from what I could make out. However I finally found a taxi service that could take me to a train station.

There was no air-conditioning, and the heat-smothered train prickled like a stick-on fur coat on a hot day in midsummer. The journey was like no other train journey I had taken before. The seats were old and broken, and the floor was un-swept. The passengers, mostly African, piled on and seemed not to notice. A scattering of whites came in and sat in what seats were available in my compartment, without speaking. It was hard to believe that this was the first-class compartment. The train chugged unhurried, picking up scruffy passengers who had waited patiently in the heat to climb aboard on its numerous stops on route.

Outside, a changing landscape moved from undulating green to the grey blue hills of what I was to learn were the Drakensberg Mountain foothills. The sun blazed down onto a brilliance of wild fields with no divisions, but open undivided spaces. Here and there an old farmstead with a windmill and corrugated outbuildings explained life among the wilderness.

I was already immensely tired after the flight and I dozed off, to wake often upon the ever-changing landscape. I seemed to have travelled half my life away. My back ached and my neck was stiff, and my mouth was sour and dry. No refreshments on this long journey. I had been warned that few white people took the train -"You should go by Greyhound," the woman from the travel bureau said - but I couldn't find where to go to catch the Greyhound, and no one seemed to know to help me, and besides, there were few who appeared to understand English. White people were simply not in evidence after I had left the airport. "Get the first bus going into the town," I had been ill-advised by an ignorant travel agent back home. There were no buses. "From there, any travel agency will get you a ticket to where you need to go." How do you explain 'travel agency' to someone who does not speak English? They all only knew 'train' and 'taxi'.

'Taxis', the only means of public transport, appeared to be *dormobiles,* packed to full capacity with Africans who gazed sourly at any white person intending to use them.

I was going to an address and people I did not know, reacting on a reply to my letter to the scant address that Lydia had left for me. It had come two weeks after I had sent it and was written by a cousin of David's.

Dear Josephine,

I am David's cousin, Eric. I am now living at the address you wrote to asking about David. I run the farm for my grandfather now as he is too old to manage it. David comes here from time to time. I suppose you know that he can't talk. He has interests with the blacks in some location somewhere, I am not sure quite where, but if you decide to come and see him you can stay here and wait for him to turn up.

Yours truly,
Eric Van Heerden

There was no telephone number offered so I wrote back to say when I would be arriving, and then received no further communication from him.

Nothing could be that difficult to find, I thought. I could always go to the town, find somewhere to stay and wait, as he said, for David to turn up. It was the only way I was going to be able to see him again.

As the train rattled slowly from station to station, it dawned on me only then how vague and impulsive my planning had been. What was I doing there? Why had I not taken more care in the preparation of the journey? I was going to an unknown address and without any information or telephone number to contact, and I had no idea what these people I was going to were like.

The train stopped at a small siding called Turner's End Station, no doubt named after some early settler long since forgotten, leaving no other trace than a name. This was where I was told to get out. There was not a white face to be seen. A few parched bushes in the dry red sand stuck out in the stark surroundings like unbrushed hair, and beyond, tall gum trees stood sentinel to what was left of an old corrugated shed, whose single hospitality offered a dilapidated bench for refuge from the weather.

Three other passengers got off from the lower carriages with me; they seemed accustomed to the place, and went about their journey. I looked around, feeling utterly lost. There seemed to be no place of civilization anywhere nearby. I approached an old man who was, by comparison, reasonably dressed in a worn-out old jacket over a frayed shirt, with oversized trousers pinched in at the waist with twine. He was busy brushing grey dust from his scuffed old shoes. He looked up as I greeted him, hoping there would be a response to my English. He looked at me from dark-brown eyes, buried in dark-black furrowed features. It was a tired but kind face. I asked him if he knew the town I was going to, and if he knew how I could get there.

He sucked his teeth, drew a long breath and said, "Ays long way. Take long time to walk, missus."

"I don't want to walk," I answered. "I want to find a taxi or a telephone somewhere to enquire how to get there."

"No taxi now, missus," he replied graciously.

"Well, what about a bus...any buses going there?" I asked, feeling a little desperate at my plight in such remote and isolated surroundings.

"No bus now, missus. Bus finish long time ago. Only taxi-bus come in morning and tonight." He put his head down, muttered something to himself, and proceeded on his way. I looked around to see if I could find any kind of building to which I could walk, but there was nothing and I was feeling distinctly at risk and exposed - to wild animals, dangerous snakes, rape, murder, theft of all my belongings I had with me. It was not the first time that I reproached myself for being impulsive over the entire journey.

Of course, I blamed it all unreasonably and churlishly on Stephan. *Ever since I met him*...I was agonizing, when a cloud of dust appeared from the road ahead and a large battle-worn truck came into sight, stopping with a screech of brakes near the station building. Several hefty-looking Africans jumped off the back of the truck. The driver was white. His face was sun-darkened and toughened like old leather. He kept it belatedly shaded with a battered brown felt hat. He stared hard at me as if I were something out of space, as I approached him to ask if I could get a lift to the town.

He spoke with a strong guttural accent, "*Ag*, man you can come along with. I live just outside Dassiedorp. Who are you going to visit?" I told him, and he looked surprised.

"I know the Van Der Walts. The old man has been real sick," he said.

I told him I was a friend of David's and he looked at me even more keenly. "No, you must be joking man, you mean that backward *ou*? *Ag*, man, he lives with the Kaffirs."

He got out, took my bags, and threw them into the back of the truck, while I struggled to open the passenger door.

"*Ag*, man, it sticks something terrible." He gave a great shove with his boot and the door flew open, crashing into the side of the vehicle. I climbed up into the cracked leather, seat filthy with grease stains and sundry dirt, but by now I was just content to be reaching a conclusion to my journey.

"Why didn't you get the Greyhound? It goes straight to Dassiedorp. No one gets the train these days; it's not safe for whites." I wondered at a transport system that was reserved exclusively for the blacks. Perhaps it was a form of retribution to the whites for the apartheid time. This was just a new kind of apartheid.

He introduced himself as Frikkie Nell, and asked a few questions about coming to South Africa but otherwise, was silent. I told him that I had received a reply from Eric Van Heerden to say that I could stay at his grandfather's place until I had found out where David was. I wished to find a hotel in the town nearby, but first I wanted to find the family home so I could establish contact. He knew the Van der Walt's place, and he knew Eric. He also advised me to locate the hotel as he was sure 'the old lady' would not receive guests in her house.

He drove with careless disregard for the large potholes in the road, which we struck from time to time with such a force that I was ejected from my seat. I clutched at the door handle to keep me fixed in one spot, keeping my feet firmly braced at every interruption. There were no safety belts. The odd loud expletive in Afrikaans assured me that he too had felt the impact, while we bounced about like ping-pong balls inside a glass jar.

The journey took about twenty minutes of strained punishment, until we reached a town which might have come out of some American West movie. The houses were whitewashed bungalows with painted red or green tin roofs. Every garden was bordered with barbed or razor wire fencing, and the name of the protection service they supported brazenly advertised at the front gates. The message came loud and clear: these people were afraid.

There were several scanty-looking shops down the main street, with many more blacks than whites walking about, and two or three unadorned churches - identified only by a single cross outside – which, you could say, granted it the classification of 'town'.

We passed through the town and hit the dust road again on the other side, and several minutes later turned into a farm track that had 'Van der Walt' printed on an old board. Frikkie blasted his horn, rousing three large dogs that came to bark noisily at us. There appeared to be no-one home.

I clambered shakily out of the truck, grateful for release, and followed Frikkie around to the back where a couple of African women were talking. He called out to them, speaking in their language, and they answered by pointing to an empty garage and then towards the house.

"Eric is out with his Oupa, and the old lady is in the house," he translated.

At that moment, an elderly woman in her seventies or thereabouts came to the back door. She was short, with an overriding stomach that dwarfed thin legs, and withered flesh that shrank her even further. Her mouth was a secondary wrinkle to those that spread about her wizened face, and behind thick glasses two magnified eyes peered at us inquisitively.

"Hello, *Tannie*," (these people seemed to call everyone *Tannie* or Aunty, I was to find out) Frikkie began, giving an explanation in Afrikaans. The woman answered in the same language, with defiance in her folded arms. She shot me a look of annoyance, like a flight of poised hornets whose nest had been trespassed.

"She says: *what do you want with David, did you know that he is not normal, and you may certainly not stay here!*" Frikkie seemed greatly amused by the translation. I was not. I was tired, very tired, and her uncalled-for rudeness ignited a flare of primal anger that I fought with, not to go and slap her.

"Tell the ill-mannered old fossil that I have no intention of staying in her hovel. I simply wanted to confirm that I had found David's family home, and that I wished to find a hotel nearby until I was able to speak with him."

"No one speaks to the boy," she answered more than competently, in a slightly Geordie-English accent. "And if it's his money his mad aunt left him you are after, he has given most of it to the blacks and not one cent to the church."

"Where will I find David?" I persisted, whilst resisting the urge to go and smack her tightly permed head.

"Not here," she pouted. "He lives with the blacks." Whereupon she turned on her heel and slammed the door behind her.

I stood there feeling isolated in my foreignness and, for the hundredth time, examined the scant motive I had for coming such a long way with such fragile arrangements made without much forethought. Yet again, I cursed my impulsive nature.

How had I been so sure that David wanted me there? All those thoughts that I had imagined he was trying to send via some telepathic message to me now hit me as crass stupidity. I sighed, and turned gratefully to the large bear of a man who had helped me so far.

"Can you drop me back into the town?" I asked, not at all sure where I would go from there.

"Of course," he said, leading the way back to the truck.

"You have been wonderful," I said, wondering what part of nature creates some with such generous altruism and others, like the old grandmother, with not a jot.

"It is not often a beautiful young woman comes into the town from nowhere and asks me for help," he said, glancing at me sideways. He was a total stranger in a strange town and a strange country. What chance it was, relying on the kindness of total strangers! I sat unmoving and unmoved by his flattery, hating myself for my insecurity and liability.

"Don't worry about old Mevrou Van der Walt," he said. "She is like that to all strangers, especially anyone who is not part of her church. You want to hear her go on about those with other beliefs, like David's *Tannie*. *Ag*, man!" He slapped his leg and roared with laughter at some joke I was not yet privy to.

"Church!" I exclaimed, "People with Christian values are like that!" Of course there are those blind religions that are passed on down the family that challenge any sort of original thought or other possibility. Visions and voices would be seen as the working of the devil incarnate

"Did you know the women that David lived with?" I asked.

"*Ja*, they rented a place from the Smidts. There has been no one living there these past six months. Why don't I take you there?" he offered. "You can rent the place while you are visiting David. The hotel in the town is not so *lekker*."

"So you knew them?" I asked, surprised that he had sat in silence for so long without volunteering any information.

"Ja. I knew them only a little at first, but the last old *Tannie*, Lydia - *ag*, man, she was a lady, I tell you! I got very fond of her. She used to come to my Pa's shop in the town to buy bread, even though we deliver."

So his father had a bread shop in the town; he must have known everyone.

"Did you see anything of David?" I asked tentatively.

"No-one saw David," he replied. "His aunt kept him indoors most of the time, and then she was sick for a long time and David stayed by her. I caught sight of him a few times when I delivered bread, though. There was something about him. He was…you know, man…I can't say. I don't know." He scratched his head for further inspiration to find the right words for David. "I just know why you have come to see him."

"You have been so kind already…I don't know how to thank you," I said.

We got back into the truck and turned back towards the town. It had been hot in the train, but the inside of the truck was like stepping straight into an oven that had been put to its hottest temperature. Outside, pale-brown tufted grasses grew in red dusty sand, bleached by the relentless sun. Tin shacks dotted about the landscape, and beyond were silent hills where the sun blasted down upon scorched earth. It drew the moisture from my face and arms, leaving me parched as the earth outside. As my tongue fused with the roof of my mouth, all I could think of was water. We re-entered the town and drove up into one of the bungalows which skirted the town centre.

Mr. and Mrs. Smidt soon became translated to Dorothy and Piet, and thankfully they had joined the rank that could describe most South Africans as hospitable and friendly. I was offered something to drink right away, and I downed at least three large glasses of water before dehydration had been staunched. Frikkie took out my case from the back of the truck while we made arrangements for letting. Finally, all was settled, and Frikkie went on his way with messages for his own family from the Smidts.

The house for rent was an annex of theirs. They explained that it had been built as a 'granny-flat' for parents who had died before making use of it. For whatever its intents and purposes, it was as large as the main house. I guessed that planning permission was not a top priority there.

There was an overwhelming sense of *deja vu* as I stepped into that house. It was a bit like revisiting Bethany's apartment in London, only this one had been tended to by African servants who had cleaned and managed it on a daily basis, a lot more efficiently than her English retainer. She must have imported a good many pieces of her furniture and possessions over the period that they had been there. I wondered if the Smidts ever had any idea of the value of their last tenant's belongings. Getting to know them, I saw that it would have made little difference to them.

Bethany by then had been dead for a couple of years, but her perfume lingered and the smell of her cigarettes still filtered through the furniture. There was some corporeal sense of her that had stayed behind. I could sense that she had been happy there, and I wondered at the life they had led which would have been so different from their lives in England.

Dorothy and Piet chatted about their last tenants as if they had been long-lost family, and how devastated they were when they had died, and when the dogs they had sent out to them had finally succumbed to old age.

"And what of David?" I asked, wondering how and when to broach the question, as the very reason for my journey.

The question elicited a direct response of furtive glances between each other.

"David?" they repeated in unison.

"Yes - does he come back here?" I asked. "His grandmother seemed so angry about him. I wondered what had happened to him."

"That woman is angry about everyone," Piet answered.

"Yes, guilt about her daughter," Dorothy added, ignoring the query about David.

"Is that David's mother Suki you are talking of?" I asked.

"Betty Van der Walt was full of spite about her daughter for leaving them with David just after she had come back from overseas, then a few years later they discovered her body at the bottom of a giant pot in their garden. They would never have discovered it if a Paw Paw tree's roots had not broken it open. The police said her neck had been broken, so they put the cause of death as strangulation. At first they said it was the gardener, but later they suspected it was her boyfriend, David's father," said Piet.

"I agree with Betty...you just can't trust these blacks, man. If I told you what has happened to neighbours around here - *ag*, you would want to turn round and go straight home." Dorothy was full of high dudgeon on the matter of violence from the Africans, but her husband stopped her mid-stream.

"You know that old *nooi* the gardener was old and feeble. She would have been able to fight him back, and the police said that considerable force had been used to crush the bones in her neck, as they found her. We all knew the gardener; he had worked at that farm since he was a boy and he was very close to David. He had been close to both Betty's girls too, when they were growing up. And why did he not run off right away? No, he stayed behind and cared for David. I think he saw something and was too afraid to speak up. No one would have listened - a black man telling on a white man, and a respected white doctor from overseas, at that."

"Did they do anything about pursuing the matter?" I asked, with a gulp of conscience. "I mean, they could have got Interpol to investigate the matter."

"Not enough evidence - only hearsay that he had left the same day that she disappeared, and he lied about her being with him."

The air was barbed with those sharp and silly aphorisms thought up to insult, as they bantered with one another over which they felt was guilty.

"Oh my God!" I was stunned. "Did either of you ever meet this man?" I asked, feeling such shame that he had been my lover for so long. I wondered if anyone there knew of my connection. They certainly never asked. I expect they thought I was just another family member concerned about David.

"No, he was never there for long enough. And anyway, even to this day Betty holds that it was the gardener."

"You realise I am here to find David," I said. "Do you have any idea where I might find him? Mrs. Van der Walt said he did not live there anymore and never came to visit, but I had a letter from his cousin Eric saying that he visited his grandfather occasionally."

"Well, he did go and visit a few times," answered Dorothy. "His Oupa was very fond of him. He had spent some time with Eric when they were growing up, and Eric did not mind him visiting. It was the old lady, as we said. Guilt, that's what it was - her guilt. You know, she sent him back to his father without telling anyone."

"I could never understand why they came out here to be with him," her husband continued. "We heard that Bethany had a large house in London, and she gave it all up to come out here and just sit here with him. She hated him going out beyond the garden. He was like a kind of prisoner but every now and then he would just go and the old lady would become sick with worry, then back he came, once with an old, old dog..."

"An ugly old thing that followed him about," Dorothy continued. "He would take it indoors and have it sleep in his room with him. You know the word was that the boy was autistic, but I just think that he was deaf."

"Now, how can that be, Piet? That boy could talk when he was very small." Then turning back to me she explained. "You know, Suki had the baby out here. Betty didn't want anyone to find out that her daughter was not married, but you know these things, man, this is a small town. Betty told her that the child must either go back to the father, or go for adoption after he was born. Betty nagged and nagged that poor girl until she gave in and took the child back to England with her for a few years..."

"Yes, and when she came back he was deaf and dumb," her husband interrupted.

"He used to scream a lot too...remember?"

"Now, what I say is that something happened to him back there..."

"And she was only back five minutes with him before she disappeared."

They bantered on and on, weaving in and out of each other's incomplete sentences about the circumstances of Suki's errant behaviour and that of her sister, until my mind began to swivel about in it all like a stirred spoon in a mug of hot tea. Exhaustion, uncertainty and heat blurred all sensation until my eyes lost their focus and I began to sway with the rotation of the room.

"*Ag*, and you look so tired, you go lie down..."

"Yes we will bring you something to eat when you have had a rest."

An African maid was sent for to prepare the house for me and make up a bed in the main bedroom. I turned on the shower and stepped into a spray of cold water. It took my breath away as it drenched hot, sticky, sweat-salt flesh, tingling me back to life. In the kitchen a plate of cold meat and salad had been left for me. I ate ravenously, remembering how long it was since I had last eaten.

The journey and the summation of the last few months' decisions, along with the Smidt's pooled catalogue of scandal, menaced my thoughts. What terrible crimes had Stephan committed in reflection of an ancient, and perhaps imaginary, vengeance? I winced at the idea of Suki's broken neck as I felt for the scar on my arm where he had snapped it in two, with the strength that madness had given him, and I rebuked my own fixation at finding his son. What for? Was I also trapped in this madness?

What chance had placed me with these people and these events where the rules of cause and effect had been misplaced by remembered dreams? Was it kismet, destiny, karma, or what you will? Was I heading into something even more terrible, where there was no mercy for ignorance? Would it make me accessory to what had happened? I only knew that I had this inexplicable compulsion to find David. Was it to alleviate my conscience, or was there some incomprehensible plan for me?

I had not slept for two days and was dreadfully tired that night. I fell like a dead branch from a tree into the neatly-made bed, and slept soundly. Then I dreamt.

I saw Stephan burning beneath the house. The underground tunnels were collapsing upon him, crushing him. He was calling out for forgiveness and my heart bled for him. I called out to him, and as I did so I woke in the pitch-darkness of the night. There was an eerie silence. It was hot, stiflingly hot, and I was damp with perspiration.

I got up, and pulled aside a curtain to open a window. Outside the night was deep in darkness. The earth-eclipsed moon was a sliver of silver and only the stars offered light. I imagined I saw something move - dark upon a darkness. I shivered; it was the shiver of some silent dread that broke through the sweat that sheathed my body.

Poor Stephan, I thought. How had he become so devious, so deranged? Was it a genetic flaw in his make-up, or was it something in his soul that had carried him on and on, with no resolve for improvement? Was there for him no amnesty - no absolution? There *was* a good and sensitive side to him. I had known it.

I asked myself all those endless questions that never get answered: do men commit evil and suffer endless attrition from it because they are separate egos, caught in time? Is sin a manifestation of self or an act committed outside time?

Nothing made sense to me. Death was the only certainty in it all, and even its promised afterlife is a presumption which we speak of with hopeful expectation, from which, at present, we can have no adequate knowledge but can only receive some dim reflection, as in a mirror or a riddle. Was Stephan's beleaguered soul in torment, or was it only in my mind as I perceived it? Could reincarnation be his ultimate salvation, or was this all mere wishful thinking?

In many ways the idea of reincarnation is a reassuring one, coming back and putting things right until we have reached perfection - but there is still the issue of a wandering soul before it finds its donor body, and I did not enjoy the prospect of Stephen lurking about in expectation of a pregnancy...I mean, what if...

Historical evidence has never been clear-cut on any particular point on the hereafter, but as Stephan once said, "Any theory which would represent the miraculous or the supernatural as due entirely to the imagination would also destroy the credibility of Christ's miracles, making Him as mythical as King Arthur. We all have a choice whether to be hard-nosed sceptics; mocking, and unvaryingly prejudiced. Universal prejudice makes it so easy to find means to dispose of evidence, but if we find room for the idea of Christ we will find evidence that is convincing enough to make a self-committal of faith."

Chapter Twelve

Waking in a foreign land, with its different and distinctive smells and sounds, alerts all those provocative senses to an ecstasy of expectation. I was roused by brilliant dawning sunshine breaking through the open window. It gave optimism to a new day, drawing attention to a promise of a great deal more. Distant dogs barked, far-away cockerels crowed above the diverse new calls of strange birds, and in the background the resonance of beetles pulsated new chords into the air.

I had just finished a refreshing shower and had eagerly pulled a loose T-shirt over my head, when one of the Smidts' maids came to tell me breakfast was waiting for me next door. How hospitable, how kind they seemed to be - such a contrast from David's grandmother from the day before.

There was more pooled chatter by the Smidts, who were curious about my visit. I told them again that I had come to see David and had no idea where to begin to look for him. No one seemed to know his whereabouts, nor did anyone seem to care. All enquiries over breakfast seemed to end in blank stares and astonishment that I should want to find him. To have come so far for a deaf and dumb imbecile…there had to be an ulterior motive. The suggestion that David had been left very well-off by his Aunt was said with sidelong glances, and there the matter remained. An unspoken implication that I had come for his money hung in the air, much as his grandmother had inferred. How could I explain the boy's brilliance, his supernatural powers, the feeling that he had drawn me there? They were as distantly off-course my purpose as I was distant from my supernatural trail, and they would have seen me as a lunatic for even thinking it.

After breakfast, Piet made a call to the Van der Walt house to speak to the grandfather. He spoke in their Afrikaans language, so I had no idea what he was saying. Only half an hour passed, and Van der Walt was there. He was a short man, stocky and rounded. His face was gnarled like an old tree that had stood many summers of intense heat, but his face was kind and gentle and there was a certain softness about his eyes that reminded me of David.

He came round to the guest cottage where I was busy unpacking a few things from my case. He introduced himself as Harold, and apologized that he had not come sooner, as he had not been informed of my visit the day before.

"Old Lydia said I was to expect you," he said.

"Did she? It's all so strange; you know, they kept their whereabouts a secret. I had no idea where they had all disappeared to. I can't think why she waited so long to tell me, and that was only after she had died," I said, hoping he might volunteer more information, but he appeared to be as uninformed about them as I was.

"They kept themselves very much to themselves. It was as if they were trying to hide something. I wish I knew more that I could tell you," he answered.

"And David...did David show any signs that he might expect me?" I asked, almost desperately hoping to justify my journey across the world to visit, when there was no sign of him nor any further indication that he wanted to see me.

"David was a complete recluse," he answered, "He shut himself off from everyone. I rather think that had it not been for his Aunt Bethany and her friend Lydia, he would have gone that way earlier. No, there were no signs that he would expect anyone. But I am sure that you know about David, that he communicated with no one. When he was small, before we discovered his mother's body..." He stopped for a while, to give an explanation. "We found her buried in this big pot that David and the gardener had grown a Paw Paw tree in." He stopped his dialogue to look at me, as if to test the credibility that David knew what he had been doing.

"He used to seem to talk to the pot, or the tree that was growing in it," he continued. "I used to think it was part of his condition. I never heard words come from him, just saw his lips moving. I thought David was deaf and dumb, not that autistic business his father said. You see, I think David is very intelligent, much more than anyone knows. My wife...my wife has no understanding of the chap. She has become so hard these days, and she won't have him to stay in case he does not leave – like before. Anyway, I don't think for a moment that David would want to stay."

"When did you last see him?" I asked.

"He left after Lydia died - that is, about seven months or so now. She needed him, see. After old Bethany died she had no-one, and David knew that. I used to visit there three or four times a week. She enjoyed company, that old girl, and I enjoyed chatting to her - and my, could she talk! David was always busy reading or writing things down, and he used to listen to music. Now that is strange you would say, for someone who is deaf, but he would sit quiet, not moving an inch and listen, then go and write things down."

"Did he ever play an instrument?" I asked, thinking of the old violin and wondering if he had ever attempted to teach himself.

"No, can't say as I ever saw him play anything. Bethany had an old violin somewhere, but no, no, I don't think I ever heard him or saw him play it."

We sat silent for a while - our separate thoughts and questions building up an invisible barrier between us.

"Well," I said, at last breaking the silence. "It seems that I have come for nothing. I sort of expected David to be around - I don't know what I expected, really. I became very close to him in such a short time. I tried to help with reading matter that he needed – and I put him in touch with a teacher." I stopped, unable to clarify my reasons. I could even less explain reasons for coming all this way, for wanting to see him, really a perfect stranger in many ways. I was confusing myself and the whole issue, and beginning to feel dreadfully silly about it all. "I suppose I have come a long way for nothing."

"His aunt left him money, as I expect you already know. His grandmother tried to get hold of some of it for her church but she found the lawyers in charge of it had already been given strict instructions about it, and David had already given most of it to an African community. There was nothing to be done. You know, it was the way the aunt wanted it, and…"

"Oh, for heaven's sake!" I burst out. "I have not come to get any money from David. That's what you all think. I can't explain why I came, I just did - and it's not the money." My emotions quite suddenly got a hold of me and I found myself crying uncontrollably, as if I had lost all that was dear to me and had nowhere to go from the grief of it all. It was so unlike me. I never cried.

"There there, miss. It's all right, I understand. I had to ask questions. It's just the wife has been going on. I understand, really I do. Look you will be here a few days at least? You can't go straight back. Let me run you to the shops so you can get yourself a few things. You will need to cook for yourself here," he indicated with his hand.

I felt so foolish and so adrift. Of course I intended waiting, how could I not? I had waited so long already for the mere chance of hearing from David again. I had been waiting to tie up loose ends that bound me to that time, that experience that I could not break away from. But there was no way to beguile waiting. I had been fooling myself by pretending that I had escaped its bondage by assuming an air of disengagement, and instead I had released all its conflicting strains upon a complete stranger.

We talked a while about other things, his farm and his other grandson Eric who was helping him on the farm, and about the situation the country was in. Then he stood up and said it was time to show me the town.

We could have walked to the shops, but South Africans, the white ones that is, never walk anywhere unless it is an official walking place, guarded and protected. I was to learn of the numerous stories that abounded of someone or other's attack when out somewhere, or alone in the house. I gave it cursory attention but rather suspected that the locals liked you to be fully cognizant of how dangerous their country had become.

There was a 'Spar' supermarket with most things I would need, and there was the bakery. It was Frikkie's father's bakery. I had strict instructions to buy bread from there only. Frikkie's father looked uncannily like him. His name was Bokkie, which I was told was the name for a small buck, but there was nothing small about this Bokkie. He came out from the back of the shop to greet us, all seven foot of him. His substantial stomach was kept in place by a large white apron. Shaking my hand with a floury white hand, he was all familiarity and bonhomie. I had all but acquired family status, for the single reason that his son had rescued me from the dangers of the railway station.

"*Ag*, man, but my boy was taken with you, hey! I expect you will have a call from him in a day or so," he assured my reluctant thoughts. Being formally courted by the wide-grinning Frikkie was a daunting prospect.

The front of the bread shop served tea to nice, neat, middle-aged ladies who came there, tidily dressed and free of decoration, to convey that open mildness that they were. They were delighted to see the old man, an obvious favourite in the town. They hurried about finding chairs for us to join them and choosing who was to sit where, as if it mattered in the order of things. I was grateful that Harold captured all their attention, to distract them from speculating upon a visiting stranger. Conversation was rapt and full of local gossip about what was going on under their very noses. *Well, she's eighteen next August, all grown up my dear – yes – really! well now what I mean is - come to think of it, yes it is fairly young - they do it all so different these days – mind you what of that case in the papers last week...*There was much girlish laughter and much use of *terribly, awfully, dreadfully, ghastly* suffixed to terms of endearment with tones that engage warmth and confidence; all hungry for any slip of the tongue, any intrigue or some sexual scandal let slip, or some family tragedy that could be reported on. How like Mother's tea parties. Countries don't change people. Poor Suki did not stand a chance, coming from a small town with small expectations beyond the necessity of survival there.

It was a good hour before we were able to liberate ourselves from the tea shop and go home. Old Harold was still smiling broadly after all the attention. This was evidently the meeting point of the town, and Harold's visit there was the social highlight of his week.

Chapter Thirteen

Back at Smidts' annex-house, I amused myself with packing things away and looking around. There was such a durable feel of Bethany that lingered there, as if she had shed a second skin and was out just growing another. She had cast her image into the very fabric of the place; it was as if her soul had not moved beyond it. There was that enduring aroma of her dogs and her cigarettes that had survived her, and those abiding strange perfumes she burnt on little tapers of sandalwood - ylang ylang, jojoba and other exotic Eastern smells which had impregnated themselves into the walls.

I could not for a moment imagine why she had gone all that way to remain there, in that so different and foreign environment after a hectic life time in London. It was such an extreme. She was exclusively *au fait* with London life - she had been all her life, and she had seemed more than contented with her apartment. It seemed inconceivable that she gave it all up to stay so far away amongst strangers she had nothing in common with. Just to be with David? But there again, there I was, going thousands of miles just to visit him when I had no idea if I was even going to see him.

Bethany had brought with her all her little foibles, her artistic diversions and indulgences, and they had all been left untouched by her landlord almost as a shrine to a worthy tenant. She must have spent a considerable time painting while living there, as the house was as splashed and stained as her apartment in London. Everything she had brought to the house was left there, as if she and Lydia had only gone out for a minute and would return at any moment. Every room was filled with the residue of her existence there.

Her paintings bore down on me with the constraint of beseeching sadness, releasing her soul's unrest on canvas; insistent, smouldering, critical and imperative. She painted fire with angry strokes of brilliant reds and oranges and violet splashed angrily across the canvas. Behind the flames was a blackened building, crumbling into crepuscular darkness. It was demonic and somehow disturbingly deranged. Her paintings put forward questions that made me think they were about some past experience she had endured. They screamed from a hollowed-out soul that suggested she was holding something in reserve. I remembered that she had never disclosed everything about herself, which gave her that interesting exclusiveness, much like her brother;

but here in her paintings, I saw that complex side of her, trying to resolve those deeper issues of life.

That last day I saw her must have affected her deeply - or was it some other experience she was depicting? I wondered at her state of mind. She had lived a lifetime with those wild images thrown about by her brother. Perhaps it had turned her inside out, as it had me. Had she always been aware of all those violent acts of evil he had committed? Perhaps it was the reason for living alone all her life.

She had brought with her a collection of Dresden cherubs. They stood out against her compelling art, which was so intense and full of cogent energy and authority. I remembered them well, arranged on windowsills, hoping that the light which caught them there would bring them to life. They were her angels, her whimsical little 'heavenly helpers' in place of those devils that lurked in the dark corners of her life.

Each piece smiled sweetly in some cherubic action of poised innocence, clasping ears of corn or with bow and arrow or bunches of flowers. They stood or sat erect like adults inanely masquerading as infants, unashamedly nude with plump folds of infant flesh, obscene replicas of their adult imitation. I have always found those Botticelli angels fondly touching female breasts all too suggestive and disturbingly sexual.

Lydia had an old sepia photo on her dressing table. It was a picture of her on her wedding day. She stood, stiffly posed, next to a tall man with a heavy moustache in an army uniform. Their arms were linked and in her other arm she carried a bouquet that dwarfed her, as they did in those days. It sort of summed up all that Lydia had been and lost: married, childless, widowed and faithful servant. There was little else that she had brought with her; only memories, and devoted dependability.

I felt like an intruder, with all their worldly possessions lying about. I could not forget that Bethany had deliberately excluded me from her whereabouts and what they were all doing - and there I was, infringing upon their privacy, invading, uninvited. I found it rather disquieting that the landlords had not taken away Bethany's clothes, or Lydia's in another bedroom. They remained hanging there, intact, morbidly waiting for a return that would never happen. There seemed to be nothing of David's there at all. It was as if Bethany had absorbed him for herself. Then I found something which stunned me.

While going through her canvases I saw one she had hidden with a cloth, bound up in raffia and tied tightly. It was of a Carthusian monk dressed in his religious attire - solemn, magnificent and absolute. His face wore that intense look of unruffled void or inner peace that Saints are ascribed with. One could read the solitude, the isolated beauty of his life fixed there in some infinite expression. It was of solitude not for its own sake, but for the privilege of attaining intimacy with God. His eyes were bright and looked not out of the canvas, but into a mirror that had no final point of view. I knew that face. I thought at first it was Stephan; then, looking closely, I recognised David. A grown David, not resembling the child I had known, but one who had come full circle with his life and moved on. I knew that look, and I felt somehow that I had once belonged to it.

Chapter Fourteen

I felt uncomfortable sleeping in that house, wondering about all the permutations of what had happened in those last few years of my separation from them all. To add to my uneasiness I sensed, or imagined, a presence that lurked around there, treading about in the garden in the night. It seemed real and stark against the silence but I reminded myself of the dogs that wondered about both gardens, and reassured myself that if it were a real presence the dogs would alert me.

Bethany's segregation from me had been an effective banishment, leaving me out in the cold so suddenly and so inexplicably. I had had so much time to think about it and wonder why. I had been lonely in those years. There was no one I could have talked to about it, of Stephen's metamorphosis or of those others who had so grown into my skin. Now, at last, I was in reach of where they had been, where David still was - and yet I was even further from them than I had been since I last saw them, and no closer to the truth or to any reunion.I had moved no further. I was still waiting, with an overriding need for resolution. There was a futility mingled with the strange sadness of it all. I came to the conclusion that I had drawn a blank to the past and I must move on, but I decided I would stay - at least for a while - before returning to my life back home, where I would try to restore some meaning back into my life.

I walked into the town each day and ran a few errands for the Smidts, who had become accustomed to my pointless presence, waiting for a boy who did not want to be found. The locals began to recognise me and raised a hat or smiled as I went past.

From the very first day going into the town on my own, I was aware of a particular elderly man who lurked about the shops as if he did not want to be seen. He seemed to watch out for me. I never saw his face, but noticed that his head was always inclined in my direction. He walked with a severe limp, doubled over his cane for support. I imagined he must have been in some accident at some time that had so disfigured him. His clothes were not like those of the locals who were attired to accommodate the heat. This man wore old suits that had once fitted, and now hung limp upon him.

He was usually on the opposite side of the road to me, standing there as if expecting to see someone. Not to draw attention to himself, he would hang back. His hat, covering most of his features, was always drawn down as if to shut the world out. I became curious about him after the third day and asked the Smidts if they knew anything about him. They had never noticed him before, and had no idea where he might have come from, nor were they curious enough to find out. There was always an abundance of old African tramps who lurked around the streets, begging. Perhaps, they suggested, he was one of them, and I had mistaken him for a white person. *Perhaps*, I thought, but there was something rather sinister about him, and I chose not to explore the question of whom he might or might not be.

Chapter Fifteen

There was an interesting walk through a part of the town that led to a considerable protrusion of rock overhanging a vast ravine, which plummeted way down into a valley below of rock and deep water. It was fed by a great cataract which gushed over its edge sending out sprays like a dense mist over the hanging rocks. Up above, African women washed clothes in the rushing streams that met and flowed there, unperturbed and unafraid of the precipice that dropped so far below them.

I had taken to walking that way each day. I liked to sit and look out over the ravine at the distance of the water below, and watch white cascades of water tumble in eternal motion down to the bubbling water beneath. There was a kind of intoxicating effect just being near that sight and sound of pounding water. I would take a book and sit there each day, accompanied by the Smidts' dogs. They had discovered my interesting daily occupation and would wait for me at the gate to get going.

It was one particularly hot day that I set out for the walk, not knowing it would be my last. I set my shoulder bag across my back, with purse and a note for items for Dorothy from the chemist on the way back.I stopped beneath a Flat Crown tree and stared out into the wide space below. I had been there several minutes when I noticed from the corner of my eye that I was not alone. The dogs had gone off into the bush to investigate some animal track that had caught their attention.

There was a movement of some living thing. I reassured myself that it might just be the wind conjuring images with darker shades in the surrounding bush. I turned, and spotted the old crippled man from the town. He turned his head as I saw him, so I turned back and wondered about calling the dogs to me. I was relieved to see that I was not entirely alone; three African youths were smoking nearby, drinking coca cola from tins.

I did not look back at him but heard his footsteps approaching closer and closer. His presence roused a tingling sense of unease and menace. I stood up and faced him. He stopped and looked at me, searching my face as if for some clue. His face was vaguely familiar but it was severely disfigured by heavy scarring, and his hair, which must have been burnt off, had re-grown in patches at distorted angles about his head.

"Hello Jo…it has been a long time," the voice said.

"Stephan!" I burst out. "Oh my God, Stephan! I was told you were dead. You and Jake were burnt in the fire. Oh heavens, Stephan, what has happened to you?" I shook, as shock and disbelief crashed over me like a wild spring-tide that pounds up a beach in unexpected suddenness, drowning all in its path.

"An aborted attempt to put an end to me by my dear sister," he replied almost nonchalantly, but calm, so calm and so composed.

"Bethany knew nothing of the network of tunnels that existed beneath the house. They went off miles away into woodland and some even into hidden places in the village. She thought everything would collapse on me and smother me there. Lydia knew, and she knew I would get away."

"But how – how did the newspapers come to think you had been burnt to death? I saw the papers. Everyone thought you had started the fire."

"They found Jake's remains but never mine. I managed to crawl away. Bethany set the curtains in my study alight. I had gone to my study to simply regain a sense of calm; I don't remember much after that. It was Lydia who found me. I don't remember much more. She took me to a hospital, but I don't know where. She thought I would die there. She told them I was her young brother and that I had lost my mind. I was there a long time. I had so much time to think and put the pieces together."

He sat down on a shelf of unlevelled rock and soothed the dust off his legs. There was a struggle going on inside him, as if sanity wished to regain its place amongst the tangled web of distorted nightmares that had become his life, as if the two separate parts of him vied with one another. There was the valiant soul who had gained enlightenment, and there was the lost soul who was still trapped in the horror of his bad actions. I think by then they had become one and the same, reaching no cessation to a painful and long journey.

"Jo, I know what I did to you. I…I don't know what to say…this is my Karma. I see that I will always be a slave to Karma, and a prisoner in this world."

"Now you believe that this life is a result of Karma? Are you suggesting that it is a kind of punishment? Surely those memories you insist on dredging up are best forgotten - surely forgetting is a balm, a means to move on without being bogged down by what has been?"

"Karma is the delusion of ego and the storm of fear and anger that besieges the mind, therefore I have resolved to cut Karma out by the roots. Jo, I…" He stopped, unable to continue, as if a divergence of thoughts was blocking reality from fantasy and he was struggling to stay on course.

"Jo," he said again but the words would not come out. Then, as slowly undividedly as they faltered in his mind, his alter-ego spoke. "The sacred relic was gone. I knew they had it...somewhere. I had never let it go - even while I was burning. I clutched it close to my breast. I clasped it in my hands, like this. Then when I came round it was gone, and they were gone. I had been cast aside once again...my God..." He shifted about nervously, as if remembering those painful moments, unable to release them.

"At first...at first I had no idea where they went. Bethany's housekeeper was told to tell everyone they had gone on a world cruise. A silly explanation - Bethany hated the sea - that's how I guessed they would come here, to Suki's family. When Bethany first saw me she collapsed and never recovered. She had a stroke. You see, she thought I was dead. She believed she had killed me." He had a look of accomplishment in his eyes as if he had contrived all this, and more. "They thought they were saving me from something. They were full of guilt, the old fools."

"Stephan," I said quietly. "Stop this, Stephan. You must understand how it has been for them. This past life business has destroyed something wonderful in you. Something I loved, Steph. Just stop a minute. Be calm and understand how it has been for us all."

"Oh Jo, what have I done to you? I have lost you, I can see that now." His voice had lost its mounting hysteria and he had softened once more. "Lydia was good to me. Lydia has always been good to me, but, but...God, if you only knew. When she knew I had come over here she found out where I was staying, and she came nearly every day to see me, praying over me. I couldn't stand it any longer. I had to pretend to go away so that she would leave me alone. I knew she must have my cross. I asked her and she denied it. Bitch. Huh! I know...it was nowhere in that nasty little house they were in. I searched it."

"How did you manage that if they were there? And surely David..."

"David...what David are you talking about? David was not there." His eyes flashed; it was as if his child had ceased to exist. He had a new enemy now, his sister and Lydia. "I searched when they were sleeping. I searched even after she had her heart attack...I saw to that... the sacred relic, that is what it was. She thought that it had turned me."

His eyes became glazed and vague. He hovered on the edge of mania, trying desperately to stay in touch with reality yet tipping all the time into that manic state.

"I knew you would come," he said. "You had to come. I have been here for two years now waiting for you to turn up."

I looked into his eyes, to find any small residue of what I had found attractive before. His face was now hideous and that part of his character which was once beautiful was being eclipsed all the time by the demons that slipped in and out of his mind. I was not sure how to handle him. If I was patronizing, he would know it and react. If I showed that I was afraid of him, he would try to dominate me as he had before.

"I cannot think why you have waited around for me. Why here? I mean, you could have appeared before me back in England, where you knew where to find me? Why here?"

"I saw you - many times - in England. I saw you come and go to *Nasiarcuth*. Then I had the place levelled, removed completely - with instructions that no one was to go there again. I could not bear to see you there. I followed you about but I could not risk being seen. I wanted people to think I was dead."

"Then what do you do for money - surely all your accounts have been frozen? How are you managing?"

"My solicitors know I have not died. There was never a funeral. I told them I want it this way. I have paid people off to acknowledge me as dead." He was so unequivocal, so categorical and confident about himself; I saw for a moment the sane and intelligent Stephan. Nonetheless I wondered who this strange man had become, the man I was once so close to. How could someone change so much; how could someone become something so different?

"I know he is here somewhere. He hides himself still from me. Now, you are waiting for him. I know you came here to find him. I know you will lead me to him. I knew you would not be able to let him go. You never did the last time. You hung around like a she-wolf after her cub, until they found you and killed you." All of a sudden his alter ego had re-emerged with schizoid unexpectedness.

"Dear Stephan, what has happened to you? I can see that you have suffered, but your suffering has not brought you back to reality...it has driven you even further into that lost perception you have of what you imagine you might have once been."

He shrank back from me as I extended a hand. He seemed almost afraid of me, and yet I saw a longing in his eyes that wanted to touch me, to hold me. I felt an invisible connection with his yearning in my heart, not with the words or actions he threw at me, but what lay blocked behind. His two worlds were so in conflict with one another, and he was standing on that tenuous ledge between past and present.

When our eyes met I saw him striving to maintain a reality out of it all, but it was as if he was unable to let go. I was sensitive to an intense awareness of something lost and gone that was whipping up over another centre of consciousness. I sat, frozen in variance with my own feelings. Who was this strange person who had taken Stephan's body, destroyed it, and was expecting me to respond as a character from a screenplay that belonged only in his mind? What was happening to him? What was happening to me?

"Why, Stephan, why? Surely all that past life business is over with you? How can you hold on to it still? Can't you see the damage you have done to others, and what you have done to yourself? You have exchanged your soul for a handful of forgotten memories. Only memories, Steph. That time has passed."

"When I was in hospital Lydia took something from me, and I want it back. I can't live without it. They have given it to David and he won't be found because, I know he wants to keep it for himself." He shifted about, looking around as if to discover something or someone who might be there.

"There is only one thing that he will come out of hiding for, and I have waited for you to come for that." He took a step towards me, and I felt mesmerised by him as I had before.

"Poor Stephan, poor Stephan," I said. "What on earth can you imagine you can do now?"

"I have come to finish what I started," he said. He made a grab towards me, and as he did, so a tall thin figure appeared as if from nowhere.

"Ah, I thought you would make yourself visible when I had her," he said.

"Let her go," the soft mellow voice spoke, breaking the brittleness of the wild and illogically specious moment.

"David," I whispered. A kind of haze had come over my mind. I had entered another central processing unit of perception. In my mind or somewhere in my body there had begun a fresh new activity. It was as if a deep-seated light was shining there and I had been blind within it, unable to know anything, except that something extraordinary existed; like an inexplicable circumstance of mind between us, connecting us.

David did not look at me, but instead fixed his gaze upon his father. I had backed up against a fall of rocks which lay behind me. Stephan was standing in front, ready to make a rush at me. It suddenly occurred to me what he wanted.

"Stop, Stephan   wait! I know what it is you want. I have it here. Lydia sent it to me. She said you wanted me to have it. I keep it with me all the time. Look!"

I pulled my bag around to me and reached down into it beyond all those unnecessary items that fill a bag, and felt for the hanky that was wrapped around the item. I took it out and held it.

"What are you doing with it?" he snapped.

"Lydia had it sent to me from her lawyers after she died. It came with words of love from you, and was wrapped in one of your handkerchiefs. She told me you wanted me to have it, and I believed her. I was bringing it here to give to David. You see, I did not want to keep it."

"Do you realise its value - carrying it about like that!" he said, approaching me more carefully now.

"No, it has no value to me, but for the value you put upon it. I see it as a fetish, and object of engrossment. It is nothing. " I reached over to pass it to him. "I would like to keep the hanky. I loved its owner once, and I would like a keepsake of that."

He hesitated a moment, and raised his eyes towards me as if recognizing something that he had once known. I had become the illusory memory and the cross had become the only reality he could cope with, now. All of his consciousness lay in the icon. He was bound to it - trapped by it. Had I not experienced, even for a moment, its extraordinary potential to absorb me? Why had I carried it about with me? It was as if the icon had itself willed it so. Now it wanted to claim its old victim once again and in that moment, that solitary moment, Stephan knew it and knew also that he was powerless to relinquish it. That was why Lydia wanted me to have it. She and Bethany must have known that he had survived, and they took the cross with them. Lydia must have known that he would come after it and all the time her lawyer had it, waiting for the right time to send it on to me. She must have thought that Stephan would never guess that I had it. While they lived, they could keep him from it. Perhaps that is why they severed all ties with me as ploy to draw attention away from me. It was as if this moment had been planned. I could not think how or why, but I felt that it was just so.

With the cross came all that meant subjection to the will of the almighty church. It had come to stand for defiance in the suppression of worship. It represented those reprisals, those threats and fear of terrible punishment. Its past was bloodied in corruption for the sake of humble obedience not to God but to the more earthly power of wealth. It was connected to the sacrifice and the suffering. It was connected to ignorance, to those who believed that to lose a life was to save it, to Martyrs who died that their lives may be tied with Christ in God - dying on the cross of mortification - dying in continuous and voluntary self-annihilation.

Stephan's eyes never left the jewelled icon. Its significance had become his torment. It had driven him to those places that would teach him transpersonal psychology and schools of meditation and positive thinking - with a strong bias to controlled thinking - and the control had misfired.

Everything in Stephan's life had been a knife edge of extremes. His passions, his moods, his temper - and here he was, falling apart, withering at the sight of his fixation. He was kneeling and muttering prayers as he extended his hand to take the cross.

David's silent figure moved slowly forward. Stephan saw him, and stood up.

"You think you are so different," said Stephan like a child jealously possessing another child's toy. "I remember you fawning upon each other once before and you think I am the obsessive fool for my jewel! You thought you had escaped, both of you - but you are wrong!"

He rushed once more towards me with his hand outstretched, making a grab at me. In that instant, as if compelled, with one quick movement I hurled the cross over the cataract into the thunderous water below. Stephan shrieked, his body leaping convulsively out towards the fetish, out into open space. In slow-motion, it seemed, they floated down together into the water below. I thought I heard a last call of my name before he became oblivion.

The splash was barely discernible with the weight of water that crashed down from above.

We stood together, watching the water swallow him up and drag him below its bubbling dark maw.I turned to see who else had witnessed the terrible scene. Mercifully, there was no-one there. The three African youths that had been standing there earlier had moved away.

Birds, like small dots, darted across the wide expanse that fell into a bubbling cauldron of white foam way below.

There was no grief in this parting, only a sense of wonderful peace that filled the air; and I could feel Stephan's soul was free at last.

Chapter Sixteen

There would be little point in reporting Stephan's death. He was already dead. There was nothing to report, nothing to mention.

"The experience is short - the memory of it is everlasting," David said softly.

We were silent, staring into that giant well of space, a vast expanse from rock face to rock face, a defiant permanence of historic resistance, a time-fashioned cradle for that massive and intimidating power of water. Insignificant; beneath that water Stephan's body would lie forever bound up with a small jewelled cross.

Way below, trailing branches of water-edged trees jerked and pulled back from the rush of driving water. Some branches had given way and lay trapped in eddies and pools way out of reach where no one could go in safety, and I knew that no one would find him.

My thoughts streaked like forks of lightening that dared and challenged possibilities, searching for random targets. All the while, David stood, silent observer, yet apart, as if the whole act was one that destiny had designed.

"Nothing is chance, I suppose. All is as it should be, all is as it has been written." I said aloud, testing how David might respond, but he did not answer. It was as if he knew but the answers were less simple, yet at the same time more complex than I could understand. And those thoughts became mine as I felt I was reading a part of his mind that was meant for me to try and struggle with, in my own limited way.

I looked up and saw the boy who had become this young man. He was watching me in his own quiet way. I was struck by his quiet beauty. It was an almost unearthly beauty, the kind that goes with those self-abnegated saints who are depicted with an effortless and awe-inspiring serenity. It was as if he had a great force flowing through him, from an ocean of subliminal consciousness. His eyes were beautiful deep pools of light. His hair bleached several shades lighter, and his face browned from the African sun. He had become the swan.

"I could not come sooner," he said. "I had to wait for the right moment."

"David," I stopped, unable to complete a sentence as all those associations of feelings arose in me from nowhere, and tied my tongue. He waited for me to speak.

"Why did Lydia send the cross to me?" I asked. "Why to me?"

"It was you who had to hand it over for its destruction," he said. "You owned it once, and only you could have lost it again."

I did not want to re-examine the last statement. If other people wanted to have these past lives they were welcome to them, but I was not ready yet to have any information about myself and another identity thrust upon me; so I ignored the suggestion that I had once owned the cross, and made another confusing suggestion instead.

"But it is not lost; it's down there in that depth of water. Just another depth of the earth, as it was before."

"Yes and it is with Stephan also, until he learns to let it go: to let go of the past."

"How do you know these things? Who hypnotised you?"

"No one...I have become attuned to many levels of consciousness. Problems from a past will always re-invest themselves in a new life, but in some different way. Forgetting the historic detail leaves behind the unimportant husk of the problem. That is only a part in a play. What is left is the kernel - the innate substance - of the problem. The problem with Stephan was that he had reinstated a particularly difficult husk, and the dual characters drove him insane. It must be remembered that the past is the past and must be left there."

What did he meant by 'levels of consciousness'? I thought of those EEG measurements of the changing voltage in brain tissue in terms of the amplitude of its waves and the frequency of the waves, but that would not make sense of what he was saying. I only knew the levels from coma to mania, and I wondered if he was referring to those 'higher consciousness' levels that people who have been on narcotics talk about. Was it what Ouspensky called 'Experimental Mysticism', or was it 'Cosmic Consciousness'? It was said to be that awareness that is purportedly beyond description, like a describing a sunset to a blind man who has never seen colour sort of thing.

"Yes, indeed, that is so."

He seemed to be answering my thoughts.

"And there are many levels way beyond that. Way beyond the comprehension of man as he is. Man can only conceive eternity or the ideas of the universe by supposition, equations and mental sums. Man has only recently come to terms with corporeal evolution, but spiritual evolution is harder for him to grasp."

"Well, if reincarnation is a means of spiritual evolution, why do we keep coming back if there has been no improvement over the centuries?" I said, with Stephan in mind.

"Oh, man has certainly improved. History is an imprecise sketch, and experience is forgotten and buried from how it really was. Man is inherently cruel and that weakness towards evil is ever present. Only self-knowledge can change him. Cruelty was bred into man over an age, and that cruelty will finally evolve out of him as man moves forward all the time with each new birth, looking back in amazement at the actions of his forefathers."

"How can someone with such obvious intelligence do something so irrational...evil, even? I mean, Stephan was all into meditation and all those higher aspects that are supposed to rake out those human shortfalls."

"A person's intellectual and emotional acuity are two entirely separate things. We all have to learn to know ourselves. Too often our emotions control rationality."

"I am not so sure what it all means. I mean, where is it all leading to?"

"As you have just observed, 'how do you describe a sunset to a blind person who has never seen colour.' The human mind in its current state can neither define nor grasp the Absolute."

"So you imply that we are stalled by an inadequate vocabulary to describe something beyond our cognition?"

"Yes, and more than that."

I thought of how often I had stumbled over words that so often could not convey a profoundly intense thought. I mean, I got lost with those crazy ramblings of worded thoughts that poets like T.S. Eliot made, where a dozen people will give a dozen different explanations of what he meant. Then there were those poets with extravagant phrases that over-emphasised a simple thing - like an over-frilled wedding dress - and turned a single thought into a complex stanza, leading translation into a dozen different directions.

"You were without speech for so long...is it that you could not find the right words to convey what was in your mind?"

"Words are often the confused echoes of inner thoughts. They are used to make sounds to articulate anything that comes into the head, mostly of little importance. There is this brain connection in which thought and speech connect, sometimes correctly, but often not. Words used randomly spread like weeds, imprecise and flawed, blocking the real expression of thought that lies beneath. I learned in silence. I began to understand expression, nuance, cadence, and I began to use my mind to control those energies that lay dormant in others. In my growing years, my brain had lost its connection with speech. My thoughts were vivid, but I was unable to express them. They stuck somewhere in my head in a blank space that would not allow me to move out of that strait-jacket new life that I found myself in. Speech is no longer important where I am now. I can convey things with my mind far easier. I had been placed in that tension between a desire to retreat into an aesthetic world in which I am familiar, and a life that had been created as a catalyst for unresolved issues of a past I had experienced a long time ago. I came back for him. A choice is sometimes obligatory. It is the binding part of belonging to one another."

"Do you think you helped him? I mean, whatever you might have done, it did not seem to work. Or did it?"

"He was looking for me. He knew me at once, and believed that I was responsible for his own crimes. It often happens that way – transference - you call it."

"What of the lifetimes in between - there has been mention of those? Why were Stephan's issues not resolved in those past lives? Did you know Stephan in any of those?"

"Every life is connected to every other and to care and to assist is only what we can do for each other, as Christ and the Buddha and all the great prophets have told us. We are all familiar with one another in some way, in some past, and we are all part of each other. You and I - I expect you have sensed that - we were close once and that closeness will remain, perhaps in no obvious way, just an awareness of something more. As for Stephan…he was always a great man, but unresolved issues with religion and fixation on the wrong things always sent him out of his mind. In this life, his parents constantly brought forward a dark episode with the use of hypnosis and the abusive use of Pentothal, until he became obsessed with those things which had never been resolved, until they became more real than the life he was living. He has, in the past, attached himself to that house and chose incarnations where he might come back to it over and over, until it became a part of him - but he never knew why. He has always been so filled with impossible ideals, fantasies and attachments to things and people that he could not let go. Those snatches of past memory are the unrecognised things that generate fear of the unknown within us. He had reached a part of faith where nothing seemed to work. It is the faith that comes when the mind has given up. His life became a dream where nothing seemed to matter in the end. He had reached that manic level you believe is the extreme of consciousness."

"And you, David…have you reached beyond that extreme manic level?"

"Perhaps, but I would not term it manic, not when you are truly acquainted with it. There is this I can recall for you, it is from a description of that poet you find so obscure. It comes close to what I am trying to tell you…or, as you say, another interpretation:

There is shadow under this red rock
(Come in under the shadow of this red rock),
And I will show you something different from either
Your shadow at morning striding behind you
Or your shadow at evening rising to meet you;
I will show you fear in a handful of dust."

I was silent. I could not respond. There were no more questions, and yet so many. I was in the presence of this beautiful, wonderful being, whose authority I had recognised when he was still that small and frightened boy. He had overcome those fears and moved on, and I wanted so much to learn from him.

The dogs returned, exhausted from their exploration of the undergrowth, tormenting some poor creature no doubt, which I hoped had out-run them.

"Bobbejaan, Boetie, Kleintjie!" called David. They knew him as well as he did their names, and came bounding towards him. "Time to go home," he said.

We looked out over the untamed and breathtaking landscape for the last time. While we had been moving from life to life, it had remained as it was for the millions of years that had preceded us. There was that fragile thought that it was here when we first came and would be there long after we had gone - and to where?

We walked in silence, and when we got to the house the dogs ran off to find water to gulp noisily. "Will you come in?" I asked David, as we turned into the drive.

"No," he said. "I have to move on. I will see you again, but not just yet."

He looked pensively at me for a moment. I thought I caught a wistful, sad look as I turned away to put the key into the lock. I opened the door and looked up to respond to him, but he was gone and there was no word of farewell. How could anyone disappear so fast! I had not asked him where he was living, or how I could reach him. There were so many more things I wanted to ask him. How had he come to know so much in such a short time?

How strange, I thought. *How remarkable.*

Chapter Seventeen

I entered an empty house. How could it be empty, I thought, when it was so full of ghosts? I imagined them circling around me, whispering and trying to reach me, but all I saw were those shades of light that move as the wind moves their mirrored replicas outside.

I sat for a long time, looking out into the vanishing evening until it became dark night. I was alone again, with yet another extraordinary and shattering experience I could not impart to another living being who would not think me mad for repeating it.

I thought of Stephan and for the first time since I first learned of his death I instinctively felt at peace for him. I thought of David, and the longing that I had had to see him had grown to an understanding of something I could not put words to.

I thought of how we are conditioned to accept this short interval of life we have. How we accept the facts of birth and death as visible testaments of life, but what happens after and in between is either dismissed or treated with suspicion. Birth and death are constrained like bookends to that pith of life. And we are always afraid to look too closely at what happens before and after life. Suspicions build upon imagination, dismissive or credulous of any ideas that might be fed to us.

Of course, all religions offer some kind of promise of eternal life in whatever form it offers. Man is too selfish to expect all that energy in worship and prayer and ritual and sacrifice without something in return, and even those hardened sceptics hope somewhere that they are wrong. I marvelled at how easily we learn acceptance, finding some superstition for each and every circumstance.

With all those images and reflections of the day, I knew that while I was peaceful now I would forever be haunted by them. There will always be those bruised corners of the mind, which, when scratched, will hurt again. We can teach ourselves to forget and to forgive but there will always be that remnant of memory that lies there, unanswered, unresolved.

A knock at the door next morning sent me flying to open it. The man who introduced himself as Eric, David's cousin, stood before me - a mockery of the genetic link, for there was no evidence of it whatsoever. He was an abbreviation of a prize fighter, with stocky muscles. He was wearing khaki shorts with matching waistcoat. It was unbuttoned and exposed a gorilla mass of chest hair as curly and unkempt as that upon his head. He put forward a grease-stained hand that I was reluctant to shake.

"My Oupa said that you were looking for David."

"Yes," I answered, not knowing how to continue.

"It is too late, you know. The Will was sorted and he left Oupa enough money for the farm and the rest has gone elsewhere...you will have to speak to his lawyer."

"I have no idea what you are talking about," I said hastily. "I came to visit David, not to find out what he has done with a Will that has nothing to do with me."

"*Ja*, okay, *ja* - well just so as you understand," said the cousin, with a wide grin that intended no animosity.

He walked presumptuously past me into the house without invitation. "I can see the place is just as the old ladies left it. You would think Piet would have sold their stuff by now, man. It must be theirs now, if they left no instructions about it."

I was rather dumbfounded at the young man's impertinence, but he must know where I could contact David so I chose to be polite.

"Have you heard from David recently?" I asked, choosing not to mention that I had been with him only the day before.

"You must be joking, man - have they not told you yet?"

"Told me what?" I asked

"David died a week ago. The blacks had a burial and service up on that hilltop location. No whites went, but Oupa went...he liked David. Didn't Oupa tell you?"

I remember nothing more of the conversation for at that point I must have fainted, as I woke up to find Dorothy leaning over me with a damp cloth to my forehead.

"So," she began, speaking sweetly and softly, "you heard. I am so sorry, man. I only learnt of his death yesterday and we were coming over to tell you. You had gone off with the dogs and when we saw no lights on in the house, we thought you must have gone to bed early. We should have been round this morning but Eric got here before us. I can't think why the old man didn't tell you...he must have known."

"How did he die?" I asked.

"He had a weak heart, it appears, and he had been ill for some time. You know, he kept himself to himself. *Ag*, man - no one hardly saw him."

"It's not possible," I said. "I saw him only yesterday."

"*Ja, ja*, like the old ladies. They used to see all sorts of people that no one else saw."

I couldn't take it all in. Who was it that I saw yesterday? Had I imagined Stephan as well? Was that Stephan's ghost? Now Dorothy assumed that I was as fey as Bethany had appeared to them.

I stood up and looked about me; everything had a different hue of reality about it. Was I going insane? Perhaps Stephan was still alive. No - how could I ask that? I had heard of his death once, and witnessed it the second time.

"Have you heard of a Dr Tyndal from England who might be living in the town?" I asked, trying to regain some form of composure.

"You mean that old guy who has been badly burnt in a fire?" she asked.

"Yes, that's him. Do you know anything about him?"

"He comes and goes. They say he has family living nearby and he comes to visit them, but no-one has seen him visit or visiting. I don't know his name, but that is the only Englishman I know of who is staying nearby, if that is who you are talking about. How do you know him?"

"I thought I recognised him in town yesterday, that's all."

I began to shake. If it was Stephan, I was the last person to see him alive. What if he had been seen talking to me, would they suspect me of giving him a shove over the precipice? I wondered if I should report what happened. How could I? The only other witness with me was ostensibly dead.

"I know that *ou*," came Eric's voice from somewhere in the room. He was still there, leaning up against a bookshelf.

"*Yus*, but you got a shock when I told you David was dead. Look, I am sorry, man. I did not know that David was important to anyone. That old man now, he also came asking about David. I know him. When I told him I was David's cousin he was interested, but he never went to see David, just asked about him. He stays at the *Ou Voortrekker* Hotel in town...he should be there now. Do you want me to find him for you, hey?"

"No, that's perfectly all right, thank you. I just thought I knew him, that's all. I am sure I might have made a mistake. No, I never really knew him, only sort of knew him. Once that is, yes, once...a long time ago, that is..."

"He was probably who you mistook for an old tramp the other day – remember? Look, you are still upset - why don't we leave you to get over your shock? Here, the maid has made you tea. You drink that and then come over and have lunch with us, okay?" Dorothy offered kindly.

"I can take you to where David lived also, when you are feeling stronger," Eric offered.

"Yes, please, yes I would like that very much - in fact, this afternoon if that's alright with you, Eric. I would like it very much indeed."

Arrangements were made, and Eric agreed to pick me up after lunch. The last thing I needed was making conversation with the chatty Smidts - but to be at last on the right track of David, dead or alive, was something to make the journey there worthwhile.

Chapter Eighteen

Eric arrived in a battered old Jeep with no roof covering. His mother had bought it for him when he had passed his driver's test, only recently, he said. It had seen better days. It rattled and rumbled its way up the driveway to the back of the house, and Eric was making as much noise as could be expected in stamping his feet at the door to rid his shoes of excess dirt, and calling out loudly to announce his arrival. We set out, with many warnings from the Smidts to take care in the area we were going to. Eric patted a revolver at his side to reassure them that all would be well in hand - to them perhaps, not to me.

Eric, with as much finesse as a male dog snatching the scent of a bitch in an interesting condition, made no pretence of his attitude towards me. After I had recovered from several rather forward and suggestive remarks about my anatomy, I was beginning to feel more *au fait* with the smutty crudeness of the man who was not so easy to deflate with a few smart rejoinders.

We seemed to travel for mile upon mile up into the hills when at last, after bumping along a dust road for half an hour, we came to what seemed like a Mission Hospital and School. The Jeep was surrounded by a dozen or so children. Two adult men came out of one of the buildings and greeted us. They seemed to know Eric; he had been there before. He spoke to them in their own language and they looked at me solemnly, and shook their heads.

The head man there was Duma (which I learned meant lightning). He spoke reverently about David and even showed me a photograph of himself standing with David, and there was the serene face that I had seen only a short few hours before. It invited my doubts of David's death, if they were indeed speaking the truth.

Duma was an educated man, and spoke reasonable English. He took me round the school and the buildings and the small hospital which he said David had funded. Of course, Bethany would have left him all her money. David had spent his money on what he had seen as an advancing cause. I learned that he had been close to Duma's father, an old man who had once worked for David's grandparents as a gardener. David had gone to find him but the old man had died, Duma explained. His father had been some kind of shaman or witch doctor, and was well respected there. Duma said little about David. It was almost as if he did not wish to disclose something that he knew about him. We had tea in the schoolhouse, and then we turned to go back.

"You will return, one day," said Duma quietly to me as he opened the door of the Jeep for me. "When you are ready, you will return."

Eric was mercifully silent on the way back. Something had affected him while we were there which had made his approach more sombre and respectful.

"You are like him," he spoke at last.

"Who?"

"David."

"How is that?"

"You say little, but all the time I can see you thinking to yourself."

"Oh."

"He helped me a lot, you know. I feel bad about it now because I was not good to him when we were children."

"How was that?"

"I used to tease him when we were small. He was different. He was my age but much, much smaller than me. He never seemed to grow into his head. You know, it always seemed too large for his body, and he had a strange way of looking like over your head and his mouth would move like he was talking to someone - really spastic like, you know what I mean?"

"No, not really," I answered, thinking of the pathetic boy I had first seen with a look of fear about him. Obviously David had more than grown into his head, and Eric's growth had arrested at a dwarfish age.

"He seemed to be...I can't describe it, really. I felt that he could read my mind. As he grew up he seemed to know what to do to keep me in my place. Then, when he came back here and...well...he was different again. He returned with those crazy aunties of his. Ouma refused to have David stay, and that fat Auntie, she turns on her heel, looks Ouma over and says "My good woman, I have no intention of leaving him here in this shell of a house. I intend to move on at once."

Then David goes walkabout for a few days and they are stuck. Oupa arranges for them to stay at the hotel, and then they rent the Smidt's place. David comes back with that mangy dog that used to belong to the old gardener they called Kethla. I don't know his real name, we just called him Kethla - it means old man. Anyway, David he comes back and somehow the aunts know to staybecause they say that is what he wants. He still is deaf and dumb like before but you know, he sort of answers questions in your mind. *Yus*, man. When I first found he did it to meI had a real fright. You seeI wanted to leave school before Matric to work on the farm and my Ma said I must stay and get a good job. Then this voice comes from David: *Go back. I will help you.*

Man, I wrote those exams knowing nothing, and somehow I passed. I knew what to write and how to answer everything. Then when the family saw I had passed, man, they made such a fuss! I said I would work on the farm and they were not happy, man, they wanted me to work in some office. Anyway, somehow David did something to Ma and Ouma one afternoon when he was there. They suddenly turned to me and said *What about you work on the farm with Oupa?* I look up and David is looking at me and he gives a smile, a small smile, and I know. Shit man, what can I say? If I tell them what I think has happened they will think I too am spooked or a bit like David. Well, you know what I mean."

"Yes," I said slowly. "Yes I know exactly what you mean."

Chapter Nineteen

I stayed in the Smidt's annex for a further week - waiting. I don't know quite what I was waiting for, but I knew that I could not be there forever. Mother had sent several messages on my mobile phone asking when I would come back, and I had ignored them. I no longer took a delight in walking to the waterfall outside the town. In fact, I now avoided going anywhere near there. I was afraid of the sudden re-emergence of Stephan from behind some boulder, or seeing a body floating out somewhere below. No one had reported him missing, so I imagine his furtive comings and goings were commonplace to the hotel owners.

The purpose of my journey was over. I did not even have an inclination to return to the hill-top mission. I packed my things and decided to make a visit to the Van der Walt's house to at least say farewell. Eric had been round several times to invite me there, and I accepted at last. I could say that it was a final salute to David - in some distant way.

Their garden was well cared for, like a tidy pattern on a plan. There were bright shrubs in the corners and the lawn in between was neatly mown. A path ran down to the end of the garden where trees grew with less constraint, and all round the perimeter to the back of the house were a row of those strange Paw Paw trees with their wide fingered leaves, like umbrellas in the sun.

Grandpa Harold was busy watering. He came over as soon as he saw me, and invited me indoors. He had those eyes that wear a permanent smile, or so they seemed. He was a gentle person with gracious manners and led me to the house where Eric had marched ahead, calling to his grandmother to announce my arrival.

The house, in contrast to the garden, was drab and uninviting, its furnishings cheerless and without any adornment. Grandma appeared from the kitchen wearing a large apron which covered most of her clothing. There was not a trace of smile upon her lips, but fortunately none of the hostility that she had greeted me with before. As someone whose only contribution in life was to be a wife, a mother and little else, she had that sanctimonious pride of someone who would not be taken lightly. As there was little within her to build upon her worthiness, she had resolved the issue of her value by becoming a staunch member of her church. Church music played constantly from a radio. Long unbroken notes from an organ moving solemnly into semibreves came almost as a warning for compulsive sobriety, as we entered her dutifully Christian home.

I was soon to learn that Grandpa, compete antithesis of his wife's religious sermonising, was a defiant and ardent atheist. Not to be outdone on wisdom, he had memorized little pearls borrowed from Bernard Shaw which he enjoyed quoting in defiance of those 'worshippers of prehistoric faith', he said. I wondered how they ever come together as a couple. Eric said that he had become a deliberate atheist in defiance of his wife's attitude towards David by sending the child away behind his back. The antagonism had widened over the years, and parted the couple even further by his taking a separate bedroom.

"I don't think David would have wanted that," I said.

"No, but it is how they have reacted to one another over the years, I guess. My Ma's marriage never worked either, and there was what happened to Suki. I think I will stay single," he said unconvincingly, giving me another of his sidelong glances.

I tried to imagine what it must have been like for David being there. Eric said he was seldom home but at the native compound, where he spent his time with the gardener. Before I left I asked if I could go and see the place.

It was one of those hot sultry days where insect life seems determined to attach itself to any living thing that sweated, and there was plenty of that. Infuriating flies orbited my head, wallowing in the humid air, challenging all efforts of waving hands to deter them.

I stood at the top of a tall rock and looked down onto the compound, which was perched on a hill overlooking a beautiful valley below. A few scraggly hens scratched at the dry grasses that peeped from the red-dust sand.

The 'compound' consisted of a few mud-brick huts, their thatched cone tops looking to be growing up from the earth like wild mushrooms; one or two square block houses with rusted corrugated iron tops stood amongst them, looking superior in their more modern shape. No one was around, and the silence was filled with distant birds calling to one another.

In a handful of dirt, a small tree was valiantly growing; its thick trunk held up its large many-fingered leaves. It was a Paw Paw tree...I recognised it. Growing there in sterile stamped earth, this tree seemed to have a special life of its own. Its roots had already dug deep into the earth to find moisture buried somewhere deep. There was something almost majestic about it. I had the strongest feeling that David was there, watching, as if he waited for me.

"David," I whispered.

I will see you again, he had said.

Chapter Twenty

Going home to my family was like returning from somewhere with an empty suitcase. The aspirations I had taken with me had melted away, and what I had come away with was hidden. Visiting my parents, I felt that stifling complacency that is so easy to fall into. That was where my parents had taken their stance in life, and there they had crystallized into their customary position in life, managing its barbs and joys with prayers and self-righteousness, packing it all into one small parcel of acceptance of normality. Anything beyond those boundaries fell into the category of absurd fantasy and foolish thinking, not worthy of discussion.

"No photographs!" Father exclaimed. "What did you see?" Going to Africa could only mean an inclination towards wild animals in wide-open bushy places. To explain that the reason for going was to see Stephen's son who was known to be autistic would have provoked one reaction. To explain the telepathic and extraordinary circumstances when I got there would fire up psychiatric investigation.

"I can't think why you went all that way," Mother considered, after reasoning with me about my life and where it was going before I became too old to marry and bear children.

The truth was that my life had stagnated. I had become stuck for a long time since the days of *Nasiarcuth* and its secrets. I was unable to move on, to put my life together again, and now those few weeks in Africa had confused me even more.

I sat outside that first night back at home, and looked up into a cold star-lit night. I thought of those miniscule spots of light from stars that could burst in a moment into fragments as they come to a completion of their life. And here we are with this complex life of ours with all its remarkable properties which make us unique - evolved from matter and localized to our little planet. Yet we are such trivia when seen on so small a scale in the vastness of the universe which envelops us. I marvelled that we have existed for no more than a moment of time as on a fragment of a star's life - a life that I can watch from here - become extinct in the matter of exploding seconds. I wondered at our coming and our going.

There is always a silence after a storm, when beetles and little things slowly and singly resume their former noises. The storm in me had abated and those things that made noise before were going on around me with an infuriating intensity. I was trying desperately to resume my own normality. I returned to my flat and my work, which was all about people with problems. Theirs were the problems that had reached an impasse and they were unable to cope with them on their own. I began to wonder how far back problems arose from. The problem with the nature/nurture theory of behaviour is that it is limited. I was beginning to see people from a much wider viewpoint, but I was also battling with the issues of reality. There were reasoned moments when I saw everything with great clarity, and there were times when I slipped back into that assumed world of delusion with incoherent memories of a strange past. They took shape in my imagination, like that confusion in a dream that made no sense to me. I chided myself that I had become too enmeshed in Stephan's speculations of a past life. I would not want to evoke unknown horrors like those that lurked unresolved in that shadowy mind of his. I could not forget that wretchedness in his soul that echoed along those empty corridors of a haunting past. I thought of those things that had attracted me to him: his mind, his charismatic charm and eloquence one moment, and a brutal coldness the next, a sort of double-edge of fascination. Was it that which attracted me, and why would it?

The idea of reincarnation filled my thoughts. I looked tentatively at Eastern ideas on reincarnation where humans could incarnate alternately with animals, or even insect life. I looked even more reservedly at the scientist's view that life was limited to the physical, and no more and dreams and mind could never be more than some wild firing of neurons - and in between were all those differing religious concepts offering eternal life, whatever that might mean. I could find nothing that was well-defined about reincarnation. It seemed to be the subject of assumption and sensation. But, then again, there is nothing in religion that can be regarded as legitimate logic because there are no standards to experience without dying first. The problem with finding out about a truth that cannot be supported by substantial evidence is that our tendency to exaggerate and hallucinate gets in the way of reality. Yet we crave fact, because it moves us away from those nightmares of the mind.

The thing is, that from the day we are born, we lose the freedom to think individually, for we are boxed in to an adoptive form of thinking by those we are born to. I began to look more closely at the subject of self-will and how to direct it, and I thought repeatedly about using hypnosis.

I first started using hypnosis as a therapy quite accidentally. I had been to a few seminars on the subject, and found the techniques not too dissimilar to meditation practice. We went through the process with each other on the courses as a means of entering a subconscious state of relaxation.

I was with a patient who had just been released from hospital after a suicide attempt. She had been in a state of hysteria over something that had happened in her life which she could not cope with. She was still very anxious and restless, so I started with a relaxation exercise and then took her into a deeper level of subconsciousness, and told her to go back in time to her childhood. She was a good subject and went back with ease to various incidents in her past. Then I suggested she go even further back, and she started to talk in a different accent and gave a different name for herself. She described the village she came from and talked of the streets with the 'bake-house' where they took their bread to be baked in a communal oven, and she talked of the 'wash-house' where clothes were washed in a communal kind of stone trench that was fed by a local spring. There only appeared to be her and her mother, whom she described rather sketchily. There were no other siblings, and her life was lonely and fraught with problems. It appeared that her mother went out each night to earn money to keep them, and she was left alone. When she grew older her mother encouraged her into her trade of selling herself and the girl, unable to cope with it, took her life. Going back further in time she had taken her life several times when things became unbearable to her, and suicide became the quick-fix resolution to her problems. This time, she had not even questioned that there might be another solution other than death. We talked about it afterwards and she was able to understand and pull her life together by working things out. It was to me a positive confirmation that memories of long-distant lives can be reached, and deep-rooted problems can be resolved by facing them.

I investigated places that were mentioned and found that they were historically accurately authenticated. Although the stories that came up were startling and interesting and certainly had a consequence in a current life, I could not say that my researches were conclusive. I was using a technique that would not be considered professional in the way I had been trained. I was often reproached and given some questioned glances of disapproval, despite success, but success was limited. That state of deep-level subconsciousness is rare and difficult to achieve, and most people resist the idea of it. In less deep-level states, subjects often reel off some idea of a past-life like a book they have just read. I found those less convincing, as if they were seeking some kind of excuse for current behaviour. But in those instances where a serious level of subconscious was reached, the results were remarkably successful.

The problem with any therapy or cure that has startling results, but with only a small percentage of people, is that because success is limited to a mere eight percent, the whole subject is abandoned as flawed and unsustainable. I could understand Stephan's parents pursuing their best subject to validate the whole idea of reincarnation. But the fact that it was their own son whose mind they investigated so relentlessly rather put a selfish slant to it, as they had confused his mind to such an extent that his basis of reality lay in two worlds.

I needed someone to talk to about all the unanswered questions and the speculations that were gathering woolly clouds in my mind. I needed to lighten the load of the extraordinary experiences that had occurred, by sounding off my doubts as well as my convictions. The problem was, how to find someone who had know-how of such regressions who was also not a fixated obsessive for the abnormal to blow things out of proportion...or harder still, to find someone who could listen objectively without censure? I realised the value of conversations with Stephan in his more lucid days, and wished that I had asked more and listened more to him without being confoundedly critical right from the start.

Coming from a family of scientific minds, I can't deny that I was afraid of ridicule. We are bred to be such creatures of conformity that we deride that which is unknown or unacceptable to the masses, and who wants to be seen as different? As Goethe put it: *Wir sind gewohnt dass die Menschen verhohnen was sie nicht verstehen.* Or to put it in another way, as in Jude 10: *But these men deride whatever they do not know; and the things they know by instinct like the dumb beasts, become for them a source of destruction.*

Ultimately, it was my brother who turned out to be the person I was able to speak to; surprising really, as I had never before even shared a confidence with him.

He had a new girlfriend in his life that ticked all the boxes, and he wished to bring her home to meet the family. Mother made an imploring request that I joined the family to meet her. I had not been home in several months as I had rather alienated myself from the family, being reluctant to talk about my newly-tested techniques which were beginning to cause a stir with fellow psychologists, and it would not be long before it came to the attention of curious and contradictive criticism at home. However it seemed a 'must' that I go home to meet someone who might become a new member of the family.

The meal was excruciatingly carefully constructed by Mother, whose knack for cheery family dinner parties were most often arranged with an ulterior motive to find out about my life, or to introduce me to some 'influential' people or person - but in this instance, the spot-light was not on me.

Gina, Brent's new attachment, was promising to be exactly what our parents would want for a daughter-in-law. She was well-educated with a good family background, intelligent, attractive and stable - that is, without any ideas beyond the regular requirements of life - marriage, children with good schools, and retirement plans with the church thrown in wherever necessary.

While after-dinner conversation was progressing, with all those subtle questions being laid upon the unfortunate Gina, Brent had managed to detach himself and join me outside, quietly ruminating.

"Good to have you around again," he said, coming to sit next to me and staring up at the dark sky. "We have seen so little of you since you got back, and that seems months and months ago. I had this feeling, somehow, that you were going to stay over there in South Africa."

"Really?" I answered. "What made you think that?"

"Well, there were rumours that old Tyndal's son had been returned out there, and I had the strongest feeling you had gone out to find him."

"More intuitive than I ever thought possible of you," I answered.

"When I was very young I had this innate belief that I was unique," he began, as if what was to follow would be a long principled discourse on getting me back on track.

"Yes, it came across. I was never able to keep up with you. Everything you did you excelled in," I interrupted, rather more facetiously.

"No, I am not talking about being excellent at anything. This was something different. An evocative piece of music or a wonderful piece of literature would stir some distant emotion from deep within. They seemed to echo a forgotten memory, and bring a kind of sadness into my life." He stopped a moment and looked at me, as if to verify any chord he might have struck within me. How could he be so astute with what he was saying without being aware of what was on my mind?

"I guess we all go through those adolescent feelings; that we are unique, that we stand in isolation," I responded, with a brusque detachment.

"I never thought it possible that anyone else might also feel as I did. Those were feelings that could not be shared. I imagined that to talk about them would be like giving away an intimate part of myself," he went on, undisturbed by my indifference.

"Perhaps we missed a lot in our childhood for not talking to each other more." I answered, feeling suspicious, and at the same time curious that this was Brent speaking.

"It is only as one gets older and one learns to distance oneself from that inherent egocentricity that one begins to see it as an indulgence of youth. Then you fall back to earth with a start, to discover that the world plays to a single tune to which we all dance," he continued, watching me to see if he had hit a mutual spark.

"What is it you are going to say to me, Brent?" I asked, with a slight barb to my voice. Where the start of the conversation seemed promising, it was only to end with one of Mother's insightful little aphorisms on life. "Are you about to launch into knowing how I am thinking, or are you really going to startle me with something innovative?"

I was hardly in the mood for swapping wild stories regarding Stephan and his past lives with my brother, even with his introduction into past cerebral insights proving to be more spiritual than I could have guessed.

"About two years ago now," he continued, ignoring my churlish response, "it could be more than that, I forget - Stephan Tyndal came to see me. I did not recognise him at first. I had only met him on a couple of occasions and, of course, Father had told me that you were seeing him - there was much discussion over that, as I expect you knew. Then we heard, and indeed read, about the fire at his house, and that some skeletal remains were assumed to be his. Naturally, we all assumed he was dead, and he was obviously the last person I was expecting to see. He turned up one morning at my office; which caused a great deal of raised eyebrows, I can tell you. He was dressed in some old priest's garb which rather took my breath away. It took a while to realize who it was. He was badly scarred, walked with a limp and bowed shoulders. I was shocked to say the least...I mean, he looked as nutty as a fruitcake and his behaviour was straight off the shelf. He referred to himself by some outlandish Latin name which I have since forgotten. He wanted to know where you were living, as you had moved from University digs and were working, and he had been unable to trace you as you had never acquired a telephone.

Well, we talked, and I decided in our conversation to tell him that you had left the country. Best thing to do under the circumstances. The man was clearly not normal. We were all well aware that he had injured you rather badly just before we learned of the fire."

"I thought you all believed I had had a fall outside the university?" I interrupted, astonished that they had known the truth from the start.

"Well, Mother invented that. She thought that if you were told that was how you had come to be in hospital you might believe it, and she did not want anyone to find out the truth."

"God, Brent, did any of you ever think how confused I was already, to then be living another lie fed by my own family? It's all about cover-up and a sense of social decency, isn't it? I have been fed lies upon lies over the past few years by everyone in my life."

Brent waited for my outburst to end, and then continued.

"His conversation was erratic and insane and he would sound off about you being his Dulcinea. Rather appropriate, as he had clearly assumed the attitude of a Don Quixote with as much mad intention to travel about the world fighting windmills on an old horse."

"Did you mention it to Mother and Father?" I asked, quite horrified that they too were aware of all this madness.

"Of course not - can you imagine Mother with this information? She would have had a fit, and Father would have seen to it that he was committed at the very least. Well, Tyndal ranted on about a past life with you, and someone with whom you had been party to a theft of some fantastic jewellery. Really, I cannot remember it all, but the man was so disturbed that I alerted the social workers in the area and saw to it that he was taken into care."

"And you never thought to warn me or to discuss the matter with me?"

"No; you had gone through enough. We could all see you withdrawing into a world of your own and I imagined that if Tyndal were carefully monitored that he would keep away. Then when I heard you had flown off halfway round the world to South Africa, I wondered if you still had connections with the family. I made enquiries about Tyndal to find that he was often in and out of the country, and I began to worry."

"As well you should have. And you would have saved me some dangerous moments, had I been aware that Stephan was still alive. I can only tell you that I was very nearly not."

We sat silent for a long time, without speaking. Brent knew not to question me further and I had no inclination to unburden myself at that moment - certainly not to my brother, who was in close cahoots with the parents and they would cause no end of problems and prying. However, my need to unburden myself was being tested by his empathy, so I thought I might begin by asking him questions of his own beliefs.

"Brent," I began hesitantly, "have you ever considered the possibility of reincarnation?"

"Well, as a child I had these strange dreams. I often felt I had been here before as a grand Duke. I imagined myself in ermine cloaks with those embroidered shoes you see in pictures. I have always been fond of restoration type music, Monteverdi and Josquin Des Prez with that wonderful choral music. I love their flutes and harpsichords...it gives me that feeling that I have heard it before. But feelings and imaginings are not enough - it's all part of that fanciful child ego, I think. Imagining something and being something are two very different things. Separate the ego from the imagination and you come a little closer to truth. Peel away the next layer of fear and supposition and you tame the imagination. No, you need to go a lot further than that, for truth is an ambiguous thing and has many angles to it. I think that is why I chose to study genetics. There is a solid basis for observation. Besides physical features and disorders of the body and brain, it is often conclusive that behaviour patterns, idiosyncrasies and mannerisms are inherited, but there are, of course, many exceptions. Of course, research into these fields is a way of standardising and categorising that which we like to control but I feel there are exceptions." He stopped a while as if to gather his clearly considered thoughts, before going off-track.

"I am sure I don't know what to believe in, but something old Tyndal said made me think."

"What was that?"

"He mentioned in his ramblings that you always wore an ancient Ankh - or was it some kind of cross? - about your neck. I forget."

"Well that is not true. I have never even seen an Ankh. All I know is that it is some kind of ancient Egyptian symbol."

"It was the symbol of enduring eternal life. When you were very small, the first thing you ever drew was a perfect Ankh and some kind of round circle with a cross."

"Like a Celtic Cross, perhaps?" I volunteered.

"Why yes, that was it! You would make patterns of them, which amused Mother no end. She was never able to understand what you were drawing, or where you had got the idea from."

"Well my memory has moved on from there and I am grateful for that. Poor Stephan was trapped in a past memory. It was as if he had walked between two worlds all his life. It must have been a terrifying sort of schizophrenia which had become so real, he came to believe it."

"You mention him in the past tense. That means you think he is dead now."

"Yes, this time I saw him go. He leapt over a precipice into a deep waterfall below."

"Dramatic. Was anyone else present?"

"No, only me. He was chasing an ancient relic that he believed he once owned. I threw it over the ravine and he went after it."

"Did you know he would?"

"No, I was confused by it all. I still am."

"I rather think you have been through a lot of experiences in the last few years that would be interesting to hear."

"Yes, and I have this urge to talk about them. But not tonight. I need time to speak of all those things that are on my mind, and without the censure that the parents will offer."

"They are that generation."

"No, Brent...a generation has nothing to do with thinking or how we should think. It is all those doubts that we are fed in our growing up. It is easier to follow current thinking, without stirring the water. It is easier to dismiss a concept than to battle with it against modern and local trends. The eye sees what it wants to see, the ear hears what it wants to hear."

"Doubt gives birth to suspicion, and suspicion is the mother of surmise - I read that somewhere. I think perhaps it's time to go inside and join the others. We will find time to talk some day, but not in front of Gina. She is strictly 'born-again' and that means of this new-age Christianity type...not the kind you are speaking of."

"Oh dear. I hope not one of those bigoted schisms of Christianity where every other division of the religion is condemned as mistaken?"

"Yes, I'm afraid so."

"Will you go along with it, or will you question it?" I asked.

"Neither," he said. "We all need freedom of choice, and this is hers."

Sadly, I was to learn as we became more acquainted with one another that Gina did not for a moment consider that we should all be entitled to freedom of choice in what to believe. She was determined to conscript each one of us into her fold. She had learnt to believe that all our souls needed saving 'the only true way'. Mother and Father were carefully taken under her wing and led to 'the one and only church' with the only correct translations of her precious Bible. They conformed beautifully and assiduously attended all the Bible study sessions. It was, after all, a socially acceptable compromise.

I managed to avoid her, not because I did not want to believe, but I wished to be allowed to keep all options open without dismissing other possibilities outright.

There never was another conversation with Brent.

Chapter Twenty One

Those events of a decade ago have become tamed and rubbed dry of emotion, as events in progress fell like winters leaves upon last year's rotting, and bit by bit I became less involved with circumstances of a past episode, watered down with shaded memory. Socially, I found myself mixing with a wide variety of people. I kept a weathered eye open against being swept along in the current of any particular sect or belief. I began to listen more to people's voices and hear the pain in their souls, and found that there was more confusion about what to think about life, let alone what happens after it has ended.

My work became more interesting, and every now and then I would find a rare and interesting subject among them who was able to go back in time and resolve current fears and anxieties from past issues. Though I no longer doubted the evolution of the soul in this way, I thought not to become too involved in regressions as the entire answer to everything. Nothing is absolute.

I never seemed to latch on to anyone in a romantic sense for longer than a few months. I suppose I kept remembering and comparing. After a while Mother even stopped trying to match me with anyone; she became far too involved with Brent and Gina's fast growing small family. They have three very adorable little girls, all as pretty as their mother and as clever as their father. They were all given currently-popular names which seemed to suit them: Polly, Jessica, and Harriet. Like all small children they are growing away from wonderful imaginations to the obedience of parental beliefs. And so a new cycle has begun.

Jessica spoke to invisible friends and talked of her 'other' children she had left behind, and everyone smiled sweetly and encouraged that she would grow out of it, and she did. On one family occasion she suddenly broke away from her imaginary tea-party with her dolls and came to stand in front of me.

"Jo, my friend says you must go back to Africa," she said, then turned and went back to her play. Her mother was sitting close by and looked up, startled. "Now, where did that come from, I wonder? I hope you don't take offence, Josephine," she said. "She must have picked something up from her father that you had been out there some time ago."

"I don't think I have ever mentioned Jo's visit to Africa in front of the children," said Brent, who had overheard.

The subject was interpreted as childish imagination, and when I tried to get Jessica on her own later to question her she had lapsed into a childish mode and said, "I forgotted it now."

I guess Gina had spoken to her.

I felt an emergent need to write down everything from the first moment I met Stephan to the present. I needed to clear things in my mind; to see exactly where I fitted in with it all by writing it all down. Copious notes I had written over the years were scattered together in untidy heaps about my desk. It took weeks to put them down in no particular order onto my computer so that I could refer to them.

On one particular morning I sat at my computer, ready to go through what I had written, wondering where I would begin. On the screen in front of me was the writing:

Behind staunch beliefs, old customs of a barbaric age, bigoted schisms of Christianity and a good helping of corruption from a government with newfound power, Southern Africa seems to be in a dilemma of regressive development. But deep within the heart of this part of Africa beats a new and fresh awareness, quite unlike anywhere else. It will take time to remove from its wrappings the knowledge that only a handful possess, but like a small fire it will ignite one day, and keep alive the rare souls that have come to inhabit this land.

I have no idea where it has come from. I have decided that when I have finished writing this all down, I plan to go back there. I want to speak once more with Kethla's son. He was so sure I would return.

Lightning Source UK Ltd.
Milton Keynes UK
UKOW051148300312

189895UK00001B/17/P